Heat of the Knight

Also by Jackie Ivie

THE KNIGHT BEFORE CHRISTMAS

TENDER IS THE KNIGHT

LADY OF THE KNIGHT

Published by Kensington Publishing Corporation

Heat of the Knight

Jackie Ivie

ZEBRA BOOKS
Kensington Publishing Corp.
www.kensingtonbooks.com

ZEBRA BOOKS are published by

Kensington Publishing Corp.
850 Third Avenue
New York, NY 10022

All Kensington titles, imprints, and distributed lines are available at special quantity discounts for bulk purchases for sales promotion, premiums, fund-raising, educational, or institutional use.

Special book excerpts or customized printings can also be created to fit specific needs. For details, write or phone the office of the Kensington Special Sales Manager: Attn. Special Sales Department. Kensington Publishing Corp., 850 Third Avenue, New York, NY 10022. Phone: 1-800-221-2647.

Zebra and the Z logo Reg. U.S. Pat. & TM Off.

ISBN-13: 978-0-8217-8013-8
ISBN-10: 0-8217-8013-1

First Printing: November 2007
10 9 8 7 6 5 4 3 2 1

Printed in the United States of America

To Elizabeth, for orchestrating the magic.

From MacFarlane's Dictionary (online)

Prepared for the use of learners of the Gaelic language
by Malcom MacFarlane
Eneas MacKay, Bookseller
43 Murray Place, Stirling. 1912

****

neart
>	nm. g.v. neirt, strength, power, might

aithnich
>	va. -eachadh, know, recognise

Chapter One

AD 1747

He remembered the smell . . . the feel; just about everything.

"*Jesu'!*"

Langston sucked in a breath full of peat, fog-blessed chill, and damp dirt. Shivers of reaction ran all along the six-and-a-half-foot frame he'd matured into, making even his hands tremble on the reins. He let the breath out and smiled wryly before pulling in another, testing the air for the lingering notes from what had sounded like a solitary piper. It must have come with the memory. He shrugged, and then the yelling started.

"Angus MacHugh! You *auld* fool!"

The woman behind the noise appeared, coming straight at him, shoving her hair from her shoulders with one hand, while the other held up her skirts, and the sky-blue eyes she looked at him with went all the way through him.

That wasn't the reaction he got from most women. It wasn't a response he got from *any* woman. Langston moved his horse sideways as she passed, swirling the mist with her skirts. She was fantastic enough to be drawn up from his imagination: gorgeous, full-figured, reckless, wild. . . . He blinked. If he wasn't mistaken, there was a pistol tucked into her waistband, too.

"There you are! You've got to stop!"

She had obviously reached her prey. Langston couldn't decide if he pitied or envied him.

"The rangers are at our steps! And you're the wretch that brought them!"

"But Lisle—"

"Don't 'But Lisle' me! I'll not stand for it! We've got but two shillings left to our name, and they'll want that for fines and such. Like as not, they'll take your pipes, too! They might even take you! You know the penalty. What will I do then? How will the lasses cope?"

"I dinna' mean to start anything. I only—"

"I already know what you wanted. We all want it. It's not going to happen. Scotland's lost, and we're the ones that lost it . . . now move! Back to the bog with you. Get your trousers back on and hide that sett a-fore you lose your hand, or worse! Stick to the rocks and doona' let anyone else see you!"

Her voice had softened, belying the harsh words she was using. Langston moved his horse slowly . . . going one step closer, then another. They weren't far; they couldn't be, but fog made the ground beneath his horse's hooves look fathoms deep, and the distance was impossible to guess from the sound of their words.

"Hush, Angus! What was that?" Lisle whispered.

Langston had heard it, too, and he pulled on the bridle, lifting his horse's head with the movement. The sound hadn't been him. It was something else. Someone was coming . . . someone big.

"Quick! Give me the pipes! Nae, I'll na' hand them over. What do you take me for, a Monteith? I can't just let you get caught with them! That plaide's going to get you in enough trouble. Quick! Hurry home. There's four Highland Rangers sitting in the kitchen, awaiting scones as we speak. They seem to think we can fry them from thin air, and serve them with sunlight for a topping. Stupid, arrogant, thoughtless men. I'll be right behind you. I promise. That's a love. Watch your step, now."

Langston smiled at her description of Captain Robert Barton's troops. They were every bit of all that, but she'd forgotten to add flirtatious. That was why they were stopped at that goddess-woman's step and visiting with the lasses she'd referenced. It wasn't for any scone. It was to receive a smile and a soft word or two from that mouth. Now that he'd just heard them, he wanted to stand in line and receive the same.

Their hooves weren't making much sound, but bridles hadn't the same muffling benefit on the soft moor. Langston backed his horse two steps up the hillside and was swallowed by mist almost the moment he did. It was a troop of Highland Rangers, riding single file and with deadly intent. He could barely make them out, and held his breath as not one looked his way. His ears told him how many there were. He just hoped they hadn't heard what he just had.

"Why . . . Mistress MacHugh. Fancy seeing you out and about."

"Captain Barton," she answered with a curt, barely polite tone.

Langston could envision how she'd look. She'd most likely hidden the pipes and pistol. To do anything other was inviting her own penalty.

MacHugh, he thought, letting the lineage run through his mind. There'd been a MacHugh in this glen since the infancy of the world. Theirs was a clan spewing out chieftains; all large, healthy, red-headed, and boisterous—all loyal to the Stuart, even unto death. He didn't know which MacHugh the auburn-haired goddess named Lisle could be. The fact that she'd just been addressed as mistress wasn't possible. It didn't seem conceivable that she was wed. She'd looked too young for such a thing, especially if it was to the elderly-sounding Angus fellow.

He eased his horse closer, turning a rock with a hoof. Langston heard it cascade onto the chipped rock path they'd used, before going over the other side and continuing down the hill. This Angus had chosen a well-placed hilltop to play his pipes. He'd chosen a good foggy morn, too, perfect for cover, and for muffling the skirl of his pipes. He'd been lax in not checking first with the auburn-haired woman, though.

"'Tis a foul morn to be out, Mistress MacHugh."

"I think it's quite lovely," came the instant reply.

"There's nothing lovely about it. There's not even enough span in front of a man's face to see if 'tis lovely or not."

"That's exactly as I like it. Keeps me from seeing certain things . . . like vermin. Our hills are being overrun with such."

She was audacious and bold, Langston thought. He wondered if the captain would catch her meaning. With the tight tone of his next question, he knew the man had.

"Have you a reason for being out and about?"

"Is it illegal to take a walk now? I'd not heard that of the Crown's displeasure with us."

"Things change quickly at the king's court, Mistress."

"It's not enough that you take away our right to wear our own setts? Now you're taking away a morning stroll on Scottish soil?"

There was a long silence after her snide remark. Langston was at the back of the battalion. He started circling them. The sun was moving, the air was warming, and the mist was dispersing, making it easier to see the ground, and the amount of soldiers the MacHugh lass was facing. He admired her courage and audacity, even if it was a classic case of Highland bravado and stupidity.

"A stroll about the moors is one thing. The playing of pipes is another entirely. We heard pipes, and such a thing is illegal."

She laughed merrily. Langston's heart twinged with the

sound. That was a new experience, and made him catch the reins up, stopping his horse.

"A woman doesn't play pipes, Captain. It would require more hot air than any woman possesses."

"We heard pipes."

"In Scotland's bogs and marshlands, beset by fog, it's easy to hear any number of things, Captain. Why, if you venture near Drumossie Moor, I'll wager you'd hear screams and groans if you're so inclined. Or so it's been said. I haven't tested it. I'm na' brave enough."

"Are you saying there was no piper?"

"I'm saying naught. I'd a bit of a brisk walk under my belt, enjoying the solitude and getting a good dose of fresh, mist-laden air, and for that I get accosted by a Highland regiment? You say you heard a piper? Well, I simply state it couldn't have been me."

The mist was slimming into fingers of opacity that were caressing the scene in front of him. The lass, Lisle, was atop a flat boulder, making her level with the man on horseback that she faced. She had her shoulders back, and her hands were on the belt on her hips. A MacHugh . . . she was a MacHugh. Langston ran the information through his mind. There'd been MacHugh clan at Drumossie Moor, where the Battle of Culloden had been fought. There had been scores of them, all decked out in their red, black, and gold plaide . . . all dead. They were all dead. Langston groaned softly.

"You saw no one else out here?"

"Dinna' you understand the word solitude, Captain?"

"Very well, actually. It's the gift we give prisoners of the Crown . . . when they deserve such, that is."

Langston knew a threat when he heard one. She did, too. He had to give his grudging admiration to her, if she didn't have it already. She was brave. She tossed her hair over her shoulder, looked at the Captain levelly, and smiled. It didn't look to have much merriment to it.

"That is not what I've heard about your prisons," she replied.

"Are you ready to tell us where he went, then?"

"Who?" she asked.

"The piper."

She sighed audibly. "I must not be making sense. I saw nae one out this morn."

"No one?"

She shook her head slightly. "*Nae* one."

"You're certain?"

"Perhaps you should take your helmet and remove it from your ears, Captain. That way you'd not continually ask questions you've already received the answers to. It might improve your looks, too."

"We heard pipes."

His voice was telling of his nonamusement over her gibe. Langston didn't have to see it, although the sun finally rising over the mountain range behind her was making it easier to do so. It was also turning her hair a brilliant burnished copper sheen.

"Well, I heard naught. Now, allow me to pass. I've bread in my oven, and four daughters to see fed. Not to mention my retainers, my uncle, three frail aunts, and my servants, such as they are."

"Answer me first."

She has four daughters? Langston repeated it to himself in disbelief. Impossible. She looked about sixteen . . . maybe seventeen.

"You Scots are forever for the doing, before the thinking. That's the reason, you know."

She didn't act like she wanted to ask it, but her curiosity got the better of her. "The reason for what?" she asked finally.

"Your loss at battle, your loss of a country, and your loss of the right of your men to wear their own . . . skirts."

"They're not skirts!" she replied angrily, giving Barton what he wanted.

"Where are the pipes, Mistress?" The captain's voice was jovial.

"I saw *nae* pipes, nor a body fit enough to play them!"

"Then what was it you were about?"

"She was meeting with me." Langston said it loudly, and moved his horse through the mounted troops. They parted easily. It wasn't due to anything other than surprise and the size of his horse. He didn't bother with the why of it. He always surprised people, and he'd chosen the stallion, Saladin, for just such a reason.

She moved her head slightly, and Langston caught a breath as their gazes met. Crystal-clear, sky-blue eyes met his, then dropped to the vicinity of his chest. He tried to tell himself that at least she'd looked at him this time.

"Lord Monteith." Captain Barton announced it.

"*Nae*," she whispered as she heard the name. He hoped she wasn't bullheaded enough to disclaim him.

"You have a reason for disturbing us?" Langston asked, arriving finally at the boulder. Captain Barton had moved his entire line back more than two horse lengths as he approached. Although it was expected, it was still gratifying.

"The mistress—"

"I already told you. She's meeting with me. We've business."

"Business?" the captain queried.

"Of course. Why else?"

The captain cleared his throat. It was a nervous gesture, confirmed by the accompanying finger he used to pull his collar from his neck. "You conduct business on a foggy morn? Out on the moors? In sight of any number of Scot marksmen?"

"I'm dealing with a member of the MacHugh clan, Captain. There's no place better," Langston replied easily. "I'm not exactly welcome at their table at present, and you already know Highlanders wouldn't be about with a weapon to shoot at me. It's as illegal as the playing of our pipes and the wearing of our . . . skirts."

His remarks got him a bit of amusement from the ranks,

and he sensed them relaxing. The woman was silent. She could be in shock. He knew why. She wouldn't want to be within sighting distance of a member of Clan Montcith, let alone being asked to agree that they were meeting. It was almost amusing.

"This is true, Mistress?" The captain asked it as a matter of course. He didn't really need an answer. Monteith's word was enough. His leanings were known. He was loyal to the English Crown. His lips twisted.

"I—"

They all heard the pistol shot, interrupting her words.

Langston saw her whiten. It was especially noticeable with how wide her eyes went as they met his again. He put out his hand and she took it, surprising him almost as much as how much thigh she was showing as she hitched up her skirt and launched herself onto Saladin's flanks.

"Ride! The bog!" She hissed the words into his ear. At least he thought that was what she hissed. It could have been anything, for the touch of her breath on his neck gave him a feeling he'd rather forgo.

He tightened his knees and Saladin obeyed. If she was impressed, he didn't note that she showed it.

"You shouldn't have given him the pistol," he remarked over his shoulder as they covered the rock-strewn grass, easily outdistancing the troop. It wasn't entirely due to superior horsemanship or horseflesh. It was because the Highland Rangers wouldn't move unless, and until, they were ordered to do so. The captain was woefully late in giving the order, Langston thought.

"You're . . . him," she said.

"Oh, I am definitely a him," he answered.

"No, I mean . . . you're *him*," she replied, emphasizing the word this time.

Langston chuckled, and the movement made her hands slip from where they were clasped about him. She refastened them and slid closer, pulling herself more securely to him. He was grateful he'd worn the black, woolen jacket atop a like-colored, knitted tunic. It made it easier to feel her. Actually, he amended to himself, it made it easier to imagine he was feeling her.

"Thank you for clearing that up," he said, tossing the words at her." Now, hush! We've got to find him a-fore they do. It's not going to be easy, either."

"But—you're the Monteith," she answered him.

He grabbed at her entwined hands before she had a chance to act on her knowledge. "Aye. Now hold to me, I'm putting Saladin through his paces. He's very impressive. Watch. Feel."

The Arabian stallion was more than impressive. He was horseflesh with wings. The bog was upon them before another word, and then Langston had to put his attention to speed without breaking one of Saladin's legs. It wasn't easy, and she appeared to know it as they dodged and ducked branches and decay and bits of moss hanging from outstretched tree limbs.

Through it all, the woman clinging to his back moved with him, making herself an extension of the horse, just as he was. Langston gave Saladin his head more often than he controlled it. Not because he wanted to, but because the thought of her breasts shoved against his back, the feel of her fingers clinging to his abdomen, and the idea that her bare thighs were pushing against the backs of his, was starting to interfere with his horsemanship. He'd never thought that possible before.

Mud splashed with each step, coating his boots, and flecking the black leather of his trousers, too. Langston ignored it. The stallion's heaving breaths were transferring to him, making his own chest fill and empty with the expenditure of energy and strength. The woman was doing the same movement at his back, and the thought of that was driving him mildly insane.

"Angus!"

She was pointing, accompanying a voice that he barely

heard. Langston shook his head to clear it, and pulled on the reins before they ran over the small, wizened-looking fellow. She was off before he was, and bending over the fellow at Saladin's hooves. If that was her husband, she'd wed poorly, he decided.

"Forgive me, lass. I dropped it."

"Where?"

"In the bog. Over yonder."

"Not that! Where are you hurt?"

"I'm na' hurt."

"But we heard a shot."

"The pistol fell. It discharged. You should na' run about with a loaded weapon like that, lassie. Think of the consequences."

"Angus MacHugh, I'm going to take the entire verse of Saint John and screech it into your ear! Do you hear me?"

"I believe everyone can hear you," Langston replied dryly. "Including the Highland Rangers we just escaped."

"Sweet Lord! What are you doing with the Monteith? Devil spawn! Get back! And take your devil horse with you!" The old man leapt to his feet and spat toward Langston.

He was spry for his age, whatever that might be, Langston thought.

"You ken what this means to us . . . to me?" The man called Angus was pointing at the woman, and then at him, and his voice warbled as he asked it.

"I had nae other choice!" she replied, too loudly once again.

"Nae Highlander worthy of the title consorts with a Monteith anymore. Especially this Monteith. He's black as pitch. Blacker."

"Your regard warms my heart," Langston said with an even drier tone.

"He gave me a ride to save you!"

"And as you can see for yourself, I'm right as rain. Or I will be once I've a dram or two beneath my belt, and . . . where is my belt, lass?"

The girl opened her mouth to howl out what sounded like absolute frustration. Langston was on the ground, had his arm looped about her, pulling her up into his chest, and a hand over her mouth before she finished. She twisted. She kicked. She bit him. The pain and stunned reflex was what got her mouth free. It didn't last.

"Unhand me, you—you—!"

He had her mouth again. "Rangers," he hissed, the word stopping further struggle. With one arm about her waist, and the other crossing between her breasts, he felt every bit of her anger, fright, and indecision. And every bit of her womanliness. That was disconcerting. He knew what she was debating, too, and his lips twisted into a shaky smile. Her nearness was intoxicating, but she was almost more willing to pay the penalty to the rangers than to continue it.

"Let the lass go. We'll na' trouble you further." The Angus fellow had lost his bravado. He seemed to shrink in the process. Langston frowned.

"I'll unhand the lass if she'll keep her voice low. These trees hide many a tale. They'll hide us, too, but not if you announce where we are. Nod for aye."

At her nod, he released his hand, then both arms. She flung herself from him and stood, bent forward with her hands on her knees, panting. That was an even more impressive sight. The girl was gifted with every bit of curve and softness that the Lord could have provided. She was also flushed in the face, making the azure of her eyes more vivid and piercing, although it clashed with the orange-red streaks in her hair. It was a true shame she was already wed. Even with what Langston thought of the institution, he'd consider it, if the bride was her. He shook his head to clear it. *Marry a Highland lass?* he wondered. There wasn't one outside the Monteith clan that would have him.

"What do you want?" she asked when she had control of

her breathing. There wasn't one emotion on her face as she stood there asking it either. Langston folded his arms and considered her.

"A graceful 'thank you' would be appreciated," he replied, keeping his features as stone-stiff as she was hers.

"I'd rather thank a snake," she finally said.

"Very well. An ungraceful, begrudged thanks, pulled from the depths of your gut. That will do," he responded.

She looked like that was what it would take. One side of his lip lifted.

"Perhaps your spouse isn't so stubborn. What say you, Angus? Will you say a proper thanks to me?"

She snorted at his words, sounding like it cleared her nose. Then she caught her middle and held onto the merriment. Langston had never seen withheld laughter so vividly displayed before. He was beginning to think there wasn't anything she did that wasn't vividly and intensely done.

"He's not—I mean . . . we're not . . . wed. He's my uncle. Through marriage." She was getting the words through wheezes of breath.

"Where do I go to find him?"

"Where do you find *whom*?" she asked, putting an emphasis on the last word.

"Your husband. There must be some man on this continent capable of making you obey. So, where is he?"

Her merriment died before his words ended, finishing off with several indrawn breaths held to the point of pain, before she let them out. She wasn't looking at him with anything other than unveiled dislike and absolute disgust. Langston pulled back despite himself.

"He's beneath the sod at Culloden. Rotting beside every other Highlander that possessed honor and bravery and strength. Exactly where you should be," she replied.

Everything went completely solid, still, and quiet, and very focused. Langston swallowed. He raised himself to his full height before bowing mockingly to both of them. Then he turned and mounted Saladin before he said something he'd regret. The sound of his leather saddle creaking and the slight clink of his reins were the only breaks in the stillness. She watched him, and it didn't look like she blinked the entire time.

He knew exactly what he was going to do: the same thing he did with every other stiff-necked, pride-filled, arrogant, and judgmental Scot. He was going to make the MacHughs an offer they couldn't turn down.

Chapter Two

Ornate, sealed, Monteith messages started arriving the very next day. Lisle sent every one back, unread, and once the emissary started leaving several of them behind, she resorted to putting them in with the smoldering peat they used for a cook fire, adding a strange odor to everything that came out of their oven. She'd have used a real fire to burn them . . . if she had one with which to do so. Building a fire took wood. Everything took something else; something that they didn't possess and couldn't afford. It was dire.

She knew just how dire it was when the west hallway collapsed, sending a wall of rainwater into a hall where royalty had once walked, and waking everyone except the youngest lass, Nadine. That lass could sleep through a war, Lisle thought as she shoved her arms into the thick, woolen, unbending fabric making up the sleeves of the housecoat that doubled for indoor and outdoor use. There wasn't anything else she could use. The trousseau that she'd spent so many years laboriously putting minute stitches in adorned her stepdaughters and aunts, unless it was of more use as a drapery or bed linen. That included every lace-bedecked, satin, and gossamer . . .

Her thoughts stalled the moment her feet did. The hall roof

had finally given into a rain that chilled and pelted and stole breath. She was experiencing all of it as she picked her way along the bricks and sod, the broken, rotted beams that had made up this section of the MacHugh ancestral castle.

"Oh, my God!" The screech accompanied Aunt Fanny as she launched her skeletal, white, bridal-satin-clothed body through the rubble. It was Lisle that had to stop her head-long flight before she twisted an ankle, or worse.

"Aunt Fanny! Stop that! You'll injure yourself." She was putting the same amount of volume into the words, but a mouthful of rain and wet hair muffled them.

"The chest! Doona' let it get the chest."

Aunt Fanny hadn't much energy left in her body, and what she did possess, she'd just used. Lisle held to her and assisted her back, over chunks of indecipherable debris: an upturned chair—that was easy to identify—and what had once been a beautiful, grand tapestry depicting a faded, ancient battle that a Scotsman might actually have won, for a change.

Lisle had to swipe a hand across her eyes to make out the safest path back to the broken-off eave, where a sleepy-eyed mass of MacHughs huddled. She was grateful for the coat, since there wasn't much that could penetrate it, rain included.

"Here. Take Aunt Fanny. Aunt Matilda? Come on, love. She's distraught."

"Poor dear. Come along. I'll get you a bit of spirits. It will do your body good, it will." Aunt Matilda had an arm around the frailer aunt, and was trying to turn the woman away.

"I canna' go yet, Mattie. You doona' recall it? I've got to get the chest. It's priceless."

There was nothing priceless in the entire castle. Lisle looked back over her shoulder at wreckage that glimmered in what light was available.

"What chest, love?" Aunt Mattie asked.

"The war chest. Laird MacHugh's personal effects. You remember it?"

"Calm yourself. There was nae chest in that entire hall."

"Was too! It was in the deacon's bench! She's got to get it! I canna' rest if she does na' get it!"

Her words ended on a wail, and they'd just gotten her over an illness that had lingered for months. Lisle set her hips and her shoulders.

"If there's a deacon's bench in there, I'll find it. I promise. Get to the fire—" Lisle stopped her own words, but it wasn't soon enough. All the MacHughs were shivering and rubbing their hands over their arms, and hugging each other, and she'd just reminded them all of it. There wasn't a stick of wood worth burning in the entire place. There hadn't been since early spring. She swallowed and turned back to the mess that used to be the west hallway. There was wood now, once it dried out enough to burn.

"Angus!" she shouted, but it wasn't necessary; he was already at her elbow.

"Aye, lass?"

"Get me something to lift . . . this." The pause came as she stumbled over a rain-soaked piece of something, ripping her coat, splashing everything else, and jarring her knee against a beam, paining her enough to make her cry aloud. She didn't. She'd learned years ago that crying, sobbing, and self-pitying didn't do much, except gain one a sore throat and an aching head, and sometimes both.

"We've na' got anything like that. If it had a use, we sold it."

"Then fetch the ladder!"

"We've got a ladder?"

Laughter was bubbling in her throat now, taking the place of any desire to cry. "You were using one to pretend to clean the rafters just this morn, Angus. When you thought I wouldn't know you were actually running about, trying to discover where I'd hidden your pipes."

"I—? My pipes? Oh, bless me, lass, you're right. I'll be back directly. Directly. That ladder's na' much good, but we can use it for leverage and such."

"And I dinna' hide them in the rafters, Angus!" She

shouted it after his retreating back. He didn't hear it. None of the others did, either. Those still interested in watching had gathered blankets about themselves, covering over the remnants of Lisle's French-inspired trousseau they were wearing. She sighed and ran her hands along her hair, plastering it to her head with the motion. It was easier to see that way. It was actually a good thing her husband, Ellwood MacHugh, the last laird of the MacHughs, had filled his nursery with nothing save daughters. God alone knew what she would have used to clothe a boy.

Angus was back, sending her stumbling several steps backward with the awkward way he held what was their ladder. They'd already bartered off the serviceable one, just as Angus had said. There was nothing left. The villagers wouldn't take credit anymore. She couldn't afford wood to cook and warm them, or flour to eat. They were almost reduced to eating barley soup without even barley in it.

All of which made it strange that she sent every unbidden letter from the Black Monteith right back, unopened. The last time, Nadine had tears in her eyes at her stepmother's stubbornness. They didn't know what it contained. She did. Monteith was buying up land and property at an amazing rate, accruing his own personal kingdom. The MacHughs would rather starve to death before taking one thin shilling from the man.

The ladder wasn't but six feet in length, maybe seven. Lisle eyed a promising-looking beam, draped over with pieces of thatch and what looked to be plaster, and some of that old, worn-looking tapestry. Of course, it could be anything else, but in the rain-blurred night, that's what she decided it would be.

She was actually grateful it was night. This might be enough to make her sit down and wallow in self-pity, if she actually saw it in the light of day

"What are you standing about for, lass? Let's get to rescuing the war trunk so we can find a spot to dry out in!"

Lisle gained as many slivers in her palms as there were calluses and cracks, but she had the thing beneath the beam, and then she was shoving on it. Nothing happened. She tried putting her entire body weight on it, testing the ladder's tensile strength. That got her a bit of sway to the pile of rubble, and a groaning sound that transferred from the wood along her palms and into her spine.

She went back down. The stack leaned back, an inch or two from where it had started. She only hoped this chest, that Aunt Fanny was desperate to own, was beneath this chunk of old roofing and decayed beams. Someone should have taken the time and funds years earlier and redone some of the castle. Maybe then, when there were only MacHugh daughters alive to inherit it, there might be something left to inherit.

Lisle was being stubborn. She should open the Monteith missive, sell off the lot for a whole bunch of his dishonorable gold, and buy them a smaller place; one with some land worth farming, or raising sheep or cattle, or anything that might bring some coin into the family coffers, rather than sending all of them flying out in the opposite direction.

She took a deep breath and launched herself onto the ladder again. The beam swayed up, dangling pieces of unrecognizable debris, and she kicked with her feet to get it to move a little farther this time before she came back down. The ladder did the same creaking motion, although the wood in her hand shivered along with it, but when she came back down, the beam had moved, and none the worse for it. She was almost in buoyant spirits the third time she tried it, absolutely amazed that something she was trying was working.

"Good work, lass. I see it. I ken what she wants now."

"What?" Her teeth clenched, and the word was whistled through them as she jumped up again, bruising her ribs a bit with it, and gathering even more slivers in her palms.

"The MacHugh war chest. It's hid in the deacon's bench. If it's what I think it is, I know why the woman will na' rest without it. It'll contain the family Bible. That's what she wants."

"What . . . why—?" Lisle held herself up, kicking her feet with a swinging motion, and moved the beam another good foot to one side. Her query didn't make much sense with the amount of air available to her to use on it, but he understood it.

"I said, it contains the family Bible. All the history. All the names. All of them, lass. Every hero. Every chieftain. Every Celt."

"I mean, why are you keeping it in the west hallway, buried in a deacon's bench, and being nibbled on by rats?" She didn't pause through the entire sentence, because that would mean she'd have to suck in more air, and every breath was so laden with rain mist, she might as well be swimming. That also meant she had to wait before coming up for more air.

"Because the chapel's lost to us, years past."

That much was true. It was already roofless, and full of ghosts. No one went in there anymore, even the ones pretending to be religious. That was all right with her. She hadn't managed to get on her knees and say one prayer since leaving the convent school what felt like years ago, but was actually only one.

The Sisters would be mortified. That was all right with Lisle, too. She did her praying standing up; she hadn't time for any other way. Such was the punishment for being in the midst of one problem or another since becoming a MacHugh, and God wasn't listening, anyway.

She scrunched her lips together, launched herself up onto the ladder's edge, and swung her legs back and forth easily this time, since the beam's weight was putting her higher off the floor than before.

The ladder was offended, and the wood was telling her every bit of it, as it shuddered and groaned in her hands, making it impossible to hang onto for any amount of time. Her own arms were stiff, and her elbows locked, and the shaking of her perch loosened her grip and weakened any kind of hold.

"I'm coming down, Angus!" She was trying to shout it in warning, because he'd ducked beneath the mass of tapestry-draped beam, and she couldn't stay aloft much longer.

He was dragging something, and not about to let go.

"Angus!"

The wood creaked loudly, drowning out her voice, but the old man was scuttling out without the chest, and glaring at her like it was her fault as he sat there, his hands about his knees in the damp and decay and mess of what had once been a glorious hallway.

"You dinna' give me enough time, lass! Try again. And stay up longer this time!"

"The ladder's not going to hold, Angus. We're going to have to leave it for now."

"We canna' leave it. The women will na' rest."

"They'll have nae choice. We can fetch it on the morrow."

"You doona' understand. That book's full of heroes!" He yelled it up at her.

"Well, they're all dead heroes, Angus! Dead!" She yelled it right back.

"That does na' change it, lass. You doona' understand. You were too long in that foreign school. It's worrisome."

"Anything I am is worrisome to you. You'd best start changing your tune, or you'll have to do it without your blessed bagpipes in future. That's what I'm for thinking."

"You're threatening me with my own pipes?"

"I never threaten, Angus. I'm only—" Lisle stopped and swiped a sliver-filled palm against her forehead to force the rain to find other channels to sluice down rather than her eyes, then swallowed around the ball in her throat. "Forgive me. I won't hide your pipes another moment. I only did it to protect you."

"I ken that, lassie. I always did, although it's a thing that canna' be done. Sometimes there's nae protection anyone can give us. It's a Scot thing. We're that stubborn, that focused, that straightforward. We'll never give an inch, na' one. You're a Dugall. You know. You lost four times more clansmen at Culloden last spring than the MacHughs did. Four times."

"Doona' remind me," she said, holding every bit of anguish deep down, so not one bit of it sounded in her words.

"Highland blood runs deep and thick in our veins. It's na' something we can change. I doona' think we'd wish it changed, even if we could. That's why that chest is so important. It's got the MacHugh family Bible in it, and that book holds the soul and spirit and lifeblood of this clan. We've got to get it."

"What clan, Angus?" she asked. "What? Where? There's nae MacHugh left. Just you. Three aunts. Four lasses. Me. We're na' a clan. We're na' much more than wretches, and very soon we'll be homeless wretches to boot."

His shoulders drooped. Lisle felt like she was kicking a wounded, great, old stag. His voice warbled when he answered.

"You're wrong. There's the lasses. They're MacHughs. They're the future. You know that. 'Tis why you protect and nourish them. You know it."

Lisle sighed. "I'm their stepmother, Angus. That's why. You speak of a MacHugh future? There is na' one. There's only the MacHugh lasses. Not one possessing a dowry, clothing to call her own, and nae schooling beneath her belt, or even a good meal, for that matter. I'm a failure at protecting and nourishing and making a future for the clan. I'm a failure at just about anything I do. This included."

"Nonsense! You're nae a failure, Mistress. You're the bravest lass in the isles . . . mayhap further. Trust auld Angus MacHugh about it."

"If you doona' stop that, you're going to start me crying, and believe it or not, I'm already wet enough, thank you very much."

He cleared his throat. "One more heft, another bit of swing, for as long as the last one, and I can fetch it. We'll all be in where it's dry, and the others will thank us for it. As well as all the MacHughs that have gone before. The dead MacHughs. The hero MacHughs. They'll thank us, too."

His voice was solemn and contained an indefinable quality that had Lisle bowing her head, despite herself. He was right. They were going to fetch the chest containing the names of the MacHugh heroes, or they weren't going back in. It *was* a Scot thing.

"Amen," Lisle replied, finally.

"One more good heave and we'll have it, lass! Trust me. You lift it, and I'll do the rest."

He was in a crouch, bare feet sticking out of his black breeches, and ready to crawl beneath the mass the moment she raised it. Lisle put her hands on the end of the ladder that was now at her eye level. That's what came of having one end deeply buried in the roof-beam mass and the other at a crazy angle, reaching up with its bare limbs for more rain. She jumped up.

The beam lifted, held perpendicular by the ladder, which was in the same position. Lisle kept her elbows locked, held her breath, and didn't move a thing. She didn't dare. The entire structure was groaning, and bending, and swaying and shimmering with raindrops, like some beast seen coming up from a deep loch by a clansman on a fogged morning, with a good dram of whiskey to fortify himself to the seeing.

The beastlike structure wasn't the only thing complaining. Lisle felt like the cords in her throat were going to come through the skin, her lungs were burning with the denied air, and everything from her waist down felt like so much dead-weight.

Then, the ladder snapped, sending the shock of it straight to her stiff arms, weakening her position as a counterbalance, and shifting everything. The middle of the debris pile rose, before collapsing into itself in slow motion, allowing her to see every bit of it, and knowing that, once again, God wasn't answering the prayers she'd been winging in her thoughts. Chunks of masonry, plaster, wood, and heaven only knew what else flew up with the motion.

Lisle couldn't close her eyes to it, although she sent the command. Everything was in open-eyed horror before Angus shot out, shoving a little chest in front of him. Then, the image of him was obliterated by what looked and felt like one of the ladder rungs, as it hit her squarely on one side of her nose, giving her the first black eye of her life.

The ground, or what could just as easily be hall flooring, was as hard, unforgiving, and cold, and wet as it had looked when she was standing on it. It felt worse, once she landed on her backside and felt it filling every bit of her own once-gorgeous nightgown with the rainwater mix. There was nothing for it. She sat there and tried to cry.

Angus was at her elbow then, all concern and anxiety.

"Poor lassie," he called her as he helped her to her feet.

Lisle had a hand to her eye, making certain it was still there, before she dared open it. She welcomed the smaller man's arm about her shoulders as he led her over the debris field and back to the dry spot of hall where everyone else had been huddled.

Lisle was grateful there weren't any mirrors left on the walls as she allowed the group to lead her to the kitchens. Not that she cared anything about how she looked at the moment, but she still possessed some vanity, and at one point in her recent past, she'd been known as a beauty. To have that changed in such an ignominious fashion would be the height of indignity.

Actually, the height of it was what greeted her when they reached the kitchens.

There was a fire burning, warming the enclosure for the first time in weeks, and shedding its golden glow onto the beautiful red bricks that lined the room. Everything felt warm and safe, secure, and eternally wrong.

"There's a fire going. Bless the Lord."

"Angus," she said, stopping his praises with the way she said his name.

"What is it, lassie?"

"We haven't got any wood."

"But we have, too. Look at the proof yourself. Feel it. Is na' that the nicest thing you've ever felt? Let's get a good look at that nose of yours. You may have broken it."

"Angus," Lisle said again, in the same deadened tone.

He frowned. At least, she thought it was a frown. It was difficult to make out through the steamed mist rising from her soaked, woolen coat and nightgown, and the way her eye was swelling.

"Aye?" he replied gravely.

"Where did we get wood for a fire?"

"From me." The black devil named Monteith pulled away from the wall and approached. He looked like he was frowning, too, in the minute glance she gave him.

"You're not welcome." Lisle moved to cup her eye again.

"You need to put some cool water to that to keep the swelling down," he replied. "It might also help with getting those slivers out."

"Dinna' you hear me? You're not welcome. Leave."

"The other ladies doona' feel the same, Mistress MacHugh."

"My aunts doona' know who you are."

"He brought us a log, Lisle," Aunt Fanny answered, her hands holding a cup of what smelled like tea; real tea. They hadn't had tea for over a year.

"You sold us to the devil over a log?" Lisle asked incredulously.

"It was wrapped in a fancy green ribbon," Fanny replied.

There wasn't an appropriate response. The MacHugh honor was stained forevermore, over a ribbon-wrapped log. It was laughable, if anything ever was again.

"You have my thanks for the log. Now leave," Lisle said.

"It's going to be frightfully painful soon, too. You really should get some cool water—"

"And if you doona' leave, I'll have you shown out."

There wasn't anyone in the castle with enough strength to make him do anything, herself included. She stood to her full height and glared at his neck with her uncovered eye.

"You should read one of my offers before sending them back, or whatever you've been doing with them."

"There's naught I'd ever sell to you, Lord Monteith. Leave," she replied, in the same calm, collected, completely false voice. Everything, everywhere else on her, was screaming it.

"I dinna' offer for anything you own, Mistress."

"Nothing anyone else owns is for sale to you, either. Leave."

"Here."

He lifted a hand, holding out another missive. Lisle took it and walked carefully over to the cheerful fire, burning in the same manner in the fireplace, and tossed it in. It wasn't easy, since her sense of depth was off. She didn't know that came from only having one eye at her disposal.

"Here. I have more."

She turned around. He had another held out. It sounded like he was smiling. Nothing could be worse. Actually, several things were. Alarm bells were ringing in her ears, and they accompanied the shivering going over both arms and ending at her fingertips. It was the chill, she told herself. That's all it was. She was wearing a satin gown, pleated and embroidered, and stuck to every bit of her with the clammy feel of moss and slime.

She walked over to him, ignoring how it felt to have her gown plastered to her legs, took the proffered, wax-sealed, folded piece of paper, returned to the fire, and tossed it in, too.

"Here," he said again.

Lisle's good eye opened wide as she swiveled to face him. Her other eye protested the movement, making her wince. She'd have given anything to hide it, especially when she saw the way his lips seemed to soften, since that was the extent she was willing to look this time.

She walked to him, but when she reached for this one, he zipped it out of her grasp the last moment he could.

"You have to earn this one," he said softly.

She reddened. At least, that's what she thought was happening. Nothing in her past six years at the French Catholic school had taught her anything about it. Well, maybe the whispers of the other girls had, but beyond that, she hadn't a clue.

"I have to do nae more than watch you leave," she replied finally, as all he did was hold the letter to his chest and wait for her.

His lips answered for him as he smiled, a soft, slow smile that seemed to be tying every bit of her belly in knots. Then, he opened his jacket and pulled out more of the letters, all identical, all written with exquisite script and sealed with wax. It pained her to move her gaze, so she had to move her head to watch as he made a fan out of them and placed them on the kitchen table.

"You really should read at least one of them a-fore you burn them," he said. "I'll call again on the morrow. Nae. I'll wait another day. You won't be up to visitors until the day after. And you really should get some cool water for that eye. Take my advice."

No one said anything in reply. There wasn't anything to say. They all watched him leave, the open door seeming to suck the warmth and glow of the room out into the rain-filled night before it shut again.

It looked much worse in daylight, or what daylight the Lord was letting them have. Lisle sat on a rock, laboriously picking out slivers with one of her needles, and scanning occasionally with her good eye, at what was left of the west side of the old, humble-looking, MacHugh castle.

The rain had stopped, but the sky was promising more of it. Lisle tipped her head back. The clouds looked like some giant had taken fistfuls of shorn wool and shoved it into place up there, to hang clinging to every other handful. Every so often, a gap came, letting every living thing in this glen the

MacHughs called home see the clear blue sky that was being denied to them. All of which fit her mood perfectly.

Monteith hadn't given her a respite. She should have known to add knave to his other titles. He'd started manipulating and conniving the moment her nose woke her, smelling breakfast. The fact that her eye was almost swollen shut, her head was thudding with every pulse-beat, and her palms were itching and paining with slivers hadn't stopped her from rushing into her dress and going down to find out how it had happened.

The entire family was circled about the covered garden gate that doubled as a table, since the ancestral one had been bartered away months earlier, and they were feasting on what could only be ham and biscuits.

"Where did we get ham . . . and biscuits?" she asked, keeping the condemning tone from her voice with a lot of effort.

Angus answered her, once he swallowed. "'Twas on the steps—with that."

He gestured with his fork to an arm-sized bundle of Monteith missives. Lisle's eyes went wide and then she had to slap a hand to cup the injured one.

"It seemed a shame to let it go to waste," Angus finished.

Lisle's lips thinned, making it easier to ignore her own belly's growling. She turned to the stack of letters, tied with a beautiful, green ribbon with gold edging. It was very expensive. It had to be. He'd used his family's colors. *Wasn't that nice?* she asked herself.

The bundle of letters wasn't any heavier than a small load of linens that needed washing. She picked the entire mass up and headed to where the log he'd given them last night was little more than coals.

"I was wondering what I was going to use for firewood once this burned," she announced loudly, and bent forward to push the still-wrapped bundle into the center of the ashes.

"Now that's wasteful, Lisle."

It was Aunt Matilda reprimanding her. Lisle stood and turned to face her.

"How so?" she asked. "They were all addressed to me. I know it. You know it. I also know what he wants, and I'm not selling. Not one speck of land, nor one drop of the loch. I doona' care if we starve. He'll not get his hands on MacHugh soil."

"I mean, that was a waste of a good ribbon. We could have used that."

Lisle's lips curved and her eye smarted again, this time with moisture. She ducked to hide it, and that just made her head thud. She'd never had a black eye before, although her brothers had suffered through enough of them; back when she was growing up, and long before Laird Dugall had sent her away to become a proper young lady, and not the lad she wanted to be.

All of which had obviously failed, she told herself.

"I'm taking a walk," she announced. "To inspect the damage."

"I'll accompany you, lass. Just let me finish," Angus answered her.

Lisle spun. She had to get out of there before the smell of ham, accompanied by fresh biscuits, made her forget her principles and give into her empty belly as she joined them.

All of which explained why she was out on a rock, picking at her palms, between surveying the remains of the castle, watching clumps of gray clouds, and wishing herself back into the confines of the French finishing school that her father had sent her to. Life had been simpler, then. A lot simpler.

"It's na' so bad," Angus said, fitting himself onto another rock at her side and pushing his heels into the sod, like she was.

"It is, too. We may as well make that tower into its own free-standing building. That hall's beyond repair."

"I mean, the eye."

Lisle smiled in reply.

"Although it's strange-looking and probably hurts like the

devil, I'll wager the swelling will be gone by evening. You may even find it useful to you again, then. Trust auld Angus. I know these things."

They didn't say anything for a bit. Nature decided they needed sprinkling, but it was a soft-starting one. Lisle couldn't even feel the drops misting the air about them. She could smell them. "Did you get your pipes?" she asked.

The grin he gave her creased his face, combining with the raindrops to make it look like he was sparkling. Lisle looked at him and felt her breast tighten. She no longer felt her eye, her slivers, her bruises, or even her hunger. She swallowed so she could speak.

"Take a bit more care where and when you play them next time."

"Not to worry. I've learned a lesson. I'll keep them by my side and nae one will hear a peep. Nary a one. You can trust me."

"I wouldn't have given them back to you, otherwise," she replied.

They looked back at the castle. The clouds had gotten lower, nearly touching the tops of the MacHugh towers, although now the west one looked like it was being orphaned.

"It looks like the courtyard wall's still intact," Lisle said.

"Well, that hall was in need of a good cleaning."

Lisle chuckled.

"We were in luck when Ellwood set his sights on you, Lisle Dugall."

"He never even saw me a-fore the ceremony. You know that. He had his sights set more on my dowry. It was considerable, you know."

"I was trying to honey-coat it."

"Doona' bother. I already know the why of it. I just wish there was some left of it. That way I'd not have to consider what the Monteith offers."

"You consider it?"

She turned her head sideways. "If you promise not to speak of it, I'll confess. It gets harder and harder to toss his letters into the fire. He knows it. He knows how dire it is. The only bright spot is that he's not going to get very much for his gold now, is he?"

"I wouldn't say that. MacHugh is prime ground. Always was."

"I'm sorry I have to do this, Angus."

The rain was thicker; not breath-stealing, like it had been the previous evening, but it was making plumes of mist rise from the ground in front of them, and making the castle look like it belonged in a fairy-tale.

"It sure is beautiful," she said.

"Aye. That is it. Come along now, lass. I'll slice you a bit of ham, on a biscuit. It's ever so tasty, and I'll not tell a soul it's for you. My word of honor."

He stood and held out his hand. After a moment, Lisle took it.

The girl was stubborn to the point of obnoxiousness, and still she was in his every thought. It wasn't her attitude toward him, although Langston had never had a woman simply dismiss him before. Never. He scrunched his eyes tighter, bringing her more fully to mind. There was something about the MacHugh woman. It wasn't her pale, perfect complexion, highlighted by sky-blue eyes that showed every emotion so clearly he could almost feel them; it wasn't her rose-shaded lips that did nothing but spout hatred at him; it wasn't the long, auburn mass of curls that caressed a very slender waist before ending at well-rounded hips. It certainly wasn't those hips.

"Damn it!" Langston swore and gave up sleeping. He rarely slept for lengthy periods. He'd long ago found it to be a nuisance and a waste of time. Too much happened in the dark hours, when everyone was supposed to be oblivious; too much that couldn't be stolen or bought back—at any price. It was almost dawn; dawn on the second day he'd given her. The luscious Mistress MacHugh might be wakeful, too. He hoped she was feeling something—maybe even the same anticipatory sensation he was, although hers would probably be colored with dread.

He was just finishing tying his cravat into an intricate design only a valet was supposed to know the execution of, when the door burst open, surprising him. He didn't let it show, and took his time to turn and face the man there.

"Come quick, my laird! The tunnel's collapsing!"

Langston lifted an eyebrow in reply. "I've an appointment with the MacHughs to keep, Etheridge," he replied in his usual bored fashion. He watched the man's lip tighten.

"We doona' have enough men to shore it up."

"Call on more."

"Already done."

"Report to me when it's done, then." Langston reached for his cloak.

"The design was the flaw, sir."

"Impossible." Langston turned his attention to sliding his hands down the cloak's folds, prior to shaking it out.

"I warned you not to go near the moat, but would you listen?" Etheridge was definitely smirking as he said it. Langston stopped his motions.

"I have an appointment with the MacHughs today."

"It may not take all day to correct," his valet said.

"And . . . if it does?"

"Sweeten it with gold. You wish water in the dungeons, too?"

Langston sighed. "The Mistress MacHugh is a very stubborn woman."

"Most are. Hurry!" The words came over the man's shoulder as he ran through the door.

Langston swore, yanked the cravat open, ruining the self-absorbed perfection of the knot that had been at his chin, and then he was running, too.

And it took more than one day to correct it. It took five.

Chapter Three

The moaning and groaning, crying and complaining, anger and spite, and looks of incredible maliciousness lasted four days. That was all the longer Lisle could put up with every last one of the ungrateful, back-against-the-wall remnants of the MacHugh Clan. She announced as much over a tasteless dinner of broth. That was what the ham had been reduced to; a flavoring of such little impact. Any barley the soup still contained tasted flat and bland, and you couldn't detect what the soup was flavored with even when standing atop the pot inhaling the steam.

They all knew it was her fault. She didn't need anyone remarking on it. They didn't. Their looks were enough. Lisle looked from her own bowl of barley-enhanced, steamed water to the cold fireplace, which wasn't making her feel as guilty. That was probably because the weather had decided to change, bringing chilled mornings followed by brilliant sunshine, followed by freezing nights, making not only Aunt Fanny, but her frail twin, Aunt Grace, ill again.

In fact, Fanny was so ill she didn't seem to have the strength to cough, just so she sat there, her body jerking with the motions. Lisle put down her bowl and stood. "All right. All right! Stop looking at me like that!"

"Like what, Lisle?" It was Aunt Mattie.

"Like I've taken everything from you and without reason. I have a reason. I doona' want him in this house. I doona' want to sell out to the devil!" *I doona' wish to suffer through the strange sensations he makes me feel!*

"We're tired of hearing what you want."

Lisle's mouth dropped open at the insult from her eldest stepdaughter, Angela. "Stepdaughter" was a stupid title, since Angela was larger, sturdier, and the span separating their ages was less than six months. But Angela was still the child, while Lisle was the parent. She raised her head, put her hands on her hips, and faced them with both eyes, although the injured one wasn't quite opened to its full extent.

"I'm not deigning to answer that, Angela, and you'd best be grateful that I'll not send you to your room, either."

"Good thing, for I wouldn't have gone."

"Hush your mouth, Angela!" Angus championed her.

Lisle gave him a smile, and then she had to force it to stay in place as he continued. "The lass has something to say to us, and I, for one, think it's what we're waiting to hear. Go on, lass. Say it."

She gulped. "It's not my fault."

"He dinna' come when he said he would, did he?" Mattie asked.

"Well . . . nae, but—"

"And there was nae more logs, and nae more food, and nae more letters of offer left, either, was there?"

"That is not my fault, either!"

"What is your fault, then?"

"That I dinna' read what he wanted when I had the chance! I'm going to correct it, though. That man is not getting away with this!"

"How are you going to do that?"

"By marching over there on the morrow and finding out why he dinna' come when he said he would, and what he wanted. That's how!"

The entire assemblage brightened. Lisle watched it with a detached part of her she could learn to dislike. A wall of non-emotion rose, making her feel like a bystander, instead of a participant. It was easier to deal with it that way, she decided, watching everyone smile and chat and look at her with pleasure instead of the black looks they'd been using. She couldn't hear a thing they were saying for several moments as her heartbeat rose to cover the noise. That was probably a good thing, too. "I'll find out what he wants, and if it's not so dire, I'll consider it," she said.

"Doona' sell him the loch. Nae clan can exist without such."

That was Angus. He was helping himself to another bowl of the broth, and acting like it was thick with ham, barley, and every sort of delicious, nutritious vegetable.

"What if that's what he wants?" she asked.

He set the bowl down and looked at her. All of them had the same expression, too. Pained. They knew it was going to be dire and hard to live with. At least it would be living. The only thing worse was starving to death.

"Make him pay triple what it's worth, then," Aunt Matilda said quietly. "I hear that's what he does. He doesn't understand the value of his gold. He treats it like it's wheat chaff, and worth as much. The man's a fool."

"I won't let him get the better of me. Never you fear. I'm a MacHugh, aren't I?" Lisle asked.

They all chorused that she was, making her feel very welcome and very needed. The emotion carried her into the sleepless night lying beside Nadine and her full sister, Elizabeth, in the ancestral bed that she should have been sharing with Ellwood MacHugh, and not his fatherless daughters.

The weather held. That was a good sign. Lisle had two things left from her trousseau: one was a traveling ensemble, made of velvet-trimmed, sky-blue satin that matched her eyes, and the other was her own wedding gown. She'd had the traveling one designed in the French fashion, the material snug across her bodice, although it was much tighter now than it had been when she'd last worn it, on the lengthy day she'd arrived and become a MacHugh, and then a widow.

Her waist had also gotten longer; it had to have. Lisle was an expert needlecrafter. The stitches were so tiny and meticulous that they were difficult to spot, and the fit had been exact when it had been made. Now the waist was an inch or more above where hers was, and consequently the hem was barely reaching the tops of her boots.

She grimaced down at them as she waited at the crossroads near Old Leanach Cottage for any type of conveyance that would save her what promised to be a very lengthy, hot walk. The cottage still stood, mutely testifying to the horrors that had taken place in the barn. Lisle shivered in the predawn light. Everyone knew what had happened there; how the Sassenach had found the wounded clansmen and chieftains hiding there after the defeat at Culloden, and how they'd bolted everyone inside and then they'd torched it. Lisle swallowed and told her own imagination to hush, although she said it softly. Ghosts didn't take well to loud voices.

She focused on her boots. That was better than imagining that she heard screams and groans. She'd shined the best pair she had left, using a paste of water and soot, which was all that was left of Monteith's missives, and still her boots looked like what they were: well worn, old, and tired. There were even three tiny buttons missing from the top of the left one. She wondered how that had happened, and also if she'd be better served hunching down a bit when she finally reached the Monteith stronghold, in order for her skirt to cover it over.

She heard the creak of wagon wheels before she saw it, and started waving as the farm cart came into view. It was the miller, and the bed of his cart was loaded with sacks bulging with flour, the like of which the MacHughs would be salivating over. Her mouth filled with moisture she had to swallow around in order to beg a ride.

It was going to be a gloriously sunny day, and her luck was holding as the miller took her nearly to Inverness itself. She didn't tell him she was going to Monteith Hall. She didn't want anyone to know. She was thinking that kind of knowledge wouldn't get her any kind of assistance with anything.

He only asked her once where she was heading in such a fine dress. She lied and told him that she was checking in Inverness for employment deserving of a lady of quality, like herself. That had stopped his chatter briefly, but he wasn't able to stay silent long, and soon was regaling her with all sorts of tales from his farm, his animals, his missus, and the seven lads he'd sired that helped him with all of it.

Lisle had ceased listening, and was nearly dozing, when he stopped, letting her off near an overhang of cliff that lined one side of the inlet known as Moray Firth. Lisle waved until he was out of sight, then turned back the way he'd taken her. The road turning into Monteith property had been passed some time earlier. The farmer had pointed it out to her, with a tone of envy in his voice. It should have been obvious. He'd told her that the Monteith laird didn't know the value of gold. Lisle decided that he obviously didn't have the sense to keep it hidden, either, for there were four stone pillars on either side of his property, a lion statue at their tops, and a gleaming iron gate between the closest two.

The gateposts were attached on either side, to a wall of stone that had looked to be chest high from the wagon. Now that she was walking along it, she realized it was actually over her head. He must think everyone wanted what he had, to fence himself in like this, she thought.

It was stupid. Nobody wanted anything to do with him. He didn't need to build a fence the size of a castle wall in order to keep anyone or anything out. She pushed on the gate and it swung open easily and with a well-oiled efficiency that either proved its newness, or the amount of maintenance he was willing to expend on it.

It was both. She had the answer to it as she walked up his road, which was covered with perfectly fitted and aligned stones. It wasn't possible to twist an ankle with the fit of the stones. It would probably feel like flying, if one were riding on horseback, or being driven in a coach.

The amount of funds he had to have expended on it was jaw-dropping. As was the army of groundskeepers it looked like he employed, all of them studiously applying themselves to grooming a tree, or a shrub, or doing anything other than watching her walk by.

The landscape bordering his drive was in a condition resembling a woolen carpet of green, and about as thickly woven. Monteith was leaving the woods beyond the road in pristine condition, though, and there wasn't much sunlight penetrating through them. It was unnerving. There could be any number of watchers and guards posted, and no one would ever be the wiser. It was also impossible to see how large this fenced-in property of his was.

It was a longer span before Monteith Hall came into view. Lisle stopped. His castle was supposed to be black and craggy like the rocks overlooking the Moray Firth, and bleak enough to contain a clan in league with the devil. It was the exact opposite. Sunlight was touching the light yellow stone of which it was constructed, making it look like it belonged in the sky rather than attached to a small hill in the center of the valley it was nestled in.

Lisle selected one of the stone benches at the side of his drive and sat for a moment, to rest the blisters forming on the backs of her heels, and also to absorb the beauty and dimension of Monteith's home. It looked to be ten times the size of the MacHugh ruin, and probably four times the one she'd been raised in.

A flag flew from the flagpole, fluttering with what breeze there was. She knew it was green, and would contain a lion

passant at the center, the heraldic beast that was a lion in profile. It would have two crossed swords in its hind claws, and
would be colored in solid, vivid gold. Looking at what she
was, she wouldn't have been surprised to find he'd paid to
have actual gold thread put into every embroidered stitch.

There appeared to be four ways to enter the walls, although
she could only see three of them. One had a drawbridge. She
knew that because it lowered, and she watched a coach leave
with a sort of detachment that had little to do with the lump
of nervousness still there, like a stone in her belly. She stood
and waited. She didn't question that it was being sent for her.
She knew it was.

"You've got . . . a visitor." Etheridge huffed between the
words, his frame holding the post upright while it was lashed
into place.

"What?" Langston took a moment to answer. He hadn't
been paying attention. He was being driven mad by visions of
sky-blue eyes, alight with something his imagination told him
he'd glimpsed, and that he wanted so badly his hands shook
on the rope pulley before he could stop it.

"I said . . . you've got . . . a visitor."

The man's words came with a curse, since water was still
seeping through the wall behind the post. He was being pes-
simistic. At least it wasn't flooding anymore. Langston
stepped back, pulling on the rope as he went. It was going
well. They had one more log to set, and the wall would hold.
It hadn't been a design flaw, either. It was an engineering
problem, and a misread of his plans.

"I dinna' hear the pipes."

"There's nae way to hear anything down here. This place
would swallow the sound of an entire band of pipers."

Langston grinned. The others stopped and stared. The grin
died as he realized it. Hide emotion. Hide everything. Always.

It was better that way. He cleared his throat. "Then, how do you know I've got a visitor?"

"Because Duncan's standing behind you, waving his arms and speaking of it. Has been for some time. You dinna' hear him. You dinna' hear much, I'm for thinking. Your mind's elsewhere. Has been for some time. Strange."

Langston turned his head. It was true. A clansman was at the steps; a dry clansman. "Well?" he asked the man.

"It appears the woman is arriving. She's on the drive."

"What woman?" His heart might have lurched. Langston's voice stumbled as he felt something so foreign he had to consciously command his body not to betray it. That was stranger than anything Etheridge mentioned.

"The one you write your notes to."

Langston's eyes widened then. He couldn't prevent it. "Here?" he asked. "Now?"

"Aye." Now Duncan was grinning, too.

"How much time do I have?" He was looking down at the mess of sweat-soaked shirt, wet plaide, and mud-covered boots.

"Little. We sent a coach."

"What?"

He couldn't break into a run until he got through the standing water. He knew they all watched. He would have, too. He was supposed to be an emotionless, demonic, Black Monteith. Etheridge didn't wait to show his reaction, though. He was laughing.

She was still standing as the coach slowed before it reached her. Then it passed by to find a spot to turn about and return for her. It could also have been because whoever was in it wanted a look at her. The coach stopped directly in front of her, making a looming shadow that reached to the toes of her scuffed and used boots. Lisle watched as the coachman secured his reins. There was also a groomsman at the rear of it. He stepped down to walk over and open the door for her, and lower a row of three steps into place.

"We've come to fetch you," he informed her, holding out one of his white-gloved hands in order to assist her in.

Lisle gulped. She had too much sweat on her hands to touch his gloves. She stood there, undecided, and watched as he smiled at her.

"It's all right, lass. We've been expecting you."

They had? That was almost enough to send her marching right back down the perfectly groomed road and back to poverty. Almost.

She took his hand and allowed him to help her enter the coach that contained two opposing newly padded leather seats, a small shelf on the far side, white satin to line the sides and top and windows, and nothing else. Lisle settled onto a seat and watched as he put the ladder back into place beneath the flooring and shut her in. There was no turning back now, and her heartbeat wasn't loud enough to dull anything.

It was loud, though. And it wasn't dimming the entire two minutes that the ride took. It was actually getting louder, pulsing through her, and making everything else feel weak and shaky. She was going into purgatory, the devil's spawn was awaiting her, and there wasn't anyone there to help her, or guide her, or even hold her hand. Lisle was afraid her bottom lip was trembling.

The drawbridge closed behind them. She couldn't hear it; she had to sense it by the loss of light as they went into his courtyard. Her mouth filled with spittle that she was too frightened to swallow, and then when she did, her ears popped with the released pressure.

She only hoped she didn't burst into tears.

The coach stopped with a rocking motion the coachman had probably needed many years to perfect. Lisle watched the empty seat in front of her with unseeing eyes, pushed another swallow down her throat, and grimaced at the heavy, hard feeling of the ball of fear she was harboring.

She told herself she was being stupid. There was nothing to be frightened over. She was simply going to ask him what he wanted from the MacHughs, and then she was going to bargain for the best price for it, and then she was going to take her leave. She wasn't going to give him the time to create a reaction of any kind within her.

The door was opened, showing her a sun-kissed inner keep that made her gasp. The rocks used to construct his keep were nearly a story high each, and constructed vertically, so they looked like they were thrusting up from the ground into the sky, before being molded to another rock that appeared to do the same. And they were marbled-looking, giving the castle walls veins of gold and amber and brown and white, and making it look like there wasn't any amount of money that would have made such beauty.

"His Lordship is awaiting you in his study, Mistress."

She thought the servant waiting for her was different from the groomsman that had assisted her in, but she wasn't certain of it. She hadn't paid him enough attention, and this one was wearing gloves, too.

Then she saw the three doormen, all wearing Highland attire. There was no stopping her jaw. It dropped, completely and mortifyingly. Imprisonment and confiscation by the Crown was the penalty for a Highlander in a kilt, and Monteith was begging for that very thing. She didn't think it possible that he was that stupid. But he had to be, or he wasn't afraid of the penalty because he was immune from it.

Her upper lip lifted in a sneer, and some of the hard ball in her throat dissipated with it. He *was* immune. How right she'd been about him! He was in league with the devil, all right, but the devil was the Sassenach. Every Scot knew that. Lisle no longer felt any fright and she smoothed her hands down the silken-feeling fabric of her traveling gown, not even caring if the motion caused more snags than it had earned with use.

She was a true Scot. She was born a Dugall. She'd married

a MacHugh laird. She could still look herself in any mirror on any wall in any castle, Jacobite or not, perfectly maintained or not.

The mirror he had in his front foyer meant this was an excellent time and place to put that to the test, and Lisle looked at herself, seeing for the first time the yellowish purple of her left eye, which still wasn't as fully open as the other one. Then she was looking at how her cheeks looked like she'd just come in from a run about the moors, because of the agitation. It surely wasn't due to anything like a blush.

She swallowed, and wondered how she was supposed to keep from looking like she was blushing. Rice powder would have worked, but if she'd had anything the MacHughs thought contained something like rice, she'd have probably found a way to make it edible by now. Lisle smiled at the thought, and watched as it made her look her age, for a change.

The expression instantly turned into a frown. She couldn't afford to look like a girl of eighteen and a half. She was here as the matriarch of the MacHugh clan, on business, and the entire family's fortunes could very well turn on what transpired in the next few minutes. There wasn't any place in that plan for being a young girl.

She untied the ribbon at her chin and removed the bonnet that had kept the worst of the sun from paining her eye. Then she patted strands that had escaped her bun, frowning further at that. Her hair wouldn't ever behave, and she'd used the last of her lavender softening soap on it, hiding it at the loch since the girls would have been in a dander over how she'd kept it from them.

"If you'll follow me?"

Lisle jumped at the voice. The woman who owned it didn't show any response, pleasant or unpleasant, to Lisle's reaction— no smile, no commiseration, no sympathy, nothing. She didn't look interested at all. Lisle kept her head high and her gaze straight ahead as she passed hall after hall, doorway after doorway, showing rooms of luxury and size, and full of so much furniture it looked impossible to move about in most of them.

The woman took a right turn halfway down the main hall; then she took another right, and then a left. Lisle's eyes widened with each turn, and after yet another left, she was in danger of getting disoriented to the point she'd need help finding her way back out.

Contrary to the clutter he looked to have filled most of the rooms with, the halls were free and clear, large and with a high ceiling span that made it feel like she was in a cathedral. The woman stopped at a door with two guards standing at attention on either side of the carved wood entryway.

Lisle nearly rolled her eyes, except she knew it would hurt too much. The expense of keeping guards here had to be offset by the need for them. That was the only reason for such a waste of gold. What enemy could possibly find a way in here, long enough, and far enough, in order to be a threat to their liege? Monteith had guards posted outside his chambers? Ridiculous. The only reason had to be because he must feel he needed them.

Then the door was opened for her, and everything she was thinking went straight out of her head as the Monteith laird stood from a position in a very large, leather chair and took over her entire vision.

She'd already proven that the men she'd seen so far, wearing outlawed Highland garb, were enough to make her jaw drop. The laird was every bit of that and more. Lisle kept her teeth clenched to prevent it from happening again as he moved around his desk and walked toward her, an unreadable expression on his handsome face.

Lisle looked down. She didn't have a choice. It was self-preservation and instinct in their most pure form. Little needles of sensation were hitting at the tips of her fingers and even at her scalp, almost like she'd had the areas asleep. She didn't know hatred and disgust felt like that. Then he spoke, and the reaction went right to the peaks of her breasts, hardening them, to her absolute dismay. She gasped and almost covered herself, except that would make him look. And make him think.

"You . . . came."

Wonder colored the words that were said in a deep pitch no man should be able to wield so easily. Lisle scolded herself, gulped, took a deep breath, and then looked up, promising herself that she was going to meet his eyes this time.

She reached his chest. He was breathing hard. That seemed fair to her. She made her eyes move higher, past the lace that was cascading from his neck, heaving with each of his breaths. She dared herself to look higher . . . his chin. . . . It wasn't possible. She dropped her gaze again.

He cleared his throat, making it worse.

Lisle tipped her foot, putting the scuffed toe of one boot against the wood grain of his floor, and chided herself for being an idiot.

"Can I offer you some refreshment? A chair? Take your wrap?"

She shook her head to each query.

He chuckled. Softly. *At her.* Lisle's back felt the insult first. Then, it penetrated her mind. Culloden widows didn't act like startled rabbits. Her head snapped back and she glared up at him, although she had to take a step back before it worked, and then she was using everything at her disposal to keep every response hidden. She couldn't prevent her lips when they parted, however. She had to let the gasp in.

Monteith was wearing a kilt of his clan colors, topped by a black leather jacket. He had more lace at the cuffs of his sleeves, cascading onto the hands he had perched to his hips. There were gold-trimmed epaulets on the shoulders of his doublet, a double row of gold buttons, and his sporran was hung with gold fringe. Even the tassels on his socks were of gold.

Sunlight was streaming in the floor-to-ceiling window, turning his black hair into shined ebony . . . wet, shined ebony. He was wet? Her eyes narrowed. The light was also causing a shadow to dust where his eyelashes reached his cheeks and the cleft of his chin. She pulled back farther, moving her neck this time, and wished heartily that he was a spindly, weak, and pale sort. It was a forlorn wish. Nothing about the man in front of her fit the definition of weak or spindly, or anything save large, strong, and innately raw. He was every definition of big, brawny, and beautiful . . . the kind of man women swooned over. He knew it, too. The smile playing about his lips betrayed it. She detested him. Completely.

There wasn't a drop of moisture anywhere in her mouth with which to swallow, so she didn't try. Lisle kept her eyes on him as she moved two steps sideways into the room, listening for the shutting of the door behind her, and yet dreading it at the same time.

She got both, and the resultant silence felt like they were in their own, encapsulated, luxurious world. Lisle had to force herself to do something other than stare at him. She blinked, and pretended to look over the books lining the walls to the right of where he stood. Then she moved her gaze to the fireplace that was of a size a royal palace could claim, and from there to the magnificence of the dark green lion passant-emblazoned shield above it, stretching clear up into the wooden rafters crossing the ceiling two stories above her.

She lowered her head from studying it, caught his gaze for more time than she dared admit to, while her heart hammered faster, stronger, and with a hum to it that was every bit as loud as anything the clan armies could drum out. Then she moved her gaze to the window, and to the picture beside it, and on the left. It was obviously a relative, one hand resting on a hunting dog, while his other lay across the chair that had to be the exact one Monteith had just risen from.

There was nothing left, save to do what she'd come to do, and somehow find her way back out of this maze of rooms and riches and furniture. Lisle cleared her throat. It sounded like Aunt Fanny's coughing had, and about as confident. She tried again, wincing a bit at how it pained her dry throat.

He was probably smiling; anyone with such a complete

win over a MacHugh would. She avoided looking. The floor
was safest . . . *again*. She concentrated on the slatted wood of
the floor beneath them, covered with enough overlapping
rugs that she could leap across from rug to rug and never
touch wood if she didn't want to.

"I'm gratified I was on hand to welcome you to my humble
home," he said.

That time she did roll her eyes, gaining every bit of the
ache she knew it would cause. It wasn't worth it. He hadn't
even seen it.

"To what do I owe this surprise . . . visit?" he continued.

"Let's na' waste time with words. You know why I'm here,"
Lisle said.

"Agreed. You've acceded to my offer," he replied softly,
and with a mesmerizing tone that could lull a beast into submission.

She lifted her head and looked at him, hoping disdain was
the expression on her face, but she couldn't do a thing about
the flush. She felt it clear to the roots of her hair beneath the
bun, and all the way to the toes in her socks, but she didn't
blink, or make any other sign of any kind. It took every bit
of her determination, too.

"I've na' even read it," she answered, finally.

His eyebrows rose. She had to gulp and move her gaze
away. There was no way to continue watching him, unless
there was a scar, or at the very least a pockmark, somewhere
on his face, to focus on.

"Would you like another one?" he asked.

She glanced over, caught a glimpse of pursed lips—
unscarred, perfectly formed, pursed lips—and moved quickly
away. The mantelpiece looked safe, and since it was over his
right shoulder, she could pretend she was looking at him.

"I won't sell any land cheaply," she answered the mantel.

"It's na' land I want."

She frowned, but didn't move her gaze. "I'll na' sell the
loch without the land."

"I doona' wish any land or any water from you, Mistress MacHugh."

"Why na'?"

"Because I have enough, I think. And what I already own is of better quality. I can raise better cattle, and better sheep."

The flush went hotter at the insult. Her upper lip curled. "What is it you do want, then?" she asked. She moved her eyes directly to his, and kept every bit of what was happening to her very own body at the locking of his gaze deep down, where she could hide it. It wasn't easy. Her heart felt like it shut down, skipping several beats before restarting, and her breath clogged her chest with how it went missing as she held it.

In reply, he started unbuttoning his vest. Lisle watched, only the widening of her eyes betraying her. Then he was reaching inside and pulling out yet another wax-sealed tri-folded piece of parchment. This time he waited, holding it toward her, and not even blinking through his regard.

Lisle had to step forward to reach it. The moment she had it, he turned, the motion making his kilt swirl as he strode to the far window and stood, hands on his hips again, and his back to her. She opened it and read.

Chapter Four

Monteith wanted Lisle. Her? Barefoot, hoydenish, poverty-stricken, wild, red-haired, hot-tempered Mistress MacHugh? And not for just one night, either, or even a week—which she might be able to live through and then try to forget. He wanted her for life, at his side, as his wife. His *wife*?

Her steps halted, knowing she had only deep-rooted mulishness to blame that she'd had to find out what his offer was in person. *His wife?* she repeated in her thoughts yet again. No. Not that. Any portion of MacHugh land was better than that. Anything.

The shock was what had gotten her from the steps of his keep and across his drawbridge without having to ask one soul the way, or wait for anyone to open a door or lower a bridge. Anger got her all the way to the castle gate, more than half a league distance, and then it became rage, which had her stomping along the fence-lined roadway outside his property. Then the emotion turned to stubbornness, making it easy to ignore the blisters on her heels that were breaking open, the way the sun seemed to beat down on her, making sweat rivulet down her back, and how even the growth beside the road tried to reach out for her, catch and imprison her.

Despair dogged every step and every breath as the sun set

behind her, sending her own shadow farther and farther along the road, and frightening her more than any deserted farm-house along the way could. It should have taken nearly the night to reach the MacHugh property, rather than arriving just as the moon was sliding from behind the clouds, stirring wind and whispers and ghosts to accompany her.

It was exhaustion that owned the final leg of her walk, making every step on the well-worn path seem endless and futile. There was more written. She'd been too shocked to absorb it, but tinges of it flew into her mind then, when all she had to look at was the moonlit path in front of her, stirring over with the first vestiges of night mist.

There was a lot written after the word *marriage* . . . some-thing about inheritances and land, supplying coin and dowries to her MacHugh stepdaughters, a payment of gold to the other MacHughs . . . children. There was something written about trusts set up for children; riches beyond her dreams. Children. He'd written the word *children*. . . .

Their children.

Her feet stopped, and her body had no choice but to obey as the emotion resembling liquid fire touched through her belly and up through her breasts again at the memory. *Children?* Oh, dear God, she couldn't! No one could make her. She'd rather starve! She'd rather walk the streets in rags than give one instant of thought to the shiver way down deep that had started the moment she read the words, and that no one would *ever* get her to admit to.

It had to become anger again, and that gave impetus to her feet and legs, turning her long strides into a semijog that put a stitch in her side and made her lungs burn worse than her thighs.

Then the resignation came, completely and totally. She knew she had no choice. He knew she had no choice. That was why no one had lifted a finger to stop her flight from the Monteith estate. He knew she was going to have to do it.

There was light coming from the lower MacHugh castle

windows. Lisle stopped and looked at the place that had been home for a year now. That was ending. It had ended the moment she'd awakened this morning. She just hadn't known it. Lisle dragged her feet the remaining steps to the door and opened it, looking at change only the devil's gold could make, and knowing that the MacHughs hadn't even waited for her to agree before accepting Laird Monteith's terms.

"Angus?" she croaked from a throat dry enough to soak up a sporran full of liquid. "Mattie?"

"Look, lass! We're in the parlor. Just look!"

They hadn't used the parlor since before the Yule, because it was too large to keep warm in, and without any furnishings it was too vivid a reminder of what they were facing. That wasn't the case anymore.

Lisle stood, swaying until she had to lean against a doorjamb to disguise it, at the three aunts snuggled into new woolen blankets and rocking in identical chairs, while the other members of the MacHugh family lounged about on what appeared to be some of the same furniture they'd bartered away before things got so dire.

"The butcher still had my chair. Can you believe it?" Angus rose from the chair that had embraced him like a lover, and approached her, arms outstretched. Then he turned and used his arms to encompass the entire room.

"And look at the settee, and the tables, and even the mirror! He still had them as well. Isn't it grand?"

"Aye," she replied, through the same dry throat.

"We've you to thank, too, lass. Now, thank Lisle Dugall, all. She's gone and saved the MacHugh clan. That she has."

Lisle's eyebrows rose a bit, but it was too much effort to move them much farther, and she let them fall back down. She didn't have the energy to lift her own brows?

"Dugall?" she asked, with the croak of voice she had left.

"The missives he sent today came with gold, lass. Lots of it. He's offered thirty thousand for your hand. We couldn't turn it down. Think of it! Thirty thousand!"

"You opened . . . them?" she asked.

"We couldn't allow you to take us to the brink of disaster again, now, could we?" It was the eldest, Angela, asking it in a snide tone.

"And me . . . to my deathbed," Fanny added, between bouts of coughing.

"Weren't they addressed to me?" Lisle asked.

"Well . . . that there is the rub, lass."

Lisle tried to find a backbone stiff enough to hold her straighter, but her own spine was giving up on her now. If it hadn't been for the solidness of the wooden doorjamb she was clinging to, she'd probably be collapsed on the bare floor at their feet.

"What's the rub, Angus?" she asked.

"Thirty thousand gold pieces is a powerful amount of gold, Lisle," he said softly, and she noticed he wouldn't meet her eyes.

"Aye," she intoned.

"We could na' turn such a thing away. You ken how it is."

"Aye," she replied again.

They'd been afraid they had to sell their pride. It hadn't happened. They were selling her. The worst part was, if they had waited, they'd have known she would have gone without a fuss. She had to. There was no other choice.

His children? she thought again and shuddered, the motion making her own body tremble against the wooden support.

"And it isn't as if we canna' look ourselves in the eye anymore, either."

"Your meaning?" she asked with a very careful, controlled voice that sounded like the same rasp as the other words, but had heartbreak attached to it. She was only grateful they didn't hear it.

Angus cleared his throat. "I thought long and hard about this, lass. I did. Truly."

"I like you better when you're straightforward, Angus," Lisle answered, although all the words didn't make it to sound, and the last were said in a whisper. She knew he heard them since he flinched.

"The offers were addressed to Mistress Lisle MacHugh. That much is truth."

"And?" she asked, when all he did was stay silent, and act like he was waiting for her to think it through.

"There was nae wedding consummation with a MacHugh."

They weren't just selling her, they were disowning her first? Lisle found her backbone, and thanked God silently and swiftly for bringing the emotion to a halt, just like what had happened last night. She couldn't feel a thing, not even one blister.

"You canna' claim me enough to sell me, Angus, and then disown me once you have the gold."

"You were na' bed by a MacHugh, therefore you aren't truly a MacHugh. You're a Dugall. Still."

"That wasn't bothersome to you when I still had my dowry," she answered.

"Well, it's gone, and with it went hope. Until now. We want our futures back. That's all we want," Angela said, and this time she was aggressive.

"You should probably give the gold back, then," Lisle replied, and her voice had sound to it after all.

Angus flinched. Not one of them would meet her eyes, and she looked at each one in turn. "I believe I'm going to bed now, Clan MacHugh. I'll thank you to save further words until I've rested. It's been a powerful long day, you see. Good eve to you all."

Lisle turned, and had almost reached the steps leading to the chieftain's bed chamber, before the emotion turned into sobs that tormented her own chest with the strength of them.

She knew why they were doing it. She could even forgive them for it. If she were a MacHugh faced with what they had been, for as long as they had been, she'd have done it, too.

* * *

Lisle woke late, took several breaths, and then remembered. She tried to sit up, and groaned at the motion before her body betrayed her and dumped her back onto the mattress, making it sway a bit.

"About time you woke."

It was Angela. She was sitting on a padded chair that looked new, and knitting with what appeared to be bleached, freshly carded wool. She didn't look up as Lisle turned her head to face her. Angela had always been the most outspoken of them. That came with maturity, and losing a motherly hand at a very young age . . . twice. With Lisle's upcoming desertion, it was now three times.

"What time is it?" Lisle asked.

"Late," Angela replied to her knitting.

Lisle's lips thinned and she rolled her head back to look at the ceiling above her. Angela was probably getting ready to assert her authority as matriarch of the clan, if she hadn't done so already. From the way she was clicking her needles and the way she'd spoken, she had probably already done it, and Angus presented no challenge. That man had the life sucked out of him over a year ago, at the battle he couldn't forget. He wasn't up to challenging over authority.

"Do you wish me to leave now, or do I get a respite?" Lisle asked.

"Now would be best," Angela replied.

Lisle sighed softly. It was time to prove that she knew what love was. She knew it, very well. There was a part of her that wanted to demand the gold back, turn her back on the lot of them, march right back to the Dugall clan stronghold, and make what was left of them take her in. With thirty thousand in gold, she'd be most welcome, until they found out why she had it, that is.

She sent a silent prayer for strength and courage, and for unlimited guile to hide all of it. That way, not one of them would know what it was costing her, because that's what love was.

Lisle knew very well what love was, because she'd spent

six years praying about it and asking about it, and then she'd spent the last year showing it, with every part of her trousseau she parted with, and every drop of sweat she'd shed over every bit of labor to try and keep this family from ruin. She was actually grateful that she had the chance to finish, and do it so completely.

"Is there a bucket of water for my use?" she asked, grateful God was granting her prayer as her voice didn't even have a suspicion of the warble she'd expected it to have.

"Over yonder. It was warmed hours earlier. It is nae more, though."

"I shouldn't have slept so long," Lisle replied.

"Nae, you shouldn't have."

Her body really did have the strength. She was willing it there, and it worked, since moving her own legs toward the side so she could stand did show a bit of an ache, but it was small compared to the one in her heart. That pain was growing heavier with every beat of it.

"Will you grant me privacy?"

"Will you be needing it?" Angela replied, not once looking up.

"I think it would be best. I've nae idea how long I'll be, and I've a very long walk ahead of me at the end of it." *And I've bruising, and torn palms from slivers, broken blisters on my heels, and such, and I need to keep it all hidden*, she finished in her thoughts.

"There's a black, unmarked carriage at the end of the drive. Just outside our property. Waiting."

"There is?" Lisle's voice cracked, despite the control she was exercising to keep it at bay.

Angela didn't seem to notice. Lisle watched as she nodded, her head bobbing along with the way her needles moved. "Been there all day. None of us had the inclination to ask what it's there for."

Lisle sighed. "You dinna' need to. It's *him*."

"That's what we suspicioned. Must you dawdle so?"

Angela wasn't going to like looking at herself very much when she was older. Lisle looked at the lines of concentration stretching across her forehead, and how she was squinting slightly, bringing creases to both sides of her eyes. The girl was prematurely aging. Lisle only hoped it wasn't partly due to her failure at nurturing, protecting, and being a mother to her.

Her shoulders set, making her wince slightly. It was ridiculous. She'd walked before. She'd lived with sliver-filled palms for days now. She'd never had the weight of censure and banishment accompanying it before, though. Well and good, then. She couldn't change her future. All she could do was make certain those she loved didn't know what she was paying in order to save them.

The Black Monteith had also promised a dowry to the stepdaughters. He needn't know they didn't consider themselves that anymore. He could hear the truth of it, along with everyone else. He could hear it from their own lips, which everyone would—as long as it was later, after he paid. He was going to pay a dowry, and put it in trust for every one of them. She'd make certain of it. She still held out hope for the other girls, but sensed that Angela, for one, was going to need her dowry.

She shrugged, moved to the edge of the mattress, put her feet on the floor, sun-warmed by the uncurtained window, and grimaced slightly at how much she ached, before forcing her legs to support her.

They may have warmed the bucket of water, but it was hours earlier. It was tepid now. Lisle shivered as she touched her fingertips to it, and then told herself she was being ridiculous. Just yestermorn, before she found out what her future was, she'd bathed by swimming in the loch, luxuriating in the smell and touch of lavender soap, and kicking through water that was ice cold. She hadn't a hint of a shiver then.

"I wish you'd leave me to this," Lisle said, pulling the tie undone at the neckline of the one nightgown she'd claimed and owned and worn and washed, until the satin was so threadbare it no longer shone.

"You'll need help with the donning of it," Angela replied
to her knitting.

Lisle's heart sank, and her eyes flew to where her wedding dress had hung after they'd bartered the armoire away.
They were wedding her off now? Without any more time to
assimilate?

"'Tis your own fault, too."

"It is?" Lisle asked.

"Yours were the fingers applying all the seed pearl buttons
and beading, weren't they?"

"Aye," she replied.

"There's nae way to fasten it about oneself without an
assist."

Lisle didn't think through how Angela's hands on her back,
while she fastened the dress, were going to feel. She closed
her eyes and sent another prayer heavenward, this time asking
for the blessing of numbness. The MacHughs were right. She
wasn't going to go to Monteith unwed, and she wasn't going
to be allowed to stay from it. She might as well get it over
with. The carriage wasn't going to leave without her, the
MacHughs weren't going to go back to being the MacHughs
she knew, and the man she was going to have to wed wasn't
going to disappear if she stalled. It was only going to loom
larger, and the MacHughs would be the ones paying. They'd
start hating what they were doing, they wouldn't have anyone
to turn that emotion onto except her, and if she wasn't available, they might turn it on themselves.

Lisle wasn't going to allow that. She was going to dress in her
wedding finery, and she was going to act like she wanted to do
it. She hoped God was listening to that part of her plan, too.

She pulled the nightgown off her and bent to wring out the
cloth they'd given her in order to sponge off. She wasn't going
to worry over her hair. It had been in a bun since yesterday,
and beneath that, it was in two braids. That should be sufficient once she had it undone and combed through.

She wrapped the dry cloth about her before walking to the

gown, lifting the satin skirt and finding the chemise, real stockings of silk, and petticoats that she'd kept hidden beneath the long, seed-pearl embroidered skirt and train. She heard Angela's reaction as the needles stopped their incessant clicking noise, and a smile appeared on Lisle's lips.

Lisle slid the chemise over her head, sliding her hands along the satin-feel of it, and frowning a bit at how it clung to her breasts, but fell from everywhere else. She'd sewn it exactly to her own proportions, but a year of toil had slimmed her. There was no explanation for the increase in her bosom, however. It was enough that the gossamer weave of tatted lace at the center of the bodice was stretched wide, holding her in place, and creating a valley of shadow where she'd never noticed it before.

She wasn't going to be able to wear the stockings if she couldn't stop the broken blisters from weeping. She went over to the white linen sheet, pulled a corner from the bottom of the mattress, where it wouldn't easily be seen, and ripped at the sewing that wasn't ever supposed to come undone. She had to resort to picking at it before the hem gave, but she had her strips of linen. She didn't look up to see what reaction Angela had, and she couldn't hear if there was one over the sound of ripping material. The linens had come from her hope chest, they belonged to her, and if she wanted to use strips of them for bandaging, it was for her to decide, not any of them.

She sat to wrap her heels, tying little bows above her ankles, before she could pull the stockings on. She only winced once as she connected with the bruise on her right buttock from falling on it the other night, when she'd helped rescue the MacHugh war chest. The memory of that time warmed her, calming her incessant shivering for a few moments. That box had a place of honor in the center of the family, and they all had to admit that without her, it would have been lost.

The stockings were sheer to the point she could spot flesh beneath them. They were also too large, and weren't going to

stay up without garters. That was also odd, but she didn't
bother with the reason. Her legs looked more slender than
before. It wasn't surprising. Everyone looked like they were
slowly starving, and getting thinner was the first sign of it.
Well, that was changing, and it was Lisle that was making it
happen.

The shivering restarted. She stood and went to fetch the
light blue garters that she'd sewn into the petticoat, so they'd
not get lost. She tied them both on, ignoring Angela's watch-
ful eye, since there wasn't one click of any knitting needle
happening, and then she stood to put the petticoat on.

If Angela thought the dress overworked and laborious, she
wasn't going to have a description for the petticoat. Lisle had
used every bit of skill to embroider small blue butterflies all
over the garment, using the stitches to add thickness by quilting a layer of stiffened lace to the underside of it. The extrav-
agance was even more stunning nearly four years after she'd
designed and started creating it, and especially after the time
they'd just gone through.

"That's absolutely beautiful," Angela said, showing that despite her best intentions, she was female, and had a feminine
appreciation for such things.

Lisle smiled across at her. "My thanks. I designed it
myself."

"You did?"

"Aye. And if you like I'll help design one when you—"
Lisle's voice stopped as a pained, shuttered expression shut
down her stepdaughter's animation of a moment before. "Forgive me," she said, after clearing her throat. "I wasn't thinking. You won't want anything to do with me once this is over.
I understand. I do. Please let everyone know. Will you do that
for me?"

Angela looked across at her, and for a moment, Lisle could
have sworn she saw the glimmer of unshed tears in her eyes,
before she blinked them into nonexistence again. That was a
good sign. This wasn't killing off every bit of her capacity for

love. Lisle didn't want that to happen. Someday, the girl facing her was going to wed some upstanding, righteous Scotsman, if there was still one of marriageable age alive, and she was going to bring future MacHughs into being, and the last thing Lisle wanted was to know Angela wasn't a loving mother because of something her second, and final, step-mother might have or have not done.

She buttoned the petticoat into place, although it didn't fit on her waist like it used to, and would probably rotate about, and then she reached for the gown.

Angela was there before she was, reverently taking the dress from the wooden hook it had been hanging from, and sliding her fingers over the creasing that hanging in such a po-sition for so long had made in the shoulders, in order to take the worst of it out. Lisle watched her and then lifted her eyes to meet Angela's. There were definitely tears in the depths, and it took the most severe effort of Lisle's life to suck the answer-ing moisture in her own eyes back in. It was better to be numb and nonemotional, and listen to Angela trying to be assertive. The smile she gave was shaky, as was the girl's answering one.

"Let's get this over with. Fair?" Lisle asked.

The girl nodded, and lifted the dress to get it over Lisle's head. It was a good thing they hadn't undone her bun and brushed out her hair yet, for the dress would have ruined every bit of it with how it clung to and scratched everything it touched. Lisle lifted her lip into a slight smile as she re-membered that part of it. Such embroidery and seed pearl en-hancement came with a price. Inner threads that itched and caught on strands of hair and on the lace centerpiece of the chemise, regardless of the satin she'd lined the inside with.

Then she was standing, facing the window as the sun moved into a position heralding dusk. She'd slept the entire day away? It didn't seem possible, but it was just as well. She didn't want the others trying to be hard-shelled and stiff-backed, and she didn't dare put her numbness through much more testing.

Angela's fingers gained competence as she started at the waistline, sliding the hundreds of little loops Lisle had sewn onto the pearls that would hold them, until she ended at the top of Lisle's neck. Then her fingers were unwrapping the bun and unbraiding the hair. Lisle let her. The girl was taller, making it simpler, and she guessed this was Angela's way of asking apology for her curtness earlier.

Lisle knew her hair was going to be like a wave-rippled section of the loch, and wasn't surprised to find it was so, even to where the ends grazed her hip. There wasn't a veil. They'd used it up as bandaging when Angus had first reached home . . . after Culloden. That was all right.

"You look beautiful, Lisle." The girl breathed the words. "It's a shame . . ." Her voice dribbled off.

"That it's to be wasted on Monteith as my groom?" Lisle supplied.

The girl nodded.

"I had a good look the other day. It's not too onerous. He's a right comely man, if one gets past what . . . he is."

"That's na' going to be easy. He's immense. I've heard tales. He's evil. He's frightening."

Lisle frowned. "I ken as much," she whispered.

"I doona' envy you," Angela said softly.

"I'll just have to keep my mind on his handsomeness, and not on what it hides." She took a deep breath. "He does have that, you know."

"I know. I saw him."

"Yes." There were those shivers again. The ones she'd die before admitting to. Lisle frowned. They didn't stop. They got stronger. She gulped. "He's tall, he's manly, and he's gorgeous. Why, if this was taking place under other circumstances . . ." She almost got it out before her voice failed, and she just let it trail off. To do anything else would crack her composure open. That, she wasn't going to allow. She was not going to let anyone know what Monteith was doing to her.

That would be the worst indignity of a whole heap of the same ever since she'd met him.

Angela put a hand on her shoulder and squeezed slightly. Then it was gone, as she stepped back and tilted her head to one side, as if surveying their handiwork, and not like she'd just put almost more weight atop her stepmother's shoulders than she could support and still go through with it.

"Doona' move. I've got an idea," Angela said.

"For what?" Lisle asked.

"A circlet about your head. We can fashion one from the creeping azalea that Mary brought back from the cliffs just this morn, although I've told her over and over not to go there. I'll be right back."

Lisle looked levelly across at Angela and nodded solemnly. She didn't trust her voice.

Chapter Five

The carriage was for her, and it was empty. The interior was just as luxurious, new, and bare as the one she'd ridden in when she visited him, perhaps more so. Lisle sat on one of the tanned, leather-covered, padded seats and looked about her. She wondered how many of the carriages he owned, and if they were all reeking of newness and wealth, and wasteful expense.

She shook her head. She was going to have to teach that man the value of his gold, before he spent all of it and made the Monteith clan look even more foolish than they were already perceived to be.

The coach halted with an unprofessional movement, making her rock like the hanging lantern at the far side. The door opened. It was Aunt Fanny, Aunt Mattie, and the ghostly Aunt Grace, who looked even more insubstantial in the lamplight and faded day.

"We've something for you, lass," Aunt Mattie said, after clearing her throat. "Something auld."

"And God be with you," Aunt Fanny whispered, stepping forward to hand her a small packet. Lisle was almost too surprised to reach down for it.

Then, they were gone, fading back into the shadows alongside the road. Lisle unwrapped her present with trembling hands to reveal a very old, chipped brooch, containing a bit of crystal at the center. She trembled with the sob, but had it under control before the coach rocked to another stop.

The coachmen were silent, but they had been that way since the first time she'd journeyed to Monteith and had a groomsman open the door for her and assist her in. This time, it was Angus MacHugh, looking sheepish, and with red-rimmed eyes that only two reasons could cause. One was too much drink; the other she didn't want to know.

"Here, Lisle lass," he said in his gruff voice, and shoved a bundle at the flooring before disappearing into the night faster than the aunts had. She didn't have to look to see what it contained; the movement of the coach starting up made the bundle shift, and any remaining air in the bladders sighed out with a moan. Her hand wasn't just trembling, it was difficult to control as she lifted the edge of the old MacHugh tartan that wrapped the bundle.

He'd given her his pipes.

Lisle sat, holding them to her breast, and letting the plaide soak up tears the MacHugh clan had just caused.

"Damn them all, anyway!" she whispered, her arms pushing further moans from the bags with the pressure she held them to her. They should have just let her go. It would have been easier.

If smitten really were a condition with emotion and meaning attached to it, he was very afraid he had it. Langston stood at the altar and watched as she walked toward him, enhancing the organ music and the reverence of the place with the slow, gliding way she was moving. She had a bundle of something wrapped in the MacHugh sett and held to her, with as much pride as a bouquet of flowers. Her head was high, making the auburn color reflect all of the candles he'd ordered and personally supervised the placement of, and there wasn't any part of her that wasn't ethereal, stunning, and absolutely breathtaking.

He nearly thumped himself in the chest to start up his breathing again, but settled with clearing his throat and swallowing around a strange lump that wasn't moving anywhere.

She was very pale, mirroring the ecru shade of her gown, even to the lack of coloring of her lips. Langston swallowed again and licked his own lips, wishing he'd had Etheridge tie the mass of white satin at his throat a bit looser, since it scratched his skin with the movement and made it all somehow worse.

She reached his side and glanced up at him, startling him with the vivid contrast of those sky-blue eyes to her pallor. Then, she dropped her gaze, while a light bloom of color touched the tops of her cheeks. *That was interesting*, he told himself. It could be a sign that all wasn't lost, and that the bit of something he'd seen flicker through her eyes yesterday was actually what it had appeared to be at the time—interest.

If he interested her as a man, despite everything she thought of him, there might actually be a rhyme and reason to why he was forcing the woman he was losing sleep over into doing something she deemed so patently horrible. Her lashes were dark brown, the length easily seen against her pallor. She didn't look up to him again; not when he reached for, and received, her cold, trembling hand in his; not when he answered his vows, with a voice he had to clear his throat to find; not even when she whispered her own troth.

If he wasn't already intrigued, he would have been then, when her chin trembled, a tear slid from the corner of one eye, and she still managed to whisper the words that were saving her family. He was so aware of her, and the strange emotion she was making him suffer, that it almost made him forget that she probably hated him.

She didn't look like she was at that emotion at the moment. She probably wasn't at anything other than shock. The one glimpse she'd given him showed him that. It was the same, unfathomable look she'd had when she'd first read what he wanted from her, right after her gasp of reaction. She'd dropped the missive, put her hands to her cheeks to cover them, and then spun and stomped right out of his house, without one backward glance. He didn't even know if she'd read through what he was offering.

All of which meant less than dust to him next to how she seemed to be shying away from the moment he was waiting for, and Langston was more than a little annoyed to find he was trembling at the thought. *Me? Shaking?* He realized it in disbelief before putting all his effort into stopping the tremor of his own hand holding hers before she felt it.

She didn't want to kiss him. She didn't want to be near enough to him to touch him. Her cold hand gave him that indication as it just lay within his grasp, holding a chill to it, when he wanted to send nothing but warmth. She was going to have to kiss him, though.

The thought that he had to force it gave him little satisfaction, but the desire to feel those lips against his made it something worth risking. He was losing sleep over it, he was being plagued ceaselessly with it, he was finding it difficult to concentrate. There was only one thing to do about it. See if the reality matched the dream. He could hardly wait for the end of the ceremony, sealing her to him, and making her his for this lifetime . . . his wife, his partner, his mate.

They were pronounced man and wife and Langston turned his head slowly, savoring the time it would take, and holding his breath at what he'd find. He wasn't disappointed, although she was looking up at him with the look that went straight through him again, just like that first time. He could have been anyone, as long as it was anyone *else*. His eyes narrowed as he knew that's what she was wishing for.

She had a bit of rose to her cheeks that she couldn't disguise, and a touch of the same to her lips. She also had more tears hovering at her lashes, but not going anywhere from there.

He turned fully to face her, and she did the same motion.

Langston was a large man. He always had been, although he'd been much more lean when he'd first left Scotland. He was dwarfing the vicar who had just said the words, and making the woman look like a waif next to him, rather than the flesh-and-blood goddess she was. Something sparked through the opacity she was hiding behind, startling her, and bringing even more rose to her cheeks.

Langston caught his smile before she saw it, but he couldn't do a thing about how his heart stumbled, his breath caught, and how all of that made his hand tremble again as he reached for her chin, tilting her upward for him. He watched the lashes flutter to her cheeks as she closed her eyes. He knew she wasn't doing it to experience it more fully; it was to shut him out.

Langston drew her closer, his arm molding about the slim waist to lift her from the floor, feeling the bundle she held as it was the first thing to touch his chest, and then his lips were at her ear, whispering words his mind hadn't cleared. "I'll na' claim a kiss until you give it freely," he said, and he could have bitten his own tongue off the moment they left his lips.

He only hoped the surprise on her face wasn't the mirror to his own as he pulled back; seized, and then held, by sky-blue eyes that hadn't an ounce of disinterest in them, but were full of life and shock, disgust, and confusion.

That would have to do. Langston felt the flush creeping up the side of his neck, and wished now that he'd had the cravat tied higher, to stop her from seeing it. He knew she was, too, for her eyes didn't leave him as he set her back on her feet and started walking, holding her at arm's length and then letting her go completely. The fact that she didn't move away from him was the only sign she was giving him that she wasn't going to die on the spot after all, although that was probably what she'd been wishing; that, and the way her lashes fluttered, and her cheeks went from rose to red, and then dead white again as she realized it.

He'd never seen anything as intriguing as this woman he'd just married, and he wasn't letting her out of his sight. The prearrangement he'd made to send her to Monteith Hall in the separate carriage was tossed right out of his head. He wanted her by him, with him, eating, sleeping, and caressing him. He wanted her to learn about him, and he wasn't going to able to give her any clue.

The walk to the carriage was excruciating, the ride was going to be worse, and there was nothing she could do about any of it. What was one supposed to say to a stranger one had just wed, giving the rights to one's body to? Especially a stranger that wasn't even going to force it?

He had no right to be chivalrous. How dare he do something so against character that it tossed her emotions up into a blur of confusion before giving them back to her? He was supposed to be vicious; taking, ravishing, stealing . . . exactly like the Sassenach had done to every woman they came across after Culloden. He was supposed to be a devil. He was supposed to have evil intent behind those eyes that looked to be so brown, they were almost black. He surely wasn't supposed to be chivalrous.

Lisle was at his side when he reached yet another carriage, where the door was opened by two groomsmen smiling—no, they looked more like open grins, she decided—at both her and Monteith, while they waited for the couple to enter, so they could be sealed in together.

That was it, she told herself. He was waiting. He'd force her when they were alone, and no one would be there to rescue her, or even hear her screams. He'd probably ordered them to drive slowly; to give him enough time to make certain she hadn't a bone left that wasn't violated.

"Do you need an assist in?" he asked, at her elbow, since she had been standing there, stupidly looking at the yawning opening of the carriage like it was supposed to swallow her up without her having to expend any effort.

"I—I . . . uh, no," she answered, stumbling over the words

and having to look away from the humor that was starting to haunt every bit of every look he was giving her.

He stood back a step and waited while she lifted one part of her skirt with a hand, showing that her slippers were caved in at the heel, and not fully on her. It wasn't because her feet were too big, although she suspected that was what he thought, since he had even more humor about his features the next time she dared to glance at him. It was because the linen wrapped about her blisters had made the slippers too small to wear.

If the other coaches were luxurious, there was no description for this one. Lisle stooped to get in, running her hand along red and black–patterned silk that could only have come from the Orient, meeting dark mahogany everywhere else, and trying to keep the gasp in where he couldn't hear it. She should have known it wouldn't succeed.

"I had it built in Edinburgh. For one occasion, and one only. Then, I'm retiring it," he informed her, in a bored-sounding voice.

"Good Lord, why?" she asked, before she could stop herself. Then, she busied herself with putting the pipes reverently at her side, arranging her skirts about her ankles, and taking up as much of her side of the coach as she could, so he wouldn't even think about sitting next to her.

He looked like he'd known what she was about, too. He entered, the carriage rocking slightly with his weight, which, from the stolen glimpses she was still trying to keep him from seeing, looked to be considerable. She couldn't imagine where he'd gained such an amount of bulk to his frame. From all she'd heard, he didn't do a thing, except spend gold.

"For posterity," he replied, with the same bored tone that hadn't a hint of depth, sense, or reason to it.

Lisle glanced at him again. He wasn't looking at her. He was settling himself on the opposite bench, opening the buttons on his black coat, and then pulling a bit at the white material he'd swathed all about his throat. She couldn't stop the smile.

"Something amuses you?" he asked.

"What is that for?" She pointed.

"It's called a cravat. Menswear. For formal dress occasions. This being one of them."

"A cravat," she replied, without inflection.

"I decided that if we have to dress in the English fashion, I may as well adopt some of their ways. You doona' like it?"

"It looks like a bundling of scarf, in the event of cold weather."

"My valets will be crushed," he replied.

"Valets?" she asked.

"Personal servants. I have a score of them. Very observant chaps, very conscientious in their duties, very precise. According to Etheridge, this is the height of fashion in London."

"Oh." It was all she could think of to say. *The height of fashion in London?* she repeated to herself.

"I'm na' very fond of it, but one must play by the rules one is given, nae?"

"If you're asking about living under Sassenach rule, and liking it, you're asking the wrong person," she replied, using the exact same, bored tone of voice he was.

"That's distressing," he replied.

"That's not the most distressing part, let me assure you," she continued.

"It's not?" he asked, almost jovially. At least, it looked like he had even more humor to his features when she looked up. It was muted the moment their glances touched, until it became almost a frown.

"I'll not be made fun of," Lisle announced.

"I'd never allow such a thing to occur."

"Good. Then we'll start this marriage by discussing your spendthrift habits and the cessation of them."

"Excuse me?" he asked.

"You. Spendthrift. It's a word attached to your name . . . *our* name, more oft' than necessary. Nae one likes a neighbor with more gold than they have. It's making enemies of us."

"Do tell," he responded and quirked one of his eyebrows.

"Someone should have told you sooner. The more you toss gold about, the more contempt you're held in. I doona' like it."

"So?" he asked.

"You'd best not mean what it sounds like you mean with that tone, my lord."

"Oh, please. Call me Langston," he replied, smoothly and easily. Almost too smoothly and easily, she was thinking.

"Langston?" she asked.

"It is my given name."

Lisle giggled.

"I've not received that response a-fore. Tell me. What is it about my name that amuses you so?"

"Langston and Lisle," she replied, dropping her tongue on the beginning consonant so it rolled. "You doona' find it funny?"

"Nae," he replied, and the word hadn't a bit of amusement or humor attached anywhere to it.

"Well, I won't allow any child of ours to have a name beginning with an L, then," Lisle continued. "We'll be worse than laughingstocks."

The sigh that came from his side of the coach must have been his reply, for he didn't say anything for long enough that she had to fill in the gap. "Is that your acquiescence?" she asked.

"You've been formally schooled," he replied evenly . . . too evenly. The lamplight was swaying slightly, highlighting him and then moving away, so she couldn't tell why he sounded so different.

"Of course. Ellwood MacHugh dinna' betroth just any lass," she said to that, lifting her chin slightly, so he could tell his insult had been taken and replied to.

"Perhaps we'd be better off partaking of wine." He was speaking, but it didn't sound like his self-assured, bored voice, nor did it sound like any voice he'd used before. It sounded young, and in a higher pitch than before. She wondered why.

"Wine?" Lisle asked.

"What wedding coach comes complete without wine?" he replied.

"I've never drunk wine," she said.

"Never?"

"I've na' touched whiskey much, either."

"Nae?" he responded.

"Does wine have the same effect as whiskey?" she asked.

"Some say 'tis worse."

"Good. I'll take two doses of the stuff, then."

He laughed, and it was such a surprise that Lisle couldn't keep from staring. He didn't look like he was in league with the devil. He looked like he was a handsome, young man. *Young*, she repeated in her thoughts.

"How auld are you?" she asked when the sound of his laughter had died.

"That would probably depend on how auld you are," he replied softly.

"What? Why?"

"I would na' wish to frighten you."

"I'm not frightened of you," she announced loudly.

"You look frightened."

"You doona' know me enough to judge such," she replied.

"True," he said, finally.

"So . . . how auld are you?" she asked again.

"Twenty-eight."

"Nae!" The shock in her voice had him laughing again. Lisle reddened, and had to turn her face away before he saw anymore of it.

"Too auld for you?" he asked.

"My first husband was fifty-seven," she replied to the wall.

"Ugh," was his response to that. She almost matched it.

So, Langston Monteith was twenty-eight. Young, by any standards, and especially youthful to have amassed the fortune he was spending. She wondered if he'd stolen it. That was probable to the point of being likely. He was a pirate. That was it.

He'd stolen it from good, sea-faring folk, taking their ships, stealing their gold, and then sending them to the bottom of the ocean. That's where the gold must have come from, she told herself.

"You're mumbling to yourself. Here." He was holding out a slender, crystal goblet, filled at the bottom with a dark liquid that rolled back and forth with the carriage's movement. She wondered where he'd gotten it, and why she hadn't even seen it.

"Is this all I get?" she asked.

His lips curved into a smile, and she couldn't tear her eyes away. Not when he handed the goblet to her, or when he touched it with the side of his own, since she hadn't been able to move her hand, or when he brought his own to his lips, took a draught, and then swallowed it.

Lisle wasn't able to prevent her own throat from doing the same motion. She dropped her gaze to the goblet she gripped with two hands now, to still its trembling. She didn't know what was happening to her, but it wasn't good.

"Until I see how well you handle it . . . aye," he said, filling the coach with the smoothness of his voice again.

"What?" she asked.

"You were asking if that's all you get. That's my answer."

"Oh."

"I'll not have it said my wife's a drunkard."

"What?" she asked. The words were insulting, but the tone was slick and warm and masculine, and making strange rivulets of something she didn't know enough about to define run her spine and then return, crawling up into the circlet of flowers still at the crown of her head before dissipating, like bubbles of froth at a fast-running burn. That wasn't good, at all, she decided.

"Take a sip. It's not lethal."

Oh, if only something was! Lisle lifted the glass to her lips and made the same motion he had, although the wine was

sour-tasting and acrid, and made her nose wrinkle with distaste before she swallowed. She didn't like a thing about wine.

"Does it meet with your approval?" he asked.

"What?"

"The wine. It's a very good stock. From France. Expensive.
I drink only the best and pay well for the privilege."

"Will you cease flaunting this wealth? 'Tis unseemly!"

"To whom?" he asked.

"Every Scot that's without it," she whispered.

Her answer settled into the carriage, changing the atmosphere so subtly that if she wasn't so attuned to it, she'd have
missed it. It was colder, too. She reached to touch the bundle
of bagpipes on the seat beside her for strength and courage,
and to curb the fright she'd just claimed she didn't have.

"I really hadn't given it much thought," he finally said,
making her gasp with the words.

She lifted the goblet and gulped it down, making a wince
at how it tasted at the back of her throat, and then she held it
out for more. He didn't say a word; he just lifted his eyebrows, before tipping the bottle and pouring her another
dollop of it.

Chapter Six

"You decide you like my wine?" he asked, with a softer voice than he'd used before, as Lisle gulped the second portion down, too, not even noticing the taste that time.

She nodded and held her glass out again.

"Oh, I doona' think so, my dear."

My dear? Her head repeated it because her ears still didn't believe they'd heard it. "Why not?" she asked, lifting her chin.

"Because you're excruciatingly young."

"So?"

"And I'm not," came the answer.

"Twenty-eight is not auld," Lisle replied.

"True. To some."

She frowned. She probably should have grabbed a slice or two of the black bread that the MacHughs had been making into rolls about their sliced beef when she'd left. She didn't know much about it, but wine probably wasn't a good thing on an empty stomach, and what little of it he'd let her have was sending warmth where she was determined to stay cold, and making him look fuzzy and indistinct every time she looked that way.

"And to others, it's ancient."

She lifted one side of her face from the frown, straightening it out, but he was still blurred-looking. That wasn't all bad, she decided. He didn't look as dark and malevolent. "You're not ancient," she announced, since it was a fact.

"I've been in Persia. Do you know where that is?" he asked.

She shook her head, then squinted her eyes, then nodded. She'd learned this at school. "At the other end of the Mediterranean Sea," she replied finally.

"Very good."

Lisle felt the blush again, and had to look down at the empty wine goblet in her hands.

"Persia has a clime that ages a man . . . and a woman. Alexander the Great was but twenty when he became king and conquered the known world. Twenty-six is the age at which Hannibal the Barbarian took over his father's armies and became a great thorn in Rome's side. All of which is ancient, dusted history, but proves my point. Age is relative when life is held cheaply, and twenty-eight can feel quite auld to some."

"That's distressing," Lisle replied.

He took a long time to answer. She wasn't looking at why. It was better to go back to studying her wine glass.

"Why so?" he asked finally, with a voice that sounded different, somehow.

"That gives me nine years and some, a-fore I feel the same. That isn't very comforting."

The meaning behind his groan was lost on her. It didn't sound like he agreed, though. "It won't happen to you. I'll make certain of it."

"I think you overrate yourself, my lord."

He rolled the amusement through his lips. At least, that's what it sounded like. "My thanks, I think," he replied finally.

"I mean . . . you're not in charge of such a thing." What was she doing? If he felt insulted, why was she softening and amending it?

This time he gave a great sigh, the breath of it nearly reaching where her hands were still wrapped about the wine goblet. "Why do you ken I offered for you?" he asked softly, surprising her with the texture and sound of his voice as it wrapped about her.

"There was naught else the MacHughs had that you . . . wanted." Her voice dropped on the last word. He wanted her? Oh, good Lord, don't make that word mean what it sounded like!

"That . . . and more," he replied.

It was better to be blurred and unreal, even more so than it already felt. She instinctively knew it. She held out her glass again. "Can I please have some more of your wine?" she asked.

"Nae."

"But, why?"

"Because wedding nights doona' fare well with drunkenness."

She gasped, insulted to the core of her being. At least, she thought she was insulted. The pit of her belly was still warming her, and the wine was making it difficult to feel anger. She actually felt like giggling, but that wasn't the correct response to what he'd just said. She settled with swallowing on the giddy reaction and sitting straighter.

"I'm not drunk," she said, finally.

"I know," he replied. "I'm na', either. I prefer to keep it that way . . . for both of our sakes."

That had her frowning again. She didn't have a ready reply, and blamed the wine again, for making everything feel like it was floating on clouds. Her brow lifted as she thought it out. His carriage was well-sprung, and his drive was crafted of perfectly aligned stones. Of course it would feel like floating.

"Why?" she asked.

"Because things might happen . . . or not happen."

That time it was her turn to gasp, as her eyes flew wide, and it wasn't just a blush, it was full-out fire licking at her cheeks. Then, it was receding, leaving her still floating, but it was on shakier clouds.

"I doona understand," she finally replied.

"And I think you do. Very well, in fact."

"Are you calling me a liar?" she asked.

"Never," was the reply.

"Then, explain your words." *Or try*, she added in her thoughts. It didn't seem possible to understand them. Wine must be very intoxicating, she decided.

"Life's held cheaply in Persia, my dear."

"What?" she asked. There was that *my dear* again, rolling off his tongue like it belonged there. It had to be the wine making it so. It must have the same effect on him to keep saying something so patently ridiculous.

She did giggle, then, and had to move one of the hands from her goblet to her mouth to cover it over. One didn't giggle over what he'd just said. Life was too cheap. That's what he'd said, wasn't it? Why would he make such a statement and what did it have to do with wedding nights?

"It's different here. Much different."

"Is it?" she asked.

"Oh, aye."

"How would you know? You weren't at the battle. Your family wasn't at the battle. Why, there wasn't a Monteith anywhere near Drumossie Moor that night, or any other night."

"I wasn't there because 'tis nigh impossible to be two places at one time."

Lisle waited for him to finish such a ridiculous statement. Or maybe she was waiting for the low timbre of his voice. He had a very nice voice, she decided, half-closing her eyes.

". . . and I already told you where I was."

"What?" she asked, her eyes flickering on the man facing her, and trying to find some spot on him that was unpleasant, or unfit, or wasted, or just plain ugly. There wasn't any. He was still beautiful. Evil . . . but beautiful.

"I was in Persia."

"Why were you there?" she asked.

"Something to do with being unfit."

"Nae," she replied, giggling again. "You're not unfit anywhere. Or, if you are, 'tis impossible to spot."

"Oh, Christ," he replied, filling the coach with the curse, except he hadn't said it like a curse. It was more like a prayer.

"What?" she asked.

"Give me your glass."

He wasn't requesting it, since he just reached out and plucked it from fingers that didn't do more than let it go. That was strange, she decided. She hadn't even fought it.

"Why?" she asked.

"Because I'm a-feared of what I might do otherwise."

"What?" Lisle was going to find a way to stop the one-word questions from coming out of her own mouth, but it wasn't going to be easy. She ran her tongue over her teeth and tried to suck any leftover wine from there.

"You're very tempting to me, Lisle. Very."

Tempting? What did that mean? "Why?" she asked, and wrinkled up her nose. There was another of those one-word questions. She had to halt that.

"Why? Doona' make me answer that one yet. We've not yet reached that point, and I'm not going to allow it to happen like this."

"What?" she asked.

"You know very well what."

"I do?" She brightened at the words, glad to have found herself capable of saying more than one of them. He wasn't making sense, but it was a very nice bit of nonsense he was making. That, or wine was very intoxicating, or she should have eaten something, or it was her wedding day. Any of that should be enough to make her feel giddy and insubstantial and like she hadn't a stiff bone anywhere in her body.

"It's evil," she said.

"What is?" he asked, with a quickness that belied any intoxicating effects he might be feeling.

"This. You. Us," she replied. They were one-word sentences, but she'd said three of them. That was an improvement, she decided.

"I'm sorrowed you think so," he said after a very long span of time.

"You are?" she asked.

"Aye."

"But . . . why? You already knew of it."

"Hearing and knowing are two different things."

"Then . . . ex—explain." The word *explain* took two tries to get it out, but he understood it. Lisle could have kicked herself, again. Why was she still trying to soften everything she said to him? That was senseless. She didn't want to like him. She didn't want to tempt him . . . *tempt him to what?* she wondered again. And she certainly didn't want to be his dear; although when he said it, there hadn't been any hesitation or pause, or anything that might be normal when addressing a lass named MacHugh—Dugall, she amended in her thoughts—that had just shamed her ancestors by marrying the Black Monteith.

"What would you like to know?" he asked.

"What?" she asked.

"You wanted an explanation. I would like to know to what, please?"

"Explanation," she repeated, looking for the sense of the word.

"Remind me of your proclivity to alcohol in the future, would you, my dear?"

Lisle kept the bubble of mirth inside at hearing the endearment, and then she thought through what other words it had been attached to. *Proclivity? What did that mean?* she asked herself. Then, she just asked it.

"It means that you canna' hold your spirits. That's what it means."

That was insulting, too. Lisle sent the order for her backbone to straighten up, so she could tell him exactly what she thought of him. Nothing much happened. She continued swaying slightly with the coach's movements and nothing on her was stiff or unbending or anything save nicely pliant. She couldn't even get her lips to tighten up and close.

She wondered if he knew.

There wasn't any way to tell by looking at him. The sway was making the lamplight move with it, sending the glow from her knees to his and back, but it wasn't far enough to penetrate his side.

"Is that why you won't let me have more wine?" she asked, a bit surprised and yet pleased that she'd linked that many words together.

"Very good. There isn't much hidden that you canna' uncover with those clear, sky-blue eyes of yours, is there? That's a very good thing. Very."

"Why?" she asked, absolutely amazed that she wasn't full-out laughing at what he'd just said. She had sky-blue eyes? No one had ever described them like that. Her frown of concentration deepened. Actually, no one had ever described them at all.

"There's a lot hidden, at present."

"There is?"

"Aye."

"Why?" she asked.

"That's for you to discover. I just made mention of it, dinna' I?"

"You . . . hide things?" she asked.

"All the time. Trust me."

"But . . . why?"

He sighed again, but if it hadn't been for the white of his shirt she wouldn't have seen it. She watched the movement and wondered why he'd be able to move such a large chest, if he didn't have that big of one to begin with. She wondered if that was the case, and knew it was by the proof in front of her eyes. That wasn't a good thing at all, she told herself.

Her chin rose, and she moved her eyes to where his had to be. That was probably a mistake, but she was making lots of them in a short amount of time, and one more shouldn't matter. Because he'd put so much dark mahogany wood to his coach, and patterned the seats in red and black, and since he was wearing black, with only the white cloth marking where he was, he was blending into the background. If it weren't for the shine of his eyes, and glint of his teeth when he smiled, he'd not be easy to spot at all.

She opened her mouth and said, "You're a very handsome man, Monteith."

He sucked in a breath and closed his eyes at that. At least, that's what she thought he did, since the shine disappeared for several moments. When what light they had slithered onto his knees, she could see he'd clenched his hands on his knees, too. He had very nice-shaped fingers, she thought, moving her glance all the way down him and back. She hadn't noted that before.

His hands were very large, too. Everything about him was large and well defined, masculine and extremely fit. Big. Brawny. Beautiful. Very. It still wasn't fair. She reached out, connecting with a shockwave that jolted through her wrist, and then ran her index finger along his, before stopping at the obstruction of his cuff.

"You shouldn't be doing this," he said.

"Why not?" she asked.

"Because regret and recriminations are terrible things to live with in the morning."

"What?" She'd opened her hand, resting her palm atop his hand, and then she was sliding the rest of her fingers along and entwining them between his.

"If any fool ever gives you so much as a drop of wine, I'm lynching him. On the spot. Without a trial. Myself included."

"Why would . . . you do that?"

"Because you hate me," he answered.

"I do?"

"If you dinna' already, you surely will, if I allow this to continue."

That made less sense than anything he'd said the entire trip. Lisle reached out with her other hand and held to his. He opened his fingers the moment she did, allowing her to easily place them within the grasp of his, where they were swallowed by the size of him.

"Why are you doing this . . . to me?" he asked. He wasn't using his low, smooth voice. It sounded rough and mean.

She'd done it more to keep herself from falling. That was strange. It felt like she was already falling. She didn't dare tell him any of that. "I doona' know," she answered, lifting her face to his.

"Doona' offer what you'll regret, Lisle."

"I haven't offered anything," she replied.

"Then, sit back onto your side like a nice young lass, and allow me some time to gather myself."

"What if the answer to that is 'nae'?" she asked.

"How long have you been without a man, Lisle?"

That was absolutely senseless. She'd just left Angus that day. She opened her mouth to say it, and then closed it again. She knew then that wasn't what he'd meant, and her tongue reached out to lick at her own lips to moisten them so she'd be able to answer.

"A long time," she answered, and then added the truth. "Never."

The fingers tightened on hers, entrapping them, and she could feel the muscles above his knees going to the same tautness. *He has muscle above the knee?* She wondered at it and wished he'd let her go, so she could experiment further with such an idea.

Instead, he was moving forward, his knees bending into a right angle to the floor of the carriage, and then he went past that, to a near-squat as he took up entirely too much room. He was definitely the most handsome man she'd ever seen, she decided, looking from the top of his shiny black hair, which he'd tucked behind his ears, down the aquiline nose, and ending at lips too perfect to belong to a mortal man. None of this was fair, she told herself. He wasn't supposed to be beautiful, and she wasn't supposed to be holding to him, and she definitely wasn't supposed to have her parted lips within inches of his.

"Do you ken what it is you're about?" he asked, using a whisper of sound she barely heard over the roar in her ears.

She nodded. Then, she shook her head. There was an answering smile hovering on his lips. She didn't look past that.

"Doona' close your eyes this time."

This time? Why was nothing making sense? As far as she knew, there had never been a first time. She didn't shut her eyes. He did. Which made it awful strange that he had no trouble tilting his head so he could fit his perfectly formed lips to hers.

Lightning struck the coach, lighting the interior to the point she couldn't keep her own eyes open. That was especially strange, since there hadn't been a hint of it in the weather before, and it had never filtered into her breast before, making her heart feel like a caged animal, and her breath hard to find. She didn't even know where it had gone to. Lisle rocked in place, worse than any coach movement could possibly make, and her head moved of its own accord, tilting the opposite way his was, making it easier for the kiss to deepen, and harder to find one part of her that didn't want it to.

There was a groan coming from his chest, the sound filling her mouth and then the coach, and then it was accompanied by such a trembling of his entire frame, that she felt it and responded to it with everything that was maternal and loving and caring about her. Then, he was pulling his lips from her with a vicious twist that felt like it tore skin. Lisle didn't dare open her eyes for several moments, and she felt none of the dizziness or blurred feeling of the past minutes that could just as easily have been hours. She felt painfully sober and cold all over.

She opened her eyes.

He was inches from her, black eyelashes shadowing what she knew was the dark ale color of eyes, and with not one expression on his face. *Damn him for being so handsome*, she told herself, pulling her right hand free so she could mold it around his cheek and cup his chin with her palm.

Lisle's eyes filled with tears. She didn't know why, or even where they came from, as his image distorted and then cleared, and he was still far too handsome. She also felt his pain, and wished she could help him with it, help mute some of it . . . and she didn't know where that insane idea came from.

"Doona' ever do that again," he said softly, brutally, and with a note in his voice that spoke of absolute finality and nothing more.

Lisle's heart stopped, and then decided it really would continue beating. She didn't know what had taken place, or why she'd done any of it, and he reacted like this? Her hand started stinging where it was still touching him, and she lifted it away and let it drop. Her left hand was still entwined with his, making it impossible to move it away as easily.

"I won't be pitied by anyone. Highlander or not."

"Pitied?" she whispered.

"You ken exactly what you did, and you also ken exactly why you did it," he answered.

"Pitied?" she repeated. He thought she'd kissed him out of pity? What was wrong with the man that he'd get such an idea? And why was she fighting it? She didn't dare think through what might be the true reason—that she'd lost her mind. It was better that he thought it pity.

"When we arrive at Monteith Castle, go to your room. Doona' touch me again."

She nodded and loosened her fingers, and then she was pulling them away from his. He didn't help her, but he didn't fight her, either. Lisle didn't think she had feeling left in her left hand from the grip he'd had on it. She didn't flex it to check. She didn't move anything on her.

"You aren't welcome in my bed," he told her.

She gasped. "I've not said I wish to be there," she answered.

"Good. Keep it that way."

Lisle sucked in on an emotion that she instinctively knew would go beyond tears and turn into full-fledged sobs if she let any of it through. There was no reason for any of it. She didn't want to be in his bed! Good Lord—that he would think such a thing! She didn't want any part of him. She only wished the place beneath the seed pearl beading of her bodice wasn't such a painful lump that she nearly clasped her hands to it to stop it.

"Why did you wed with me? Why dinna' you just buy up the land, like everywhere else?" she asked finally, wishing the words from existence almost before they left her lips.

"Remember how I spoke of hidden things?" he asked.

She nodded. She only wished she could move her gaze down, and not keep it linked with his like they were strung together with pieces of spun wool, or worse, jewelry wire.

"That's good. That's very good."

He blinked slowly at the end of his words, releasing her, although nothing on her obeyed the newfound freedom. She was still gazing raptly at him when he opened his eyes and caught her at it.

"We haven't much left of this ride," he offered.

Lisle would have answered any of his words, if she had a voice left. She was afraid of what might come out of her mouth if she opened it, so she didn't. She just sat there at the edge of her seat, looking into dark brown eyes and a handsome face, with perfect lips that were spewing unintelligible words at her, seemingly without end, and wondering how such a thing had transpired.

He was the Black Monteith. He was the enemy of all that was Scot, and detested by every Highlander with faith and integrity and honor, and little else, left to his name. He was a spendthrift, a fool, and a coward. He was her husband; the man she was supposed to give herself to . . . and the man who had just told her she wasn't welcome in his bed.

"I would appreciate it if you stay on your side of the coach, and allow me the other."

She nodded.

"You agree?"

She nodded again.

"Then cease looking at me like that!"

Lisle turned her head away, and it wasn't easy. She didn't know what expression she'd been looking at him with. There weren't any mirrors, and she'd die before she admitted any of it.

"And doona' touch me when we arrive. I won't allow it."

She nodded again. The mahogany strips on the side of his coach were set in a slanted wood pattern. That probably added to the expense of it, for it had probably taken longer and cost more. She hadn't noticed that before.

"You're to go to your rooms, and stay there."

"I doona' know where they are," she replied. All of it was ridiculous. It sounded like he was telling her to report to her prison and stay there; exactly like what had happened at the French school more times than not.

"They're at the top of the right stair, next to mine. Doona' bother checking the connecting door. I'll make certain it's locked."

He had a connecting bedroom to hers, and he was going to make certain the door was locked. What on earth for? Did she look like she was going to try to get through it, and attempt ravishment on a man who had just told her she was not welcome in his bed? She was very grateful there weren't any mirrors so she could have seen the look on her face that would have him thinking such a thing as locking his door was necessary.

And there wasn't anything she liked about wine.

Chapter Seven

Lisle lay on her belly, stretched in the length and width of a bed that she couldn't tell the size of even if she flapped her arms and legs, and wondered why she felt so grand. There wasn't any reason for it, save the obvious. She'd been wed to a man known to consort with the devil, gotten a bit tipsy, actually kissed him without compunction, been denied access to his bed, and not one thing else had happened, other than the bidding of a good night. She felt like she'd been given a reprieve, at the last possible moment, and knew how prisoners must feel who'd been granted the same.

A long, low-pitched tone, coming from a horn of some kind, filtered through the maroon-colored, drape-lined window, or maybe it came from one of the smaller windows that were all along the top of her two-story-high room. She rolled over, wincing at the bruising pressure from the row of pearl buttons up her back, and looked at those windows with her forehead wrinkled. Placing windows so high up made no sense, unless it was to catch a ray of sunshine and send it through the light-tone wood that latticed across the ceiling of her room. She looked at it through the sheer white canopy that topped her bed. Everything in her new suite was either white, or a shade of maroon. There wasn't any other color. Even the wood bureaus were painted white, with little knobs painted with maroon flowers on them.

The note ended, leaving a haunting feeling behind. She'd heard that same tone more than four times already, and had thought it part of her dreams. She didn't know what she was supposed to be doing, but that melodic note demanded investigation, and she was never one for sitting abed, waiting for what the day brought, anyway.

Lisle slid from beneath bleached, white, muslin sheets, woven so tightly they made the ones she'd called her own look amateurish and cheaply made. They'd felt luxurious against what skin felt it through her wedding gown, and they hadn't even been snagged by the hundreds of seed pearls. Her abilities as a seamstress had been tested by sleeping in such a gown, but she didn't have anything else to wear and there hadn't been a soul around to help her with the unfastening of it, save her new husband. She wasn't letting him touch any part of her, ever again.

That's how much she wanted to be in his bed! she told herself.

There wasn't anything hanging in the room off to the left of her bedroom. She knew it was supposed to be a dressing room; only that sort of room would have rows of empty rails, and pegs along the walls for holding the heels of her shoes, if she had any with heels. She found out the same thing about the room off to the right, for it held rows of railing and pegs awaiting the same thing.

No woman could possibly have enough clothing to fill one of those dressing rooms, let alone both of them. She sincerely hoped Monteith didn't expect her to. She'd have to wear a different outfit every day of the year, and probably twice every day, too. What a waste that would be.

The door that must connect to his chamber was on the other end of her right dressing room. She didn't test the handle. She told herself she didn't care enough to. She returned to her bed chamber. Neither dressing room had any windows, save those high up on the outer walls.

Lisle approached the window, pushed the drapery aside, and then she was grimacing at diamond-paned, cut glass that had been polished until each facet shone. The amount of gold that could buy such craftsmanship had to be staggering. She ran a finger along one of the edges, feeling how it had been rounded after the cut of it, by a master at his art. Unfortunately, it was also difficult to see anything through it, muting and distorting anything she might have been able to see outside. That wasn't helpful to her investigation.

Her belly growled, reminding her of its emptiness. Aside from the two dollops of wine—that was all he'd let her have—she'd not eaten or drunk a thing since . . . she couldn't remember the last meal, but thought it was the watered-down ham broth sup from the MacHugh Castle.

"Good morn, my lady. It's time to be up and about. We dinna' know what time to expect you to awake, or what you favored, so Cook Higgins, Letty, and Dame Margaret-Lily sent up everything they thought might tempt you. Oh. There you are. I dinna' know you were such an early riser. Here. Let me assist you into a chair, and fetch you a bed jacket. We doona' want those shoulders catching cold."

The door had opened, letting in a loud voice that was attached to a very large woman, followed by a train of servant women bearing smells that turned her belly into a roar of emptiness. As the entourage bore down on her, Lisle had the insane desire to run for the safety of one of the dressing rooms. It wouldn't have helped. The woman was holding up a waist-length, sky-blue jacket, knitted of large, looped, thickly spun wool, and finished off with a dark blue velvet collar. She could just as well have been using it to cut off any such escape route, as anything else she was doing with it.

Lisle's eyes were wide as the woman helped her into it, although the high-necked wedding gown wouldn't have allowed a hint of cold to get to her shoulders, anyway.

"Set them down there, and there. And over here. Now serve. And send Mistress Beamans in. There's sheets to air and such. There's no time for her staff to laze about. There's a lady of the house to impress. You could have knocked us over with a whiff of air over that news, my lady. Just let me say it and get it over with. We dinna' even know the master was inclining himself toward courtship of that nature. We're ever so proud to be able to serve you. Move smart, now."

Courtship? Lisle wondered. *Sheets to air?* They already smelled of sunshine and dew and everything else that was fresh and vibrant, and they hadn't had but one person sleeping on them—her—and that was for one night. Then her attention was moved to where they were placing trays, taking off covers, and setting out food; sending the smell and sight of scones, and cooked oats, and breads, and honey melons, and grapes, and every kind of meat, prepared in various different ways; some with sauces, some heated, and some cold and thinly sliced, while everywhere was the gleam of silver plate.

Her mouth hadn't shut yet, and she was afraid it was about to drool, too, so she put her own hand on her jaw and forced it closed. There was enough food there to serve the MacHughs for a fortnight. Lisle was appalled enough at the waste that she didn't think she could take a bite without it sticking to the roof of her mouth and making it impossible to swallow.

"What do you feel like having for your breakfast, my lady?" Each one of the servant women hovered above one of the trays, a large spoon in one hand and a plate in the other, as it looked like they were actually preparing to fetch anything she wanted for her.

"I—"

Spittle choked the word, and she couldn't say what she wanted before the door opened again and more than six chambermaids entered, making the enclosure spin with womenfolk and talk, and perfectly ironed black outfits, with crisp, starched white aprons, and cleaning rags and such. Three of them attacked the bed, while the others were intent on wiping cleaning rags all about the base of furnishings that hadn't time to think of catching dust. Lisle watched it and could actually hear the women humming to themselves.

Then, the sheets were pulled from the bed, and someone exclaimed at how there wasn't any blood speckling them before being hushed with words over how the new wife was a widow, and hadn't they heard. That's when she put her hands to her ears, and told them all, in no uncertain terms, that they were to leave, and leave immediately.

For a lady who was supposed to be the chatelaine of her own home, her order was instantly and complete ignored, although they all stopped what they were doing and stared at her.

"You want us to leave? But we haven't finished. We've just started, and His Lordship—"

"Am I the lady of the house, or na'?" Lisle asked through clenched teeth.

The woman who had been standing, directing the work crew, and who must be the main housekeeper, nodded.

"Good. Then I expect to be obeyed. Instantly and perfectly. Leave. Now. Please."

"I'll have Her Ladyship up and about when she's breakfasted, Mabel Beamans. You can come back then."

The large, jovial one who had first attacked her chamber was the one whispering it and escorting all of them out, although they took the bedding with them, and once they left, Lisle noted that they even had the maroon drapery and sheer white canopy with them. They were airing out such things?

She was going to put a halt to this senseless waste of time, effort, and coin, and she was going to do it before she got much older, too.

"Them, too," she said, when the kitchen serving women just stood there, hovering over their trays, with their utensils and plates.

"You heard my lady," the fat one said.

The women didn't look pleased, but they each put down their

weapons of interruption, making a clang against the silverplate, and then they, too, went out the door.

"I dinna' say you could stay," Lisle said as the fat one shut the door, locking everyone else out and returning to her.

"I've got the personal responsibility for your comfort, my lady. His Lordship entrusted it to me two days past, when you first visited, and he told me to prepare myself to be of service to you. I doona' take my responsibilities lightly. Not at all. Why, there's no Highland woman around that's as efficient, or trustworthy. You'll see."

"But I've nae need of a personal servant."

"His Lordship has more than twenty for his own use."

"He—he . . . what?" Lisle couldn't stop the surprise and disgust from coloring the word.

"His Lordship likes his home kept to a perfect degree, my lady. It's a matter of pride with him. He's been redoing the place, and he's right proud of the old castle, and his other estates. We are, too."

"You are?"

"My, yes. We'd keep it polished and perfect, even if he was na' paying excellent wages for the chore. Excellent."

"Triple what you can get anywhere else?" Lisle asked sourly.

"I wouldna' say that, my lady."

"Nae?" she asked snidely.

"Oh, nae. 'Tis nigh impossible to find wages for anything anymore. You doona' ken what it's like, or you'd understand."

"Understand what?" Lisle asked, although she already knew she wouldn't like the answer. She *knew* it.

"If His Lordship dinna' employ me, I'd be forced to resort to begging again, and that much sooner, I would. We all would have. You doona' understand."

Lisle looked at her solemnly, seeing lines of suffering etched on that pleasant-looking face, and she immediately knew what Langston was about—damn him anyway! Those that wouldn't take his gold, he hired to work his already overworked properties, or maybe it was those that had nothing left to sell.

"Are you wed?" Lisle asked, standing to inspect the bounty all these Highland lasses must have been paid very good wages to bake and cook and serve to her.

"Nae more, my lady. My poor dear man met his end at Culloden. I've a son, though, a strong lad, about your age."

"And where is he?"

"He's one of His Lordship's groundskeepers, keeping game and such away from the lawns, and out in the wilds where they belong. That way, there's not a blade of grass out of place, anytime, anywhere."

"I see . . ." Her voice dribbled off. She did see, and was surprised she'd been so blind, and she was angry. He had no right to put so many to work, and make more Highlanders take his gold, cheapening them to the point they'd wish they'd perished at the battle! If she had anything to wear besides her wedding gown, she'd march right out and tell him of it, too.

"So. Now that's settled, what is it you'd like to partake of this fine morn? Toast? Cakes? They're special, they are. Crumb cakes. Dame Margaret-Lily Burton makes them. Every day. Makes the kitchens smell just lovely, they do."

"I think I'd like a bit of cooked oats. Perhaps a scone, too."

The woman had it served onto a platter and set on the table in front of Lisle almost before she finished.

"And now I want all that food marched right back to the kitchen and put to use. I won't have wastefulness in my house."

"Oh my, nae, my lady. It's not wasted. His Lordship has an army of menfolk to feed. It will all be gone within the hour. I'm certain they're famished about now, too."

"Why? Does he work them through the night, too?"

"I—I'll be seeing to removing this, promptlike. Doona' move from this chamber while I give the order. Are you certain you wouldn't like a nice spot of tea with that scone?"

Lisle smiled, but it felt as false as the cheer on the woman's face had to be. Langston was going to rue the day he'd put this into effect, she decided, watching the woman who was pretending to have her pride and dignity intact.

"That would be nice," she replied. "And I can na' possibly leave this room. I doona' have anything else to wear but my wedding gown."

"And a very lovely gown it is, too, my lady. Very."

"Will you call me Lisle?"

"Lisle? That's your given name?"

"You say it strangely. Try again. Like weasel, only with an L."

"Lisle," the woman repeated, bobbing her head.

Lisle was hating everything about being Langston Monteith's lady, especially knowing these women received gold to agree with her and serve her. She hoped it didn't show on her face.

"Oh my! I forgot. There's a dozen castle seamstresses, and they've been given free rein to purchase bolts and patterns and fancy laces and such, to get you outfitted as befits the lady of Clan Monteith. I'll just step out and see if—"

"What's your name?" Lisle asked.

"Mary. Mary MacGreggor. Pleased I am to meet you, my lady. I heard tell you were a MacHugh a-fore you wed. Theirs is a fine clan, my lady. Fine."

Lisle bowed her head right back. "Aye. That they are. Go now, Mary MacGreggor. Send me your patterns and fabrics and such. I'm a very good hand with a needle. I won't need a seamstress to assist."

The woman went nearly white. Lisle wondered what could cause such a reaction. She didn't have to wait long.

"But—but they were just hired! His Lordship put out the word to find women handy with a needle, and he hired seven of the best. The very best, my lady."

"I thought you said there were a dozen seamstresses," Lisle replied, without one bit of inflection to her voice.

"We always have five on staff. There's no tear or rip allowed on any fabric in any room. Everything has to be perfect, just like the master orders."

"So . . . he hired seven women, and paid them excellent wages, all just to make me a wardrobe?"

Mary nodded her head.

"I suppose he wants me to fill the dressing rooms on both sides of this one with clothing befitting my new station?"

She smiled widely. "Oh, aye, and you've the use of yet more, if you go through this door. . . ."

Lisle cocked her head and watched her open the door at the end of the left dressing room. She could see, in the sunlightened interior, what was her privy, followed by yet another door. She didn't need to follow the woman who was cheerfully showing her what was probably more dressing room space to know what it was.

The woman returned, closing the door behind her, like she was guarding a secret.

"What would everyone do if I said I dinna' need such a grand thing?" Lisle asked.

"Those lasses just got the employment of their prayers, my lady. They're very good with a needle. You won't have a complaint, nary a one. I promise."

"I doona' need so many clothes," Lisle replied. "Nae woman does."

"That's not what His Lordship says. He says he plans on traveling. He has interests and such, in other countries, and with other kings and personages and in other courts. His wife has to look exactly as he wishes. He's such a perfectionist. You've nae idea how hard it is to please him. He has an aversion to dust. Canna' abide any of it in his home, and told Mabel Beamans in nae uncertain terms about it. We had to hire more staff."

"I'm beginning to get a clue," Lisle replied stiffly. The one thing she hated was having her choice taken from her, and Langston Monteith was doing it without a bit of effort. If she didn't accept and order a very large wardrobe, it would be her own mouth sending those women back to poverty.

"Are these new seamstresses wed, Mary?"

"Wed? I doona' recollect as much. I think they're widows, my lady."

"Widows?"

"With children."

"With children?"

"Aye. Culloden Battle dinna' discriminate on such a thing."

"Where are their children, then? Do we also employ them?"

Mary laughed. It was a merry sound that didn't have a bit of distress to it at having her own choices taken away. Lisle wondered why Langston Monteith hadn't just hired Lisle's services. Or . . . maybe he had.

Her own face whitened. She watched it happen in the chamber mirror atop one of her new white bureaus. The MacHughs wouldn't take his money; he knew she'd never work for him . . . so he married her to make them take it?

"Children? Nae. His Lordship does na' employ children. He makes certain they're not left on their own, though."

"How does he do that?" *Send a nursemaid he hired, too?* she wondered.

"He matches any funds the towns can raise, for schooling and such. I swear he more than matches it, but that's his own personal business."

"He's building schools, too?" It was too much, and it was getting cloyingly sweet in the room. No man was such a saint.

"Dear me, nae. The man's not stupid. He doesn't toss his gold away. He makes the townspeople earn it, and they have to build it. If you have a chance to visit Dearglen, you'll see. There's ever so many folk busy, building, making a future for themselves and their bairns."

The room was spinning, everything Lisle thought she knew was being churned about with it, and she didn't think she'd be able to look him in the eye when next they met.

"These matching funds . . . where do they come from?"

"I already made mention. His Lordship. He matches them."

"Not that. The ones he matches. Where do they come from?"

"The Good Lord's labor, that's where. And doona' think it any other than just that."

"Doing what, please?"

"Working for His Lordship, of course."

Lisle was going to be sick. She only hoped it didn't look like it on her face. The man was creating new futures for his countrymen, and they couldn't even see it? "Why do they do it?" she asked in a little voice.

"Do what, my lady?"

"Work for him."

"Because they can. They have skills no one thought of much use, until His Lordship came along and hired their services. You see these knobs, painted so delicately?"

Lisle nodded.

"Made by my own family. We're mighty proud of the carvings my mother does. Right proud."

"Your mother made those?"

"And painted them. Always loved her paints, she did. I'm certain she put the funds Lord Monteith gave her to good use, too."

"But where does he get it? Monteith were no richer than any other clan, yet he throws gold like it runs in every burn."

"That's the rub. His Lordship was tossed out when he was but a lad, and he dinna' return until he had his fortune. His return was the death of the auld laird. It had to be."

"His return killed his own father?"

"If you had sent your only heir into the world when he was little more than a lad, and he returns with not one, but seven ships, all laden with riches beyond your dreams, wouldn't it have killed you off, too?"

"He . . . has ships . . . too?" The room wasn't just spinning, it was rocking and waving and distorting, and all those beams above her were gyrating along with it. Lisle sat down in a chair before she fell there.

"Aye. Seven of them. All fancy caravels. All plying the waves, trading. Taking those silks and spices and tea that he gets in that foreign place, and selling it. Makes a tidy profit with each voyage, from what I gather, but I canna' stand jawing away all morn, my lady. We've a breakfast to get into you, and then a wardrobe, or two, or three, to get started on."

"Two . . . or three?" Lisle choked between the words.

"You wish to send those lasses back to starving?"

Lisle hated him. Very much. She didn't say a word about it as her new personal servant stood, a smile on her round face, and waited for approval of The Plan. She had no choice but to approve of it, and no choice but to portray a rich, spoiled woman, who needed more clothing than she could possibly wear. To do anything else would be worse. She smiled falsely, and it felt like the emotion stuck in place on her cheeks with the way she had to force it.

"We'll start as soon as we've had all this bounty taken away. You'd better be very certain that it's all partaken of."

"It will be. I promise it. It always is. His Lordship employs very good cooks. Nae one leaves any of his tables hungry."

"Now leave me. Go. I'll ring for you when I'm ready."

The other servant women must have been hovering at the door, awaiting the order, for how quickly they were back in the chamber, putting covers back on platters and bearing them back downstairs. Lisle waited until the door shut behind all of them before picking up the cooked oats and shoving them into her mouth fast enough that she choked, and then she was forcing each bite down with a scone that melted in her mouth, and washing the lot of it down with tea.

She had no other choice. If she took any time over it, she was going to be unable to eat a thing with the way her throat was closing off.

She had the bowl in the air and was scraping the last of it into her mouth when what had to be another horn note floated through the windows, although it wasn't long and piercing anymore. It was in three short, quick, staccato bursts.

She used her fingers to slide the last of her meal into her mouth where it had fallen onto her chin, and then she put the bowl back down. That horn demanded investigation, and the only other option she had was awaiting an army of seam-stresses that she'd have to simper and posture for in order to make certain they left for their homes each night with gold, and their pride intact.

She hated him for doing this to her, and there wasn't much reason for why he'd done it. She hadn't done anything to de-serve it. There wasn't any explanation to why he'd picked her to marry. It was obvious he could have had any lass, Highland or no, and without much effort.

He was handsome. He was rich. He might not be from a clan that had been blessed to be at the horror that had been Culloden, but he wasn't remotely evil. He was a very good actor, though.

Chapter Eight

There was something severely strange about Monteith Castle. Lisle noted the strangeness the moment she tiptoed over to her chamber door and opened it to peer into the hall. She didn't decipher what it was until she'd walked down the steps, her hand running along a banister of rounded wood, so highly polished there wasn't a sliver that would dare mar the surface of it, let alone be there to get into her palm.

It was as if the three short blasts had meant something . . . to everyone but her . . . something like desertion.

She knew she had the description down perfectly as her stocking-clad feet touched the polished stone of the lower hall, and the movement didn't disturb so much as a whiff of dust. There wouldn't have been any allowed in the keep anyway, but it was unnerving. Lisle hadn't known desertion and silence felt like that. She'd never felt so alone.

The kitchens weren't hard to find. She just followed her nose, and just as Mary MacGreggor had said, there was the smell of crumb cake filling the four-room enclave at the back of the keep. At least, she thought it was the back of the keep. There weren't any windows in the kitchens, unless one counted those high on the walls, where interlaced beams were fitted.

That had her squinting, and she knew she was right as she

walked from room to room through his kitchens, her chin back and her neck craned while she looked at the beams that all seemed within easy reach of one of those little windows. That didn't make much sense. They weren't large enough to gain access through, and since the walls looked an arm's length thick, it would be nigh impossible to do more than lie up there and look out of them.

The keep wasn't a freestanding building. She knew that from her first look at it. It was connected to the back wall, with more yellow-hued stone, and the access to that wall was through the back of the kitchens. It had to be.

Lisle drew her head down when she reached the last room of his interconnecting kitchens, and looked back the way she'd come, through a span of building no other laird could think to own. She wondered why such a span of room was necessary. Why, the MacHugh Castle would fit in the space of the Monteith kitchens, she decided, with room to spare. The Dugall stronghold was farther north, in the glens near Halkirk, and didn't boast a kitchen one-fourth the size of this one. She didn't know much about wealth and position and power, but there had to be only one reason for such a thing. The Monteith laird had kitchens this size because of the volume of food that must be needed.

Lisle started chewing on her cheek as she walked, looking for the part of the castle that had to connect to the outer wall, and looking for anything else of interest at the same time.

There were four mud-brick ovens at the center of each room, their funnels venting toward the windows. There were also fireplaces on the inner walls; one even held a full carcass of what looked to be a boar, and upon further investigation was exactly that. Whomever had the chore of turning the spit was being very lax in their duties, as the fat kept dripping onto the flames from one side, and that side was getting a nice blackened shell to it, while the top wasn't getting cooked at all. Lisle mindlessly turned the crank a half-turn, waiting until the meat was fully rotated before securing it with the chain cord there for the purpose.

There wasn't a soul in the kitchens, there wasn't a speck of all the food she'd just sent down, and that was almost as odd as the fact that there wasn't anyone, anywhere, in any of the lower rooms. Lisle gave up trying to find the connecting passage and put her mind to finding one servant, even if it was a minor one, anywhere in the lower rooms.

The mass of furniture that she'd seen cluttering the lower rooms wasn't as much in the way anymore. Mainly because he now had it suspended from more of the ceiling beams. The beams looked to all be of the same dimension, although of different grades and types of wood, almost like the architect of such a design had thought about which shading would be most aesthetic to each room. It probably would have been striking, if there wasn't furniture dangling about, looking like a fest of some kind was going to take place, with fairies as guests.

Lisle shook her head. She suspected what Monteith was doing. He was putting more of his gold into more hands, but he'd probably be better off building storerooms for the items he kept purchasing and didn't have placement for, than hanging them about in his rooms.

"'Tis a good thing you have such high ceilings, my lord," she commented aloud, although her voice had dropped to a whisper before she finished. The words had echoed back at her, and that had the back of her neck feeling like someone had brushed against it, and that had her jumping and looking over her shoulder and making her feel a bigger fool than she already did.

Her wedding gown hadn't been made to conquer dragons and demons and other imaginary, but very real-feeling, creatures, and it wasn't doing a thing to keep her from shivering. She held the bed jacket closer to her and wished the weave hadn't been made as loosely, letting the draft feel like it was going right through her. She should also have found her slippers again, since the sheer stockings weren't any protection against the cold of his floor. It was a good thing she was used to going barefoot, she told herself.

She gathered her skirt in a hand that was visibly trembling, despite her telling it not to, and looked up at the towering height of the main foyer ceiling, nearly four stories above her. Her heart was hammering and her breaths were coming swift and hard. It would have been impossible to disguise.

There was a thump above her, and then a curse, or what sounded like a curse. Whatever it was, it sounded like it had come from a real person, and not her imagination. It also sounded like it had come from the side that held her bed chamber, and that of the Monteith laird. The only thing it hadn't sounded like was him.

The sounds of a scuffle grew louder, blocking out the hammering of her own heart, as she reached the door that had to lead to his chambers. Another curse came; another thump. She turned the handle.

"My . . . lord?" she asked, biting on her lip and wishing she'd slapped a hand to her mouth instead. She'd sounded like a little girl, and little girls didn't investigate possible attacks on their husbands in their own chambers!

She waited a few moments, with her head against the door, before daring to push on it. She was almost afraid of what she might find on the other side, and she'd yet to come to terms with what she'd say, or how she'd let him know that she knew what he was doing, or any slew of other things. She opened the door and listened. There wasn't a sound, except maybe that of rustling material, and her own heartbeat.

The door didn't open directly to his chamber, and Lisle stood in the small antechamber room, wondering what sense this made. There was a small bench-thing on one side, a large painting on the wall behind it, a marble-topped table with a vase of flowers on it, and, on the opposing wall, another door. Chieftains needed antechambers before reaching their beds?

She cleared her throat before trying again as she went to the inner door and opened it. "My lord?"

No chambermaids had been in to steal his drapes or his bedding, or even the thick, green canopy that fell all the way from the very top of the ceiling, splitting midway down to reveal the gold brocade–embroidered interior of it, before ending by wrapping about both sides of his headboard.

The opulence and magnificence, even seen with the hazed, rain-cast light, was amazing, and like nothing she'd ever seen, and if she'd thought her own bed large, it was nothing in comparison to his. She could barely tell where his feet probably were, and that was more near the middle of his mattress than the end. If that weren't enough, they'd placed that bed on a three-step-high pedestal, in order to make it look even more overwhelming and larger, almost deifying the being that got to sleep there.

Lisle shook her head, tossing that imagining away, before forcing her feet to move. She had to climb the three steps of the pedestal, and then she was moving along the side of it, following where his legs and feet were, until she forced her eyes to move to him. It didn't matter what she'd been thinking, or how rampant she'd allowed her imagination to roam, for there wasn't a thought left to her the moment her eyes touched his.

It was definitely Monteith, for none other could have such black hair, perfect features, or take every bit of sense left to her and toss it up to where the ceiling beams had better catch and hold it and hang onto it before giving it back to her. Lisle's eyes widened, for he was all-over large, from the heaving strength of his naked shoulders, to the sweat and muscle smell of him, and he was soaking wet.

"What's happened to you?" she asked, reaching a hand to his forehead, and then having to crawl up onto her knees on the bed to reach it since he moved away.

"Are you ill?" She crawled after him and finally reached him, but only because he hadn't anywhere else to go, unless he wanted to fall from the mattress. That would have brought a smile to her lips, for it looked to be a powerfully long fall, and he didn't appear to be wearing much, but she was too worried for smiling.

"It's all right. I've been around illness a-fore. At school, they had an outbreak of ague, and I've been raising daughters, and—and my aunts were never well . . . much. Good heavens—you're burning up. And sweaty."

Her hand told her the truth of it, and she frowned. She wondered if he realized just how ill he was, and then told herself that he didn't. He couldn't. He probably wasn't even lucid. "Now, cease that, and let me have a look at you."

His eyes grew wide and Lisle nearly giggled as she moved closer and pushed the sheet down to his belly, revealing what appeared to be an amazing amount of muscled abdomen and chest, with only the slightest dusting of hair to mute it. He'd been deep in the throes of his fever, too, for he was heaving for breath, and that movement on such a span of him had her moving her gaze to look at him wide-eyed.

He licked his lips, and that made her gasp.

"I—I . . . I've tended fever a-fore," she stammered.

His eyebrows rose. That was somehow worse, for she didn't want to be mesmerized by those dark, amber-colored eyes, even if they were shadowed by lush lashes, the drape of his canopy, and what little daylight managed to penetrate the enclosure of his room. Her heartbeat wasn't the only thing filling her ears. Her breathing was vying for volume and space with it.

"And—and . . . we've got to get you sponged. The chill's good for the heat. It takes a fever away quicker."

His eyes went wider, and then he was sucking in on both cheeks, narrowing his face, and making her heart do antics in her very own breast. Then he smiled, and it had everything wolfish and enticing, and not one thing about it that was weak or sickly looking.

"You are . . . fevered, aren't you?" she asked.

His brows lowered; he nodded. Lisle let her breath out slowly, and she hadn't even known she held it. She'd been right. He was barely lucid. The entire morning had been senseless, but this was something solid, something stable, and something she knew all about. She'd tended Aunt Fanny through the worst of last winter, and in early March, when they'd almost lost Aunt Grace. She'd learned it at the convent school. You needed to wrap a fever when shivers took a body, but sponge away the worst when sweat and heat took over. If you did that, the fever wouldn't get worse and start cooking a body from within.

She checked his forehead again, and then knelt forward to put her lips to it. He wasn't as hot and wet-feeling. That was a good sign. In fact, it felt like a pulse was throbbing at the skin her lips were touching, a pulse that seemed to speed up.

She was frowning as she went back onto her knees and looked him over. He didn't appear as agitated as before, or maybe it was the same, but in a different fashion. And his continued silence was unnerving . . . as was the glitter of his eyes on her; unblinking, watching, waiting.

Lisle forced herself not to look at the amount of man right beside her, but it was nearly impossible, especially since he raised one leg, crooking his knee, and that made it look like he was making an enclave for her to fit into. She told herself she was being ridiculous, and then had to make herself believe it as he turned onto his side to face her, showing that the muscles in that chest were large and well defined, and moved easily beneath the skin. Then he was making it worse, by supporting his head onto one uplifted hand. That movement only made bulging sinew come out everywhere on his arm, and it looked like he was preening for her. She told herself she was being silly, and it could just as easily have been he was studying her, as anything else.

She watched as he moved the sheet upward with his free arm, covering himself, until he had it to the bottom of his breastbone, and for some insane reason, she almost told him to stop.

One thing was certain. She didn't have to worry over what

she'd say when she next saw him, or if she could look him in the eye. She couldn't. But there wasn't much left that she could look at. She tried looking at the wall behind him, where light from the high windows was just making a shadow of itself known. She tried looking at the door over by his armoire, which probably went to her own chamber; she tried looking at her hands where she'd put them in her lap. That was very dangerous. He was right next to those.

"Did you pick up one of those jungle fevers while you were in Persia?" she asked, stretching her knowledge a bit, since she hadn't paid that much attention at lessons, and she couldn't even remember where Persia was at the moment, or even if there was a jungle attached to it, or not.

He didn't answer. Lisle didn't know what else to ask, or even if he understood. She didn't know what she was doing, and began heartily wishing she'd just stayed in her maroon and white bed chamber and awaited the seamstresses like she'd been told to do. The gold weave of his bedspread wavered for a moment, and then what had to be his free hand blocked her view of it. She flinched, but he adjusted for the movement, moving to put a finger beneath her chin to raise it, making her face him. Lisle found herself looking into very solemn eyes in a very unfeverished-looking face.

"You should na' be in here," he whispered.

Her eyes couldn't get any wider. She could feel the air on them from the extent she had them opened. He didn't look remotely ill, and his black hair was drying, curling slightly where it reached to his shoulders. He moved up onto his haunches, making an angle of his body as his lower arm straightened out to support him, while the sheet made it impossible to look elsewhere as it dropped to pool in his lap, and all he did was pull her closer with the hook of one finger beneath her jaw.

Lisle begged her own body to stop acting like a fish caught on a lure, but nothing was working. She rose, almost to her knees, while her thighs took the brunt of the thrust. The bodice of her wedding gown had definitely been measured too tightly. Either that, or her breasts were supposed to feel weightier, heavier, and like they ached for something she hadn't the expertise to know of, but was totally certain that he did.

She was also certain he was going to kiss her again, and there was nothing she wanted more. She wondered how he knew.

"You really should na' be in here," he repeated, this time from a distance that had his breath feathering across her nose.

"Why?" she asked.

"Because we're wed."

"True," she answered.

"And I'll na' take any woman paid for the chore."

Paid. The word went through her consciousness, and parts of her told herself to stiffen and start spitting invectives, and act like it was momentous and insulting, while other parts of her weakened, became even more pliant. Her lips parted, her body started relaxing, her tissues opened, softening, dampening. . . .

"Unless she's here of her own free will," he continued.

He was speaking of free will, and she didn't have any left. He had all of it. Was he too obtuse to know that much? "Are you going to kiss me?" she asked.

His eyelids lowered and he shuddered, the motion transferring to where he held to her until her head felt like it shook with it.

"You're a very enticing woman, Lisle Monteith," he said.

"I am?"

"Aye. So enticing a man forgets—" He cut his own words off, and they didn't make a bit of sense.

"Forgets?" she offered.

"Time. Space. Sense. Duty."

He was speaking of sense, yet was making none. "There's nae wine anywhere about." She whispered it.

"Your meaning?" he asked the bedding.

She had to say it aloud? Lisle didn't think the words could get out of her throat. She was there—in his bed—and it wasn't with any wine to make him more enticing for her. He'd chosen a good word, she decided, a good, strong descriptive word. It was very enticing, and she wanted more of it.

She licked her lips, gathered every bit of her bravery, and asked it again, before she tossed herself into his arms and made him give her a kiss, and everything else her senses were tempting her with, and being denied.

"Monteith, are you going to kiss me, or not?"

"Nae," he finally replied, although he was speaking to the bed.

"Why not?" she asked, absolutely disgusted and appalled at herself for not just taking his rejection for what it was and moving from his bed, and never, *ever* going there again.

"Because there's na' time enough."

Lisle stopped the movement before she made it, to yank her chin out of his grasp and stomp from there, and it was at the strangeness of that statement. Then, she just wished herself anywhere else as her own mouth betrayed her again. "For one kiss?" she asked in a small voice.

This time, she heard the groan, and it had to be as deep and earthy and full of anger and denial as it sounded like it was. "Damn you, Lisle! One kiss will na' be enough! Never! I won't be able to stop myself, and I've got parts to play, and murderous bastards to fool, and I swore I'd never say a word about any of it to any other soul on earth! And here you are making me lose sight of my vow, and my goal . . . and just about everything else . . . that matters . . ."

He had her pulled into his arms before he finished, and was not only kissing her through the words, but was sending needles of sensation shooting through every nerve ending. He put both hands through her hair, pulling it back and holding her in place so he could suck on her lips and breathe heavily onto her nose and hold her so tightly, the beading was probably putting small pocklike dents in a large portion of his chest.

Lisle wasn't letting him get the best of it, either. She didn't know where the primitive urges were coming from, or what it meant, but anger and energy flowed through her, making her arms beat at his sides, her fingernails rake down every ridge, and then back up again, sliding over the bare span of chest and around his shoulders, and then she was entwining them about the ends of his thick, shiny, black hair. It was all to make certain there wasn't a whiff of space allowed between them. She'd never felt anything like it, and her body knew it.

He must have known it, too, for the groan that tore through them came with even more depth and timbre to it, almost enough to make the beams laced above his room rattle with it. It was accompanied by his fingers, moving from her hair to the fastening of pearl loops up her spine, and he was flipping each one from its mooring without benefit of anything except touch. He was very adept, but that didn't occur to her until later. Now there was just the smell of freshened rain, sweat, heat, and flesh. Then there were three more of those piped notes, filtering through her senses and adding to the rhythm of emotion her body had been in its own creation of making, before it was making him go completely and utterly still and solid and unmoving.

She didn't know what was wrong with him, but the next moment he was yanking himself from the embrace of her lips with a spate of cursing that was so different than the emotion he'd spun about her that she didn't actually hear it, at first. She thought she heard her name, and some damning to it, and more cursing of devil's spawn and blood, and something about hellfire. She clung to him throughout it, although it had to hurt him, because he pulled her fingers awry where they were still gripped in his hair.

Lisle forced her eyelids open, although they felt too heavy to move, and watched the enormous chest heaving before her eyes, while everything else on him looked taut, angry, pulsatingly large and heavy and absolutely fascinating, and that was just the part she could see above the bedding.

She licked her lips, and he bit at them, stunning her into flinging her eyes wide open to stare.

"Nae! Not now, I tell you!"

He was pushing her onto her back, and there wasn't any problem with pearls anymore, because they weren't there. And then he was lifting his head to send his voice to the rafters, making cords bulge from his throat with the effort, and he didn't stop until he ran out of breath, although his face and neck and shoulders went bright red with the effect of it.

His howl had one other effect, too. It made every bit of her senses that had left her earlier, and were balanced up there on those beams, fall, and then they were filtering back into her, turning her into a proper Highland lass, who'd never be enticing and begging and clinging to any man who so clearly didn't want her. Her fingers opened, releasing him.

"Go to your chamber, Lisle. Stay there. Posture for whoever comes in. You hear me?"

She nodded. Her voice wasn't available for her use, and if she dared open her mouth, pain was going to come out. It was better to be silent.

"This dinna' happen between us. You ken?"

She nodded again at such nonsensical words, and then he flung the covers aside and stood up, showing her the rain-dampened, green-plaid kilt he was wearing, as well as the gold-tasseled socks, and the one shoe he still had on, as well. Lisle gasped, and had a hand to her mouth to hold it in.

"Go. Now."

He turned from her and had his hands on his hips, his fingers defining a cord of strength that wrapped about his waist, and broadening the span of his back that she already knew was large and muscled and nothing like a gentleman of leisure should ever own. He kept his back to her as she left.

She only wished she'd had the sense to turn away before she had the image emblazoned on her eyelids even when she did close them.

She wasn't left on her own again, but the Lord had decided to grant her numbness. That was a relief. She didn't need to posture for anyone, like Monteith had ordered her to, because she didn't even feel them about her.

The seamstresses were efficient. They only needed her to stand, lift her arms occasionally, and then sit. Then, they wanted her to stand again, lift her arms, and repeat. Lisle watched the fire they'd built for her, burning behind the white and maroon grill, and wondered why she hadn't tried to find this state before. It was almost as pleasant as drinking the wedding wine had been, making everything muted and dull, slow and indistinct, and very numb.

At one point, she asked her own personal servant, Mary MacGreggor, if she could have some wool to card, thinking maybe if she had something in her hands, she'd be able to feel something. What she got instead was two younger servant women, to sit and card wool for her. Lisle watched them with a sense of detachment, and wondered if she asked Mary for a muckle wheel with which to spin it into thread, which girl was going to get that chore, and further, which one would have to knit for her, too.

Both girls looked adept at either, but Lisle could have outdone them with her eyes closed. At one point, she put her head back and sighed, which got her the attention of not one, but four of them, who decided amongst themselves that she needed a restorative, such as tea. They didn't ask her if she wanted it, they asked Mary MacGreggor. Lisle watched that, and decided it was amusing, but just barely that.

If this was her future, she would just as soon face it numb, since it felt like she wasn't living anything, just sitting on the edges and watching it get lived.

"I understand His Lordship had the Highland garrison visiting with him today. Early. I understand they're preparing for another visit from Cumberland. I doona' ken how His Lordship can abide having that man in the same room with him," one of the seamstresses said, as they were serving tea.

"Not that I've leanings that way, but I do find him rather handsome."

"Butcher Cumberland? Dear me! I'll have to see your eyes looked at yet, Maggie. The man's as fat as an ale barrel, and half as smart!"

There was a bit of giggling after the outburst, and then the first one clarified her meaning, by stating that she found Captain Barton handsome, and didn't they all recollect that he was still unwed and available?

"But he doesn't like Highland lasses, Maggie."

"Actually I've heard he likes the lasses fine, just not as well as the lads," another snickered.

That had them all shrieking with laughter and then they were pointing at where Lisle sat, in little more than her chemise and stockings, and they were calming their noise the moment they did. The numbness was a blessing. Otherwise she'd have been screaming. The Duke of Cumberland was known as Butcher Willie, and he was the man who'd caused all of this poverty and discontent, and aura of defeat . . . and the laird of Monteith was going to be hosting him? Which meant, by marriage, she was going to be his hostess?

That was the only time that entire day that her numbness was in danger of dispersing. Lisle had to concentrate on the fire with every fiber of her being, in order to stave any such thing off. She wasn't going to be ill. She wasn't going to faint. She was going to endure and make certain her body never gave another sign to Monteith that he was anything other than a base, lying traitor.

"They won't stay at Monteith Castle. From all accounts, they doona' think it grand enough. His Lordship never allows them beyond the front four rooms. I don't know what ploy he uses. Probably the crowded rooms."

"He has to say such. Otherwise, they'd probably want him to give them the castle to garrison in. You know how the Sassenach are."

"That's right. They take what they want, and torch what they doona' want, so nae one will want it, either."

"I hear the duke is going to stay with Captain Barton, over at MacCullough Hall."

"That would be your chance, Maggie," one of the ladies teased.

"I already told you, I just find him a bit handsome. I always find that about a man in uniform."

"They're only handsome in their plaide. That's the only way I want to see a man. 'Tis a pure shame it's outlawed. A man always looked more like a man when he was in his kilt. Isn't that right, ladies?"

Lisle shut her eyes, saw Langston as easily as if he were standing in front of her, looking extremely manly in his, and caught her breath at the immediate ache. Then, she opened them on the sight of a dozen gossipy women, with cups of tea at their sides, and needles, knives, pins, fabric, and trimmings everywhere else.

"I believe His Lordship is even paying for renovations to make the auld MacCullough stronghold a fitting abode for a visit from any son of King George. It's costing a fortune, too!"

"Everything he does costs a fortune," one of the women said archly.

"It's also putting meals on tables all through the glens. Remember that, ladies, when you gossip about it. His Lordship is hiring craftsmen from throughout the Highlands to do the work."

"It's a double-edged thing, that is. They're being paid good wages to do work that will bring comfort to the man who brought all the pain and anguish to them in the first place. I doona' envy how that must feel."

"About like this does," one of them whispered.

There were several gasps, as most of them looked her way, and then there was a collective sigh as they went back to work. Her numbness was a blessing and Lisle silently thanked God for it again.

Chapter Nine

The long, low, moaning note from the pipe woke her, floating into the chamber again, just like it had yesterday morning. Lisle stretched in her bed, heard a tear as one of the seams in one of the shoulders of one of her new nightgowns tore at the movement, and twisted her lips at it. She was going to have to find a needle and thread and resew it, the way it should have been sewn in the first place. It wasn't the women's fault. Mary MacGreggor had made them hasten to get at least three nightgowns finished, and one daydress before they finished for the day and could return to their own hearths, in their own crofts.

They were even given carriage rides to the gate, to save them the walk. Laird Monteith would have taken them all the way to their doors, but only one of them took up the offer. Lisle knew why the others didn't. The same reason she'd stomped out of here less than a week ago. They didn't want to be seen associating with a Monteith.

Her lip curled with distaste at their actions, and that was strange enough to have her wrinkling her brow. She wasn't supposed to care.

The note came again, and then, if she wasn't mistaken, came the faint sound of drums. That was incredible. There wasn't an army allowed on Highland soil, unless it was the Highland Regiment, and there was no drumming of drums or playing of pipes or wearing of kilts or . . .

Lisle was out of bed and tearing open the maroon drape before another imaginative thought came, breathless as to what it might be. The frustration of staring at diamond-paned glass had her snarling at it. She wondered if he'd designed it that way on purpose. To let in light, but not allow anyone to see through it. She tried another window, and then another, going beyond the rooms that Mary MacGreggor had shown her, and all that she found was another diamond-paned window, and then more of the same.

She turned back around and retraced her steps, stopping near the privy room as another long horn blast came, followed by what her mind told her was a perfect cadence of chanting. It hadn't been drums after all. It was the sound of thousands of feet marching with a drumlike rhythm. It had to be. Her eyes went wide and she looked up, and then her gaze was following the ceiling beams from each of their little windows to where they were positioned, starting at the wall that framed the four-story Great Hall.

If she wasn't mistaken, she could access one of those windows, and her instinct told her there was clear glass in them that she could see through.

Lisle ran to her headboard. The white canopy made an excellent handhold as she scaled the smoothed wooden sides of her ceiling-high headboard. Luck was with her, too, since he'd had cornice pieces carved onto the structure, and they made excellent footholds for this sort of thing. Then, she was straddling a beam, and listening to even more of her nightgown tearing.

The beams were sturdy. They were just right for supporting a man, and Mabel Beamans had a fault, after all. There was dust up here. Lisle looked across at the other beams, all leading to a window that she could tell had a latched pane of clear glass covering it, and noticed that all the beams were covered with a fine film of dust.

She was going to have to take that up with the head housekeeper—allowing dust in His Lordship's house! Lisle giggled before she could help it, and started scooting along the beam before giving it up and going to her knees. Then she was balancing on her toes, in a crouch, because it felt safer, and then she was upright and looking down on the room that wasn't just white and maroon. It was immense-looking and a very long way down.

She dropped back to her heels, holding the beam while she shook with the reaction. Fright wasn't going to get her to the window, and there hadn't been another pipe note played in so long, she was beginning to doubt her sanity. She stood again, although she stayed bent at the knees, and she didn't look down this time. The beam held her weight easily. It could have been designed to hold a man of fighting size . . . or an archer . . . or even a marksman with a musket.

She instantly knew that was the reason for all the beams, and the placement of the windows, and all the positioning of all the rooms. Castle Monteith was beautiful, and it had a secret. If she wasn't mistaken, it was being built to defend a siege from an army the size of Cumberland's.

Lisle nearly gave sound to the cry when she reached the window opening and couldn't do more than flail her arm toward the latch. Whoever was supposed to be accessing these windows must be bigger than she was, and have longer arms. There was no help for it. She was going to have to crawl into one of the alcovelike spaces, and it looked like there was even more dust in there.

Mabel Beamans was safe from any censure over her house-keeping abilities at the moment, because no one was going to hear of such a thing from her. Lisle jumped slightly, putting her upper body into the space, and then she had to pull herself up, using the window latch for an anchor. The window's size was deceptive, for once she was seated in it, there was room to sit upright, with crossed legs, and more.

Lisle's hands were shaking almost too much to turn the latch. She didn't know if it was the excitement at what she knew she'd see, or if it was the exertion of what she'd just done, but the window opened without a hint of protest, and she peeked out and swallowed the disappointment.

There wasn't anything except an enormous span of green grass that didn't have the slightest dent to show a footprint had just been walking across it, let along marching on it. There wasn't anything except a perfectly groomed lawn, acres of forest land beyond that, and she could see, over the tops of the trees, what was going to be a cloud-strewn day dawning. Lisle sat and watched the sun rise, tinting the clouds rose and yellow. She looked down at the grime on her new, muslin nightgown, and rubbed her palms on it, making it worse, but getting most of it off her hands. It was just as well. All she'd managed to prove was that she possessed an overactive imagination, and that was already well documented from school.

When the sun was up, reaching the tops of the trees, and from there the green lawn that hadn't a blade disturbed on it, she pulled the glass back in and relatched it. Then she peeked over the side at where her bedroom looked very small and very far away. It hadn't seemed stupid when she'd first done it, but it certainly felt that way now. She had no idea how she was supposed to get down, and to ask for help was going to have everyone referring to her as a lady who was touched in the head. No lady of the house climbed among the rafters.

She could always say she was inspecting for dust. That would set Mabel Beamans's smug confidence back a bit.

The door opened, looking like it was also a long way down, and Lisle watched as Mary MacGreggor came in, leading just one servant woman bearing one silver-plated tray, rather than the number of them she'd brought yesterday. Lisle knew why. She'd already given her order for breakfast, and knew what was beneath the cover before it was placed on her table and lifted.

"My lady?"

Mary MacGreggor's voice floated eerily up to where she still sat in one of the window ledges. She wasn't going to be easy to spot. That was comforting, for the moment. Lisle was going to worry about what to do next when she got her privacy back.

"My lady?"

Mary MacGreggor was starting to sound frantic as she opened door after door, and then came back. Lisle watched as she went into the dressing chamber, and even tried the connecting door to the laird's rooms, rattling the locked doorknob.

"Dear me! We've lost Her Ladyship! Alert His Lordship. She's loose. I doona' know for how long. Now, go! Go!"

She was pushing the serving girl in front of her, and moving faster than her bulk looked like it could move. All of which was interesting enough to give it some thought when, and if, she got down from her perch, and had scrubbed off the worst of the grime, had another nightgown on, and was ensconced back in that bed. She grinned. She could hardly wait to see Mary MacGreggor's face when that happened. She got back onto her knees. The door opened again.

"You see?"

"Calm yourself, Mary, and tell me what you saw again."

It was Langston, and he was dressed as she'd almost always seen him, exactly like a Highland laird would be when he was denied use of his ancestral wardrobe. He was in tight, form-fitting English slacks, which had the added advantage of showing everyone exactly how strong his legs were. He also had on a white shirt with button-down front, and the size of his starched cuffs showed they were the kind that had to be put on separately, and required a valet to assist. He didn't look remotely like he could be the same damp and intense man that she'd seen wearing a green and gold kilt with little else, and kissing her within an inch of her sanity before sending her away into numbness yestermorn.

"Did you lock the chamber last night?"

"I always lock the chamber at night, my lord."

"Then, where could she have gone?"

"She was here last night, although she was na' saying much."

"She was na'?"

"Nae. In fact, I dinna' hear her say a word all day. Nor even all eve. Na' even when I wished her a good night."

"Is that normal?"

"I doona' know the lass that well, my lord."

"I mean, is that normal for a lass that's just been wed?"

Lisle was afraid she was going to giggle, giving away her vantage point, and she wasn't going to do that for anything. She'd been locked in? She'd suspected it was a prison, but to find it was true was worse.

"I would na' know, my lord. It's been a powerful long time since I was wed, and well . . . my spouse was na' Your Lordship, you ken?"

Now, that statement was going to give her the giggles, if nothing else did. Lisle had to put a hand to her mouth to stop them.

"I want her found, and I want her found now. Start the search in the house, with this floor. Keep it quiet. Nae alarm. Alert the staff and report to me. I'll be in my study."

He was angry, if the way he shut the door was any indication. The sound of it traveled upward, in a thundering sort of way. Lisle wondered why he was so angered. He wouldn't think his bride had run away from him, would he? And if he did, that was priceless. She already had the gold, the MacHughs already had their dowries, and he had what? A wife that had deserted him, and he hadn't even gotten a consummation out of the deal. As the man betraying everything, it was priceless if he thought a portion of that. She might just keep her mouth quiet, and let him.

Her legs were beginning to ache from how she had them

scrunched, or maybe it was the exertion she'd just put them through, of actually climbing her own headboard. Lisle looked back down at her bed, and gulped. She wondered if she dared walk out onto the center of the beam, put her arms out, and then just leap outward, and hope she'd bounce on the mattress. She didn't know that much about it, but that sounded like a logical way to go about it. She could also go back the way she'd come up. The canopy material was still firmly attached to the wall above the bed, and she could just hang onto that and slide down onto the bed. She might even be able to do it without ripping the material . . . too much.

There was no use for any of these beams, save as holding the walls together, and maybe for stringing excess furniture from, as he'd done in the lower rooms. They certainly weren't for supporting an army of archers, or marksmen, as they protected the castle from an invasion. Lisle didn't know where she got her ideas from, but she was going to curb them in the future.

Just look where this one had gotten her. Sitting high in the rafters, covered in grime and dust, and wondering how the devil she was supposed to get back down without breaking her neck.

She ran her eyes along the beam she'd used, looking for where it connected with the perpendicular ones that made up the lattice frame. Then, she followed where her beam connected to the one closest to her dressing room, following it to the one running back to the main wall. That's when she saw the way the beam narrowed before meeting the fireplace wall. Beyond that, it disappeared into the wall from which it had come, where it probably became one of the beams laced above the Great Hall.

Lisle narrowed her eyes as a shadow caught what could be a groove. She leaned forward a bit to look better and saw that it actually was a groove, indented into the wall with such a perfect precision, it was impossible to spot unless the sun had lightened it for her. She followed the six, shelf-looking things that were molded into the walls, until they met the side of her fireplace. Then, it was easy to spot the way the rocks were put together, by such a master crafter of mortar, it looked like the shaping of the rocks.

It was a series of uneven steps. It had to be.

"I had you fetched because 'tis such a fine day. I'm going to teach you to ride."

Monteith announced it to her when she was finally dressed in her only daygown and escorted under a heavy guard of six serving men, two on each side and two behind, to the laird's study. There were two guards on either side of his door—again, she noticed absently—and they both appeared to be large, strong, well-muscled types. She decided they were just the kind a Sassenach-leaning laird would want for his personal guards. She eyed them for the few moments it took for one of her escort fellows to reach out and open the door for her, before preceding her into the room. Lisle hadn't looked to see if her escort stayed in the room behind her, or was planning on leaving. She couldn't. Langston was too visual and had snagged her attention with his words the moment she saw him.

"I already know how to ride," she told him finally.

Langston smiled mirthlessly and waited for the door to shut before answering. "I beg to differ. You already know how to hitch your skirts up, jump onto the backside of a horse, cling to a man, and chase down where you think your uncle just shot himself. That, my dear, is not riding."

Lisle frowned at his use of *my dear* again. "It's na' a good day for it, I'm afraid," she countered. "I've nae riding attire sewn yet. I'll have to beg off."

"The dress you're wearing will do nicely."

"There's nae split for straddling a horse."

Again a mirthless smile touched on his face. Lisle sucked in on both cheeks to hide what promised to be a bubble of mirth that would have her laughing if she didn't keep it tempered. Monteith was in a quandary and it was one of his own making. He couldn't let his wife out of his sight, now that she'd disappeared for a horrendous span of twenty minutes, and he couldn't tell her that he couldn't let her out of his sight.

He'd never admit to any of it. If he did, he'd have to let on that he knew she'd disappeared, and he'd have to confess how he knew it—and that he was locking her in, making her a virtual prisoner in her own room every night. If he did any, or all of that, he'd have to explain why . . . and that had to be a very interesting explanation.

Lisle watched the emotions crossing his handsome face and wished it was a full-out rainy day, rather than holding some promise of sun, and sending rays of it into his study and across the planes of him, highlighting every part of him for her to watch.

It was also glinting off several well-placed grooves cut right into the wood of his study wall. Lisle had to counsel her eyes not to follow them upward, where she knew they'd connect with a shortened beam, making it easy to reach any of the alcove windows, if one were so inclined.

"As I've already seen your legs, it shouldn't present an issue for us. Get Her Ladyship a cloak. We're going riding."

She sucked in the gasp and held it. He'd seen a glimpse of her legs, and the only reason was she'd been distraught over Angus. He had no right to infer what he was inferring. Worse was the way her cheeks reddened, and she knew that they were. She let out the air and watched him glance to her bodice before he could help it. That was hardly her fault. The dress had been sewn a bit tightly, as was the fashion. The fact that the buttons up the front looked like they were having trouble staying fastened was probably her fault, however. Since she'd been numbed all yesterday, she hadn't been conducive to puffing her chest out to make certain her feminine charms were fully measured and the space accounted for.

All of which was a moot point, besides the fact that he was taking her outside his castle, and into the scattered bits of sunshine. She didn't know why she was against it, except that it was because she had to do it with him at her side. The servant fellow was also a hardy size, she noted when she turned her back on her husband and watched him instead. He was going to fetch a cloak, since he'd been requested to do that very thing, but he hadn't much to do other than open the door and accept the one that was being handed to him, as if they were already well aware of what was required. Lisle stored that bit of information away for looking at later when she was locked back into her suite again, and everyone pretended that she wasn't.

The cloak wasn't hers, or if it was, it was newly acquired, for they hadn't progressed to outerwear of any kind yet. Five of her seamstresses were engrossed in creating all the undergarments that a lady, who was particular enough to need the services of twelve seamstresses, needed. Five others were busily assembling daygowns of varying degrees of elegance and expense, while the remaining two seemed dedicated to putting together evening attire that was sure to make a man stand and gaze in adoration. At least, that was how the seamstress named Maggie had described it. Since she was also the woman who had spoken of Captain Barton's handsomeness and his possible acquisition as a husband, Lisle didn't quite trust Maggie's taste, though.

None of the seamstresses had yet to turn their attention to cloaks and such, since the weather was turning warmer and they had other necessities to design and produce first. All of which went through Lisle's mind as she stood there, looking at the green and gold cloak that was being held out so someone could wrap it about her shoulders.

"From my wardrobe," Langston offered, when all she seemed capable of doing was looking at how large, well muscled, and fit the servant-fellow looked to be.

"It does na' look capable of being your cloak," she answered, turning around again.

"I was a lad once. I wore cloaks. We still have some of

them. Only the fancy ones, of course. The rest became castoffs necessitating removal to the nearest compost pile."

"That's highly wasteful, my lord."

"How so?"

"Such items should be used."

"They nae longer fit." He added to that statement by lifting his hands, and strengthening a portion of his chest or abdomen, and a good portion of his arms as well, in order to make everything bulge through the fabric of his shirt. That way, she had no choice but to notice the accuracy of his statement.

Lisle had to swallow around the spittle, and telling herself she was acting ridiculous had no effect on her own body. She only hoped that begging her own face not to redden was actually working.

"They could have been handed down," she replied, finally.

"To whom?" he asked.

"Servants need cloaks."

His eyebrows rose. "My servants all have cloaks."

"Are they new?"

"Of course," he replied.

He was still puffing himself out everywhere, if such a thing were possible, and making certain his frame was still holding her eye, but at least he dropped his arms.

"What do you intend to put . . . on your own children?" she asked.

"My children?"

"Most lairds possess children. I assume, at some point, you'll act the same, and get some." Her command wasn't working. She knew she was pink.

"Oh. In that event, they'll wear new cloaks, of course."

"That's ridiculous. You've no idea of the value of your own gold."

"I beg to differ, my dear. Gold is for guaranteeing a certain lifestyle. My children, when, and if, they arrive, will have nothing but the best. That's the goal of wealth. 'Tis my life pursuit, anymore."

He'd called her *my dear*, and it didn't mute her other reaction. Lisle's upper lip lifted, despite her command to her body not to do anything to show how his words disgusted and upset her. "You should have offered them to the nearest child," she managed to reply.

"You're under an assumption that it would have been accepted, and gracefully, at that," he replied.

Lisle's color changed as her eyes widened. She knew she paled. "You could have done it anonymously," she said in what sounded like complete stillness.

"True. There is a slight problem with that plan, too."

Her chin rose. She waited until the cloak was upon her shoulders and then she was tying the ties at the neckline by herself, before some servant fellow jumped in to assist with the chore. "What would that be?" she asked, directing the words to her hands at her chin.

"They're all crafted in my family colors. Very distinctive. Hard to disguise. Especially hard to look at, when one dines on principles and clothes oneself in stubbornness, and makes one's children suffer the same. Surely, you ken the feeling?"

He breezed past her as he said it, giving an airy quality to words that felt as weighty as stones, and were having the same effect in the pit of her belly. She watched him nod to another servant, who was also almost the same height as he was.

Lisle caught up at the first bend in the hall. "Your wastefulness is still appalling," she told his back.

"Appalling? Are you certain?" he asked.

His walk was with a side-to-side, rocking motion, she noticed absently, and he only tipped his head to speak to her as he led the way out. He expected she'd be following him, without even checking. Of course, she would be. Some of his hulking servants were behind her, guaranteeing that very thing.

"You make us look like fools, my lord."

"Oh please . . . call me Langston."

His reply was said to the top of the button placket at the neckline of her dress, since he was the first one down the steps and had turned to address it to her, but wasn't quite at the same level. Lisle watched as his eyes widened, and then he moved his head up to reach her eyes.

"Perhaps this is na' such a good idea," he said, narrowing his lips into slits of pink-toned flesh.

"As I've already listed some of the pitfalls in this plan, doona' look to me for help with that remark," she answered.

"Come. We'll pick out a mount for you."

He had one leg on the step between them, making the material of his trousers work at clinging to a muscled thigh, and Lisle had to look away before he heard her gasp. If he had to wear English fashion, he should craft his clothing of stronger, thicker material. That way, a woman wouldn't have to watch things get defined every time he moved. He was tipped slightly forward, one shoulder just beneath her chin, and had crooked his arm at an angle, silently offering it to her for an escort. Lisle looked upward for a moment before returning her gaze to the mass of man in front of her.

"I have nae trouble walking about on my own, my— Langston," she said, as evenly as possible.

"I would na' wish you to trip."

"I've nae problem walking about . . . without tripping," she replied.

"There's an awful lot of men and horseflesh at my stables, Lisle. Take my arm," he said with the same nonchalant air, and then he added, "We're being watched," with a quiet earnestness that didn't match any tone he'd used thus far.

Lisle took a step down, reached out to put her hand on the inside of his offered elbow, and wished she'd had a ready answer, since he brought his arm close to his body as soon as he felt her. His movement tucked her hand effortlessly into the bend of his arm, imprisoning her in place at his side. They set off, walking on a stone-set path, across the length of his courtyard, and then they were disappearing beneath the shadow of one of the gates that had a spike-tipped portcullis raised out of the way.

He took her to the original castle stables, and it hadn't been built to house the amount of horseflesh that it appeared to contain. Lisle looked about her, as it appeared every stall had at least two horses in it, and there were more being curried in the yard out front.

"How many horses do you have, my lord?" she asked.

"At these stables, or the ones I had built because these weren't sufficient."

"You have other stables?"

"Several, actually. Most are near the town of Glousburg. It's still full of Monteith clan. Very loyal. 'Tis the only place I trust with my Arabian stock. I have more stables there."

"Why?"

He turned, looking down at her, and blocking out just about everything else. "Why do I have more stables, why is it near the town of Glousburg, why is Glousburg still loyal to Monteith, or why do I have Arabian stock?"

Lisle shook her head; opened her mouth. Closed it again. Her voice was missing. It was ridiculous. She cleared her throat. "What is . . . Arabian stock?" she asked.

He smiled. Her belly reacted. She barely kept her eyes from showing how horrid that sensation was.

"Arabians are horseflesh from Persia. Beautiful animals. Lots of stamina. Fast. I've an idea to raise and sell them all over this country. The English pay good gold for prime horseflesh, and they have an excellent eye to value. Arabian horses are unique. Much faster than our Clydesdales. The one I rode the other day when we first met? He's my favorite. His name is Saladin. I named him after one of the Arabic generals, since he won the Sassenach in one of the Crusades of centuries past."

"Someone won the Sassenach?" she asked, shaking her head to clear it.

"It must have been a bad day for them. It does happen. Na' oft', but it does happen. Have you a choice, or do you wish me to decide for you?"

"I wouldn't have the first idea what to select," she replied.

"Truly?"

His voice told her he was laughing at her. He already knew she was no expert! No Highlanders owned a horse, unless they catered to the English and were wealthy enough to have coin enough to house and feed a horse. Her back went straighter, and she said the first thing she could think of: "I've rarely been atop a horse. Women ride in wagons and coaches. We doona' ride atop horses."

"Well, as the lady of Clan Monteith, you're going to have to put a change to that. I'll tell you what. We'll take two horses. You!" He waved his other arm, moving his body with the motion, and since he had her gripped into his elbow still, she moved with it. "Bring out Blizzom and Torment. Get them saddled."

Her eyes went wider. They didn't sound like comforting names for horses, and when the pure white and almost purple-black stallions were trotted out, she knew they weren't comforting horses.

"My lord, I—"

"Doona' worry, Lisle. I only select these for their stamina. I'll na' allow you to ride Torment . . . by yourself, anyway. Blizzom is another story. He was named for his color. He's actually quite gentle."

He may be gentle, but he was also nearly the size of Langston, muscled everywhere, besides, and he was pawing at the ground as she watched.

"And I'll have your rein. Here! Fergus! Hold Her Ladyship's reins."

The name Fergus belonged to a man with a large beard of an orange-red color that was attached to another large, strapping, well-muscled physique. Since he had a tam covering his head, she couldn't tell what hair color he had. She didn't have any time to try, either, as her feet left the ground.

"Allow me to do the honors."

Lisle's senses assimilated how it felt to be held off the ground by Langston, and then she was above him, sliding into place in the saddle, and wondering how she'd had the presence of mind to open her legs enough to do that much.

He didn't look like he'd enjoyed the contact, if the set of his jaw was any indication. Lisle decided it was safest to look over and beyond him, and turned her mind not to wondering why he had so many groomsmen, but to why they'd all look so fit, robust, healthy, and muscled. Then she answered herself with what everyone kept telling her. They must be the best his gold could hire. She already knew he'd pay for more men than he needed, and their wages would be triple what they could get anywhere else. It also included meals, and she knew he fed them well. She knew that from Mary MacGreggor.

Lisle decided that the best course, when surrounded by so many men, was to ignore them, including the one parading as her husband, and it was easy, until he reached over to take the reins from the Fergus fellow. Lisle looked along the line of his arm, where he was bent over slightly; up to his profile; reached his ear . . . and then suffered through a flare of something so amazing, it sucked the air right into her chest and kept it there until it burned.

Lisle's eyes were wide and her hands on the pommel shook until she got the reaction under control. She didn't know what the feeling was, and she wasn't going to find out, either. It was enough that it was related to what she'd experienced when giggling and gossiping about men and carnal pleasure, and everything that was illicit and sensual, and best said in the dark, in whispers, beneath the sheets, where one of the Sisters couldn't hear. She tried telling herself that it wasn't the same thing now. It couldn't be. There was nothing she felt about Laird Langston Monteith except the basest hate and disgust. She had to blink the sheen of moisture from her eyes.

He was leading her out over the drawbridge, and when they were halfway up the perfection of that stone-lined road, he turned. Then he was setting out across landscape that had been cropped recently, and groomed so closely that it wouldn't have looked churned up, even if a thousand feet had

just been walking across it. Lisle watched the ground between
them absently as he led her, letting his own horse have more
and more lead, and nothing was making sense.

They were almost to the line of forest that he'd left in a
pristine condition when the question hit. Why was the grass
up here in such a condition? Excitement in her grew as she
realized what it had to be. The army that she'd been imagining out on the front lawn hadn't been on the front lawn at all.
It had been over here, on a side lawn!

Her eyes looked at the proof, and she swiveled her head to
look back at the pathway of it. It didn't seem possible, but
Langston Monteith could be drilling and training an army!
But if he was—why?

It was immediately damp, dim, and colder beneath the
canopy of trees, and there was solid undergrowth beneath the
horses, obliterating any trace of a path, although it appeared
they were still on one. That had to be the explanation for
shrubbery and tree branches that looked like they'd been
snapped off and why the overhang of limbs was just above his
head at any given point she looked at.

Lisle wrapped her cloak closer, looked to either side of her,
and noticed the same thing. There wasn't anything hanging
low enough that a man would have to dodge while riding on
horseback. Her eyes went back to the man in front of her that
she was using as a gauge for such a thing, and a twinge hit her
belly, twisting it, and making her eyes widen with the gasp.

She looked aside, as quickly as possible, and waited for the
sensation to fade. The forest on either side was safer, and the
amount of space that appeared to be a cleared area looked about
the same width as the path on the lawns had been. She wondered now, not only if there was an army, but if Langston was
training them for his own use. If he did, it was an interesting endeavor, and had to be for a reason. She could think of several,
but the most glaring was the most frightening. He needed it.
Scotsmen only had one enemy they could still fight . . .
each other.

The thought that he needed such an army of protection had her glancing about nervously before she had her mind under control. He must know sentiment against him was high. *The laird of Monteith needs this much protection?* she asked herself, and then answered herself—only if his back was turned.

She narrowed her eyes on the thought. Langston Monteith was in front of her, riding with a side-to-side sway, almost like his walk. He had a very nice back, she decided, and some very wide shoulders. She watched as he stretched, putting his arms wide, and pulling her horse's head up with the motion on the reins. That was interesting, and broke into her thoughts, making her lose exactly what they were and why. This Langston fellow must be quite a catch, if she'd been any woman other than a Culloden widow, that is. He was young, robust, handsome, rich . . . alive—as many other Highland lairds were not—and he was extremely interesting to look at, as well. Handsome . . . masculine . . . virile . . . muscled.

Her thoughts mellowed on the descriptions. Langston had well-developed arms, and she already knew he had a very thick, hard, and warm chest. Lisle shut her eyes and experienced such a thrill of gooseflesh over her entire body that it slackened her thighs and shook her to the point she had to reopen her eyes before she slid off her saddle, embarrassing herself.

She looked at the man in front of her unblinkingly, questioning reason and sanity, and wondered why she was losing both of hers at the same time. Creatures like Langston Monteith were to be spit on and detested; maybe even put on a little, pointed, objective type of thing and examined by men with very long, white beards, and nothing of any interest to say, one way or the other, about it. Then, they were to be discarded.

Lisle smiled slightly—sickly, if she thought of it—at the imagery of that ever happening. If it did, it would have to be a very large, pointed thing. She gulped, and went back to trying to decide if Monteith had an army, and why; and then she wondered what he was supplying them with for weaponry, since it had been outlawed after Culloden. Scots weren't allowed anything that could be a weapon of war; no swords, no claymores, no muskets. The Sassenach even considered the kilt and bagpipes weapons of war!

Her thoughts stalled as she remembered. Langston ignored the law. He flirted with imprisonment or worse. His men had worn kilts. Langston had also been wearing a kilt—tight about his waist, draped down over buttocks that probably carried as much muscle as the rest of him. . . .

She shuddered at the unbidden memory of it, and rocked backward until the saddle stopped the movement.

"Are you tired? Chilled?"

Lisle yanked herself forward, grateful for the dim shade, and was unable to look at anything except her hands on the pommel at first. She wasn't remotely chilled. Anywhere. She knew the reason. He was sitting right beside her, looking at her. She only hoped her face wasn't giving her thoughts away.

"Well?"

He'd slowed the horse, Torment, and pulled on Blizzom's reins, bringing her right next to him, and she hadn't even noticed? Lisle shook her head.

"You shouldn't let him have his head that way."

He tipped his head and slid a glance to her. She moved her own away the instant their eyes touched.

"Who?" she asked.

"Blizzom."

"Oh. Him."

"Doona' take offense, but a horse is like a woman."

"Excuse me?" she asked.

"Women need a gentle, but firm hand, you see. One that guides, directs, but doesn't interfere, unless necessary."

"Are we speaking of horses?" Lisle asked.

"Of course."

"Are na' stallions male horses?"

"Aye."

If he hadn't answered that with a grin that went right to his eyes, Lisle wouldn't have had the reaction she did. As it was, she was grateful he had the reins, because she wasn't in control of anything on her body, or anywhere else. There was no way to ignore the gamut of shivers she was suffering; all she could do was prevent him from knowing about them.

"Then . . . why would you speak of women?"

"Because they react the same. Stallion. Mare."

Lisle sent a prayer upward, begging for help to stop the immediate response those words created, and then she was cursing the Fates that decided her prayers must not be worth answering, *again*. "Is this how you . . . teach riding?" she asked.

"I doona' know how to train a woman to ride a horse. I only know how to train a rider."

Lisle looked at the ground. It looked like it was as far away as her mattress had looked earlier. She looked at the side he wasn't on. The trees looked sturdy, woodsy, exactly like a forest should, even one that had been pruned to allow riders through. She looked at the horses' ears in front of her. She did everything she could not to look at the man on her right side.

Nothing worked.

Chapter Ten

Lisle knew then that it was going to be a day of surprises, and some of them were not going to be pleasant. The emotion that dried her mouth, that made her heart hammer and her palms sweaty on the pommel was definitely one of them. It was unpleasant and disconcerting, and had everything unsafe and unplanned and uncertain anywhere in the world in it. So much so, her eyes went wide with it, and she watched as what had to be an answering movement happened to his eyes, too.

"What . . . are you doing?" she asked.

"Teaching you to ride," was the reply.

"Is this how you do it?"

His eyebrows lifted higher. "Not usually," he finally said.

At least, that's what she thought he was saying. She couldn't hear anything above the steadily increasing beat of her own heart in her ears.

"Why?" she asked.

He gulped. Lisle saw the motion it made as the lump in his throat moved. Then, she moved her gaze back to his. The sun wasn't giving them much illumination, and that tended to make his ale-colored eyes darker . . . blacker . . . and much more mysterious.

"Because it's normal to tie a lad on and give his mount a good smack."

"What happens then?"

He shrugged, moving her glance to that. He had barely enough room in his English-tailored coat for that type of motion, she noticed with a portion of her mind. That was a good thing, since his close-fitting trousers weren't about to give an inch. That wasn't a good thing, she decided, wondering where on him it was safest to look.

"He rides."

"What?"

"Or he falls off. Either way, 'tis the start that's behind every good endeavor."

"What?" Lisle asked again.

"A good endeavor is only good if it's done. And that only happens if the thing is started to begin with."

"What are you talking about?" she asked.

"Riding. What are you talking about?"

"Not riding," she answered.

That remark had his eyebrows moving again, and drew her gaze to where she least wanted it, on his. All of which started that amazing, pleasant, warm, drumbeat sound about her ears.

"At least . . . not the kind of riding you are," she finished with a whisper.

His eyes were wider than hers could possibly go, and Lisle felt like giggling at his expression. Then there was nothing amusing about anything. He pulled Blizzom's lead, putting her right next to him, and he was too much male to do such a thing and not have it affect her. All of which added to the unpleasantness of this surprise.

"You doona' ken what you say," he answered.

Lisle swallowed and winced at the dryness. "Are you raising horseflesh, or not, Monteith?" she asked.

He nodded.

"And are there nae mares in your plan?"

He gave another nod.

"Good thing. A foal canna' come from a stallion."

He reached out, grabbed the front pommel of her saddle with one hand, and the back of it with the other, and pulled himself closer by using her saddle for leverage. Lisle felt it move absently, since he was inhaling and exhaling air, and making his coat look like it wasn't tailored with much room, after all.

"Do you ken what you're about, Lisle Monteith?"

She nodded. Then she shook her head.

"You canna'. Otherwise, you wouldn't be so bold with me."

He called it bold. It was more like insane. She pointed at him. "You are my husband, Monteith."

"Na' because you wanted it."

"True. That does na' change the fact of it. You are still my husband."

He licked his perfectly formed lips, drawing her eye there. "Aye," he said.

"Then, how can you call my words bold?"

"Because you're a Highland lass."

"True," she answered again, still speaking to his mouth.

"And all Highland lasses detest me."

"Why?" she asked, moving her gaze back to his. There wasn't one expression on him.

"My absence from Culloden. My affiliation with the Sassenach."

The words made the unpleasant even more so, she decided, sitting straighter and wondering what is was about those dark, now brownish black eyes that unhinged her mind and set her mouth to talking so boldly.

"Mayhap . . . things change," she whispered, and knew for a certainty that her mind was unhinged. That was what happened when he hovered just above her and there wasn't anything safe to look at, anywhere on him.

"You should save such talk for when we're alone. In my bed

chamber again. Without disruption. Without company . . . and without clothing."

His voice had lowered. Lisle's heart did the exact same thing, only it fell to the pit of her belly, where it started pounding heavily.

"We are alone," she answered finally, lifting her chin a bit to breathe the last word onto the lips she was almost kissing, while everything else on her seemed to be shoving toward that very thing.

He closed his eyes on her statement, tightly enough that small wrinkles accompanied the act. Then he released her saddle with a push, making it rock back upward, the span of it going askew. Lisle sucked her bottom lip into her mouth, wishing it was his she was nibbling on, and wondered where the unpleasant idea for that had come from.

It wasn't entirely her fault. It couldn't be. She couldn't find emotions of hate and disgust when faced with the physical specimen of Langston Monteith. She only worried over why he wasn't doing anything about it.

"Come. I dinna' bring you out here for such."

"What did you bring me out here for, then?"

He didn't answer at first. He simply moved forward, letting the rein slide from his hand as he did so, until there was a respectable distance of about a horse-length between their mounts. Lisle watched Torment and his rider sway as one, and tried to do the same on her mount, and then she was watching kilt-clad men drop from the trees, and come from around shrubs to surround both of them.

Lisle's heart stuck in place, right against the meshlike chemise, and directly behind the row of buttons up the front of her gown where Monteith had looked, what seemed like days ago, instead of just this morning. Then the pounding got worse than ever, filling her throat and ears with painful beating. Monteith didn't do anything except sit there. He didn't so much as try to defend himself.

"You'd best rescue your wench, my lord. She's about to fall from her saddle with the shock."

One of the men waved her way, and Langston looked over his shoulder at her. The expression on his face was a very unpleasant surprise in a day that was just starting to show how many of them it held. Lisle couldn't move as those lips sucked into a withheld smile, held it for a moment, and then turned it into a grin, with flashing white teeth.

"These are my groomsmen," Langston revealed.

"Groomsmen?" she replied, in what she hoped was an icy tone, but it sounded like it warbled to her own ears.

"I believe my wife is wondering where your mounts are," Langston informed them, turning his head to the left and right to encompass all of them.

"Wife? You went off and wed?" one asked.

"Without a betrothal?" another one piped in.

"And without the banns?" yet a third man was asking.

"It was a short courtship," Langston replied, drawing out each word.

There were sounds of amusement given his statement, as well as the droll way he'd said it. Now that she knew she wasn't being threatened by a band of murderous Highlanders spotting the green and gold of a Monteith, she found it easier to breathe. That was also assisted by her heart, as it moved back from lodging at her breastbone and frightening her with the strength of its pounding.

"How short was it?" another man asked.

"I would say it took me less than an hour to select her. She was a trifle slower with her decision. Weren't you, my dear?"

She sincerely hoped he didn't expect her to answer to anything. His words were taking her voice, and there were too many men chuckling and milling about, making it patently obvious that the forested space they were in had been cleared to accommodate such a horde.

"Groomsmen, my lord?" she finally managed to ask.

He sighed in an exaggerated fashion, moving his shoulders

with the strength of it. "Come along. Show my wife where the horses are."

It wasn't far. The trees thinned, opening into a meadow, where hundreds of horses were hobbled. They weren't Arabians, either. They were the Scot Clydesdales. Lisle's eyes narrowed as she looked at all the horseflesh, carrying either a saddle or a pack on its back. It didn't look like Monteith was just raising horseflesh to her untried eye. She hoped he didn't think to fool an Englishman with such a fable. The groomsmen started filing through the horses, bobbing and weaving amongst the distinctive, dark red coats.

"How many horses do you put with each groomsman?" she asked, while Monteith sat there on his horse and watched her watch the scene in front of her.

"Two," he answered.

"Two." She didn't state it as a question, because it wasn't one. She didn't know anything about it, but that sounded absurd. "Is that normal?"

He shrugged. "I doona' care. My horseflesh is the best quality. Their grooms will also be, and overwork makes for shoddy care and grooming. I pay for the best grooms. I can afford it."

She was well aware of that. Lisle looked at him, wondering if the expectant look on his face meant what it did. She decided to ask it. "You want me to ask why they're not Arabian stock, doona' you?"

His lips twitched, and then he got it under control. "Perhaps," he answered.

"You bought Clydesdales?"

He nodded.

"Why?"

"I dinna' like the alternative."

"What?"

"A horse is the first thing a clan parts with when they're at the end of their luck. 'Tis also the first thing an English soldier dumps once he's raped and pillaged and plundered the countryside, and has goods to sell."

"You know they did that to us?" she asked.

He nodded.

"You bought such ill-gotten goods?"

He nodded again.

"Yet, you play host to them now?"

Again, he nodded, although there was nothing mirthful anywhere on him anymore.

"I doona' think I like you much, my lord."

"Please . . ." He brought his horse alongside her, imprisoning her there, and pulling on Blizzom's rein to guarantee it, and then he finished his words. ". . . call me Langston."

There was a long low note filtering through the woods, not as distinct as she'd heard it before, but at the same exact pitch. Lisle felt the flesh at the back of her neck whisper with it, while Langston didn't look like he'd even heard it.

Lisle glanced about her, looking for the groomsmen, all of whom still stood, hands gentling and petting their mounts, yet with an air of expectancy she couldn't see but had to intuit was there. The long note was followed by one short one, then silence. Lisle waited for the two that always accompanied it, but there was nothing but silence.

Then there were smiles and movement, and men mounting to file from the meadow. Lisle frowned, and Monteith watched her do it, with the same shift to expectancy that his men had possessed just a few moments before. She knew he expected her to ask . . . but what?

"Something annoy you, my dear?" he asked.

"Your endearments," she replied automatically.

"That's unfortunate. I've grown quite fond of using them."

"Try using my name. Lisle. It's a good Gaelic name. Ancient. My da used to tell me I was named for a Celt goddess. There are so many, it could be true, I suppose."

"Did your da tell fables oft?"

"What makes you say such a thing?" Lisle stared.

"The way you suspect his word to be false. I dinna' think it so. I thought much the same."

"What?"

"Your name. You. Celt. Goddess."

Lisle's heart leapt forward, pushing liquid heat into her cheeks and making it impossible to keep his gaze. She moved it to her hands on the pommel. That was safer.

"Come. I've a surprise for you."

Lisle started, wondering how he'd known the trail of her thoughts. "I doona' think I like your surprises," she replied to the saddle.

"You'll like this one. I promise."

"How would you ken what I like and what I doona'?" she asked in an aggressive tone.

"I know you'll like this surprise because you like to eat, doona' you?"

"I eat," she replied.

He chuckled. Lisle looked about them. The groomsmen had melted into the forest at all sides of the meadow, although the trampled grass and wildflowers and horse droppings had left mute testimony of the volume of horses that had just been there.

"Good. I'll have Widow MacIlvray prepare us a picnic. I fancy a bit of one today."

"Are you na' late for something or another?"

"Why would I be that?"

"You must have pressing business of some sort to see to."

"I have business. It's never pressing. Or, if it were, I'd make arrangements to change it so I could have a picnic with my wife today."

"Why?" she asked.

"Why? Why do I have business? Why would it be pressing? Or why would I change it to be with my wife?"

"I'm na' your wife because I want to be . . . remember?" Lisle lifted her head and faced him as squarely as possible. The clouds had been gathering while they dawdled about the woods, and now there were only shafts of sunlight tipping the meadow vivid and colorful in spots. Unfortunately, one of them was directly beside him, putting half of him in perfect silhouette.

"And you have a very strange way of showing that . . . remember?" He returned the taunt, and she knew exactly what he was referring to, since he put three of his fingers against his lips and kissed at them before lifting them away.

There was nothing Lisle could do but face him as bravely as possible and try to keep her chin from quivering, while keeping him from guessing how rapidly her heart was pounding and how sweaty her palms got, or how every moment seemed prolonged to the point of eternity. Langston's face went stiff, too, making him look like a carved statue, and about as warm.

"I doona' think I like the games you play, Mistress Monteith," he said finally, although it looked like he'd rather crack his face than move it to say that much.

"Well, I know I detest what you play, Master Monteith," she answered, in exactly the same tone.

"How do you know I play a game?"

"I think you play several. I just happen to know of one, for certain."

"Your meaning?" he asked, lifting his brows and forcing what sunlight there was to turn the highlighted eye a dark amber color, while the other one remained a cool, dark shadow.

She looked at the beautiful side of him, highlighted so perfectly it might as well have been chiseled by a sculptor, contrasting with the dark, shadowed half, and wondered how God could so distinctly show her exactly what Monteith was. If she had a talent for paint, she knew what portrait she'd do.

"I dinna' leave my chamber this morn," Lisle offered and watched a twinge go across his shoulders, although if she hadn't been watching as closely as she was, it would have gone unseen.

"I see." His answer was short and simple. He added to it by tilting his head, putting shadow across all but half of his cheek and his chin, leaving the only light to glint on the perfection of his lower lip.

"And I dinna' do it on purpose."

He blinked. She could see it by the flash of light on the eyelash ends of the highlighted portion of his face.

"I was . . . beneath the bed."

That knowledge made his eyebrows rise. She wished he'd cease doing that. It put a small crease across his forehead, and put too much emphasis on his eyes. She swallowed.

"You hide beneath the bed oft', do you?" he asked.

"I was na' hiding." Lisle hadn't much of a gift for lying, and her voice was probably giving her away.

"Nae?"

"I lost a seed pearl from the bodice . . . of my wedding gown. I was searching for it. I was beneath the bed for that reason."

"I see." He said it again, with almost the same tone and inflection. Then he turned his head the opposite way, putting light across most of his face, while the dark side only managed to hold onto his nose shadow, a bit of the bulge of his upper lip, and the cleft in his chin. Lisle hadn't been exaggerating to Angela MacHugh when she'd spoken of his handsomeness. He was the most comely man Lisle had ever seen or imagined.

"You heard?" he asked solemnly.

She nodded. "I heard."

"Very good, then. Come. Picnics doona' fare well with rain, and it looks like that is what we'll be dining with, in short order."

"Why do you lock me in?" she asked, stopping his movement to turn away.

"Security," he replied.

"I would na' steal anything."

He narrowed his eyes at her. She'd only seen this expression once, the time he'd told her not to pity him when she'd held his cheek after kissing him. It was making all the blood rush to the top of her head and pound there since it had nowhere else to go.

"Doona' ever say such a thing again. Ever. I meant for your security."

Langston turned his back on her, pulling on the rein as he started forward. Lisle pushed her knees into her stallion, and was surprised when it worked. Blizzom stirred himself into a trot, catching up to Torment and matching his stride.

"Mine?" she asked when he ignored her.

He slid a sidelong glance at her, and a muscle bulged out one side of his jaw. She didn't think he was going to answer her for a spell. "I pay my help well, but that's nae guarantee of security."

"From what?"

"Hatred."

"Hatred?" she asked.

"I'm hated among my own countrymen. 'Tis of little consequence to me. I'm very familiar with the emotion already. I was detested by own father. From birth. I've lived with it my entire life. I know all about it. When such a thing exists, you practice measures. Security is one of them."

"Nae one hates me," Lisle replied.

"You wed me."

"Those men back there . . . and those at the stables this morn. They dinna' hate you."

"Monteith clan. They know the truth."

"What is the truth?"

"Something with consequences too vast to trust this thing between us. 'Tis too fragile, at present."

"What thing between us?"

"You ask without reason. You feel it, too."

"Uh . . ." Lisle said the one word, and let it falter. For some reason, he knew exactly what she was saying.

"It's not something either of us expected, nor what we wanted. 'Tis there, though. Very strong. Like a clan drum beating. Over and over; incessant. Sometimes it gets louder and faster and stronger. Sometimes it's muted and dull. Still there. Even when I close my eyes and sleep. Still there. Beating. Deny it."

Lisle gulped.

"Try," he prompted.

She shook her head. The matching description was a definite surprise. She just couldn't decide if it was pleasant or not.

"You ken why you doona'?"

She shook her head again. That seemed like enough.

"Because you lie so poorly."

"I doona'!" she exclaimed.

He sighed hugely again. "Tell me where you truly were this morn, and we'll see. Come. I canna' go without sustenance. My business requires such."

Lisle's frown was going to be permanently embedded in her own forehead at the rate she was thinking. She dropped her eyes and wondered what motion would make Blizzom go back to the end of his leading rein.

Chapter Eleven

If Widow MacIlvray could cook, it was unfair. Lisle watched the tall woman with the swaying curtain of black hair, the womanly shape, and the melodic voice and wondered why, if Monteith had such a beauty at his own doorstep, he would have taken a second look at Lisle. That question became even more difficult to answer when the woman turned from her singing and saw who was at her doorstep.

If Langston thought all Highland lasses detested him, he had a strange way of thinking. This MacIlvray woman launched herself at him, with a call of "Monteith! You dark devil! Where have you been?"

She was almost upon him, and capable of making any man pick her up and hug her closely to his body, except Lisle stepped in front of him, folded her arms, and stared the woman into a halt in front of them. She didn't know where the urge to do such a thing came from. It was another nasty-toned surprise for the day. She also didn't dare look over her shoulder to see what expression Monteith had on his face.

"Katherine," Langston said in that slow way of his, "allow me to introduce my wife. Lisle, the Widow Katherine MacIlvray."

"You've gone . . . and wed? Wed? You? Wed?"

She was having trouble saying the words. Lisle watched

her. She wasn't paying the slightest attention to the woman between them. She was watching Langston.

"Aye," Lisle answered in the stillness. "Him. Wed. To me."

"Nae."

Her lower lip trembled for a moment, and then she flashed such a look of venom Lisle's way that Lisle swayed backward into the solid block of man that was responsible for this entire nonsensical scene.

"You said you'd never wed. Anyone. Ever. It's a horrible institution, you said. You promised."

He lifted his left shoulder and dropped it with a shrug. Lisle felt the motion. "The urge came over me. I wed."

"But—you promised."

"If it helps at all, he dinna' truly wish to," Lisle offered.

"I doona' need your help," Langston said from over her shoulder.

Lisle's lips twisted into a smile. "Very good. I'll just see to fetching a bit of a repast, and leave you two—"

An arm snaked around her middle, pinning her to him. That wasn't entirely unpleasant, or it wouldn't have been if there wasn't a tall, exotic-looking virago facing her, ready to spit at both of them. Since Lisle was shorter, she was bound to receive most of the projectiles. Lisle didn't know much about it, but this Katherine woman had too much of a sense of possessiveness not to have some claim to the same.

So, if Monteith had to have a kept woman, he should have had enough sense not to bring his new wife to her and expect a basket of foodstuff handed to him when he did so. Or if he were that stupid, he should know the food would probably be spoiled, and any ale acrid and without the proper age to it.

This Katherine was all woman, too. That was easy to see by the way her chest sucked in breath, held it, and then breathed it all over Lisle. She also appeared to have all her teeth, and kept them in good condition, if the sweetness of her breath was any indication. Either that, or everything about the kitchen smelled good. Lisle wasn't certain where to start on her suppositions, nor was the arm about her allowing her any motion with which to do so.

"What did she mean . . . you dinna' want to?" the woman asked.

"Wishful thinking. On her part," Langston offered smoothly.

"Wishful! So . . . you did want to?"

Lisle's expression was probably comical. She was only grateful the woman wasn't interested in anything about her, and missed seeing it.

"I'm na' in the habit of doing things I doona' wish to do, Katherine. Now, cease this bickering. It's senseless and serves nae purpose."

"We had an understanding."

"We had naught. You put things into being in your mind. 'Twas never anything save that."

"I really think I should leave—" Lisle started to say. Monteith lifted her, cutting off her air enough she had to let the rest of her words die off.

"By all that's holy! Monteith!"

A large, gray-haired fellow entered, blocking what light there was in the doorway, and then he was inside the room, making it look even smaller. He had a hand outstretched and then he had two of them, and then he had them on Katherine's shoulders and was moving her to one side and holding her there.

"The lass giving you more trouble than usual?" he asked.

"A bit," Langston said dryly.

Lisle looked from where the woman seemed to have shrunk, to the hands that were being gentle, but not allowing her much room.

"You should have sent us word. I'd have seen to it that she behaved."

"'Tis all right. She frightened my wife, was all."

"You've a wife? You? Nae."

He looked down to where Lisle was trapped. She lifted one hand and waved her fingers at him.

"God love you, Monteith! That's a Dugall as I live and

breathe! Where did you find one? The entire clan was na' just forced off their land, but they were put on a ship and sent away, along with the MacDonalds. I dinna' think any of them survived the decree."

"She was a MacHugh."

"That there is Duncan Dugall's lass. Has to be. Tell me I'm wrong, lass."

"You're wrong," she replied.

His face went into a frown and then he brightened. "Elias Dugall, then. He had eight strapping lads, and one lass. Sent her off to a fancy French school, some years past. You're her. You must be. Tell me I'm wrong, now."

Lisle nodded slowly. This was another surprise, she thought.

"I doona' know what magic you spun to get a Dugall lass to agree to wed with you, Monteith. If I dinna' think you in league with the devil himself a-fore, I surely do now."

"Why is that?" Lisle said.

"You dinna' tell her?"

He was addressing the man above her. Lisle turned her head and looked in the same direction. Langston wasn't meeting her eye.

"Why would I say anything? I dinna' know she was a Dugall."

"Tell me what?" Lisle asked.

The gray-haired man cleared his throat in the awkward silence that followed her question. Lisle turned back to him. "You dinna' let my daughter, Katherine, frighten you overmuch, did you? She's the best cook in the entire glen, and further besides. She's just a bit overpowering toward the men ever since she lost her own, and it was na' to some glorious battle, either. Nae. He took sick with the ague. Two seasons past. I canna' get another man to offer for her, although they like her cooking just fine. Isn't that right, Katherine?"

She nodded, looking vacant, but her eyes were sharp when

she turned them to where Lisle was still being held against Langston's chest.

"I could sweeten it with a dowry," Langston offered.

"That's na' the problem. She's a tad too friendly with her charms. She has her eyes on any man, but especially on you. You should have let me know about your visit beforehand."

"It was a surprise. I've decided to fill the day with them."

Lisle knew her eyes were huge. She was only grateful Langston couldn't have seen any of it.

"You have, eh?"

"'Tis the best way to intrigue a woman, I've found."

"You dinna' have that problem with my daughter, here. She's had her eye on you for some time."

"That's na' the woman I'm speaking of."

"The wife?" Katherine's father asked.

"The wife," Monteith agreed.

"Take her to the weaving rooms. That should do it."

"I rather fancied a picnic," Monteith replied.

"Katherine. Pack the laird a basket. Doona' take your temper out on him. I'll stay and oversee it. Show the woman your weavers."

Langston sighed, lifting her with it. She supposed that went for a reply.

"They've about finished with what you provided them already. 'Twas quite the undertaking, but go. See for yourself. I'll bring the basket when she's finished."

Langston started walking out the door, taking Lisle with him. He didn't need to hold her as tightly as he was; she didn't have any fight in her. That changed in the next moment.

"And I would na' tell the lass you bought up all the Dugall land!"

Langston stopped . . . inhaled, and then started cursing. Lisle sucked in on air, and held it until it burned to keep from screaming. He bought her family's land after they were forced off of it? She started struggling and squirming, and all that happened was she got his other arm around her, and then her air denied to her with the pressure of it.

"Stop it! Can you na' see anything? Stop!"

Lisle only struggled further. They were out in the open now, between two crofts of the same size, with thin stripes of smoke coming from them, and not a soul came to her aid; not when she kicked, not even when she got a breath and tried to screech.

"Things are na' as they seem, Lisle! Think! Stop this and think!"

Tears clogged her throat, and then they were spilling from her eyes, and splashing onto his arms. That was what got her the easing of them so that she could suck at the air like it was water, and she'd rather perish than let him see any of it.

Monteith spun her in his arms and shook her twice. "Stop that, and listen to me!"

Lisle bellowed a reply, which only got her another shake.

"This is why I canna' trust you!"

"Trust me?" She spat the word in an unintelligible fashion, and said it again. "Trust me? Me?"

"Aye, you. Now, take some of that shock and use it to calm yourself. That's it. That's a good lass."

Lisle pulled in a breath, narrowed her eyes, and looked up at him. He was holding her near his chest, and the expression on his face was severe, but not stony. She centered on trying to put the wall of numbness back into place. It wasn't working. She didn't know why. She exhaled.

"You've a redhead temper, haven't you?" he asked, finally.

"I am a Dugall," she answered.

"So I've just been informed."

"What did you do with the land?"

He shrugged. "Naught."

"You have crofters there?"

"Only those that were left. I wasn't in time to do more."

She went still. "You still have it?"

He nodded.

"Find a Dugall and deed it to him, then."

His lips lifted. "They wouldn't take it."

"Why not?"

"Did you take my gold willingly?"

Lisle knew she flushed. She only hoped the air was laden with enough damp and dimness that it wasn't easily seen.

"I had to force the MacHughs to take it, dinna' I?"

"I wouldn't take it because you're the Monteith. You're in bed with the Sassenach."

"Very visual description. I am not in bed with anyone. Haven't been for some time, either, Sassenach or nae."

Lisle lifted her chin. "You want me in your bed, do you? Find a Dugall and gift the land to him first."

"You're putting a condition on this thing between us? You doona' ken yourself very well."

It wasn't easy to continue locking eyes with him, but she managed it. She didn't say a word.

"Good. Think it through. Doona' let emotion guide you. I learned that years ago. Emotion has a place. Negotiation is na' one of them."

"Negotiation?"

"That is what you did. You put a condition on something. I'm preparing to answer it with one of my own. That is called negotiating."

She still had his glance, but it was her eyes widening. He didn't change by a flicker of a hair.

"In answer to your question: Aye, I want you in my bed. Willingly. All woman. All open and trusting and loving. I will na' take it any other way."

She couldn't hold the glance another moment. It wasn't anything like a dark-ale color, or anything except black, and the obsidian darkness of it was reflecting back at her what she'd hid from herself, mocking her. That wasn't a pleasant surprise, at all. She dropped her gaze to the third button down on his shirt.

"And I will na' gain such a thing through the purchase of

it. I dinna' guess at the thing either, Lisle Monteith. I already know it."

"Find a Dugall and put the deed in his hands."

"You're still negotiating?"

She nodded.

"What is it you offer?"

"Me. Willing. Womanly. Open and trusting. In your bed."

"And I still say, you doona' ken yourself very well to say such a thing." He sighed. "Come along. We'll check on the weaving room, just as Master MacIlvray suggested."

He was lifting his hands from her upper arms, and waiting for her to react. He had the look of humor about his mouth again. She didn't know why.

"He has the same surname as his daughter?" she asked.

He lifted his lip to a smile. "I already told you things are na' as they appear. *If* you were listening to that part when you weren't screaming at me, *you* would have heard it."

"I dinna' scream."

"You raise your voice loudly enough to scream. 'Tis very visual, too. Almost too much so—for most men, anyway."

"Explain."

"I like to think I'm na' most men," he replied.

Lisle let every facet of her face drop. "That isn't what I asked," she replied.

"Oh. My mistake. You're very visual. I noted that about you when I first saw you. You do everything with such a disregard for the consequences that it tends to draw in, and intrigue, a nonemotional man such as myself."

Lisle tightened her lips. "I dinna' ask that, either."

"Oh. What did you wish the answer to, then?"

He thought she was very amusing. She could tell by his continuing smile. Lisle stared at it. It was much safer than looking farther up into his eyes.

"This Katherine. She has the same name as her father, yet she was widowed. Explain that."

"The Widow MacIlvray has an eye for the men. You heard as much?"

"Aye."

"And he canna' get anyone to offer for her. You heard that as well?"

Aye."

"Why would she wish another man, when she already has her own father-by-law, and he's within easy reach?"

"He's her father-by-law?"

"And if she had any offers for her hand, why would he tell her of them if such a thing guarantees his loneliness, and loss of the best cook in the clan?"

"He's her father-by-law?" Lisle repeated, not hiding the surprise very well, especially the second time.

"And sometime lover . . . when another option isn't at hand."

"Such as yourself?"

"Nae. Never that. I have better taste."

"She's very beautiful."

"I suppose she is . . . to some." He reached out and swiveled Lisle in place, facing her toward one of the funnel-shaped crofts.

"But I thought you and she—you . . ." Lisle lost her words. She didn't know enough about it to describe it.

"I ken exactly what you thought. What she wanted you to think. You were wrong. Things are na' as they appear. Look beneath. Trust nae one, not even the proof in front of your eyes. Think everything through. Keep emotions out of the negotiating. Such a thing makes the bargaining more difficult, and adds insult where none is intended."

Lisle was grateful she was facing away from him. That way he couldn't see her face. It was probably flaming. She nodded.

"Aside from all that, I couldn't deed the Dugall property back to a Dugall, even if I could find one who would take it."

"Why not?"

"Because they will forfeit ownership the moment it happens.

I signed as much when it was sold to me. The English have strange codicils put into their deeds. That was one of them."

"Why?"

He sighed. "I expect for the same reason they deported the entire clan, and the MacDonalds, as well. They had too much influence in the Highlands, too much hatred of the Sassenach, too much gold, too much responsibility for the uprising, too much of a chance it might happen again, there was too much desire to punish. All of that, I suppose."

"Where are they, then?"

"Who?"

"The MacDonalds. The Dugalls."

"You doona' know?"

"You should have listened, too, when it was spoken of. I have been away for years, Lord Monteith. I was sent away to a convent school. I have na' seen my family since I was a child. Back then they were a proud clan in a green glen with beautiful, deep lochs and flocks of sheep, and life to each and every one of them. Now I find out they're na' only homeless, but deported as well . . . those with life still in them, that is. I doona' think I like your surprises very much."

"Did it work?"

"What?" she asked.

"Convent school."

"For what?"

"Taking the life force and sucking it out of you, leaving a shell of religious fervor that only a monk would find desirable."

"You already called me visual," she answered.

"Aye. That I did."

"Then take that 'nonemotional man' part of yourself and puzzle it out . . . *after* you tell me what happened to the rest of my clan."

His amusement answered her, although he didn't produce much sound. She had to guess at it from the increased breath of air at her neck, where the cloak didn't quite reach, and her hair wasn't covering.

"I'm na' certain I should say."

"You doona' know?"

"I dinna' say that. Come. Here is the weaver shed." He opened the door on a larger, round building, and waited for her to enter. He didn't follow her in. He waited at the door as she went from loom to loom, each one slanted in place by a window for light, and looking over the quality of work before complimenting the weavers, one of whom was a little boy.

It didn't occur to her until she'd reached the end of the row of them that they were using a large amount of green strands to their patterns, and it was a very recognizable shade. Lisle turned and looked at him from across the room, but that was no help. He was leaning against the open door frame, his arms crossed in front of him, chin bowed slightly, and one leg before the other, in a pose guaranteed to interrupt the women weavers at their looms. And he was looking at her with an unblinking, baleful expression.

Lisle narrowed her eyes and started back down the rows, and this time she was checking more for the yarns coming from their muckle wheels and spools, rather than the patterns and setts. Nothing about it bespoke of its origins, but it was screaming the name Monteith into her consciousness, and she couldn't quite decide why.

She arrived back at where he still posed, portraying nonchalance, but meaning other. It wasn't something she could see. It was something she had to sense. She looked up at him.

"Show me the spinners," she said.

He lifted one brow slightly and sucked in his cheeks to hide the expression. The response was immediate, as a flare of pleasure went through her, frightening and exhilarating her at the same time. Lisle ducked her head, but he didn't see it. He was already leaving, and she trotted to catch up. They hadn't far to walk. The croft he stopped at was another round one, indistinguishable from the others.

He pushed the door open and motioned her in that one, also. Lisle stepped down into the building, smelling of smoke, ash, and drying wool, while everywhere was the sound of spinning wheels and ripping cloth. Lisle waited for her eyes to adjust, while those in the spinning shed must have been doing the same, because all the industrious sounds came to a halt.

"You looking for something, lass?"

It was a jovial woman approaching her, hands outstretched in greeting.

"Nae. I—"

"She's with me, Mistress Hume."

Monteith announced it, stepping in, and then he had to slant his head slightly in order to fit beneath a roof beam. There was ample room for a man even as tall as he was, but everywhere you looked bales of wool were hanging, interspersed with the green and gold of Monteith colors.

"My lord. Greetings! You like what we've done?" Mistress Hume asked, waving her hands about.

"You've done wonders, as I've already taken note. There's nae strand being sent over that will be recognizable as what it once was. You have my congratulations."

"They're ripping apart your old clothing, and the Monteith linens. Why, hanging over there is a covering that should be gracing the laird's bed, and probably did for years," Lisle said.

"You think so?" Monteith answered.

"That coverlet does look rather threadbare. Was it auld?"

"I'll just be over here if you need me, my laird." The woman called Mistress Hume didn't want to be anywhere near the couple standing in the center of the room and looking about. Actually, it was Lisle looking about. Monteith wasn't doing anything except looking down at her.

"I believe it was the part of the prior laird's linen closet. I'll admit to that much," Langston replied, finally.

"Your father?"

"Aye."

"You dinna' send anything to the compost heap, did you?"

"Perhaps."

"And you dinna' hand anything down to your servants, because if you did so, there would be nae order placed, and nae need for it to be created, filled, and paid for."

"Go on," he replied.

"And . . . as you ken, nae Highlander will wear garments of Monteith green and gold, even if they'll freeze otherwise, so you have them taken apart and created into something more palatable to them."

"You think so?" he asked, airily.

"And you pay good coin for the destruction of such a garment, so that the threads can be put into other setts, and woven into other things."

"Very good coin," he replied.

"But it's destructive."

"I have superior taste to my father's. I will na' allow anything save the best to touch myself and those I term mine. I have the gold to make certain it's done, too. That's what wealth is for, remember?"

"You're a very good liar, my lord," Lisle replied.

"You doona' say," he said.

"Oh, aye."

"I'll wait to take the proper offense to that, I think."

"You may take any offense you like. I can see what's in front of me. Finally."

"What would that be?"

"You speak of selfishness and waste, but that's na' what it's about at all."

"Nae?" he asked.

"You're using your gold to create futures, my lord." Lisle breathed the words, barely above a whisper, more to herself.

"Are you certain you wish to think along this line?" Monteith asked, almost at her ear.

"And then you posture and pose that it's for other reasons entirely."

"Me? Posture and pose?" he asked.

"At will," she replied.

That remark got her a grin, and there weren't just crinkles about his eyes, they were full-out creases. Lisle felt the blood flood her face.

"You're na' sounding much like a Highland lass. You ken?" he said.

"And you are na' looking like the devil's spawn, either."

"You doona' think so?"

"You are very wasteful, though. That much is true."

"There is some waste that is na' waste," he replied easily.

"These garments—"

"Dinna' fit a man my size. I already told you. I outgrew them."

"And I already noticed as much," she answered. "So, doona' put your frame on display again, please."

"Me? Put my frame on display?" he asked.

"These women have chores to do. They canna' do such a thing if you interrupt them at it with your presence."

"I have na' done a thing."

"You stand there, preening and posturing and posing, and putting everything on display for all to see. Such a thing is disruptive, especially to women. We'd best leave. Now. I'm hungry, and you promised me a picnic."

All of which got her another grin.

Chapter Twelve

The afternoon was still promising rain, the clouds gathering and thrusting farther down until they were touching the tops of the trees, and yet nothing felt so alive, free, and vibrant, or as lightning-charged. Lisle inhaled deeply of the scent all about her, and kept her eyes on the man leading Blizzom's reins.

It wasn't a difficult chore at the worst of times, back when she'd hated him. Now that she suspected all the good that was in him, and the self-sacrifice involved to make it happen, it was an absolute joy to sit and watch him handle his horse, and sway from side to side as he did so.

The first splatter of rain splashed onto her nose, then her cheeks; then she watched them pelt into Blizzom's white coat, ruffling the texture, and knew it wasn't going to be a light sprinkling, but a heavy deluge. She opened her arms wide, rocked back onto the saddle, tilted her head, and opened her mouth.

"You've a look of a child about you, Lisle."

She brought her head back down, looked across at him through drops that curtained her view, and stuck out her tongue. That had him staring, and on him that was as disconcerting as his grin was. Lisle hooted with shivers the rain couldn't possibly cause, shoved the cloak aside, and opened her arms wide to it. That way, she could pull as much of the chill and wetness into herself as possible. Then she was leaning back again, running her hands through her hair, and fanning it out for the rainwater.

"You should have more care with that cloak. It's the best gold can buy."

"I know," she replied loudly.

"And Monteith colors doona' take well to such abuse."

"Why? Do they run?" Lisle asked, opening her eyes to the conical look of drops that were falling in earnest abandon from the sky.

"What?"

She brought her head back down, licked off her lips, and smiled. "I asked if your colors run. You ken . . . bleed? Well? Do they?"

His face was shuttered and impossible to decipher. "Na' so much that my laundresses ever let on," he replied finally.

Lisle hooted again at the serious expression on his face. "Perhaps we should test it."

"Now?" he asked.

"Of course, now. You see a better time?"

"I see a basket of food, two horses, and a lass who has lost her wits. That is what I see."

"You wish to eat? Fine. Pick a spot. We'll eat."

"You canna' have a picnic in the rain."

"Why?" she asked.

"Because good bread and meat does na' take well to such effects."

"How about wine? How does it fare?"

He shook his head. "Most folk seek shelter in rainstorms."

"Do you always do what most folks do?" she asked.

"When it makes sense? Aye."

Lisle looked over at him, putting her face and body in the same level stance he was in. "You ken what your problem is, Monteith?" she asked in the same solemn tone he was using.

"I've a wife with nae wits?" he replied.

She reached down and pulled on the rein, bringing her horse closer to his. "You only wish she had nae wits, my lord."

"Can I get you to call me Langston?" he asked.

"Of course. Langston," she replied, lowering her tone to try and match his. "Langston. Langston." She repeated it twice, every time dropping her tongue on the first consonant.

He shook his head. "What has gotten into you?" he asked.

"You never had a childhood, did you?" she asked instead.

He pulled up, straightening his back. The rain was plastering his black hair to his head and neck, and the parts of him that the clothing was supposed to be covering. Lisle reached out and touched her hand to one of the wet, muslin-covered humps of muscle between his shoulders, and pushed slightly. Nothing so much as moved.

"Very nice," she commented.

"This is absurd," he replied.

"Oh. I know. There are enemies behind every bush, the glens are peopled with secrets, and there's darkness lurking in every gurgle of every burn. I doona' ken how you manage the responsibility. I truly doona'."

"Are you making sport of me?" he asked.

"Me?" she asked, opening her eyes wide, although that expression only got her pelted with a big drop, and that had her blinking and wiping at it, and laughing again.

"Of course, you. There isn't another in sight, is there?"

Lisle looked about. The grass he'd been leading them through was flattening with the force of the rain, and little splashes of them were spurting back up when they reached the ground. She looked back at him.

"Nae," she replied finally, and licked at the moisture dripping off her nose.

"Then, you were making sport of me."

"Show me a picnic, and I'll show you sporting. Why, I'll

even wager I can outrace you. Take me up on it. I'll prove it. That's what I'll do. Gladly."

"Dinna' you spend years in a finishing school?" he asked.

"You already know I did. Seven of them. Long ones. I was sent there to keep me from turning into a lad, like I wished to be."

"It dinna' work?"

"Oh, aye. I was finished, too. Just draft one of your pretty missives and ask them. I was barely kept from getting the boot applied. Daily. Or should I say . . . nightly?"

"If this is the type of conduct you displayed, I doona' doubt that, at all."

She stuck her tongue out at him again.

"You do that again, Madame, and I'll take a forfeiture."

"You have to catch me first!"

Lisle slid off the side of her horse, wondering where the expertise for that came from, hitched up her skirts, and started running. Wet grass slapped at her legs, soaking her skirts further, and she was almost to the trees before he caught up with her. He was cheating, too, for he didn't just pass her up, but caught her up to him. Then he was heaving her over his shoulder, all without breaking stride, not even when he had to dodge and dart through shrubbery and trees that hadn't been groomed for such a thing any time in the recent, or faraway, past.

Lisle was hooting with laughter. Then she was shuddering with the giggles. She pushed herself up from the position draped over his shoulder, and that movement forced him to a walk. Then she was sliding down into his arms, with her own wrapped about his neck, her legs gripping about the hips she'd straddled, and looking into black-hued eyes that had the strangest look about them. Without waiting permission or rebuttal, she closed her eyes and put her lips to his, in order to cling and absorb and send the power of the kiss right to him.

The drumbeat he'd spoken of had her solidly in its grasp, filling her ears and head and soul with the pounding of it. Lisle lapped at his lips as he was hers, tasting flesh and rain and salt, and everything that was manly about him. There wasn't anything nonemotional about him as he did the same to her.

Lisle hadn't any experience with kissing, but Langston must have, for what he was doing had everything virile and lusty and passionate, and every other description the girls used to taunt each other with, about it. Lisle sucked at the scratchy feel of his upper lip, moving her tongue along the ridge, while he did the same to her chin.

And then they weren't standing anymore. Langston went to his knees, taking her with him, and that put hard, warm, damp, English-clothed thighs against parts of her that had never felt the like. Lisle glided along him, moaning with the motion, and heard an answering response from the chest within reach, touch, and caress of her fingertips. Lisle skimmed her nails along the muslin of his rain-wet shirt, barely hearing the sound of it, and answering every flinch of his with a corresponding twinge. Then she was pulling the ends of it from where he had it tucked into his trousers, and wadding it into balls in each hand.

"You ken . . . what you do?" he asked, moving his lips the span from hers he had to in order to make the words.

Lisle had him right back, pulling on the wads of shirt to make him stay in place, and locking her ankles behind him in order to make it impossible for him to move. Then she was filling her palms with the wet heat of his flesh, following the lumps of his abdomen to the mounds of his chest, and from there, to the tops of his shoulders, feeling the shirt moving and bunching as she went, in order to make a pathway for her.

The long, lonely, haunting sounds of a horn filtered through her consciousness, joining the sounds of their breathing and her heartbeat. The atmosphere was defined by the forest carpet, the sponginess, and the damp. Lisle barely heard it, and knew if Langston had, he was ignoring it as he had already this day, when they were in the meadow surrounded by clansmen and Clydesdale horses.

"I ken it . . . very well," she whispered.

"I doona' wish regret . . . and recrimination in the—"

"Will you stop such nonsense?" She nipped at his lip, stopping his argument with her motion as well as her words.

Her action unleashed something, and then she was down, rolling onto her back and covered over with a bulk she hadn't experience enough to make note of, and gasping with the weight of him.

"You are one glorious woman, Lisle Monteith."

Heartbeats filled her ears like drums, drowning out the sounds of breathing, the rain moistened leaves and limbs, and the three, short, muted, blasts of another horn.

Lisle barely heard it, and knew he hadn't, as hands moved to her temples, holding her in place. Then he was moving, stabilizing himself on his bent elbows and looking down at her with such a tender expression that she didn't dare blink, in case it changed.

"I will na' do this now," he whispered. He licked his lips.

"Why?" she asked, in a like rasp of voice.

"Because you're special. You're my wife. You're the woman I have chosen for my own mate, and there is nae portion of this meadow, and this forest, and this entire estate of mine that is safe enough yet."

"Safe from what?" she asked.

There was a loud thud directly behind her head. Lisle's eyes opened wide on what looked like an arrow shaft, quivering with the motion of its embedding. It was gone the next instant, as Langston did a push-up motion, drawing her eye to the movement of muscle as he did so. When she looked back, the shaft was gone, but what could be the arrowhead was still there, since there was a split in the dark bark, contrasted and filled with a sliver of freshly cut wood. Langston was the only one who could have affected the change, but he wasn't acting like someone who had just broken off an arrow shaft with his head. He was on all fours and moving away, looking back the way they'd come.

"Someone . . . has just fired at us!" Lisle put her shock and fright in the whisper, and was actually surprised she wasn't screaming it.

Langston twisted his head, put a finger to his lips to hush her, and then turned back around.

Lisle was shaking. There was no disguising it. She wasn't in control of her limbs, either, as she gathered her feet beneath her and went into her own crouch, to scoot after him. There wasn't a thing to be heard, except the plop of rain, and the whisper of leaves as they received the moisture. There was less to be seen, and she had to do it with eyes squinted, and a hand atop her forehead to keep the droplets away.

There was nothing in the meadow behind them except the two stallions, and they looked miserable, wet, and lonely.

"Someone has fired at us!" Lisle said again, using a bit of sound to her voice this time.

"I heard nae shot," he replied, from over his shoulder.

"With an arrow. In the tree. There!" Lisle was looking and pointing, but it was useless. There wasn't any sign on any tree near them, at any level, that looked like it had an arrowhead recently entering it.

She had to let her hand drop when she couldn't spot it. That was made worse when she rubbed at her eyes, moving rainwater around, and not much else, and there still wasn't anything looking like an arrowhead. She narrowed her eyes. The carpet of deadfall they'd been atop might have hidden it if the weight of their bodies had crimped it first. She moved backward to get to where they'd been, so she could push down at the sponge of it, but Langston was there first. He moved very swiftly for a man in a crouched position, she noted.

"You're seeing things, lass," he said.

"I am na'!"

"Keep your voice down," he replied with a sharp tone. Then he was rising to a standing position, and pulling the wrinkled portion of his trousers apart, to give himself room to do it. She told herself to ignore it.

"Why need I do so, if there is nae arrow?" She had to tilt

her head up to ask it, and blink away the wetness in order to look up at him.

"Because things are na' safe. I just spoke on it. Give me your hand."

"There was an arrow."

"There could na' have been."

"Are you telling me I see things?" Lisle ignored the proffered hand and raised herself up to face him. He was near his stone-faced expression by the look of it, she decided.

"I tell you it was a mistake. Such a thing couldna' have occurred, you ken? We were na' exactly paying attention." He tried to soften the words with a smile, although it looked forced.

"I dinna' mistakc what I saw."

"You had your eyes closed," he replied.

"I dinna'!"

"Hush!"

Lisle folded her arms. "Why must I hush if there's nae arrow that was spent after barely missing your head, nae threat in the woods except from me, and naught happening save the threat of a caress or two from your wife? All I can see is a man who must be afraid of such things."

"Afraid? Me? Afraid?"

"Aye. You. Afraid."

He sighed heavily. "If it will save argument, I'll admit extreme discomfort," he replied. "And it has naught to do with fear."

Lisle stuck her bottom lip out, caught raindrops on it, and then sucked them off. He was watching the entire thing. "Admit there was an arrow, and that it barely missed being embedded in your thick skull, which I doona' doubt the thickness of, since that was what broke it off. Do that and there will be nae further argument."

"Nae fool would be about with anything that could be used to shoot an arrow. They'd be imprisoned, or worse."

"Nae fool allows his servants to wear kilts, either," she replied.

Langston gave her his stone-faced look. "Are you naming me a fool?" he asked. He was tucking portions of his shirt back into the waistband of his trousers. She told herself to ignore that, too.

"'Tis your argument. You fill in the words."

"You name me a coward, and now a fool?"

Lisle lifted her eyebrows and thought through it. "Aye," she replied. "I do believe that is exactly what I have just named you. What say you to that?"

"I say that I must be both."

"What?" Lisle's lips parted on the surprise.

"I stand here and listen to a wife argue with words when I've nae time for such a thing. I'm either a fool to do so, or afraid of her temper should I na' do so."

"Why doona' we have time?"

"Because we're na' safe, and—"

"Ha! You admit it!" she crowed.

"Hush!" he said again, this time accompanied with such a swift movement she almost didn't see it. Lisle's lips went past parted, and dropped open as he filled the space directly in front of her, and moved his index finger from his own mouth to hers.

"We must leave. Now."

"Why?"

"We have to reach the horses."

"Why?"

"Because otherwise we look like we're hiding something. And someone might be inclined to check on what it might be."

"What?"

"God damn my own tongue for saying anything so stupid!"

He had her hand to march her back, and there wasn't anything subtle or hidden about the situation. Lisle only glanced back once, trying to mark the spot for further investigation. Then she turned back around. She'd never be able to find it again. She sighed in resignation. Nothing was making sense in a senseless, surprise-filled day.

It wasn't finished with them, either.

They reached the horses, after thrashing their way through waist-high grass that clung and saturated worse, and latched onto the material of her skirt while it did worse things to him. He *really* shouldn't be wearing the English-tailored clothing, she surmised, watching as it looked like the material was painted onto, rather than being worn by, him. The shirt was rippling with every movement of his back, and the tan cloth of his trousers was now a dark brown, and clinging to every bit of muscle on him. He didn't remotely look like a man of leisure.

Now that she had that thought, she got another. He hadn't chased her down with any difficulty, and he hadn't hefted her over his shoulder and continued running with her with any effort, either. She wrinkled her forehead at the memory. She didn't even recall that he'd been breathing hard, or if he was, it wasn't because of any exertion.

Langston was a very careful, nonemotional man. He was also a very physically active, strong man. That needed looking into, she decided.

"Here."

They'd reached the horses, and he pulled her into his arms. It wasn't for anything other than to shove her up into Blizzom's saddle before letting go. He didn't wait to see if she managed to straddle the animal herself. He didn't wait to see if she wasn't going fall off. He moved over to his own horse and launched himself up and in with such an easy motion it looked like it was something both he and Torment were used to doing, and often.

"Ride," he hissed when all she did was look at him.

"You have my rein," she replied.

His stony expression was added to by a movement to make his jaw jut forward, and that had muscles in both cheeks pushing outward. If anything, he looked even more dangerous, almost like a coiled snake. It could be a product of her imagination, she decided. It could also be an illusion of the rain, but she doubted that.

"Must you argue everything?"

"Stating a fact is arguing to you?" she replied.

"Will you ride?"

"Why?"

He made a reply that sounded like it came through clenched teeth, and then added words to it. "Because we have to."

"Why?" she asked again.

"Because we've been on a picnic."

"But . . . we have na' been," Lisle replied.

"And picnics doona' leave trails."

Lisle held to the pommel as he moved, thinking through, and then knowing exactly what he was saying. She glanced over her shoulder at the definite pathway they had made when they'd been moving through the meadow grass. It led directly to the woods, and showed very clearly that they'd been hiding . . . but what?

Lisle turned back around. The only thing he'd been hiding was a tryst on a very rainy day with his wife, when they should have been finding a dry spot in which to wait out the storm. She didn't see what the harm was in that.

They reached the other side of the meadow and from there, he had them climbing a very definite pathway around and over boulders the size of a horse belly, with shale sides that looked like the slightest slip would send it skittering down the side to join the jumble of them already littering the hill below. Lisle kept her eyes on the man in front of her, in what view the rain allowed her to, and not anywhere on the fall that would face her if she lost her grip, or Blizzom decided to act like his namesake, or a thousand other things happened.

The trail they were on topped on a rise, overlooking what could be the Moray Firth Inlet seen over the tops of trees, and could also be another view entirely, since she hadn't any idea which direction they'd been going. Then she saw the top of a pole that held the English Union Jack, a pole that a flag bearer for the Highland Regiment always held high enough

that it was the first thing to come into sight just about anywhere they went.

Lisle's lip curled, despite her telling it not to. Monteith
brought Torment to a stop, and once Blizzom reached the
back of the other stallion, her horse stopped, too. Lisle forced
her mouth into a position of nonexpression that hopefully
mirrored the one on Monteith's as she watched the regiment
approach in single file, marching to their drummer's tempo,
until they came to a stop right in the pathway in front of them.

Lisle hadn't any estimation of size, but the number of
troops Captain Barton had at his disposal was large enough.
It looked like the line of them snaked out of view with the
quantity, and only then when the column had turned onto
itself twice. If she had to hazard a guess, she'd have to say
four hundred . . . at least. She hadn't seen him out and about
with so many before. It gave her chills she'd never admit to,
and started a pulse beat in the pit of her stomach that had fear
at its core.

She gulped. Captain Barton put up his hand to stop the line
of soldiers, although it was a moot gesture. The line had already
stopped. They had to. Lisle and Langston were in the way.

"Monteith! Devilish weather to be out and about in, isn't it?"

Lisle watched as Langston inclined his head. Then he was
moving forward and clasping hands with the man, making
Blizzom move.

"What but devilish weather would suit the devil's spawn?"
Langston called out the agreement with a jovial manner. If
Lisle hadn't been watching and listening, she wouldn't have
believed it.

"I see you've a Highland lass at your side. And—God bless
you, Monteith! That's Mistress MacHugh."

"Aye," Langston agreed easily, turning on the saddle and
giving her an indecipherable look.

"What are you doing with a Highland lass . . . and worse,
the MacHugh one?"

Langston lifted a shoulder that seemed to say more than his

words possibly could have. Captain Barton must have intimated what he was supposed to, because he started grinning
wider. The seamstress, Maggie, was wrong. The man wasn't
remotely attractive, even if he was available.

"But . . . her? A Highlander? Ugh. You can have any lass—
willingly or no. I myself prefer them clean, even if they are
unwilling. It makes the pleasure that much more . . . intense
is a good word, eh, my friend?"

He nudged Langston, who smiled readily, and with an ease
that looked more comfortable than any grin he'd ever given
her. Lisle was the one sitting with the stone-faced expression.

"And just how is the MacHugh lass, if I may be so bold?"

"Filthy," Langston replied. "Aren't all the MacHughs?"

Captain Barton roared his approval of that comment. Lisle
felt like she was turning into stone, although her heart wasn't
listening. It was filling her ears and her mind with a cadence
of ache and pain and gut-choking sobs she repeatedly swallowed to shove back down to where they were coming from.

"You know . . . I had heard that. It's part of the inbreeding
and barbaric practices of the Highlanders."

"Inbreeding?" Langston asked.

"You know. Brother to sister. Father to daughter, son to
mother . . . and all the other barbaric customs that are, you
know . . . too inhumane to speak of. We only hope some of
our measures have made it safe for civilized folk to walk
about up here without fear of being tainted."

"I see . . ." Langston replied.

"So tell me, my friend. Is it true?"

"What?" Langston asked.

"That they're all alike. Beneath the clothing, that is."

Langston sucked in on his cheeks. Lisle didn't find it made
him look more handsome, more interesting, or anything other
than detested. She didn't know where her mind had been all
day, she truly didn't.

"I thought you had experience, Captain."

"Not with one of her kind."

"Her kind?" Langston asked.

"You know . . . a Highland wench, from the farthest reaches of this Celt wilderness. Is she . . . as they say . . . a passionate wench?"

"Passion?" Langston asked. The look he was giving her was nothing save uninterested and dispassionate to the point of boredom. "Oh . . . she is that, Captain. Very much so. Very."

He was wounding her and he didn't even have a weapon with which to do it. He'd also lost even a hint of a Scot's brogue. Lisle was rocking in place, yet nothing was moving. She didn't think through the why of it. She only prayed for the blessed numbness back . . . anything to dim the words that wouldn't cease.

"Passionate, eh? I almost envy you. I do, although I'd have to post a guard at my back to make certain she hadn't found a way to stick a dirk or two into me. She looks especially ready to do such a thing to you, Monteith. You'd best guard your back."

"I'd rather leave it bare, actually." Langston leaned toward the captain, and said the rest of it with a loud whisper that carried. "She rakes her fingernails down it."

"Lucky man, Monteith. Very. I'm certain I envy you now."

"Really?" Langston replied.

"Oh, yes. Except for one thing. I don't like my enemies in my bed. Too many stings when there should be nothing but bliss."

"I've always found it best to keep them close at hand, myself," Langston replied.

"Good Lord, why?"

"Because the devil is easier to fight if you know where he is."

"I never quite thought of that," Captain Barton replied.

"In point of fact, my business partner, Solomon Hussmein, was once my fiercest enemy in Persia. He had all the contacts I wanted. I had all the guile he needed. It was bound to chafe."

"You partnered with your enemy?"

"It's a very lucrative partnership, Captain."

"As I've proof of. Your ships are the envy of the royal fleet.

You'd best hope King George doesn't take a liking to them, my friend."

"He only has to ask, and they will be put at his disposal, of course. As it goes without saying, for all of my holdings."

The captain sighed, filling his chest with air, and making a tasty target if Lisle really did have a dirk and knew how to throw it.

"You have the luck of the devil, Monteith, and I already know you have his wealth. I envy you completely now. But satisfy my curiosity, if you will."

"You have but to ask. You know I'll comply, of course."

"However did you manage to get this Hussmein fellow to agree to go into such a partnership?"

"Only after proving my worth, of course. And his."

"How did you do that?" Captain Barton asked.

Lisle would have given anything not to have heard the answer. She didn't even realize it until she heard it.

"I married his littlest sister, of course," Monteith replied.

Chapter Thirteen

Lisle now knew there was such a thing as hell. It wasn't buried deep in the bowels of the earth. It wasn't the black underbelly of a mythical place called heaven. It wasn't full of devils and fire and condemnation and smoke. It was in every raindrop that hit her with a stinging blow, every shallow breath she kept taking, despite wishing them done with, and it was in the burning sensation right in her breast.

It was the choking pressure of the green and gold ribbon tie at her chin, holding the Monteith cloak to her body, and making her accept it.

Lisle reached up and pulled on one end of her tie, making it a surreptitious movement. The cloak slid off her shoulders with the same stealthy motion, and came to rest on Blizzom's flank before it fell off with the motion of his step, and landed somewhere on the rocky path they were following. She didn't look back and Monteith didn't notice it, only because he wasn't noticing anything about her.

The rain had a chill to each drop now that her back and shoulders were uncovered. It stung like little needles, and Lisle tried to concentrate on that. Rain hadn't had such an effect before. It usually felt fresh and vital. And cleansing.

He'd called her filthy. Her. His wife . . . or was she even

that anymore? He'd said to trust nothing. He should have been more specific. He should have said to not trust *him*. The stab of what might be anger, but felt a lot more like hurt, raced through her, dismaying and disgusting her. She had no choice but to face why, too. The dismay and disgust belonged to her and she had to own every bit of it, because if she'd stayed with hating him, she wouldn't care what he thought of her, what he was doing with her, or what he said about her.

A hoof slipped, sending a rock down the side of the pathway, where it continued its descent, gathering more of them as it fell, until the sound of so many rocks and boulders and chips of stone landing in the gully beneath them echoed back up to them, loud even in the rain.

Lisle listened for the end of the rock slide noise, watched the pathway in front of him as they descended the same one the Highland Regiment had been climbing, and did her best not to watch the man causing all of it.

He'd called her filthy, inbred, and barbaric. Her mind replayed his words, and the way he'd said them. The effect was a stiffening of her spine, and put a dryness to her eyes that negated the rainfall filling them, making the burn intensify more with each moment she prolonged blessing her own eyes with a blinking motion.

He'd called *her* filthy.

Lisle stared straight ahead and saw nothing. She knew the incline straightened out from the decreased slant of being atop Blizzom's back. She heard the change in ground cover, but saw none of it. She knew he turned back then, meeting her eyes for the briefest of moments, and then he was turning forward again, and yet she saw none of that, either.

All she saw was hate, making her eyes burn with it, and it was colored with red—the color of hell. It made the wash of rain no longer feel clean and fresh, but more like it contained brimstone and smoke.

"Here. Eat."

He had pulled Blizzom's rein, or slowed Torment's stride,

to bring him level with her. Lisle heard his words and didn't move her head. She ignored him, although from the corner of her vision, she knew what he was doing. The rain wasn't slackening, but he must no longer care about the effects of it on his bread and meat and cheese, and other foodstuff that Widow MacIlvray had packed for them. He was fishing about in the basket tied to the side of his saddle, and then he was holding something out to her.

"I'm na'—" Lisle stopped the slurred word, and made herself consciously change it. "I mean, I'm *not* hungry," she finished.

"I dinna' ask if you were."

Lisle closed her eyes, making them burn worse somehow, at his use of the Scot slang. She shuddered through a breath she'd die before she admitted to.

"Then, doona'—" She stopped again, and forced herself to ask it with perfect Sassenach dialect. "I mean, do not offer it."

"Lisle—"

"Doona' speak with me, Monteith! Na' now. I mean . . . *not* now."

"You have to eat. Here."

"Why?"

"Because a body canna' exist without sustenance."

"A body can exist without such bounty. I ate this morn. I do not need more. I have just spent a year proving thus."

"I know. I'm sorry."

"Eat your own meal, my lord. I repeat. I am na'—*not* hungry."

"Neither am I," he replied, although he was filling his mouth, chewing, and swallowing at the end of the words.

"Then why do you eat?"

"Because that's the business I am in," he replied.

Lisle tipped her head and looked at him, although her eyes burned worse, and her head started throbbing at the motion. He was filling his mouth again, chewing again, and it looked like he was forcing each swallow when he'd finished.

She went back to looking straight forward.

"My business requires force, power, strength, stamina, and health. Mine. Every day, more of it each day. I can't afford to slacken and sicken. A body does na' get to such a state by starving it."

"I dinna'—*did not* ask," she said finally.

"I know."

She tried ignoring him again. It didn't work. She knew he ate another bite before he spoke again.

"What happened to your cloak?" he asked.

"I determined that I nae—I mean . . . no longer need it."

"Will you cease that?"

"What?" she asked.

"Forcing Sassenach words through your lips."

"Why?" she asked.

"Because it is na' you."

"I would ask you what you feel is me, my lord, but as I have already listened to it, I doona'—I mean, *do not* feel the need to hear it again."

"Lisle."

"Doona' say my name! Never again! You ken?"

"Why?"

"Because I was named for a Celt goddess, and you have just vilified everything I value in that. You are na'—I mean—*not* worthy of having the name on your lips or your tongue."

He didn't answer. He simply took another large, vicious-looking bite of his bread, chewed it, and then lifted his chin for the swallowing motion it required. From the corner of her eye, it looked like it scraped his throat as he swallowed. Lisle sneered slightly. She only hoped it scoured him all the way down into his belly.

He tore another bite off and watched her as he chewed it. Lisle wasn't looking; she didn't wish to. She knew he was looking because she felt his stare.

"You canna' ignore me forever," he said.

"I can do whatever I wish," she replied.

He sighed heavily. "You see nothing, know nothing, and sit in judgment on the whole. I doona' ken why I bother talking to you now."

"If it's any comfort, neither do I," Lisle replied.

"If I explain, I tear it apart. If I stay silent, I am hated."

"You doona' have to stay silent to be hated, my lord. I hate you just fine with or without your words. Trust me."

That got her a larger sigh. Lisle tightened her fingers on the pommel, and thanked God for making the rain as disguising as it was.

"I dinna' mean any of that . . . none of that," he said.

"I prefer brutal honesty, my lord. I always did."

"I know. That's why everything has to go as it is."

"Canna' you simply eat your meal and leave me be?"

"'Tis na' palatable," he replied.

"Then why do you still eat it?"

"I already told you. 'Tis the business I am in."

Lisle turned to him, hoping the rain blurred him, and yet knowing it wouldn't. He was still the most handsome man she'd ever seen. And now that she knew he'd do whatever it took to keep that physique as strong, muscled, and filled with as much stamina as he could, even eating an unpalatable meal, it was worse. He was also the most insidiously evil, beautiful man she'd ever seen.

"I doona' care to hear anything further about what business you are in, my lord."

"As my wife, you have to address me by my given name . . . at least, some of the time."

"I am na' your wife. I heard as much. I may be inbred and stupid, but I am not deaf. Never was."

He swore, and tore another bite from his bread. The stone look was back on every bit of his features, but it was tempered by something new, something intent and tormented. Lisle watched him chew in silence, and wondered what it was. He swallowed, tensing his cheeks with the motion.

"If you refer to my first wife, Shera, let me assure you, she presents no impediment to our marriage. None."

"Shera would probably na'... I mean *not* agree, *monsieur*." Lisle said the last part of her words in perfect French, and watched him look at her. There wasn't a bit of surprise on him anywhere to hear it.

"She's na' in a position to agree or disagree."

"She has my sympathy."

"She does na' need it. She's gone," he replied.

"That must have been uncomfortable for you," Lisle replied in her perfect French. She should have been surprised when he understood every word, but she wasn't.

"I dinna' ask for her hand."

"As I have already heard. She was probably part of the business contract that you and your partner arranged. She has my sympathy... and my thanks."

"Thanks?"

"For freeing me from you. Nae man can have two wives, Lord Monteith. Such a thing makes a man a bigamist. Even up here, in the barbaric Highlands, such a thing is still frowned upon. Always was."

There was silence for a bit as he shoved the last of his bread roll into his mouth and ate it. Lisle watched him and forced herself to ignore the twinge deep within her as he pursed his lips once he'd finished.

"The MacHughs will find life uncomfortable without their gold."

Lisle sucked in the shock, and hoped he didn't see it. "Are you threatening me?" she asked.

"Oh, I never threaten," came the reply. "'Tis too time-consuming for my taste. I like the word *negotiation* much, much better."

Lisle's eyes widened without her allowing them to do it, and the raindrops that slid into them didn't obliterate where he sat, taking a bite of his cheese block this time, although it didn't looked like he was enjoying the taste or texture of it, either.

"Or, you could try finding someone on Dugall property that would take you in . . . and keep you hidden from their landlord, who just happens to be me. That should prove an interesting endeavor. There might even be a poor crofter or two willing to risk his livelihood to shelter the last laird's daughter. I doona' know the success of that, since they would lose their livelihood if they thwart me. Trust me. I doona' have a reputation of compassion toward those who deceive me."

She was reeling in place, and watched as black edged its way all about her vision. It made Blizzom feel like he was swaying, rather than standing placidly at rest. Lisle gripped the saddle pommel with hands that were afraid of the alternative.

"Or you could try and find the Dugall clan in their exile. If you knew which part of the West Indies that England had sold them to."

"S-sold?" she stammered. At least, that's what she thought her lips moved enough to say.

"Sold. Into slavery. Every last one. The ones that survived the journey, that is."

Lisle's grip slipped, and then she forced the black at the edge of her consciousness away. She didn't know how she did it, but she was not going to faint. She refused. Not in front of him and not over anything he said or did. Such a reaction was for women who possessed emotions and things like hearts, and if it killed her, she was going to make hers cease tormenting her with its presence.

"What . . . do you want?" The shell of a woman still sitting on the horse asked it, and that had to be her.

Monteith raised both eyebrows, putting that crease into place in his forehead again. "You," he replied easily. "In my bed. Willingly. Lovingly and caressingly."

She was so thankful she hadn't taken a mouthful of food as her stomach revolted on his words, gagging her with bile that choked and burned. Lisle swallowed it back down, watched him through a sheen of moisture that she couldn't blame on the rain, and then blinked the tears into existence down her cheeks, so her eyes could fill with more.

"Why?" she asked.

"Because you have assigned me a part, and I have no choice but to play it."

"What?"

"And there are things too large to grasp, and too fragile to put to the test. I'm playing a part. One of many, I assure you. I have been for years. I'm very good at it. That is the talent for which my partner went into business with me. He could na' tell a lie. I can. I can live one. I am very well paid for it. Doona' you listen to anything when you hear it?"

"Why do you still use the brogue?" Lisle could hit herself later for allowing the emotion to stain her voice. She could only hope he didn't hear it for what it was. It was a forlorn hope.

He sighed heavily. "I *am* still a Highlander."

"Only by birth. Na' by choice."

"Such a language is mine to use. Doona' take that from me . . . too."

His voice had cracked slightly on the last word. Lisle couldn't believe she'd heard such a thing, and upon searching his face, she knew she hadn't heard it. "I did nae such thing. I wouldn't."

"Every Scot does. You included."

"But—back there, you spoke of barbarism, and inbreeding, and . . . and filth." She didn't have his reserve. She knew it as her voice broke, and broke hard. It sounded like a sob, even to the shell of a woman she was pretending to be.

"I did," he agreed easily. "What of it?"

"Why do you use the brogue . . . if you detest it so?"

"You are still not listening to what you hear. We'll work on it."

"I doona' wish to work on anything with you."

"Isn't that too bad," he answered, and took a bite of what looked to be a sausage. This time when he chewed, it was absently, as if the taste might be enjoyable, but his mind was elsewhere. There wasn't a hint of discomfort as he swallowed and took another healthy bite.

Lisle told herself not to continue watching him, but nothing was working.

"Do you have an auld pair of shoes you like wearing?" he asked after the fourth or fifth bite. Lisle had stopped counting. The woman she was pretending to be was still watching every movement he made, however.

"My shoes are auld," she replied, "and I have but one pair."

He smiled. It wasn't pleasant. "Bad example. Better one— do you have a book you liked reading, even when it became threadbare and worn? Perhaps at school they allowed you something?"

Lisle blinked the instant tears down her cheeks, and licked at them when they reached her mouth, the salty flavor joining the rainwater taste of it. She shook her head and had to wait while he swallowed yet another mouthful of his sausage.

"How about that MacHugh wrapped bundle of pipes? You treasure that?"

Lisle's body decided it did have a heart, and it was huge and full of hurt and pumping it into every portion of her body that she hadn't been successful at numbing.

"Are you threatening . . . I mean, negotiating . . . over them, too?" she asked evenly, making every effort at her disposal to do it without one sign that her heart was breaking with each and every word.

He smiled again, and there was nothing warm about this one at all. "If need be, I'll use anything at my disposal. Anything."

"Anything?" she asked in such a careful tone, the word croaked.

"You. Pipes. Love. Passion . . . anything. Trust me."

Lisle sucked in on his words, afraid she'd heard them wrong, and then knew she hadn't when she continued watching him watch her.

"Good. You're finally listening," he said.

"What do you want . . . for the pipes?" Her being dropped

into shards about Blizzom's hooves, laying bare everything she couldn't hide. She wasn't in control of anything in her voice, and the words too clearly showed how much Angus's bagpipes meant to her. There wasn't any way to hide the moisture slipping from her eyes in a nonstop torment of blur and clear, blur and clear, and then start again. There wasn't much reason to hide anything. She wasn't like him. She didn't think she ever wanted to be.

She knew for certain she'd sold her soul to the devil. Lisle didn't guess that he knew the pipes were hidden beneath her bed. She knew he knew. It was in the eyes that were still watching her. He took another bite of his cheese as he considered it. Then, he swallowed.

"If I gave you new pipes, would you want them?"

Lisle shook her head. She didn't trust her voice.

"Na' even if they were the best? The very best?"

She shook her head again.

"Na' even if I gave you enough bagpipes to supply every piper in every glen, and got you permission to play them?"

Lisle pulled in a shuddering breath at the line of his questioning. He wasn't threatening her with the pipes. She instinctively knew what he was saying. The relief felt like a cool water wash running over hot coals, and the effect like so much steam dispersing over it, too.

"I doona' know," she finally replied.

"Would you consider it?"

She nodded.

"What more do you need?"

"To give up Angus's pipes?" she asked.

He nodded.

"Never to see you again," she replied.

A look of such agony crossed his face, Lisle almost felt it. The instant she blinked, it was gone, and all that was left was a shine of obsidian where his eyes were watching her. She sharpened her eyes on him, and the only sign he'd been affected by anything she said was two spots of color high on his cheeks, but that could be an illusion of the light.

He took another bite of his cheese then, using a tearing motion of his teeth, and even to Lisle's eyes it looked like it was choking him. He had to turn aside, and she waited patiently until he finished his swallow and turned back to her.

"I doona' wish the pipes," he finally said, softly. "You can keep them."

"I know," she replied.

"You said that to hurt me?" he asked.

"Did it?"

"I'm afraid to answer that, I think," he replied.

"Good. Maybe now you can see what you do, too."

There were some prices that were too high to pay. Langston had heard this, in one of the dark corners of one of the opium dens he'd frequented, a long time ago, in another lifetime, and when he was playing the part of another soulless addict with open ears. He hadn't known what the words meant, but had stored it away for future reference. Now he knew what the old, underhand dealing, ex-pirate he'd been keeping company with had been saying. The price for this was high, almost too high.

He knew it when the pain he'd put in those transparent, sky-blue eyes had ferreted out and sought every bit of him that could feel hurt, and knew it was him who was doing it to her. That price was high. Then she'd said the words that left him feeling like he was cut open and bleeding. He'd rather have taken a deathblow at Culloden than continue doing what he still had to do. She was too volatile. She was too passionate. She was too full of life and emotion and joy and pain. She was too transparent.

The last was most intriguing, especially to one so used to darkness and hiding and lying. Having passion and abandon and the freedom of showing it was intoxicating to the point he almost forgot time and space and reason in the glory of kissing her and knowing she kissed him back willingly. So much so, that one of his own archers had to remind him of it with a perfectly aimed arrow.

It would never do. She was too open, too honest . . . too easily read. She was alive with each and every emotion, and they were so easily seen on her, it was frightening to one who stayed hidden. Why, if the Lady of Monteith was happy, it wouldn't be possible to keep it hidden. Langston knew it, and cursed himself for the knowledge, and the stamina and strength and all the other words of description he'd just used for her. He had to have all of that. It was the only way. If she was happy, it wouldn't stay hidden. Everyone would want to know why. It would be questioned. Everything would be looked at closer—including her husband . . . especially her husband. It would be Captain Barton and his rangers that would do the looking, too, and a Highland laird with what he had in mind was stripped of all his lands and titles, and then his head. There was too much at stake. Too many relying on what he was doing . . . too much to lose. He couldn't chance it. Ever.

There was definitely a price to pay, and it was Langston who had to pay it, and keep paying it. That was the only way he could get the English to trust him enough to sell him back Highland properties. It was the only way he could get good wages back into Highland hands, get food and comfort into the bellies of their bairns. It was the only way he could get the Sassenach to look at, but not see, what he was actually doing, and why.

It was also the only way he could get Butcher Willie under his control, so he could use him. It was just like he'd told Lisle. He'd do anything. Even if it meant slicing open his heart for the beautiful, passionate, Celtic goddess he'd married, so she could seek her revenge on it. He'd do it. He'd do anything. Still. Again. As many times as it took to get Scotland back.

"So," he said brightly, after pulling in another dry, tasteless bite of cheese and managing to swallow it by force of will. "Do we have a bargain or na'?"

"To what?" she asked.

"You already said you heard me," he said softly. Then, he

took another bite of his cheese using a rough tearing motion of his teeth.

"You've said a lot."

He smiled wryly. "True," he replied.

"What is it we've bargained for this time?"

"You. Still."

She gasped. Her eyes went a darker blue that struck straight to the heart of him, making him flinch inside.

"Still?" She whispered the word.

"Oh, aye. I find you very passionate. Very. I want that. I wanted it the first moment I saw you. I want it now. That's why I bargained for you and would accept only you. That's why I wed with you. Your passion. I want it. Still. Like in the woods, yonder, only with even more abandon. That is what I am negotiating, Lisle Monteith. Right here and right now."

"Now?" she asked, and he had to lean forward to hear it.

"Aye," he said.

She reached for the top button of her dress, but it wasn't slipping easily from its hole. The rain had made it slick, and it didn't look like her fingers were working.

"What are you doing?" he asked.

"Complying," she replied.

Langston caught the sound of self-hate before he vocalized it. It was one of the hardest things he'd ever done.

Chapter Fourteen

Lisle's eyes opened instantly, and she stretched in the big bed that was her own. There wasn't any man, resembling Langston or not, in it with her. It wasn't a horn that had awakened her, although something had. She lay, looking up at the long beams above her canopy, and wondered why it was taking so long to decipher what it was. Then, she knew. It was the aftermath of what had to have been the horn, moving like an echo of silence immediately at the end of such a note, through her consciousness, and then her bed chamber.

She sharpened her ears and concentrated. There wasn't a hint of marching feet, or horse hooves, or a cadence of drums, or anything other than a large bedchamber with one person in it. There also wasn't any rain. Morning sunlight was tipping the top of her room light yellow, and from there it reached toward the floor. It was at odds with everything else.

Lisle felt like she'd been kicked by a horse the size of Blizzom, or worse. Even the motion of moving her arms seemed to take forever, and there was no stopping the torture of memory. He had a wife. Her name was Shera. She'd left him. Lisle was going to find out why, and where she was. Freedom was behind that quest.

Monteith was a traitor. He was Captain Barton's confidant.

They were close enough to banter words about women. That was horrid to consider. Lisle scrunched her nose. It was almost as horrid as remembering what he'd done when she'd reached the second button.

He'd grabbed her to him, pulling her so swiftly from Blizzom that her hands had been smashed against her breast. He'd kicked his stallion into a gallop, something she'd have gasped at experiencing if he wasn't filling her ear with harsh words, said through thin lips, atop a set chin.

Lisle almost groaned at the remembrance of them. He'd told her she still didn't listen, and he was not fond of repeating everything. If she had to be a Highland lass, the least she could do was pay attention the first time. He wanted her in his bed . . . and only in his bed. He didn't want her anywhere else or any other way. He didn't want her if he had to force her. He wanted her in his bed, willing and warm, and if she was complying, she'd best wait until they were at the castle. Perhaps she could prepare herself for that.

The horse Torment showed every bit of the strength, stamina, and speed Langston had already informed her an Arabian was noted for, and nothing could stop it, nothing could prevent it, and nothing could save it.

The morning silence was unnerving. Lisle lay in the empty bed, watching beams of sunlight crisscross among the beams of wood, and wondered why, if Langston had raced to get back to his home, he'd done nothing more than carry her up the staircase, put her on her bed, and tell her to seek some sleep, she'd need it, and then . . . he'd stopped at the door and told her only one thing mattered in this whole thing. He'd called it *neart aithnich*. The Gallic words for power of knowing. Not guessing. Knowing.

Lisle turned her head and looked toward the entry door, envisioning the entire thing again, despite every attempt not to. Someone had left a torch burning in one of the sconces, and it had flickered on one half of his face, leaving the other in complete shadow. Lisle shivered in her bed, an entire night away from it. He'd looked sinister and enigmatic, and something else . . . something he'd told her to use all her senses to observe and pay attention to. *Beachdaich*, he'd said, using the Celt word for that, too . . . *beachdaich;* and not just with her ears, her eyes, and what she thought was knowledge. He'd shut the door then, locked her in, and had not done one other thing no matter how long she waited, or how many times she went on her knees, or how many circuits she made of the room.

She was exhausted. She was insulted. She was hurt. She was shocked. Just about every surprise he'd given made her feel that way, and then Mary MacGreggor was knocking and entering, leading a servant with a breakfast tray, followed by three men, carrying what was either half of a very large barrel for ale, or a large tub. Lisle sat, pulling the covers to her chin. Not that anyone would be able to see anything through the thick cotton of her newest nightdress, but she wasn't used to having Langston's large male servants in her bed chamber.

"His Lordship has ordered you a bath," Mary called out cheerfully. "I've had the water heated. It will just take a moment, and we'll have you up and about and sitting in such luxury, you'll cry."

She was going to cry all right, but it wasn't at the luxury. Lisle pulled her knees to her chin, ruffling the almost perfect white span of coverlet into a slope, and watched them. She was totally insulted now. It was obvious to her. He'd called her filthy. He was changing that.

Steam rose from each bucket they brought in, adding to the heat they'd started with a new fire in the fireplace, and making the air heavy and moist when she breathed it in. Then Mary was sprinkling something into the water that made the chamber fill with the scent of rain and flowers and the same sort of feeling you got when smelling the crumb cakes when they were in the ovens. Lisle sniffed the air.

"His Lordship has these salts kept under lock for special use. He gets them from that godforsaken land his ships keep visiting. It's ever so nice-smelling. Isn't it?"

"Under lock?" Lisle asked.

"And I had to access the cabinet by requesting such a thing through that Mabel Beamans. She had to check with His Lordship before she'd grant me access, too. You'd think she had all the power of the household, that woman. I'm telling you. One of these days, there's going to be—"

"Why?" Lisle asked, interrupting her.

"Why what, my lady? Here. Just put your knees down there, allow me to put this jacket atop your shoulders, and we'll be seeing to your breakfast."

Lisle's face went expressionless as she did the requested move, and waited while another blue wool jacket was draped across her.

"Why are my bed jackets in blue?" she asked absently.

"His Lordship wants everything done in blue for you. Everything that doesn't have clan tradition, that is."

"But why?"

"You'll have to be asking him that yourself. He's na' one for telling me the whys of his actions, you ken? You could check with Mabel Beamans. That woman thinks she knows everything. Why, just ask her."

Langston wanted to clothe her in blue. Lisle thought that over and then set it aside. She had other worries, like this bath.

"It takes a special dye to make them in every shade, too. That was His Lordship's orders, and they were most specific. Blue. Every shade, every hue. It's very costly to produce, and takes a flower called a hyacinth. Available only from parts of the world he's been to. That Persia place . . . or a place called Africa. Beautiful blue these hyacinth be. We had to hire two more men, skilled in the dye process, in order to follow his orders."

Lisle made her expression go completely blank.

"They're powerfully proud to be of service, my lady. Why, to be able to please His Lordship, and be able to put food on their tables and clothing on their bairn's backs is everything they hoped for."

"What if I doona' like the color blue?" Lisle asked, amazed she'd kept the snide tone out of her voice.

"You . . . doona' like it?"

The thought of saying it to put a large knot in the middle of Langston Monteith's little plot was almost too delicious to keep silent about. Lisle glanced toward where her personal maid, Mary, stood, and although she'd paused midquestion and her voice sank, she was doing her best to hide it. Lisle put a smile on her blank face, but it felt and had to look as false as everything around her felt and looked.

"I happen to like blue just fine, Mary. I'm just surprised Monteith guessed it."

"Oh! He dinna' guess it, my lady. That's what marriage is, you understand? Doing something special, just to show how much you care. Why, I recollect the time my man and I—"

"I'm actually quite hungry," Lisle interrupted her before she had to listen to anything more and started screaming something vile that was bound to have both women staring at her.

"Martha! Step smart. Get Her Ladyship's breakfast set up."

Lisle watched as the servant girl set a tray across her lap, and then put a newly cut sprig of heather in a crystal vase at the corner of it.

"What is this?" she asked.

"Griddle cakes. We thought you'd fancy a change, and since I dinna' hear from you at all yesterday, you being out with His Lordship and all, I thought you'd like to try them."

"What is this for?" Lisle pointed at the heather.

"Fresh cut. From the meadow. We thought you might like it."

"We?"

"You mustn't sit and dawdle so, my lady. You've the seamstresses to see still. There's patterns to approve, and dresses to decide, and then you've got instructions to give."

"To whom, please?"

"Your staff. I'd start with that Mabel Beamans. I'd make her give me the key to everything. That woman has too big a head. It's dripping over to her mouth, and her words. I only wish someone had something bad to say about her house-keeping. She thinks she's perfect."

Lisle looked levelly across at where Mary was smiling and bobbing her head, and kept the words inside. All she had to do was speak of dust on the beams and Mary would have her ammunition. She didn't.

"Now go, Martha. Check on the towels. Knock when returning."

"Towels?" Lisle asked.

"We're having a stack of them warmed for you, my lady. It's what His Lordship ordered for you. Every morn. He's hired an extra laundress to make certain you're treated to such."

"Every morning?" Lisle asked.

"Oh my, yes. He says you're worth whatever his gold can buy. He wants you to have a heated morning bath delivered with your breakfast, a stack of freshly laundered, heated towels, and anything else you need. It's quite impressive, it is."

"What?"

"How much he cares about you."

Lisle put her tongue between her teeth and held it there. It wasn't care. It was diabolical deception and worse. It was confinement and gaol-keeping, and adding insult, as well. Langston Monteith was making very certain she didn't disappear anywhere, and reminding her that he'd found her filthy at the same time. One thing she had to admit, though. He got his way. She wondered if he ever didn't get it.

"And he wants all your laundry done in this wonderful scent. He wants it to surround you. It has the scent of jasmine to it. And something he called opiate. I doona' know what that is."

Lisle clenched her jaw, and when that didn't work at allaying the emotion, she moved her gaze down to the breakfast that was beautifully arrayed on her lap, and toyed with pitching the whole lot at the wall. Perhaps if she aimed sufficiently, she could make more work that would earn someone more gold by having to do more laundry, and they might even need to pay to get the wall redone, besides.

She settled finally for cleaving her way through her cakes with a two-pronged fork, and making very little bites on her plate before she started eating.

"He keeps it locked up because it's so special. They kill each other for it in that Persia place. It's called *aphrodisiac*. I believe that's the word, although I doona' understand what it is. Mabel Beamans thinks she knows. She's always laughing beneath her breath at me over it, too."

Lisle's eyes went wide and she choked on the bite in her throat. She only wished she had enough experience to hide any, or all, of that.

"But you mustn't sit, listening to me. Your bath's cooling, and Martha will be back shortly with your towels. Come along, now."

Lisle put the plate aside. She wasn't hungry, and even if she was, her throat wouldn't open enough to get anything down. Langston was clothing her in a scent designed to titillate, create sensation, and heighten sensual pleasure? Daily? She was shivering when she slid out from beneath the covers, and it didn't have anything to do with the water's temperature.

The sensation of being beneath silken water, warmed so it pleasured, rather than water so cold it made her gasp, was such a new experience, Lisle almost forgot that she should be hating every moment of it. Mary MacGreggor helped her with her hair, giving her another potion to rub into it, and when she finished, the woman was handing her large, warmed towels, directing her to the fireplace, and making Lisle so comfortable she almost forgot her hatred again as the woman worked on her hair.

Langston Monteith was a devil. He had to be. No other man could make her feel secure, comfortable, and pampered, and able to fall in love with every sensation, even though the inner Lisle was cringing at the waste, and screaming her hatred of all of it.

Lisle watched the fire. She should be trying to do something, but her mind wasn't working as quickly or efficiently as it usually did. That was odd. She felt Mary making a braid, lacing a blue ribbon throughout the length, and saving the ends for a bow at the bottom of it.

"Where is Shera?" Lisle asked when the woman finished the braid and was just getting ready to stand.

"Shera? I doona' know any Shera. Is there one we should search out for you?"

"Aye," Lisle replied, and bit down on her own tongue.

"Is she a village lass, my lady?"

Lisle looked at Mary MacGreggor's face, decided she wasn't capable of hiding a thing, and wondered if Langston had chosen her for that quality, before knowing instinctively that he had. The only thing she didn't know was why it didn't bother her like it should.

"I believe Shera would have been with His Lordship when he arrived back . . . from Persia."

"My lady! I'm shocked!"

Lisle looked at her. She did look that.

"His Lordship never travels with a female, and had he done so, I would na' be for telling his wife, now, would I? I doona' think I would keep my position long if I went about telling such tales."

She looked like that was the truth, too.

"Besides, I was na' hired until the auld laird passed on. Lord Monteith immediately set about improving the estate, knocking out walls to make the rooms larger, and having more ceiling supports put in to make certain it was stable. He set about paying for men to fell trees and have them made. He's turning the castle into a place of luxury and beauty. 'Tis enough to make the auld laird roll over in his crypt. That it is!"

The woman broke into giggles at the end of her words. Lisle smiled, although her face wasn't making much of the effort. She actually didn't feel like taking the effort to do anything. She licked her lips. Such languor wasn't going to get her what she wanted to know.

"What of a war chest?" she asked.

"War chest, my lady?"

"For his personal effects. For safekeeping. Lairds keep them. At least, I know of one who did. Did the auld laird keep one of these?"

"The only thing the auld laird Monteith kept was a weak spine. He had that in abundance. That, he did."

"A weak spine? Was he deformed, then?"

Mary giggled more. "Oh nae, my lady. That isn't the type of weakness I speak of."

"He was a coward." Lisle didn't ask it. She already knew it, anyway.

Mary nodded. "So much so, his only son would na' claim him. You should have seen the row when that happened."

"What?"

"Laird Langston's return. You could hear it out on the moors—or so they tell me. I was na' hired yet."

"They fought?" That was interesting information, Lisle decided. She just couldn't decide why.

Mary nodded. "Oh, aye. The auld laird retired to his rooms. These rooms, actually. Or mayhap it was the laird's rooms on the other side of that door. I canna' tell, although back then they were cold and made of stone and there was nae hint of luxury about them." She looked about. "They were also smaller. His Lordship wanted space. He's got fancy ideas of things, but it's his coin." She shrugged.

Lisle licked her lips. "A family Bible, then. Does the family have one of those?"

"Family Bibles, and such, are kept in the chapel."

"We have a chapel?"

"Oh my, yes. We attend service each Sunday, too. Those of us that know what thankfulness is and what it isn't. Take that Mabel Beamans. That woman hasn't been to church in over a month of Sundays. Why, someone should talk—"

"Where is this chapel?" Lisle interrupted. It had to be the scent he'd had them use. Her mind wasn't working like it should be, and Mary MacGreggor was turning into a font of useless and trivial information.

"On the east side. That way, they catch the morning rays through the stained windows. Those windows go back so many years, nobody knows the count of them. I've heard that if you sit in one particular pew, and the sun is coming in just right, you'll actually have it looking like Mother Mary is sitting right there with you."

"What?" Lisle asked, shaking her head.

"The place is full of statues, and one of them is of Mother Mary, holding the bairn. It's said when the sun comes in through the right portion of that stained glass, it looks just like—"

"What does this have to do with the family Bible?" Lisle asked.

"Oh. That. I doona' ken where they keep it, but I would check the chapel first. You'll need to ask for the key, though. It's kept locked."

"We lock our own chapel? Whatever for?"

Mary shrugged. "I doona' ken the whys of Lord Monteith's reasons. All I know is he keeps it locked. I doona' know where the key is. You could check with that Mabel Beamans. . . ."

Lisle groaned. It didn't stop the woman.

"You're the lady of the house. I'd make her give you every key she has. That should take her head down a size or two, it should." All of which sent Mary into giggles again.

The day went by in a blur of activity, punctuated by feminine titters of amusement, gossip, the shimmer of material called silk, embroidered panels of cloth from China, gasps of amazement at designs, and yet the strangeness kept growing. Lisle had never been around so many women in her entire life, and there didn't seem to be a man among any of them.

By the time they brought a tea service in, with enough small cakes and scones to keep all of them from drowning in their tea, it was getting irritating. Lisle had already decided she wasn't going to get any more information from Mary, because she didn't have any more to give. She was going to get her answer, though. The feeling of euphoria and lassitude had melted away, leaving her stubborn again, and about one thing. She was going to locate this Shera, and she was going to make the woman claim Langston. Then Lisle was going to run as fast and as far from him and his conniving and manipulations as she could.

It wasn't going to be easy. She was surrounded by women. They were better than gaolers. They had to be, and the lack of men anywhere about the estate was grating. She hadn't seen one fellow since the three of them had lugged out her hip bath, after the used water had been laboriously drained, bucket by bucket, in order to use it on the castle's herb gardens.

Lisle begged a moment for her privacy, gained herself Mary MacGreggor and another young lass at her elbow, and left what had been a sitting room, but was now resembling a torture chamber full of women and pins, needles, and nonsensical gossip.

"I would like to visit the chapel, Mary," Lisle informed her the moment they were out of the sitting room.

"Oh nae, my lady. That is not possible. I have na' got the key."

Lisle thinned her lips. "Then, show me where it is. Surely we doona' lock the halls on the way."

Mary looked at her with a blank look. "Nae body can lock a hallway, my lady. 'Tis na' possible."

"Very good. Show me, please."

More halls and turns and twists later, they arrived at a set of wooden doors that had been carved by a master, buffed to a sheen of warm, shiny brown, and were almost reaching the ceiling more than two stories above them. Lisle tipped her head.

"His Lordship had this wood shipped over, my lady. Quite a row ensued due to that."

"Someone argued with him over it?"

"Oh my, nae. There's not a soul argues with His Lordship. It just took extra help to get it from the port at Inverness to here without damage done to any part of the wood. It was na' carved then, either, and His Lordship dinna' want one bit of it scratched, before the carver he selected touched it. They had to design a special wagon bed, they did."

Lisle craned her neck, checking and finding where at least two beams split the space above the doors. She shivered, wondered at her own sanity, and stopped her own reaction. She'd never been so high, and she still had to find out which room she would need to use to access them.

"As you can see, there's the scene of the Creation near the top, and the lines coming down represent Knowledge."

"They look more like sunbeams," Lisle commented absently, moving her eyes to check both sides of the walls on either side of the monstrosity Langston had created. There wasn't a step in sight.

Mary sighed. "That's the beauty of it. It looks like the sun is shedding its light. 'Tis actually Knowledge coming down to us. See. That's us. At the bottom."

Lisle moved her head down. There were Highland personages about the bottom, most of them in kneeling positions. It was incredible, and very artistic, and looked difficult to break through, if not impossible.

"How thick is it?" she asked.

"Thick, my lady?"

"Deep. How deep?"

"Oh. Very. About a man's arm length. Very heavy, too. I already told you the trouble they had getting it here."

Lisle stepped forward and turned one of the long handles down. It was locked. She shrugged and tried the other.

"I told Your Ladyship, he keeps it locked," Mary said from behind her.

Lisle sighed. "You still haven't told me why. Does he keep his gold in there?"

"He has a treasury, my lady, for such a thing."

Lisle picked up one of the heavy door-knockers and dropped it, making a thud that echoed through the hall behind them.

"Now, my lady, you're scaring Betsy. She's new, you ken?"

"Your name's Betsy?" Lisle turned about and smiled at the younger of the two. She didn't look frightened. She looked young, and excited at new employment, and pleasant-tempered, and not a bit curious about anything they were doing. Lisle ground her teeth. Langston had chosen her specially, too.

"It never hurts to knock," Lisle noted, and then they all heard a bolt lifting, followed by a chain, and then there was the distinct sound of one of the handles moving.

Chapter Fifteen

If the trio of gentlemen facing them were clergymen, they had chosen the wrong profession. Lisle looked over the three large, well-defined men, and wondered why even here, where no man was supposed to need more muscle than it took to turn a page, or lift a quill, the men looked fit, strong, and healthy. She was almost surprised to see them in long, black-cassocks, rather than kilts.

The last tone of a note filtered down from the heights of the Gothic-designed chapel, easily recognizable as the same note she always heard, although it hadn't come from a horn of any kind. It had come from the organ that another clergyman was just rising from.

"Thank you . . . for opening the door," Lisle said, although she had to clear her throat midsentence.

"You should na' be here," the older of them said.

"Why, please?" Lisle asked.

"And we should na' have opened the door."

Lisle smiled slightly. "You're right. Such a thing is monstrous to consider, because you should have had it opened and unlocked to begin with. Such a thing is normal with houses of worship."

He frowned. "We weren't aware of visitors."

One of her servants giggled. Lisle could see why. Men who were this fit, muscled, and smooth of voice and charm were difficult to find, especially in the lower echelons of Monteith Castle on this morning. Lisle looked askance at Betsy, who had been the perpetrator of the giggle. She was also rosy with a blush.

"I am nae visitor, Father. I am the new lady of Monteith," she announced. The sound of her words carried upward, sounding like they gained in volume, and showing the acoustic qualities of the room, as well as how gifted the designer had been. She was just surprised it hadn't been one hired by Langston.

"Oh."

The other man had joined them, making a united front of four men facing them. Lisle told her imagination to hush. "So, you see, I have every right to be here, right here. Right now. I have every right to every room in the castle."

The older one, who had been speaking, reached out to pull on his collar. Lisle watched him gulp before speaking.

"We had heard the laird had taken a wife."

"Good. Your hearing is fine. Now, if you'd be so good as to assist me with my business? I'll na' be long."

"What is it you're wanting?"

"To look about."

They all looked like they'd been expecting her to say something horrible, and her words were it. She watched as eyes widened, they all looked to each other, and then to the floor. Only the speaker was watching her. Lisle tempered the satisfaction she felt. She'd known they were hiding something. She just didn't know what. She smiled.

"I'm looking, in particular . . . for the family Bible."

"The Bible?" His face was carefully blank as he asked it.

"We do have one, doona' we?"

"All clans have such," he agreed.

All four men were nodding in agreement. She sensed it was with relief, although she couldn't prove it. All of which could mean anything, but she guessed it meant that whatever they were hiding wasn't anywhere near the family Bible.

"Good. I would like to see it then. Now."

"Now?"

Lisle smiled again. "The sooner I see it, the sooner I will leave you to your duties. We'd all like for that to happen, I think."

"I'll see it fetched." He inclined his head.

"Where is this window you spoke of, Mary?" Lisle asked, turning to her servant, who looked more prepared to run than stand behind her mistress.

Mary walked farther into the chapel and pointed to where blood-red hues, vivid green, and yellow washes touched onto the floor directly below it, before taking the eye to the work of art responsible for them. Lisle followed to it, smiling inwardly that time. The motion of looking up had her eyes following beams, checking for steps. If she wasn't mistaken, they had to be secreted near the massive organ that was framed in the middle of one wall, and topped by one lone beam.

"I've set up the Bible, my lady."

Lisle dropped her head, looked across at the man, who, now that he was smiling and bobbing his head, didn't look threatening at all.

"Very good," she replied, and followed him to a podium where the sunlight didn't quite reach, but if she'd come earlier it definitely would have. The book was opened to the center, where the register was. She flipped to the last of the center parchment. There was no entry of any marriage with Langston Leed Monteith—not to her, and not to anyone named Shera, either. Lisle bent closer, checked the date of the previous laird's death: July 1746. Such a thing matched Mary MacGreggor's story, and Langston's excuse of being out of the country. Such a thing had happened two months following Culloden, so it might be true that Langston was a traitor, not a coward. All of which was less than nothing next to the disappointment of not seeing a Shera.

"Where is the entry of Lord Monteith's marriage?" she asked finally.

"We've but heard the news recently, my lady. We're awaiting the ink."

"Ink?" she asked.

"Uh . . . His Lordship wants every entry done with a special ink—from India. We're awaiting its arrival."

"Of course we are," she replied. "What is your excuse for not listing his first marriage, please?"

All four faces held the exact same look of surprise, and Lisle guessed if she turned around, she'd see the same expression on Betsy's and Mary's faces.

"Were we out of ink then, too?" she continued.

"I . . . uh . . . his first marriage? His Lordship was wed a-fore?"

"I believe I've seen enough, Father. You may show us out now. Or, you can trust that we'll see ourselves out. Thank you for allowing me in to see my own chapel. I look forward to the sermon on the Sabbath. We all do, doona' we, ladies?" Lisle kept saying words, sounding like a fool, as she backed from them toward the doors.

Then, one side of that enormous wooden structure was opened, showing that every servant man who had been missing was now in the hallway outside the chapel, and more besides. They looked prepared to do more than serve anyone. They looked ready to do battle. The longer Lisle and her retinue stood facing them, the more the impression grew. The large doors shut behind them, relocked loudly, and then the bolt drew down, rasping into place.

Lisle told herself she probably should have stayed in the sitting room as her heart jumped to lodge in her throat, and from the corner of her eye, it looked like Betsy was going to faint. Lisle didn't dare move her gaze to check on Mary. She was looking at her own husband. If she'd thought him a devil before, it wasn't a far-flung thought, especially with the claymore that was held directly out, pointing unerringly at her bosom. She longed to tell him it would have been useless to strike her there. Her heart was still in her throat, sending pounding pressure with each beat of it. She swallowed around it.

Langston pulled back a fraction and the tip of his sword lowered, showing the sinew all along him, since he was clothed in sweat and exertion and heavy breathing, and not much else. He was bare-chested and he was in a kilt. Lisle caught her breath. They were all dressed like her husband, although she couldn't tell if anyone else had a weapon.

Something clicked through her mind, and she'd die before she admitted it had anything to do with the way his upper lip lifted as he passed the large broadsword to a man at his side, who then passed it farther. Lisle lost sight of it after the third pair of hands.

"Good day, Lisle."

"Doona' color this anything other than what it is, my lord," she replied evenly.

"And what is it?" he asked, in the same tone she'd used.

He was folding his arms, leaning slightly to one side, and if Betsy hadn't sighed, Lisle was afraid she would have.

"Not a very good day," she answered.

He smiled broadly, showing white teeth and the small crinkles about his eyes, and making it nearly impossible to look anywhere else, although something told her it was too staged, and thus it wasn't quite perfect. She watched as behind him the edges of his horde were dispersing, stepping backward, one by one, and sliding around a bend in the hall, without making much sound. Lisle sharpened her ears. She couldn't hear that they were making any sound.

"I thought you engrossed with your new wardrobe," he said.

Lisle's chin lifted and her focus returned to him. If anything, he'd preened himself more, and the two humps of his chest had striations of muscle going through them now. She wondered how that was possible, and why he did it. She didn't like the answer the moment she got it, either. He was using whatever it took as a diversion . . . even his own body.

"I got bored," she said.

Beside her, she heard Betsy gasp. Lisle didn't think it was due to her words, and she turned her head to check her instincts. It was because Betsy was watching Langston with such a wide-eyed look of adoration, Lisle clenched her hands to keep from hitting something with them, something that was probably going to be him.

"Truly? Fitting a new wardrobe . . . bores you?"

"Anything, if done to such a length of time, is boring, my lord."

"Anything?" he asked.

"Even that," she replied.

That got her a wider grin. Betsy was coughing on her reaction. Lisle nearly rolled her eyes.

"If you were bored, you should have said something."

"Why?"

"I make arrangements to that effect."

"You make arrangements to keep me from being bored?"

His eyebrows lifted; then he nodded.

"How, please?"

"You have but to say the word. Whatever you desire will be proffered. Without exception. Even me." His voice was lowering. "Especially me," he finished.

Now Lisle was gasping. She couldn't tell what reaction Betsy had. Her ears were too full of what had to be her heart pounding as it got harder and faster, and she was very afraid that was exactly what it was. Then her eyes closed, reopened . . . narrowed. His throng was down to twenty, maybe less. She knew then exactly what he was doing. He was making certain all eyes were on him, and not anything else. And, with an audience of three women, he must not think it presented much of an issue. She just couldn't believe he was as good as he was.

"You can cease this," she said.

"What?" he asked easily.

"You're a very handsome man, Monteith . . . very. Manly. Strong. Virile. Good to look at." Lisle made her voice purr the words.

His smile fell. His eyes widened. Betsy choked.

"And I believe I've seen enough."

"I beg your pardon?" he replied. Betsy's reaction wasn't describable as it sounded like she couldn't catch any breath, let alone choke on it.

"It's nae longer necessary. They've gone." Lisle knew she was right, because she'd moved close to him to whisper it, and those dark brown, ale-colored eyes had sparked.

He looked over her head. Lisle felt the bubble of mirth as he swallowed, and the lump in his throat moved. "Mary?" he asked.

"My lord?" the servant woman answered.

"You have strange ways of serving your mistress."

"B-but . . . Her Ladyship wished to see the chapel," Mary MacGreggor continued, her voice unsure and sounding like she would rather cry than have to answer.

"I see."

Lisle's back straightened. She was being treated like she'd been at the convent school, back when she'd transgressed. She hadn't liked it then, and she didn't like it now, especially when it was turned on someone other than her.

"Mary is accompanying me. I wanted to see the Bible, my lord," she said loudly.

"I would have shown it to you."

"I have two feet."

He looked down to them, and back. It felt like a caress, and she didn't know much what one felt like. Lisle told her own body to hush, but her lips parted to allow the pant of breath she didn't want him to see. It was ridiculous! She was in a hall, outside locked chapel doors, with two servant women watching, and he wasn't being genuine, anyway. It was for show. Everything he did was. He'd been truthful to her only once. He'd said he was living a lie, and he was *very* good at it.

"True," he said.

"What?" she asked.

A smile tipped his lips again as he looked back to her. "You have two feet," he answered.

"Oh. Aye. And I can use them to walk. By myself. Unescorted."

"This is a very big castle," he responded.

"I ken as much. 'Tis also a very interesting castle."

His lips lost out. He smiled again. This time, it looked genuine.

"How so?"

"'Tis full of secrets." She whispered it.

His smile dropped. He looked over her head at Mary again. "You followed my orders this morn?" he asked.

"Aye."

"Her Ladyship had a bath?"

"I smell like I had a bath, doona' I?" Lisle said before Mary could reply.

He bent his head toward her and sniffed. "Aye," he replied.

"Well, you doona'," she said.

"Nae?" he asked, pulling back a bit to look down at her.

"You smell like a horse. Make that two horses."

His smile was back. "I see. If I ordered a bath, would you assist me with it?"

Betsy was going to break into tears if she listened much longer. Lisle looked at the poor girl's red face, and turned back to Monteith. "Why doona' you instruct my maids to see to it, and we'll negotiate for such a thing while they're gone."

"We will?" he asked. He waved his hand, and Lisle listened for the steps as the women left. She knew they were, too. They were almost running.

"Ah, aye. After you show me where your first wife is, of course."

"My first wife?" he asked.

Lisle thought she saw real confusion behind those amber

eyes. It was an exhilarating feeling to know she was the one causing it. "You doona' even have her listed in the family Bible. For shame, Lord Monteith."

"The family Bible?"

"I was in the chapel for a reason. I was looking for the entry of your first marriage. It isn't there, but you know that already. You probably ordered it that way."

"I did . . . did I?"

He had his self-assurance and the personae he was showing back in place. Lisle watched as it dropped, like a film across his features. She shivered despite herself.

"I was in the chapel for a reason, Langston. I was checking for this woman."

He grinned down at her. She couldn't fathom the cause, but a moment later he answered it.

"You've just called me Langston," he said.

"So?"

"Without being prompted. Without any hesitation."

"So?"

"I'll save further words for our negotiation. What is it you're offering, again?"

"An assist . . . with your bath. Tonight. In your chamber."

His eyes shut and she could have sworn a tremor ran through his frame, but it couldn't have, because when he opened them and looked back at her, nothing looked like it had changed.

"And what is it you want for such a momentous thing?"

"Your first wife. I want to know where she is."

"Why?"

"Because if she's wed to you, I am na'. That has merit."

The brown ale color of his eyes all but disappeared as blackness colored over any hint of personality not only in them, but everywhere on him. He had a stone look to every feature, too.

"You want me to show you this thing?"

Lisle moved another step closer, almost touching him. He

caught his breath at it, and if he didn't want her to see such a thing, he shouldn't be running about his estate with nothing on to hide it. She reached out and traced her index finger down the center of him, halving him, and following the bumps of his abdomen before reaching his belt. She removed her finger and touched it to her lips, parting them so she could touch her tongue to it. He tasted salty, very salty, and she'd never felt so wicked.

"I'll wear my chemise for this bath . . . and naught else." She tipped her head up to say it. This time she knew a tremor scored him, and it was followed by a groan.

"Why are you being like this?" he asked in a rough voice.

"Like what?"

"Vixen. Wanton. Jezebel. Reckless."

"I'm a very quick student, Langston," she replied, watching as the mask slipped slightly. "And you're a very good teacher."

His jaw tightened, and then he had a hand on her upper arm, tightening it, too. Then he was marching her along the hall, beside him, everything about him looking closed and angry, viciously angry. Lisle couldn't imagine what she'd done to cause it.

"You want to visit my first lady?"

They reached a door, Lisle didn't know from which hall, or which floor. Langston had stopped, one hand on the doorknob, the other still gripping her.

She nodded.

"Badly?"

"The chemise I'll wear," she replied softly, "'tis made of softest lawn. Very insubstantial when wet. Very."

He shook completely. Then he twisted the doorknob with an effort that should have pulled it from its moorings and they were outside, marching through perfectly groomed lawn on perfectly fitted stepping stones, and then they were at the entrance to the family crypt. He let her go, and Lisle swayed in place for a moment before she caught herself.

"She's dead?" she asked.

"I could na' wed with you otherwise, could I?" he answered roughly.

"Show me. Doona' touch me. Just show me."

He pushed on the gate. It opened with a well-oiled, well-maintained efficiency that was just like everything else on the estate.

"You'll follow?" he asked.

She nodded.

The world behind the gate was slower, darker, and now that twilight appeared to be descending, it was more quiet and muted and had an air of mystery about it. She followed Langston's bare back as he walked, in that side-to-side fashion of his, and tried to keep her mind completely blank. Lisle knew she possessed too much imagination. Her stories had kept the girls enthralled for years. It was a gift. It was also a curse. She glanced once to both sides, to make certain no mythical creatures accompanied them, and then forced herself to keep her eyes on the man in front of her.

It wasn't difficult. Langston Leed Monteith was a handsome specimen, especially since he'd decided to display all of him in little more than a kilt and tasseled socks. Lisle looked down him and back, sighed, and then had to put her mind back on what they were doing. Langston was extremely beautiful, and he knew how to use it to best advantage. She hadn't been exaggerating earlier. He knew exactly how to use it to negotiate, and she was a very good pupil.

She just didn't know what she was supposed to do with any of this when it came time to pay her part of their bargain.

He approached a door that was attached to a strange Grecian-looking building. It looked too small to house a statue in, let alone a coffin. Lisle watched as he twisted the handle down, and then he reached up to lift a lit torch from the entrance. Then he was going down steps, taking her into a yawning cave, although it had carved rock to both sides and the floor.

"My own crypt."

He'd stopped and Lisle barely avoided smashing her nose into the middle of his bare back by the sense of it. She hadn't heard or seen any of it. The place was full of creatures and noises and whispers of time, and every hair from every pore along her neck seemed like it was standing up in reaction.

"And this is my wife, Shera."

If she gave the relief sound, he'd have heard it, and Lisle was pretending there wasn't anything frightening or intense about any of this. He was holding the light over a slab that couldn't hold anything like a wife.

"This is her marker. This is na' her grave. She was buried at sea. On the journey over."

"She died during the voyage?"

"I dinna' toss her overboard, if that is your question," he answered.

She moved forward and read the inscription, and then everything was swirling in a whirlpool of black. This Shera had been born in 1736, and perished in 1745. Nine. His first wife had been nine. Lisle reached out for the first thing on which she could stabilize herself, and didn't even care that it was him.

He didn't ask if she was all right. He simply lifted her into his arms and carried her, and took her back to the twilight-littered gardens that they buried their dead in. She didn't even realize she was crying. Someone else was crying. Lisle Monteith couldn't have been. She'd rather die than let him see that.

"She was a child," he informed her.

"Oh, my God," she whispered.

"She was the only sister he had left to sell."

"Oh, my God," she whispered again.

He looked down at her once and kept walking, past the gate and out into the gardens that hadn't such evil attached to them. Or, if they did, it was well hidden.

"Her older sister by two years was already wed and carrying a child. Solomon apologized to me for it."

"Doona' say any more. I beg it."

"I told you life was cheap in Persia. It is. Still is."

"Damn you, Monteith. You wed a bairn. 'Twas probably that which killed her."

"I dinna' consummate it," he said.

She was choking. It didn't make it better and he kept talking.

"She was frail and she was sickly. She'd had the best of care, Solomon assured me, but she was all he had left to offer. He kept apologizing to me for that. I didn't let the disgust show. It was nae surprise. Women are of little value in that part of the world. I plied her with food. I made her swallow broth. I forced her to move from her bed. I hired her playmates. I hired the best physicians. She never got well. She still died."

"Oh, my God," Lisle said.

"That door leads back to the main hall. Follow it. Go to your chamber. Wait for me there."

"Wait for you?" Lisle asked. Everything about her was swirling still, and there was a handsome, black-haired man at the center of it, beckoning to her, owning her . . . enthralling her . . . frightening her.

"I've got things to see to a-fore we finish our bargain."

Chapter Sixteen

Langston's room was comparable to hers, although his bed was twice the size of hers, and set up on a pedestal. That left less floor space, and consequently less room to pace in. Lisle looked about at the two sofa-sized benches, two opposing chairs in front of his fire, and then she was skimming her glance over the four marble-topped tables. He had sprigs of heather all about, putting the purple into prominence and making the air smell sweet. With the fire that was crackling and popping from a rock fireplace that looked like the stones had poured over the wall leading to his antechamber and flowed down to make a rock hearth, it looked comfortable and warm, and not at all like the den of iniquity that it had to be.

Lisle selected one of the chairs by his fire. She needed the warmth. She put her legs beneath her, folding them more for coverage than safety, and waited. The chemise reached to middle-thigh, grazing skin and raising gooseflesh, and she pulled on it, tucking it beneath where her knees met the front of the chair. That helped. Now, she had a tentlike enclosure, and nothing was clinging like it had been. She shouldn't have been so specific, but that was of no help now.

She only had one chemise made of lawn, but it hadn't been sewn with support and coverage in mind. There wasn't much of the blue material across her bosom, making it nearly non-existent, even with the added backing material in order to shade where it was cupping and lifting her, and making her very aware of every inch of her.

Her dozen seamstresses were each vying for creativity and jaw-dropping effects, and the woman who had designed this chemise had received sighs of pleasure from everyone but the wearer. There were little green-embroidered stems starting at the hem, climbing up the material and making it bunch and gather slightly with every thread in every needle hole. The stems got larger, crossing at her ribcage, before opening into two large tulip shapes, and that was what Lisle had been given to support her breasts.

It wasn't working. It looked more like she was being lifted, and held out for display. In fact, the chemise wasn't conducive to anything except drawing and holding the male eye. It did that job efficiently.

The door opened. Lisle craned her head over the top of the chair, and hoped her heart wasn't pumping blood as rapidly into her cheeks as it felt like it was.

Langston was still attired in his kilt, although there was a vest tossed on for some reason. He hadn't fastened it. That was unfortunate, Lisle decided. He'd also found his way into some mud, if the splatter of it on his socks was any indication, and he was either heaving with his exertions or he was having the same problem she was.

Lisle stood and watched as not only did his eyes go huge, but he took a step backward as well.

"Jesu'! Get something on!"

"But—" she began.

"Now! Get to the bed!"

"We . . . made a bargain," she said softly.

"And you're framed in the cursed firelight. Oh, my God!" He slapped a hand to his eyes with a definite smacking sound and then turned away, adding more words, said beneath his breath.

Lisle climbed the three steps to his bed and slid beneath the covers, placing her so far above and from him that she had to crane her head to see where he was.

He hadn't moved, and if the firelight had been reflecting on her, it was being just as kind with him. Lisle watched as it flickered over flesh that had rivulets of what had to be sweat still glistening on it. Then he removed his hand, put both of them on his hips, and moved his head toward her.

"I am na' sufficiently exhausted for this."

"I doona' understand. A bath requires exhaustion?"

"If you're doing the assist . . . aye."

"We had a bargain. I am paying it."

He sucked in a huge breath before sending it back out. That was very interesting to watch. "You are a woman who knows the value of her word, once given. I admire that."

"You ordered a bath, I trust?" Lisle was amazed her voice didn't have any of the breathless quality he was making her feel, just by standing there, watching her. He should probably put more than a vest on his upper body, she decided.

"This is na' a good idea."

Lisle's chin lifted and she swallowed.

"Yet it is a very good idea, at the same time."

The pillows at her back were as soft and flexible as they'd looked. Lisle leaned back into them as he took a step toward her, and then another. He stopped when he reached the bottom of his structure, framing his upper chest and shoulders and that slicked-looking black hair with the white wall at his back and the coverlet at the bottom.

"You ken my meaning?" he asked.

"Nae." She shook her head.

"You used your body to bargain with."

"I dinna'!"

A slight smile touched his lips. "All right. I'll say it with better words. You used my desire for your body to bargain with."

Lisle's eyes went wide. He was making certain she knew

his intent, as he took a step up onto his platform, changing her view to include his abdomen.

"If I used such, it was na' what you think," she said through lips cold and difficult to move.

"Only because you doona' know what you do, nor how to use it properly. I do."

"As I already saw. Very well," she interjected.

A smile touched his lips and he lifted a hand to push back at the hair that had escaped from behind his ears. "There's a very big difference between us, Lisle . . . love."

Love? Oh, sweet heaven! There was no stopping the instant flash of fire that hit her, making every part of her feel like it seared. Lisle shut her eyes, licked her lips, pulled in a breath, let it out, pulled in another, held it. Nothing was working. When she opened her eyes, he'd moved, leaning forward to support himself on his arms as he perched at the foot of his bed and watched her.

"Do you ken what this difference is?"

The words were spoken softly, or she was having trouble hearing over the drumbeat of sound pumping through her own ears. She shook her head again.

In response, he reached forward and pulled himself onto the bottom of the bed, using his arms and shoulders and the tucked-in coverlet for support and leverage in order to make the movement. Lisle wasn't certain where her heart had gone to, because the beat was filling every portion of her. She didn't dare blink.

"As I already made mention of it, I'm too exhausted to fight this any longer. I'll cease the denials and just enjoy. I have nae other choice. I have tried this entire day to exhaust myself."

"You have?" she asked.

"Aye."

He reached forward again, shoving entire sections of himself into full, muscled view, and then he was wrapping his fists about hunks of coverlet and using it to slide himself farther onto the bed. He wasn't but halfway onto the structure, and she had her knees nearly to her chin, but she could swear her toes were tingling.

"Why?"

"Because lessons doona' come across well if they're colored with passion. Naught much else does, either, now that I think on it."

"Lessons?" she asked.

He licked his lips. Lisle's entire body betrayed her as it pulsed. He saw it. She knew he did. "And passion," he replied, and then he raised himself onto his hands and knees.

"P-p-pas . . . sion?" She stammered the word, and the last half of it was whispered.

"You ken what it is I see in you, Mistress Lisle?" he asked.

"Me?"

He licked his lips again. Her entire frame moved with it. It was the most horrid, unexpected, amazing experience, and accompanied by such an increase in her pulse, and senses, that her eyes went even wider. He knew all of that, too.

"You. Blue eyes. Endless blue eyes, without a hint of guile, and more than a fair share of passion. Aye. You."

He took a crawling motion toward her, and the mattress moved with it. Lisle couldn't move her eyes. She was very afraid she'd forgotten how to blink. He'd reached the area below her curled-up feet, and went to his haunches, sliding with a seamless-looking movement. Then he was lifting one leg and wrapping his arm about it, and there wasn't a bit of him that wasn't worth looking over, more than once. Lisle did that very thing, although her eyes hadn't received the command.

"You ken what the difference is yet?" he asked.

"You're a very handsome man, Monteith."

One side of his lips lifted. "I know. 'Tis one of my weapons. Actually, that part of us is the same."

"What?" she asked. *Weapons*, she thought. He was talking weapons.

"We have the same weapon." He said it in a soft whisper of sound, and moved, putting weight against her feet with the way he leaned forward.

"We do?"

"Oh, aye. You are a very beautiful woman, Lisle Monteith. Although there are thousands of beautiful women. You have something more. You have fire."

She licked her lips and watched as a tremor ran through him when he saw it. The thrill of observing it surprised and scared her. She wondered if it was the same with him, and instinctively knew it was.

"Fire," she said finally.

He nodded slowly and eased himself forward, until he was resting his chin atop her bent knees. There was a trembling going through where he touched her, even with the white coverlet between them. The tulip cups on her chemise were restrictive and scratching skin that had never felt the like. Lisle watched him glance there and grimace, before closing his eyes and making his trembling worse. It was some moments before he had it under control. At least, that's what she suspected he was doing. Then he opened his eyes, showing the ale-colored warmth of them.

"And I am going to get severely burnt," he said.

"You are?"

"Oh, aye. Mortally."

"Why?"

He was moving closer, his weight bowing the support of her knees until they caved apart, placing him at the base of her stomach, and forcing the pounding to strengthen into a ear-filling beat.

"Because you doona' comprehend what you do."

He rolled onto his back, taking the coverlet with him, and if the chemise wasn't fit exactly to every part of her, it would have gone, too. Lisle looked down at the man in her lap, and wondered at her sanity. He folded his arms across his chest, making the masculine bulging even more visual and distinct. She frowned.

"What is it?" he asked.

"You," she replied. "This. Your strength. The ease with which you put all of it on display."

"'Tis a weapon, Lisle. Doona' mistake it for anything else."

"Your body is a weapon?"

"As is yours."

He moved his vision to include her tulip cups. Then he moved it back to her face. Lisle colored.

"There the resemblance ends. I know the penalty."

"Penalty?" she asked.

"Aye. And I pay it . . . every time. Effortlessly. Without thought. Without regret and recrimination. You are different."

"I am?"

He sighed. Everything on him moved with it. "You are a very handsome woman. Worse, you are a woman of passion, fire, and endless ecstasy."

"Ecstasy?" she asked, although her lip quivered on the word.

"And I am doing my level best to ignore all of that."

That had her frowning. He was reaching up and running a finger along the side of her cheek, ending at her chin. "Why?"

"Do you wish to be here?" he asked.

Lisle looked away, focusing for a moment on the fireplace that had seemed so warm and inviting earlier, and felt now like it was endless leagues away.

"Doona' look away from me to answer that. Look here. Right here."

He was lifting his head and pointing to his eyes. Lisle bent her head and complied, looking as deeply into his eyes as he would let her. There wasn't a hint of anything save opaque black to be seen on the surface. She wondered why.

"Now . . . do you wish to be here or na'?" he asked.

"I . . . doona' know. Perhaps," she replied softly.

The amber was back, accompanied by a groan. "I am not

exhausted enough for this!" He exclaimed it, and then proved the words by rolling back onto his hands and knees and putting his face very close to hers. That way, she had to feel every breath slipping over her face, watch every heave of his chest, and tremble all over with every bit of what he must be referring to when he called it passion.

"For what?" she asked right back, snarling slightly with the words, and sending her eyes all over him, since he'd arrayed himself for that purpose right in front of her. That much she understood.

"This!"

He reached forward to grip her shoulders; then he slammed her to his chest, crushing her tulip-encased bosom against the thick, heavy smell of him, melding himself into lace-covered sweat, and making her think her lawn chemise was too much material after all. Then he was looking at her, like he was asking something. Then he was filling his nose with the smell of her lips, her cheeks, and moving to an ear, and doing everything except the one thing she wanted.

His arms were as hard as they'd looked, and weren't giving her much room to breathe as he continued his exploration.

"So sweet." She thought she heard him murmur it, but it could be a mistake of the drum beating through her temples, and thumping everywhere along her. There was definitely a drum, pounding hard and in perfect rhythm to every one of her increased attempts for breath.

"So . . . passionate. So trusting. So open. So . . . clean. Fresh. So innocent."

Lisle tried to turn her head to find his mouth, but he was denying that, too. She should have had Mary take out her braid before she'd dismissed the woman. It was just making it easier for him to slide his lips and breathe his words along her neck and over her shoulders, and everywhere but against her lips, where she wanted them.

"How . . . do you ken such?" she asked in the room he gave her.

"You reek of it, love. I doona' trust only my nose, either. I trust all my senses. All of them."

Love, she thought. There was that word again, but coming from him it couldn't mean what it was supposed to. It couldn't. The devil didn't know what love was.

"Langston?" she asked.

He was inhaling and breathing all about the back of her neck and making shivers that were moving from there to the tips of her bosom, making little pinpricks of sensation that were tormenting her with the proximity of male flesh they were pressed against. From there, it was a quick drop all the way to where the chemise hem was, and that part of her really was on fire.

"Aye?" He whispered it, sending more rivulets to follow those already in motion, and that had her squirming and shoving, and doing her utmost to unlock his arms. All of which got her a chuckle, and that made a worse sensation as it traveled over her back, and settled into the same path that the other shivers had gone.

"Langston!" she tried again, sharpening her voice.

"You doona' ken what you do," he replied harshly.

"I know I doona', but I want to do it!"

The shuddering that shook him with those words was made worse as he shoved himself onto his back, taking her with him and lifting her free of the remaining coverlet. Then he was running his arms all along her back and over her buttocks, and along the backs of her thighs that had never felt such a thing. Lisle gasped, and he had the motion, holding her lower lip between both of his while he sucked on it. That had her moaning, and he moved his mouth then, opening it to capture the sound, while his hands shifted, holding her loins tightly against a part of him possessing heat, and strength, and solid rigidity.

The sound of a long horn blast filled the room, growing in intensity and stridency, and it was followed by three shorter ones. Langston matched the cadence, moving her with it, the motion bringing her upward, and then back down, using the strength of his upper body, and nothing else.

"The horn."

Lisle pulled her lips from his to say it, but he didn't allow her time to say more before he had her mouth again, and this time he wasn't allowing her any resistance at all. Lisle felt the straps holding the tulip cups in place moving as he peeled them down, rolling them into snakes of ribbon atop her arms.

She heard pounding, and it wasn't any internal thing. It was nearly shaking the bed with it.

Langston lifted his head away, stared sightlessly at her for several moments, and then rolled his eyes up as he flung his head backwards. He was in luck that the mattress was soft, she thought, with a reaction such as that.

"My lord!" There was a frantic knocking at the antechamber door. "They're at the drawbridge! At the bridge!"

"Run, Lisle." Langston lifted his head and his look pierced her in place. "Run. To your chamber. Doona' look back. You make me forget everything. I canna' allow such a thing. Not now. Bloody hell. My arms have the weight of boulders."

He was heaving great breaths when he finished the words, and it might be true, since his arms slid away with the weight of them.

"Why?" she asked.

"Are you still here?"

She nodded.

"Why?"

"Because you need help."

He must have thought that the most amusing thing he'd ever heard, if the laughter that came from him was any indication. Lisle went onto her hands and knees, and then she was crawling down over the side of the bed.

"Go through the connecting door."

"'Tis locked." She checked it anyway. He raised himself. "How did you get in here?"

"Through the hall."

"In that attire? I'll have you across my knee if you attempt such a thing again."

"Your Lordship!" The voice was calling louder.

"Where is your key?" Lisle asked.

"Somewhere out in the bushes."

She stared. He sighed heavily.

"Open the armoire. Get a cloak. Put it on and sit in one of those chairs, and try to be invisible." He motioned with his head toward the same chair she'd already been in.

"They're in the courtyard, my lord!"

Langston groaned, rolled to the side of his bed, and stood, watching her. He didn't have much time, and he wasted it watching her? He had control of his arms again, because he had no trouble making a motion with his fingers for her to keep walking. She had the cloak wrapped about her, covering even her head, and then she was perched back in the chair.

"Come in, Etheridge. Assist me. I'll be a moment."

Lisle slipped open the cloak a bit and wished she hadn't as Langston was already stepping into Sassenach attire, slapping a belt into place while his valet buttoned the shirt and started tying a cravat-thing about his neck, all without stopping for anything that looked like a bath. They were doing it in such silent efficiency it looked like something done often and without wasted effort. They were also being silent for a reason. Langston had put his finger to his lips to guarantee it.

The valet was combing his hair and handing him a walking stick thing, and then they were both gone, Langston looking dapper and cool, and just like a Sassenach-leaning laird should.

Lisle let out her breath. She hadn't even realized she was holding it. She'd given away her knowledge. She only hoped he'd been so caught up in the same emotion her body was still suffering through that he hadn't caught it. She'd heard the horn and knew it meant trouble, because it had come in three blasts. One blast might mean the opposite. She'd never heard two. She wondered what that meant. The long, lone tone she heard throughout the morning could mean anything, but today it had meant rescue was needed in the chapel.

That certainty she'd be willing to bargain with anything over.

Chapter Seventeen

If he expected her to go back to her room, he was sadly mistaken. She wasn't letting an opportunity like this go. She already assumed the horn meant trouble was arriving, and that could only mean the Highland Rangers, although if that was the case, then everything Langston had portrayed with the captain had to be false. She was going to find out, and she only had the cloak to cover her, but it would have to do.

She was going to sneak out, get to the top of the steps, and look down. She was going to find out the truth; just as soon as her legs would support her sufficiently, and she had her breathing under control. Whatever emotion Langston had started within her, her body wasn't willing to let it go. She felt like her legs had the consistency of a sapling atop a bog, her belly was pulsing with heat, followed by cold, and the tulips weren't doing anything except chafing and rubbing and making her wonder why women had to be cursed with breasts before they had a child, anyway.

Lisle paused at the door to the antechamber and watched her own hand shaking on the handle. She didn't know if anything like this was affecting Langston, but if it was, and he still managed to look calm, cool, and perfectly in control, then he was a much better actor than she already suspected.

The antechamber didn't have anything in it except the same chair and table and painting. Lisle's legs were still a bit shaky, and she had to wait another span of time before she thought they might support her enough for stealth, all of which was stupid, and feeling more so the longer she tarried. She shook her head as she rubbed at her own knees, and even that felt erotic and sensitizing. How had Langston managed to look so diffident and cool? It didn't make sense.

She stopped her own questions, her eyes wide. Maybe he didn't suffer anything like this. Maybe it really was all a bargain, and he was just paying it. What had he said . . . something about how he used it, and then paid the penalty easily, without regret and remorse?

She was going to make herself ill with thoughts such as these, but they were helping with one thing. Her legs were gaining strength, and her belly had decided to settle back into one place. She couldn't do a thing about her breasts. They still felt heavier, and enlarged and sensitive to the brush of the cloak across the tulip cups. There must be something wrong with her.

She opened the door handle, dropped to her knees, and crawled over to the banister, all of which probably looked as ridiculous as it felt, except there wasn't anyone or anything in the main foyer to see.

Lisle went to her feet and took the steps at a pace that resembled a run by the time she reached the bottom, all of which made her painfully aware of her chemise's shortcoming as bosom support. She wrapped the cloak more securely about herself. This was worse than the first morning, when everyone had disappeared.

She knew the horn meant change, or hide, or run, or any number of other maneuvers, but to find no proof made her grit her teeth and approach the main, massive door to shove one side open herself, since there wasn't a servant, in Highland kilt or not, in sight to assist her.

The door was just as well oiled and maintained as she

suspected it would be, and despite being more than two stories in height, it opened easily. Too easily, as Lisle stumbled
out onto the front steps, gaining her feet in time to see the
last of a column of men on horseback going over the rise
leading to Langston's big lion-statue-guarded gate. The glee
that sight gave her was tempered by the realization that the
door had latched when it closed behind her, it was darker
than before, and she was outside in a chemise, with only a
Monteith cloak to shield her. She didn't even have on socks.

Lisle picked her way around the right side of his keep,
thanking her luck that Monteith kept his property as well
groomed as he did, and that his stone walks were as smooth
and perfectly fitted as they were. Her bare feet were very
aware of how it felt more like a cool, stone-lined bog than
castle grounds. She didn't stay on the stones, although they
were the easiest to see. The path they made meandered back
and forth, and she had to take the closest route to another
entrance.

Lisle shivered, wrapped the cloak closer about her, and
wondered whether anyone saw her running about outside
they'd let her in . . . assuming, of course, that there was someone in the castle to see her. They had all disappeared the other
morning. What if they'd all done the same thing now? She
could be wandering about all night. She shivered again. She
could always try to find the access way that the army of men
had used. They'd all appeared in the hall outside the chapel
yesterday, and they probably hadn't gone through the front
doors to do so. That gave her hope. She was going east. She'd
be at the chapel soon. She could even climb the beam and see
what he really had hidden in there, too.

Lisle shook her head at her own nonsense. She wasn't
dressed for such an adventure. She didn't think her legs
would support her climbing to a beam that appeared to be
three stories high, either, and she certainly wasn't in the mood
to do anything so adventurous.

Lisle stubbed her toe, went to her knees, and while she

rubbed at both her toe and her knee, she wondered how she could get so soft in such a short time. She was used to running about the MacHugh estate, bathing in the loch, and walking leagues around the properties in search of something edible that might still be growing in the ground.

This softness was ridiculous. She patted the ground in front of her toe for the offending object, and when her hands closed on it, she gasped. It was a key; a very large key. She instinctively knew where it went. She looked up, guessing by the windows that were three and four stories high that she was directly below his rooms. She knew she was right. It was the key to the connecting door between their chambers. He really had tossed it out into the shrubbery.

"Well!" She spoke it aloud and slid the key into an inner cloak pocket. Such a thing might come in handy later.

Lisle got back to her feet. She was probably in luck that she was wearing a dark green cloak, and that it was a soft-black kind of night, with mist starting to creep about, and the moon still not making an appearance. If it was anything other, she'd probably end up hearing tales about a castle waif, or banshee, or any number of other creatures roaming about the grounds, and that, only if there was anyone watching.

Lisle shivered again, rubbed at her arms, wrapped the cloak more securely, and started walking again. This time it was her nose, and then her forehead, smacking into a wall that shouldn't be there. Lisle had been walking, running the tips of her fingers along the golden-cast stone for lack of other guidance, and there was this wall. She rubbed at her face and looked up, although in what light there was, it was impossible to see the full height of the obstruction.

She wasn't at the chapel yet, or if she was, it was connected to the old castle walls at some point. That made sense. Mist was swirling about with each step, coating her feet and ankles and chilling everything it touched. The moon came out, finally starting to assist, and making it very easy to see that the wall belonged to a stairwell, and that there were stairs snaking about the outside of the keep to join up with the wall at some point. Lisle checked it with her eyes, and then she was climbing it, although with the slight rise of the steps, it wasn't much of a climb.

The stone here was slick, smooth, and had a buffed quality that had her wondering if he paid craftsmen to polish his stairs, too. It was also slick with damp that the night was causing. Lisle counted more than three hundred steps, all flat and long and with a rise of less than a finger-length between them. That was odd. Everything was.

The stairwell turned into the top of the outer wall, right beside one of the towers. Lisle stood, framed in one of the crenellations, and looked out over the countryside, bathed with a soft hue of moonlight; long, disjointed fingers of mist that looked to belong to a banshee hand; and spikes of foliage that was the forest all about his grounds. She caught her breath. She had never seen anything so darkly beautiful, nor so frightening . . . just like its master.

Lisle shook her head to stop the images. It didn't help to rail about her imagination. It had gotten her in enough trouble back in school, when everything was unimaginative and dull and coated over with lecture and punishment. Lisle had always had a following of other girls, under the covers, at night. The tales she'd told had them all giggling, shivering and begging for more. All of which did absolutely no good out on a castle wall in the middle of a moon-filled night, when she was supposed to be in her own chamber sleeping.

Lisle sighed and turned, and barely caught the scream from sounding as a shape loomed out at her from beside the tower. She couldn't do a thing about the way her heart froze and her legs wavered, sending her to the stone walkway before she could stop any of it. She didn't even feel the bruising as she landed and started to scramble backward until she was stopped by a stone side.

It took a few moments to get her breathing under control, blink away the instant moisture she'd die before she admitted to, and calm her heartbeat enough to listen. The thing wasn't moving. It was just a thing, covered over with something in order to make it less noticeable to the casual eye.

She got to her feet, although everything on her legs was weak and shaky and complaining over the use, and walked over to it. Perhaps it was an extension of the tower, although that didn't make much sense. Perhaps Langston had his craftsmen sculpt great lion statues for up here, too, to give them employment, so they could feed and clothe their families. Perhaps it was any number of things, except what it was: a heavy woolen blanket, in the same colors as the walls.

Lisle ran her hands over the weave, done so tightly she couldn't get a fingernail beneath it, and attached with something to the stone at her feet, so that it couldn't be removed . . . or couldn't be removed easily. They'd used the heaviest of wool strands to weave this blanket. Her hands knew that. There was little give to the fabric, no nap, little more than strength and durability. Such a textile was useless as anything except a floor covering. She had even seen it used as walls.

Her fingers smoothed across what felt like wire, and that's exactly what it proved to be, once she put her tongue to it to be sure. No man ordered a blanket woven with wire in it, and if he did, what would such a thing be good for?

Lisle knelt, forcing the cloak to do its job as a covering for her knees, and tried to pry part of the blanket up from where it was attached. It was nearly impossible, although there was a gap of a foot or so between the spikes that were driven into the stone to secure it.

She ran her fingers along the rounded top of a spike. It would take a man with great strength, using an implement with a hook, to pull these spikes out and expose whatever was hidden. And since there was no dearth of strong men about, posing as everything from servants to groomsmen, that meant there was probably a lot of these hook things hidden in the chapel . . . unless, of course, it was normal for a laird to put a carpet-covered thing atop his castle wall.

Lisle stood, still running her hands along it, although the covering didn't move enough to define anything except a massive object the size of a horse belly. She sighed. Even if she possessed the strength to get one of the spikes out, she hadn't anything to do it with, and there was nothing she could use to put the spike back in.

All of which was moot next to the fact that the moon was out fully now, the ground had misted to the point that any number of things could be hiding far below her, and she wasn't getting any nearer her own chamber. She looked that way and could see her pathway, although it looked like she might have to climb over a closed portcullis on the way. Lisle started walking, and she hadn't gone twelve steps before another thing loomed out from the far side of the walkway, stopping her and making her run her hands over it, and then go to her knees, with exactly the same results as the first time.

She stood slowly, looked up, and narrowed her eyes. There was another one twelve paces off, and past that, another, and then another. She still didn't know for certain what they were, but excitement was growing as she suspected it. They might be cannons. That meant he had lots of cannons. She didn't know much about what they looked like, but the tentlike drape of the thing could easily conceal not only a cannon, but cannon balls beneath it, as well. The only thing he'd need was the gunpowder. Cannons required powder, and to make such a thing required buildings and fires and workers, and all kinds of things that probably looked a lot like dye sheds for producing blue dye. Her heart was pounding, and it had nothing to do with any drumbeat. It was the excitement. It was the discovery. It was the shock.

The ability to get such a thing done, and do it beneath Sassenach noses, was staggering. He'd had to do it over time. He'd had to make it look like he was importing any number of other objects; things like chunks of marble for carving lion statues, or enormous spans of wood to make church doors, hyacinth plants for dye, or any number of other foreign-looking objects that a free-spending, notoriously foolish, English-leaning laird wanted to own. That way, none would have noted or checked closely what he was bringing in, or if they did check, they'd see nothing other than what they were supposed to see.

What did he tell her? *Beachdaich*. Observe. See beyond her eyes and ears and what she thought was knowledge. Lisle couldn't stop her own mind, and she ran from cannon to cannon, pushing on one to see if there was any give to the thing, and finding it just as substantial and sturdy as a cannon should be. She was laughing before she got to the portcullis, after counting more than fifty of them. She knew it was the truth, and she didn't have to check with anything other than her instinct. That's what he'd told her to do, too. *Neart aithnich*. The power of knowing. That's what it was.

The laird of Monteith was outfitting and supplying an army . . . a Highland army, and he was doing it right beneath the nose of Captain Robert Barton. And the very best way to guarantee that no one looked closely enough to discover it was to make certain Barton never looked closely.

Lisle's hands shook with the excitement . . . and something else, something that wasn't going to get her over the portcullis easily. She didn't want to look at it too closely. It was enough to know what he was doing and that he was no traitor. He was too late, but that didn't seem to matter. Langston Monteith was a fool.

No man could change history. But he was a Scot fool, and that meant the strange, fluttery kind of feeling in her belly that was transferring to her breasts and showing the tulip's failure at their job again had a reason and a rightness to it, making it impossible to temper. She used *neart aithnich* for that, too.

Lisle looked up the iron bars of the portcullis, saw there wasn't much to use for a grip, even if her arms supported the effort, and then she had to see if she could squeeze beneath it. That proved easily done, and she knew she was going to have to alert him to this. A slim lad could easily shimmy between the spikes at the bottom of his gate. He needed to put up wire of some kind to make it impregnable.

Lisle stood on the opposite side of the gate, looked back where she'd just been, and if she didn't know where the things were, she'd have trouble seeing them. What was she thinking? She never would have seen them . . . just as Langston wanted.

Langston sat atop Saladin and watched without one expression on his face as the prisoners were cinched together and counted. When Barton had first greeted him with the news, his stomach had roiled with it. That was his fault. He'd put himself through too many lunges and squats, and too much swordplay, and too many push-ups, and too lengthy of a run over muddy bogs of ground. All of it to temper and hold in check the male reaction he was afraid he was going to suffer the moment he'd seen her. And all of it had failed . . . miserably.

He sat atop Saladin and willed strength into his arms to continue holding the reins, and his legs to stay sealed to the stallion's heaving sides. The ground mist helped. It was cooling horses flecked with foam, and helping him stay alert when he most needed to. Captain Barton hadn't had to ride this viciously. The little band of men didn't look capable of running, and the rangers already had them under heavy guard. He knew Barton rode like he did because there was something about the man that heightened his enjoyment if there was torment and torture involved, and this little, ragged group of MacDonalds was going to do exactly that for him.

Langston looked over their heads at the depths of forest they should have had the intelligence to hide among, opaque white fog that was enveloping trees and muting night sounds, and looking a lot like her little lawn chemise had when he'd first seen it, made transparent by the firelight and showing a form any sculptor would have to dream about in order to bring to fruition.

He groaned and moved on the saddle to make the leather creak and cover it over. What he'd most feared was happening. He'd lost his heart, and with it his mind. She didn't know her power. She didn't know a lot of things, but what she did know was dangerous.

"I suppose we'll have to march them to MacCullough Hall, although the dungeons are in use. Blast! I should never have had the gunpowder stored down there."

"May I make a suggestion, Captain?" Langston said smoothly, and moved the stallion forward with the twinge of his knees.

Captain Barton's face glowed with the sheen of moisture. It wasn't from sweat or the mist. It was the excitement. Langston hooded his eyes. "Monteith Hall has very good dungeons. Very strong irons. Lots of moisture. Lots of dark, dank, rotting walls. It's got something else, as well."

"And what would that be?"

"Time." Langston said the word softly and waited.

"Time for what?"

"To fatten them up, of course."

"Have you lost your wits? Who fattens up prisoners?"

"Healthy prisoners last longer. Torment further. And they'll make the journey to London in fine shape. Makes it much more amusing to judge, hang, and then quarter a healthy man than one already dead on his feet. Trust me."

"Why should I?" Captain Barton said. "For all I know, you're one with them. Fatten them up? You're daft."

Langston chuckled. "Very well. Kill them with the march. Arrive in London with nothing. Don't say I didn't speak with you about it. I have no love for my fellow countrymen. It's because of them I have to work so much harder than I'm used to."

"You? Work? What work would that be?" Captain Barton asked.

"Why, spend gold, of course. If it weren't for these wretches, and their uprising, I'd be spending much more of my time counting it than having to spend it buying up useless bits of land."

The MacDonalds at their feet were shuffling and straining, but there wasn't much else coming through their gags and the ropes about them. Langston looked down at them without a hint of emotion on his face.

"I suppose I should thank you, actually," Langston continued.

"For what?"

"Ridding my ground of such vermin."

"Vermin, are they now?"

"They've never shown other, have they? I heard a rumor there were MacDonald clan hiding near Loch Shin. I suppose I should thank you for going in and finding them for me."

"We didn't find them."

"You're ruining your own legend, Captain. Never admit such. It makes you sound like a man of nonaction, rather than one of action."

"We didn't need to go in after them. They were on the move. Something about joining up with another clan."

"I can see the wisdom of that. Being a MacDonald is very bad for one's health at the moment." Langston laughed at his own words. No one else joined him.

"There's rumors of another clan, one with strength and power and pride. That's what they were moving toward. They wanted to join."

"Good heavens! Where?" Langston asked.

"No one seems to know, at present. They'll say more under torture."

"Good for you, Captain. We've got to stop the hellions before they rise again. We can't afford another bloodletting like last time."

"That's all right, Monteith. 'Twas mostly Highland blood that got let. I look forward to it, actually. There's too many of them about still."

"Captain, *I* am also a Highlander," Langston replied smoothly.

"I keep forgetting. You're so much different, but as you've reminded me, you are a Highlander. That being the case, I can't possibly turn the prisoners over to you, Monteith."

Langston would have been clenching his jaw and biting his own tongue if he allowed himself the emotion. Lisle had too much power. He was exhausted, and his mind wasn't working, as well as a slew of other things.

"Very well, Captain. Have it your way. I wouldn't give them a state bedroom at MacCullough, though. I spent an awful lot of gold getting those redone in the English fashion. I'd hate to see a MacDonald wretch in them."

The Captain sighed. "There are outbuildings."

"Too luxurious. These are prisoners. Worse, from my standpoint, they're MacDonalds. Why, a live MacDonald is worth less than a sheep."

"What's a dead MacDonald worth, then?"

"Good sheep grazing land, of course. Why do you think I purchased it? Civic pride?"

This time, Captain Barton joined his laughter. There was a rumble of noise coming from the group at their feet, although after several of the soldiers shoved musket butts into them, they settled back down.

"Monteith has dungeons still?" Barton asked.

"But of course. I don't have gunpowder to store, Captain," Langston replied.

"And you'll not treat them too well?"

"I promise to fatten them up. Nothing more. I doubt I'll even check on them." He shrugged. "Good Lord, why would I? They brought this on themselves, you know. Stupidity has a price. I insist they pay it."

"I don't want them too fat."

"There's no such thing, Captain."

"What?"

"There's no such thing as too much health or too fat of a

prisoner. Trust me. I already know all this. I learned it through my partner."

"Your partner keeps prisoners, does he?"

"Of a sort."

"He know much about torture and torment, does he?"

"Only if he has to, I assure you."

The Ccaptain chuckled. "I think I like this fellow better the more I hear about him."

"Don't let words fool you, Captain. Solomon deals in slavery. Afrikaners. Very good profit. Very good cargo . . . if you keep them healthy. He makes twice as much as any other slaver, just because he knows the goods at the other end are what people pay for. The goods on the other end, Captain. London. The courts. Trust me. A healthy man bleeds better, lasts longer. Makes a better spectacle."

"I vow, Monteith, you make even me acceptable to these barbarians, if the other option is yourself."

Langston chuckled, tightened his hand on the rein, and convinced himself it was to keep them from slipping.

Chapter Eighteen

A thump woke her, and it was followed by a bolt being dropped, a swish of coat falling to the floor, and heavy steps that were what she'd have expected of Monteith's arrival . . . except for the heavy steps. Lisle swiveled her head from where she had it pillowed atop the armrest of the chair and looked for him.

It was Langston, all right. She could tell that much from his size, and the blackness of his attire, and everything else the last of the fire coals and the first vestiges of dawn were showing her. He looked haggard, drawn, and was moving like an old man . . . all of which she would have expected of a man out and about all night when he'd already admitted to exhaustion before he started. Lisle lifted her head and watched him take first one step up, and then the next, forgoing the top one to simply fall forward onto his mattress, landing on his face.

She put a hand to her mouth to stop the giggle. She needn't have bothered, for Langston had turned his head and was making a rumbling noise loud enough to cover over anything she might have voiced. She unfolded her legs with difficulty, since she'd curled into a ball to wait for him and it hadn't been conducive to sleeping comfortably. She hadn't planned to be that way for as long as she had. She'd been waiting for him to return, so she could tell him she wanted to be in his bed and in his chamber, and very much so. Now there was no telling him anything.

Lisle had to wait for the deadened sensation to leave her left leg in particular before she could sneak toward the bed, although she told herself even as she was doing it that it wasn't necessary. Any man falling into bed and starting up a snore of racket when he hadn't even taken off his shoes first wasn't going to hear anyone, whether they approached on tiptoe or not.

His legs were still hanging over the side. Lisle started unbuttoning his shoes, gently at first, and then with as much efficiency as if she did it every day. He didn't move. He didn't even break the rhythm of his snores.

Getting his legs onto the mattress presented a challenge, and it was only by going to a semisquat and putting her shoulder into it that she managed to heave him onto his own bed. That didn't stop his snoring, although he had rolled over. That position just made him louder. Lisle shook her head. If this was his normal sleeping mode, she was in for some very wakeful nights. Unless she found sleep before he did. She giggled again, and climbed up beside him.

Langston was even more handsome, without a line showing anywhere on that face, and not one sneer touching his lips. Lisle reached out and ran a fingertip along his lower one, making him snort a bit, but not much else. This was not what she'd planned. All through the night . . . or at least in the time she'd been awake, she'd been thinking through what would happen, what she'd say, what he'd do. Then she'd had to take herself to task for making her own breasts feel like they were overflowing the chemise, and putting such a wellspring of something illicit and wicked-feeling everywhere else that she shook with it more than once. Now, in the light of early dawn, there wasn't much of the breathless, stirring, shaky feeling left.

There was interest, however. Langston Monteith was a very

handsome man. She wondered how many other women had thought so, and then answered it to herself. Probably every one he'd ever met.

She reached out again and slipped a lock of his hair behind his ear.

Then, she started untying the necktie thing that was wrapped about his throat more than once. Such attire still made no sense, and she wondered why the English designed such an item. All it did was hide a man's chin, force him to hold his head high enough to look down at others, and make it difficult to get it off, if he was unconscious and blowing snores of breath across where the stupid chemise really needed more material.

Lisle's fingers got clumsy, but she finally had the cravat undone, and there wasn't much farther she could go without having him awake and helping her. She lifted it up and out of the way of his shirt placket. The Sassenach had taken a good design and added a line of ruffles to either side of his buttons. That was interesting. They'd gone a step further and double-layered the placket with some sort of starched material, making it hold the buttons like they were tarred there.

Lisle got onto her knees and leaned over him, and stuck her tongue out to concentrate and not fall on him in that position. He had his shirt tucked too far into his trousers to pull out, so she did the next best thing. She parted the shirt opening and put her hands inside, placing her right one on a very healthy-sounding heartbeat, and flesh that was very hot to the touch. He hadn't been snoring for some time and Lisle looked up into surprised, amber-colored eyes.

"Tell me I'm dreaming," he said.

"Uh . . ."

"I'd better be dreaming," he replied to that.

"You're dreaming," she said finally, although her hands were still inside his shirt, and his heartbeat seemed to be increasing at the same tempo her own was.

"Good thing. I'm too tired for much else."

His eyes closed again, and he sighed heavily before resuming the deep, even breathing. Lisle pulled her hands back out and reached forward to put a kiss on his forehead. Then she was crawling from the bed and going back to her own chamber, and preparing herself for another wonderful, luxurious bath, with the expensive softening salts he'd brought over special that made her feel like she was floating and everything was warm and muted, and pleasant.

All of which made accepting his plans easier.

It wasn't until she was bathed, pampered, and sitting amidst the dozen women still sewing and gossiping and making her ears hurt with the barrage of words that Lisle found out what he had planned. It was a good thing the warm cocoon of well-being was still firmly in place when she was told, too.

The ladies were working on a special dress and all the accompanying undergarments such an ensemble needed. It had just been started yesterday, and His Lordship wanted it finished before the tea hour. It was a ball gown. He was escorting her to a ball at MacCullough Hall, the same castle he'd given over to the Highland Regiment for its use. The same castle that had seen centuries of Highland lairds birthed and put into the ground when they had died, and that was now so full of Sassenach evil that there had been a secret Celt ritual performed on the entire estate before the captain and his troops had moved in.

The real Lisle was afraid of the place. This Lisle, that had been bathed and towel-dried with heated towels and had her hair massaged with oils prior to braiding, didn't feel much, especially not fear. She'd suspicioned what Langston was doing just yesterday—although her mind was fogged with dates and recollections and suppositions, and watching the blue material they were fashioning, and not hearing much the entire time—when they'd been met at the chapel doors by an armed Monteith who had stolen her breath because he was so barbaric, muscled, and very Scot. That was when he'd aroused her suspicions about this bath he'd ordered. Mary MacGreggor was following orders . . . his orders . . . about the bath . . . and about the salts. Lisle stirred herself. Monteith was putting her into this fog on purpose.

This was no aphrodisiac, although if it was, it was wasted. She'd felt much more aroused and sensual, and a hundred other emotions, when she was with him, in control of all her faculties, and without this strange, muted feeling overpowering everything. Lisle lifted her hand and noticed how elegant the motion was, and also that there was no wedding band on the third finger of her left hand. He hadn't given her a wedding band. She hadn't noted it earlier. She wondered if that meant something, but couldn't get her mind to work on what it might be. She wondered if he wanted her like this: compliant, weakened, loose-feeling, free. . . .

That was a strange word for it. She wasn't free. She was locked in a fancy prison with a dozen gaolers, all dressed like seamstresses, and all talking ceaselessly, in time to their fingers, as they sewed. They held up the light, silken gown for her inspection. Lisle smiled vacuously. It was blue. It was floor-length. It had little gathered cap shoulders, with transparent blue material floating down to cover her arms and pretend to be sleeves. It was in a myriad of hues, from the royal blue band that was supposed to be her bodice, all the way down to an almost translucent white blue at the hem.

She supposed it was beautiful. She would probably look beautiful in it. She might even feel beautiful in it . . . *if* she was wearing it anywhere except to the MacCullough estate, and doing anything other than attending a ball with Captain Barton, his troops, and the hussies from Inverness who didn't know how to be loyal, who were posing as their dance partners and feminine companions.

Cannons. The instant thought filtered through the cacophony of voices and words and giggles that was surrounding her. Monteith had cannons on his walls. He had an army. He wore a kilt. He was training an army. He was playacting. It was all for show. She was being put on show, too. He was an actor, and such a good one no one suspected differently. And if anyone did—such as his own wife—then that person was going to be put into a semidazed state to ensure continued acquiescence to every bit of his every plot. Such a thing was diabolical. It took a diabolical mind to envision it. She should be insulted and angry and anything except soft and compliant and very feminine-feeling.

Lisle looked at her barren left hand again and let it drop, once again with an elegant motion. That was strange, too. She didn't do much that was elegant, although they'd certainly tried to instruct her often enough about it at school. It must be the salts making it feel so. She wasn't going to allow it to happen again. Mary MacGreggor wasn't going to follow that order again, if Lisle had to invent an accident to spill the potion all over the carpet, rather than into her bathwater, to guarantee it.

Someone rang a gong at the hour of two in the afternoon. That was odd, too. They never rang anything on the hour. They only piped long, slow, notes into the air that alerted everyone in hearing distance of some unknown event.

Or maybe it was known.

Lisle tried to puzzle through it while she was escorted to her suite and prepared. That was better than sitting at her mirrored table and watching as one of her servant women brushed out the dried braids of hair and started looping it into a mass of curls. They were doing the impossible, and Lisle almost giggled at that. Her hair wasn't going to obey long enough to stay anywhere atop her head, but that didn't seem to stop the woman.

It took more pins than there seemed to be strands, and two more sets of hands to hold everything in place, but at some point it was finished. Lisle looked at the finished result with interest. A reddish shine touched every strand as she moved, and it made her neck look elegant and long and very bare.

The chemise was a different one, although it didn't have much material to support her, either. Perhaps Langston ordered them made this way. That would explain it. A man might want all this flesh on display, whereas a woman would rather have the support and enclosure and not be bouncing with every step and every movement. Lisle giggled at that, and the ladies all about her seemed to think that a good sign.

There were gossamer, blue-tinted stockings for her legs. He'd had the stockings dyed blue. Lisle shook her head as someone helped her don them, although she roused herself enough to tie the garters into place herself.

There was an undergarment, with wires running through it, to hold it the proper distance from her legs, and Lisle pushed on one of the heavily stitched pockets where they'd put the wire. She wondered absently if it was the same that he'd used in his cannon covers, but didn't let the question leave her mouth. Like as not, the ladies in her own personal sewing group didn't know a thing about more than lace, fabric, patterns, needles, and thread. If she even mentioned cannons and blood, and a word like the Celt *neart aithnich* for strength of knowledge, they'd probably scream with laughter at such words and ideas.

They were serving a light tea and Lisle ignored it. Her mouth was too dry for cakes and sweetened tea, and anything else they might give her. She was also afraid if she partook of anything, it would dissolve the haze of comfort and warmth and safety that was still enveloping her. Mary had probably used too much of the potion. Lisle giggled at that, and then had to stand and hold her arms up so two of them could climb atop chairs and drop the gown onto her.

She could see why that was necessary. They hadn't left themselves much room, and there wasn't any part of the material marred by hook and eye closures or anything of that nature. It was fit exactly to her figure, or it would be as soon as they finished tugging it over her bosom, the material shaping around her breasts to make them a focal point, with a small draping effect at the center of the low-cut, widely spaced neckline, and then all the women seemed to step back, clasp their hands, and sigh.

"His Lordship sent up diamonds," one of the ladies remarked after clapping her hands. "Blue diamonds. I've never seen blue diamonds. You are so lucky, my lady . . . so lucky."

Lisle had never seen blue diamonds, either, although the Dugalls had possessed more than one neck strand with the white stones. They had probably been sold to pay for the uprising. She rather hoped that was what had happened. The alternative was that a Sassenach had pillaged them and added to his blood money. That would be worse.

She turned and regarded the vision looking at her in the mirror, and had to focus and stare to prove it really was her. Her jaw dropped. That made all the women twitter like robins, and Lisle frowned at the sound. She wondered why the fog had to start dispersing now, when she needed it most.

It turned out the stones Monteith owned were all in graduated shades and sizes of blue, culminating in a robin's-egg-sized one at the center of the strand. As soon as it was clasped, that big one settled into the valley of shadow they'd pressed her bosom into place to create. That was eye-catching and uncomfortable; as was the tiara that was set at the front of her coiffure, contrasting with the red strands.

Highlanders were starving throughout the glens, shivering without wood in the winter, and going without food all the time, and here she was wearing a king's ransom in jewels and fabric. The strand at her throat might as well be choking her.

"You look absolutely beautiful, my lady!"

There were murmurs of assent, and Lisle had to lower her eyelids to hide the disdain. She didn't know how she was supposed to get through an evening of posturing and parading and being on show.

Then they released her from her chamber, led her through the maze of downstairs halls with their dangling carnivals of furniture, and through to yet another sitting room. What was there made everything go crystal clear, and perfectly focused, and absolutely dead silent.

Langston Monteith was in full black evening wear, with his hair pulled back into a little queue that made a loop of black before it reached the volume of white material all about his throat, and the look on his face was probably the match to hers.

"Oh my," they said in unison.

Lisle had to duck her head to hide the blush. Langston wasn't as quick to show anything. He was across the room and lifting her hand to his lips and making little shivers go all over her shoulders and center where she least wanted them. It was making little darts out of her nipples, and showing everything she was trying desperately to hide.

"I had a strange dream this morning," he said when he pulled her hand away. He didn't release it, though. He tucked it in the crook of his arm, just like the day he'd decided to teach her riding, and smiled down at her, with a devastating show of white teeth.

Lisle ducked her head farther. That made him chuckle. It was ridiculous and it was exciting, and it was going to be an hour carriage ride in a coach and six of his black stallions, and she didn't know how she was supposed to get through any of that.

He walked with her to the front door, his side-to-side style of movement not as evident since he was slowing it to match hers, and Lisle was having difficulty looking at anything other than the shine of his black shoes and the tips of her perfectly dyed-to-match evening slippers.

Then they were out on the large, marbled landing, looking not at one coach-and-six, but two of them, and she already knew the blue painted one was probably for her, while the black one was his. Her eyes went wide with the surprise and dismay and disappointment.

"You're . . . na' riding with me?" she asked, turning her head and managing to center on a diamond stickpin he had at his throat.

"Nae. I've found it makes a better statement to show off wealth. You doona' like my arrangements?"

"Are you planning on exhausting yourself again?" she asked.

That made his lips twitch. Lisle tried to look above them, at his eyes, but wasn't quite successful.

"Is there a need?" he answered instead, and then he had her moving down the steps and toward her own carriage.

This traveling chaise was in padded white silk everywhere she looked, and it was difficult to tell where the benches ended and the blond wood began. It smelled new. It looked new. It also looked incredibly lonely.

"I've had a sup arranged for you. You should avail yourself of it. Sweetmeats, peaches, plus black, rye, and barley breads. Help yourself."

Lisle settled onto the side facing the coachmen, and kept every reaction carefully inside, so the crying wouldn't show. "I see nae basket," she finally murmured.

He reached in, opened the bottom of the seat she was facing, and pulled out a lap-sized, woven basket, setting it on the seat beside her.

"'Tis less than an hour to MacCullough. Rest. You'll be needing to avail yourself of that, too."

He was lifting her left hand to his lips again, and frowning at it for a moment before he let it go. Lisle didn't know what that meant. She only wished he'd given her a potion to make the next hour move swifter and with less vividness. The door closed, turning her entire world into white satin and blond wood, and she opened her basket.

He'd forgotten to mention the spray of what had to be hyacinth flowers that adorned the top of her basket, and also the little jewelry box. Lisle opened it with shaking hands, and dropped it into her lap the moment it opened. The man was in league with the devil! He had to be. She hadn't said a word, and yet there, on a little swath of black velvet, was a circlet of Celtic ribbon design, wrought in gold and silver.

She lifted it carefully, and checked the inner band. "Langston and Lisle" it read in tiny, scripted words. She was shaking as she put it on her wedded finger. Then she turned to her picnic.

Langston swayed against one of his traveling companions and nearly shoved the knee aside. He envied his wife her lonely carriage. At least she wasn't smashed in with nine of his most nondescript clansmen, all dressed in Captain Barton's particular shade of red and white that he demanded be worn by his servants, and all trying to keep from trespassing into space owned by the man on either side of him.

He wondered if she liked her little surprise, and guessed she would, if the look he'd caught on her face this morning was any marker. He caught his own open grin by tipping his head down and looking at nothing except how many pairs of boots they had managed to fit into this floor space. The way her bottom lip had trembled when she'd seen her own carriage had his heart flying, and filled him with such emotion, he'd had to sniff it away before she'd seen any of it.

If only what he was suspecting was true! Langston would give his right arm for what he'd seen in her eyes this morning when she'd had her tongue caught between her teeth and her hands buried under his shirt. He shifted again, and then pulled a bit on his collar. She'd asked him if he needed exhausting? Actually, he needed a good swig of whiskey. Maybe that would dispel some of the joy, excitement, and anticipation, and temper it with a bit of the reserve he was noted for.

He groaned softly and pulled at his pant leg, giving himself a bit more room. This was necessary, for it was hot and stuffy in the carriage, and there wasn't a hint of air allowed through the blackened windows. It was on his own orders and he didn't know if it would work or not. He only hoped Lisle would be too great a diversion, and they wouldn't even check this carriage closely.

She had certainly diverted him enough. He was losing track of everything he'd worked for. Such a thing was dangerous at the worst of times. Since it was getting near the point of fruition, it was worse than dangerous. It was certain death.

She knew too much, too. That was very dangerous. Solomon had counseled him on it when they partnered, but he'd already known. A woman with knowledge was worse than a hundred men with the same. A woman who thought she had knowledge was even worse. That was matched by a thousand men. Women couldn't be trusted; not with secrets, not with lies, and especially not with what he was doing now.

He had Clan MacDonald to save. It seemed like ever since he'd met Lisle, his luck had been changing. Not only was the captain getting more and more lax, but Langston was being granted a chance to redeem himself to the very men who had fought and died at Drumossie Moor. Every Monteith clansman knew what they were being given, and that was why he'd had to hone this group of men down from the hundreds that had volunteered for this mission.

Monteith had twenty-seven MacDonalds to save, and they weren't assisting him with it, either. From all reports, they were refusing every piece of food sent to them, and if anyone managed to toss something at them, it was rifled right back, with an intent to injure.

Langston grinned further. It was exactly what he would have expected from a MacDonald who had escaped death at Culloden, evaded capture and slavery as a punishment, and now faced the hangman in London. He was rather proud of them, even their curses of hatred toward him. That reassured him. He was portraying Langston Monteith, the Highland traitor, the Sassenach lover, and the man who profited from every other Highlander's spilled blood. He was glad they cursed and hated and spit at him.

It didn't matter. It had to be thus. He was saving them anyway . . . every last foaming-at-the-mouth, spitting-mad, ungrateful man.

Chapter Nineteen

Angela MacHugh was attending the Sassenach ball at the ancient Highland MacCullough Castle . . . as was her sister Mary. They were both on the arms of handsome Highland rangers, and looking like women in the first bloom of love were supposed to. They didn't look at all like MacHughs who detested everything about the English.

Lisle stood in complete shock as she saw them, and knew Monteith would feel it. He wasn't letting her far from his side, and the fact that she'd stopped, her eyes had widened, and she'd sucked in air so rapidly she was in danger of coming right up out of her bodice were very good clues for him.

"Something bother you, my dear?" he asked, bending his head to do so.

The endearment started her heart pumping again, which was a good thing. The proof in front of her eyes that she'd failed as a stepmother, and that she'd failed in such a momentous way, had been enough to give any mother heart failure. It was making her own chest feel too tight to contain what she hoped wasn't anguish, but knew was.

"It's my daughter," she replied, tipping her head a bit while she said it, and nearly grazing the lips he had at her ear.

Langston's eyebrows rose and he pulled her more securely

against him. Not that he'd let her get more than an arm's length away, but pressing himself against her entire side was not only against logic, but probably against several social codes as well.

"Where?" he asked finally, scanning the crowd.

"In the pink. With the white lace."

"The bit of fluff with blond hair and no brows?"

"Nae. That's her sister."

"Is na' she also your daughter, then?"

Lisle narrowed her lids and fluttered her lashes up at him. "Aye," she replied evenly. "That she is."

"There is na' much family resemblance."

"I think they look like each other. Everyone else does, too."

"I mean . . . to their mother."

Lisle thinned her lips this time. "You are na' amusing, my lord."

"Oh dear. I've regressed," he replied.

"What?"

"From Langston. I really wish you'd refer to me by my given name. Especially in public like this. I am trying to pretend we're wed."

"We are wed." Lisle rotated the ring on the finger of her left hand, and couldn't resist glancing down at it. It just looked *so* right, on the hand resting on his arm. She knew he saw her.

"Oh. Then, I'm trying to pretend we're wed, and we want to be."

"Langston Leed Monteith," she said in a low, and what she hoped was a threatening-sounding, tone.

"Very good. You got all of it that time. It's just as you said. You are a very good pupil. You do learn fast."

He was smiling down at her and making every decent thought fly out, to be replaced by several indecent ones. It was as if he knew it, too. Lisle had to drop her gaze and that had her looking right into Angela's stiff face. She'd lost her escort, if that was what the young soldier was.

"Good eve, Angela," Lisle said.

Angela didn't so much as nod. She did look straight at her and then move her gaze beyond her, to something at her back. It was insulting and it was meant to be insulting. Lisle colored, despite herself.

"I hope you're well?" Lisle tried again.

"As well as gold can get one," Angela said finally.

Lisle stepped forward to say, "You should na' be here."

"I deserve a future, doona' I?" Angela asked.

"You deserve a good Highland man."

"There are only Highland traitors left, dearest Lady Monteith."

Lisle's teeth set. "I doona' wish an Englishman for a stepson, Angela."

"And I doona' wish an English-loving traitor for a—oh. He's naught to me, is he?" She smiled brightly, turned, and moved away before anyone could reply.

Lisle was sucking in breath and letting it out as rapidly as possible. It was to dim the shock into a manageable emotion.

"Shocking. Absolutely shocking," Langston said at her side.

"What?" Lisle's voice showed how surprising that description was, coming from him.

"This filial respect thing. You doona' appear to have much. I suppose I should have warned you."

"About what?" she asked.

"I'm na' particularly well thought of in these parts. These Highlanders are stubborn, self-righteous, and judgmental. You ken?"

"I already knew all that," she replied.

"And if they've taken my gold, they really detest me. It ups the amount of evil attributed to me, if you will. It's almost like they feel I forced them to take it, and self-hate is such a destructive emotion."

"Self-hate?"

"Aye, and if someone has to be hated, and it's not going to

be the individual taking the gold, then it's got to be the one making them take the gold. It's going to be me. Dreadfully obvious."

"You understand all this, and you still make them take it?"

"Social change requires gold, sweet. Always did."

Sweet. It was a different endearment, and the ease with which it had rolled off his tongue made it even more effective. Lisle had to swallow around a dry mouth she hadn't had a moment earlier. She only hoped he didn't know the reason.

"How much gold do you have, Langston?"

"None," came the reply.

"Oh, that's ridiculous. Everything about you reeks of wealth. Everything."

He sighed. "Perhaps you should ask the question the proper way, if you wish an answer you'll like."

Lisle stuck her bottom teeth forward and looked up at him. She wasn't willing to flutter one eyelash, let alone two eyes of them. "And what is the proper way to ask that question?" she asked.

"You should ask how much gold we have," he answered. "Marriage does make it a plural arrangement. What I have is yours, and vice versa. 'Twas what we vowed to . . . if you listened to that sort of thing."

"You got the short end," she replied.

"Oh . . . I doona' think so."

His voice had lowered, as had his head. Lisle was very aware of those eyes, looking deeply into her . . . and there was a dark brown with a reddish tint along the outsides. She didn't think he'd actually kiss her in such a public room, but she parted her lips slightly just in case he did.

"In fact, I think I got a treasury beyond price."

Someone cleared their throat. Since Langston was breathing the words onto her nose and it wasn't a far span to her lips, Lisle had been absolutely enthralled. He really would kiss her in a public room!

"I'm dreadfully sorry to interrupt you, Lord and Lady Monteith."

It was a soldier, almost too young to shave. He had Mary on his arm. She was in pink, like her sister, and it had white lace, but there was too much of one or the other to make it visual and elegant-looking.

"Mistress MacHugh wanted a few words, if it's not a bother."

"Prepare yourself, love." Langston put his lips very near her ear to whisper it. The endearment or the whisper was sending shivers rampantly over her shoulders. She sucked in a breath.

"Mary?" she asked.

"You should na' have let Angela hold the coffers. She hasn't let anyone have their fair share. We need more. In separate accountings."

Lisle's eyebrows lifted. "You should speak with your uncle Angus over such things, Mary."

"Angus does nothing but drink. Why would I ask him anything?"

Lisle's heart fell. Her body felt like it might be right behind it. As if he knew, an arm snaked about her back, pulling her even closer to him.

"Have Angus MacHugh report to Monteith Castle on the morrow. Noon. I shall handle it, young woman."

"Do I have to answer him, Lisle?" Mary asked, making even her escort look uncomfortable.

"If you will na' get my instructions to him, I'll send them through your sister," Langston replied easily. "Or with a payment. That should get a reading."

Mary turned her back on them. The escort smiled slightly in apology as he escorted her away. Lisle watched them with no emotion whatsoever.

"Your brood appear an ungrateful bunch. I hope the same does na' happen with ours."

"We doona' have a brood, Langston."

"I know." He grinned down at her.

"What are you going to have of Angus?" she asked.

"Well . . . I'll take him to task first for misusing good whiskey. Then, I'll probably put him to work fashioning bagpipes. I feel a need for more of them, for sales purposes, you understand. It's strange, but the one thing we're denied, the world seems to want to have. Odd, isn't it?"

Lisle couldn't contain how it felt. The sides of her lips were splitting with it. "You're giving him back his self-respect," she said.

"I'm using his talents for my own ends. I'll be getting good gold out of the bargain. I'd not do it for any other reason."

"You canna' fool me much longer, Langston."

"Oh dear. You're looking at me with an expression I'd rather na' comprehend. You should cease that before someone sees it . . . like you."

"Me?"

"Self-hate . . . remember?"

"You think that I—?" She was choking on the rest of her sentence. She had turned the hate to him. She stumbled, but had the matter under control the moment it happened.

"But, of course. Such a thing is vitally important, at present."

"You want me to hate you?"

"Does that possibly mean . . . that you doona?" he asked instead.

The entire roomful of others dropped out of sight, and there was only Langston, looking down at her with those odd-colored eyes, amidst that handsome face, and making a yawning chasm open up everywhere else. Lisle clung to his arm to keep from stepping over the edge and disappearing. She didn't hate him at all. She was terrified of what she did feel.

"Oh dear," she heard him say again, from what sounded like a long way away. "This may mean what I think it does."

"And what would that be?" she whispered.

"That I'd best step up everything . . . this evening. Balls

begin to bore me. That's exactly what it means. Where is that Captain Barton?"

"Captain . . . Barton?" Lisle's legs were giving her trouble.

"Bother that. We'll dance."

He was shaking his head as he rotated her within his arms, and moved her into another dance so effortlessly, he looked like he'd been trained in it and did it often. He also looked less fit than she knew him to be, and she wondered what tailor would design a suit that made him look loose, and paunchy, and unfit around the midsection, and also how much it would cost. He was paying men to fashion clothing to make him look fat and lazy. She wondered how offended his tailors were.

She giggled.

"Something amuses you, love?" he asked.

There was that particular endearment again, and Lisle's feet stumbled, despite everything she was immediately exerting in a effort to subdue it.

"Why . . . do you use such endearments with me?" she asked.

"Someone might be listening to us. I'm attempting to act like I'm in love with you. Isn't it working?"

He pulled back to show an expression of surprise, and that put the line in his forehead back into place, drawing her eye there, if, of course, she managed to look past the sparkling sheen on his ale-colored eyes.

"It's working quite well," she replied, drawing out every word.

His response was a groan that if she hadn't had her hand to his chest, she wouldn't have known.

"I believe we've danced enough. I'm parched."

They'd taken a total of ten steps, maybe eleven. Lisle pursed her lips in thought. If she wasn't mistaken, he had a flush of color rising from beneath his neck-thing. He wasn't meeting her eyes. That was interesting. This man, who was such a good actor, who was capable of fooling everyone, was having trouble with his facade tonight? She could only guess at the reason, and hope it was true.

The refreshment tables were set all along the stone walls of MacCullough's banqueting hall, or, if the real chieftain was in residence, it would be known as the Great Hall. Either way, it was an old castle, with stone-lined walls and a feeling of history and lore and mystery about it. Lisle stood patiently as Langston reached forward and accepted a goblet of liquid from a servant, then handed it to her. Then he reached for another one. Lisle looked up the span of his arm from over the rim of her wine glass, and right into the cheerful face of the Monteith groomsman, Fergus.

She blinked. Stared, blinked again . . . stared again. He'd shaved off that carrot-orange beard, and there was still no telling if he had the same shade of hair or not, because he was wearing a curled, powdered wig atop his English service uniform. Langston was looking at her, and Lisle moved her eyes to him. There was a distinct frown on his face now.

"Something wrong, love?" he asked.

She took a deep gulp of her wine. The stuff was still acrid and slid across her tongue without even feeling like it was liquid, but it was starting a very warm feeling the moment it landed in her stomach, which was exactly what she was looking for. She took another gulp, swallowed it, and looked directly up at her husband.

"You control his servants. That way, you'll know where he is. You'll know his movements," she said softly. "That's the horn. That's what it means."

He went still, and breathed very shallowly, if what she was observing was any indication. Then, he reached out and took the goblet from her hand to place it back on the table. The line in his forehead was in full force as he looked down at her, and then he smiled.

"You have very interesting ideas for conversing at a ball, Lisle. Very. Come. We'd best get some air."

* * *

Langston had gone cold all over, but had it under control
before he reached for her glass. He'd known better! Everything he'd been taught, and lived through, and created, and
sacrificed for, using his wits, body, and mind for, had shown
him never to trust a woman with anything! Yet here he was,
with everything in such a delicate balance, while the woman
he loved was announcing part of his plan . . . aloud!

He'd forgotten her propensity for alcohol, especially wine.
He'd forgotten that liquor loosens the tongue. He'd forgotten
a hundred other things the moment she'd looked at him with
those sky-blue eyes that he'd made certain were the match to
her every outfit, and intimated that she didn't hate him.

Everything he prided himself on had deserted him, but
there was no excuse. It was as if he'd done it to himself on
purpose. He could drown in the depths of her eyes, worship
at the altar of the bosom he'd ordered put on display, and
match every part of his frame to every trembling section of
hers, and the dance hadn't changed a thing. He couldn't rotate
with her in his arms. He couldn't think with her scent in his
nostrils. He couldn't plan, think, decide, act. He was beginning to think she truly was a Celtic goddess; one that took a
man's wits and smoked them into nonexistence, like so much
opiate.

He was grinding his teeth now, and she was looking at him
with a not-so-innocent, sly type of glance, and even that made
him want to take her, hold her, caress her. . . .

"Why, Monteith! 'Tis a pleasure seeing you at my ball. I'd
about given up on seeing you at all. My prisoners giving you
trouble?"

"Prisoners?" Lisle asked.

Langston pulled her to his side and held her around the
middle, looked deep into her eyes for the slightest moment,
begging for her trust, and then he forgot what he was trying
to ask. She had the most amazing way about her . . . the most
stunning eyes . . . the most fire. Captain Barton was clearing

his throat and speaking again. Langston had to shake his head to clear it.

"Why, that's Mistress MacHugh. Whatever possessed you to bring her to an English ball?"

"Her beauty," Monteith said smoothly, turning his head and putting Lisle fully in front of him. "Don't you agree, Captain?"

He watched as she gasped for breath, making the captain move his eyes from where he'd been staring at the blue diamonds, to where every other male glance had to go. Langston felt Lisle's back go stiff. He put his left arm about her ribs and tightened it, lifting her breasts farther.

"Why, Monteith. You're quite right. She's astounding. How did you guess at such a thing, when she was running about barefoot and covered in muck all the time?"

"I've an eye for such things, Captain. It's another way I made my fortune. Allow me to amend that. It's how I still make my fortune."

"Really? In women?"

"We don't only deal in Afrikaners, Captain. Women sell for a very good price, too. In the right parts of the world, that is."

Lisle was sucking for air now. Langston pulled her closer to him, almost lifting her from the floor with the motion. If she decided to start screaming, he had to be able to cut off her air.

"You truly are the devil, Monteith. I congratulate you, but I believe I'll do it from a distance. Mistress MacHugh looks ready to slice you alive with that look."

"I am not Mistress MacHugh, Captain Barton," Lisle said. Langston groaned inwardly, and all anyone heard was his sigh.

"Truly? Why is that?"

"I am now the lady of Monteith."

"No! You married her? You? But . . . why?"

"Because she's increasing, of course."

"These barbarians breed well. You should have been

more careful with your seed. I am. I wouldn't want my progeny tainted."

Lisle's breath was coming so rapidly, Langston was afraid she might faint. He held onto her, his arm still about her ribcage, and it wasn't to push anything out farther. It was to hold her, protect her, and try to keep her from the devastation of the words he had yet to say.

"I haven't your strength of character, I guess. 'Twas all right, though. I put her through a ceremony, Captain. She insisted on it."

"Was it legal, then?"

"Ask me later, Captain. Do I look stupid enough to say something guaranteed to get me a knife blade between my shoulders when I'm sleeping?"

Captain Barton thought that was very amusing and tossed his head back to let the laugh out. Lisle's arm twitched forward, like she was going to swing at him, and was keeping it to herself by force of will. Langston moved his other arm about her, giving her more to rely on.

"Monteith, you refresh me. Makes me realize that there are more devious fellows in the world than I could possibly be. I thank you."

Langston inclined his head. "Accept my regards on the morrow, Captain. That will be thanks enough."

"What have you planned?"

"I have some of my Arabians ready for you and your officers. I'll have them delivered. Free of charge, of course."

"I have forty-one officers, Monteith."

"I'll go you one better and have fifty head delivered; mares, geldings, and stud. You can make use of that many?"

"Why would you do such a generous thing? You're not noted for your generosity, Monteith."

"That's where you're mistaken. I do nothing unless it benefits myself. Absolutely nothing."

"You may explain."

"I can think of no better test, generating more publicity,

which will guarantee myself better sales once I get a shipload to London, than to put the Highland Regiment officers aboard my own Arabian horseflesh."

"Toss in the horse you ride."

Langston checked the reaction very carefully. "Saladin?" he asked.

"The big black one. I rather fancy him."

"I trained him myself, Captain. He doesn't like other riders."

"Are you denying me?" the captain asked.

"You wish Saladin? Very well. I'll have him delivered directly to you. Go gently on him. He's a devil when crossed."

"I can handle any number of devils. Even a Highland one like yourself."

"And here I thought I'd risen in your esteem," Langston replied.

"Such a thing has merit, but no possibility. You're a Highlander by birth. Such a thing cannot be erased, no matter how many times you prove your loyalty. It will always be there."

"What will?" Langston asked.

"Distrust. Suspicion. Questions. Speaking of . . . you also never answered mine. How are my prisoners faring? Not too well, I trust?"

"It's been reported to me that they're not eating, as of yet."

"Pity," Captain Barton said.

"I'd have more to say, but I haven't ventured down there yet. They detest me, and they're far too accurate."

"Accurate?"

"They throw food back," Langston said slowly and with a bored tone. "We've ceased giving them joints with any bone in them."

The captain roared with the amusement that time. Lisle's arm didn't so much as move. Her heart was hammering rapidly against where he had her held to him. Langston dared a glance down and wished he hadn't. She had too much on display, and was too soft in the right places, and had such lengthy eyelashes and perfect lips, and everything on him was responding, and all of that was absolutely terrible.

"Your plan may backfire. I'll have the gunpowder here moved."

Lisle stopped breathing on that word. Langston noted it, and put it aside. "I wouldn't say so, sir. I'll be trying again when they dry out."

"Dry out?"

"My moat was overfull. It empties into the dungeons. It makes it very uncomfortable to try and find a place to sit, let alone lie down. I understand the misery is doubled when you add rats to the picture."

"Rats?" Captain Barton asked.

"What castle dungeon doesn't have rats, Captain?" Monteith replied.

"I see. I'm beginning to think you're worse than the devil, Monteith."

"I haven't finished yet."

"Do tell."

The man's eyes were gleaming with interest and he craned himself forward slightly. Lisle could be gagging. That's what it felt like. Langston lifted her up a fraction, put his nose against the mass of curls they'd put atop her head, and inhaled deeply before replying. He lifted his head.

"They're receiving moat water at certain intervals."

"Intervals?"

"Aye. Makes it worse."

"How so?"

"A man knowing something is coming can prepare himself for it."

"I don't understand," the captain replied.

"Such a man can prepare himself for it and prepare himself for it."

"This is a good thing?"

"Torture of the mind is the worst kind, Captain."

"Explain please."

"If a man is prepared and no water comes, then he's left in that prepared stance, dreading it, and yet wondering where it is."

"You vary the intervals?"

Langston nodded.

"You really are a fiend, but I like that. I truly do."

"There's an added benefit to all of this, too."

"Really? What is that?"

"They smell. My dungeons are starting to smell. They need washing. Badly. Tomorrow . . . I'm adding soap. Chafes the ankles."

The captain pulled back and regarded Monteith with undivided attention. He looked and acted like he was watching and smelling something distasteful. He didn't notice Lisle, at all.

"You're as barbaric as they are, Monteith. Remind me not to get on your bad side," he said finally, and swiveled.

Chapter Twenty

The carriage may have been constructed of white satin and blond wood, but with the gas lamp dimmed the interior looked dark and sinister and any number of other things. Langston stretched on his side, watched where the light swayed toward the goddess on the opposite chair, wishing it were even dimmer, and tried to halt the ache in his chest that seemed to be doubling the closer they got to the future.

She seemed to want the quiet. That was all right with him. He didn't feel up to conversing lightly or falsely, or with anything other than the burn that was making his shoulders hurt, too. He probably would have been better off not knowing this beautiful Highland lass named Lisle. She was so full of life, it was impossible to be close to her and not have some of it transfer over. It was what he feared most.

Those who experienced life had to suffer through the bad, too. That was the only way you knew how good the good felt. He blinked rapidly at moisture God was cursing him with, and shuddered through a breath she'd never be able to detect. He was very good at what he did. He acted. He played falsely. He cheated. That was what he did.

Then, she said his name, surprising him, and changing everything.

"Aye?" he answered after a moment.

"This ball . . . was na' what I expected."

"You go to many balls a-fore?" he asked.

"Nae," she replied.

"What did you expect?"

"I doona' ken, for certain. I thought it would be gayer. There would be more laughter, more wine, more music . . . more false-sounding words. You know, like the girls used to describe to me."

"Girls?"

"At the finishing school. There was a lass from Paris. She told tales that would scald your ears."

"That's highly doubtful," Langston replied.

She made a sound that could be amusement. He could turn up the lamp to be certain, but he didn't want to see amusement. It jarred against what he was feeling.

"Then there was a girl from Germany. I forget where, exactly. There, everything is so strict, a woman does na' even get to meet her husband until they're wed."

"There's naught wrong with that plan that I can tell."

"They were appalled, but also envious and a bit impressed that I had the run of the moors, I was welcome in any croft, and I could play with any of the lads I wanted to, anytime I wanted to."

"Nae wonder you were sent to this finishing school. You were a veritable hoyden."

"I turned out well enough," she answered.

Langston sucked in a breath on that one. He didn't know how to answer. He didn't know where she was going with her conversation. That was another thing that intrigued him about her. She surprised him, daily . . . hourly.

"You doona' agree?" she asked.

"I—uh . . ."

She giggled at his response. His arms twitched at the sound. He wondered why, if everything horrible happened to her, she still had such joy within her. That was the part that drew him, singed him, and was probably going to destroy him.

"You doona' have to answer. I ken what your answer is just fine."

"What do you ken?" he asked.

"This dress. This presentation. You did it on purpose. You used this body that you call a weapon to your advantage, to divert attention. You did very well with it, too. I was impressed."

Langston swallowed. "As I've already made mention, you're a very quick pupil."

"Doona' do it ever again," she said.

That had him sharpening his eyes on where she sat, or rather, where she was reclining, since she'd decided to lie across the seat, and use the blond wood for a backrest.

"I'm having a bit of difficulty following your conversation, my dear. It must be the quantity of wine I consumed. What is it you're referring to again?" he asked.

"You dinna' drink much, Langston."

"Enough," he replied.

"Enough to open some more negotiations with me?" she asked.

"What are we negotiating for this time?" he asked.

"Me. In your bed. Open. Willing . . ." Her voice lowered to a husky note that went right to his groin. ". . . wanton," she finished.

The reaction was immediate and constant, and started a throb of activity where he least wanted it. Langston looked down at himself in surprise. He still had plans for the night. He had MacDonalds to sway. He had eighteen more grooms-men to select and prepare, since he already had the nine poor souls they'd stolen from beneath Barton's nose. He had to get the opiate started that would put Barton's English-bred servants into a drug-induced stupor, to render them men who looked very like MacDonald captives, who'd had their will broken. He had Saladin to bid good-bye to. He wasn't looking forward to any of it, and he certainly hadn't time for what she was doing—whatever that was.

"Do you know how?" he asked, tossing his own mental card onto her table.

"How what?"

"To be wanton," he replied.

In answer, she reached up and twisted the knob on their gas lamp, making more wick rise from the oil, grab the light, and consequently shed more illumination throughout the coach cabin.

"Do you doubt me?" she asked softly.

"Aye," he replied, and licked his lips.

She was sliding down, onto her back on the white satin cushion, parting her legs slightly, arching her back, and everything on him was jumping at the sight. Then she did more, rolling onto her side to face him, and then she swiveled onto her knees, leaning out over the coach floor, and raising her upper torso in an arc of motion, that was forcing the dress he'd designed to nearly give up the effort of holding in her breasts.

Langston had never seen such a vivid display, and his entire body was tormenting him with it. He had to clench the padded satin cushion beneath him to keep from reaching for her.

She stayed in that back-cracking, poised position, with every inhalation sending parts of her closer to exposure, for long enough that he was in danger of losing his sanity. Then, she pulled back, slid onto her haunches, with bunches of that blue-dyed fabric about her knees, and regarded him with an unreadable expression.

"Now . . . do we have an understanding?" she asked.

"Of what?" he croaked it out.

"That I ken very well what wanton is . . . and what it is na'."

"Aye," he answered, and licked his lips again, and he watched how a tremor ran through her as he did so.

"And that it's a very good thing to have."

"Aye," he replied again.

"And . . . that you'll negotiate with anything to have it."

Langston opened his mouth to say aye, but that was what she was looking for, and his mind decided to come back from wherever it had been hiding, in order to assist him with this. "That depends . . . on what it is," he replied finally.

He watched as she went on her knees again, and slid first one of those little puffed effects at the tops of her sleeves down to her upper arm, and then the other. That was making the front part of her bodice stretch and pull and define, and Langston really was going crazy.

"Let's redefine what we're negotiating again," she whispered, and then she rolled her shoulders, pressing first one nipple against the fabric, and then the other, making him push the padding into a solid block of crushed feathers with the pressure of his fists on it.

"Wanton . . . passion . . ."

"Oh, my God," he murmured.

"And what you'll do to have it."

"Oh, my God," he repeated.

"Say it," she requested.

"What?"

She was leaning out over the chasm of the coach bottom again, only this time there wasn't much holding her in place at all. Langston was howling inside; he didn't know what the outer Langston looked like.

"That you'll give anything . . . for it."

This time it was a howl that came out first, although he had his teeth clenched to keep it from being too loud. "That . . . depends. On what. It is." He repeated it, in blocks of words that were all his body would let him have.

"You are na' a very quick learner, *cherie*," she whispered, and reached up to push the fabric down and away from herself, exposing . . . everything.

Langston launched himself, gathered her into his arms, ball

gown and all, found one of her breasts, and had it in his mouth before anything on him had time to say no.

Lisle screamed with the only portion of her that wasn't flying about the coach cabin, zinging this way and that with flashes of ache and weakness, and moisture and excruciating heat. Langston pulled her tighter, his mouth a thing of sensation and fire and eroticism, and he wouldn't unlatch from where he suckled no matter how she tried for that very thing.

He was too big. He was too powerful. He was too strong. Lisle settled finally with running her fingers through that black hair, pulling it loose from the queue, and then she was offering herself up to him, moving him to the breast he'd been neglecting.

"Oh . . . dearest . . . sweet . . . heaven."

He was murmuring more of the words, and she had to hold him in place in order to make certain he knew she wasn't interested in words, only action. Lisle had never felt what she was now, and he was taking all the weightiness and enlarged feeling she'd been tormenting herself with, the longer he stayed on his side of the coach and just watched her, and turning it into a version of mist and clouds, rain and heat.

Langston trailed his mouth to her throat, his hands moving from where he'd had her pinioned at the waist, up to cup the flesh where he'd just been, and the motion of his thumbs was just as arousing, just as torturous, and just as hot.

"Love," she said, just before he moved his head. His lips captured hers, stopping anything else from being said, and made everything disappear in a spin of smoke-gray fog with fire at its core.

Hard, heavy breathing filled her own nostrils, slid over her cheeks, and tickled her ear. Lisle couldn't stand another moment of it. She pushed at him, and pushed hard, until he moved, giving her room to find the stupid ties of his collar, so she could find the buttons of his coat, then his vest, and then, she was facing the overly starched, double-thick placket that the English put on their men's dress shirts.

She tore her head away to give vent to the cry, and he had to chase her back down, so the last of it finished in the caverns of his own mouth. Fingers shoved at the dress, making a ripping sound, until he could hold her bosom in each hand, squeezing gently. His actions made her hands that much more clumsy, her fingers that much more sensitive to everything, even the hard, slick surface of his buttons . . . the tiny, minute stitches of each button hole.

Langston was sliding his hands down her ribcage, and the dress was parting for his exploration, although it wasn't doing it willingly. They both heard ripping and tearing, and then she didn't hear a thing past the drumbeat of heart that filled her left palm, and then her right. He had a chest made for running her hands over, glorying in each lump, each section, each bump of muscle that flinched away from and then pulsed into being again as if for her delectation and adoration.

And then her hands were against his belt, and beneath the waistband of his slacks, and sliding all about and around and finding nothing that felt like a button entry. Lisle pulled her mouth away to let that anger out, too, but he wasn't allowing it. She hadn't a gasp of air away from him before he had her lips again. Then he was parting them, and he was flicking his tongue, and with each touch, her entire body was pulsing and sliding and moving. The feel of the heated, male, naked flesh of his chest against her own nakedness was enough to make her cry again. This one didn't make sound, and had to contain itself as a moan of resonance that swelled through where she was smashed against his chest. It sounded an awful lot like his groan, too.

Lisle tried to get to him again, but this time she started with his belt buckle. That wasn't as unfamiliar as his English trousers. The clasp gave, falling onto her belly with a thump of cool-feeling metal, and then she squirmed in a sideways roll, in order to make it slide off.

Langston's hands had reached her waist, and he was pushing the waistband of her wire-stiffened petticoat apart, pulling

out more of the laboriously crafted stitches. Lisle was helping
him by undulating her body against him; going upward, then
back down; arching away from him, then against him . . .
upward, back downward. Upward . . .

It was definitely a groan that came out of him then, and
he moved from her kiss to give it sound as the slip ripped free.
Then he was helping her, lifting himself into a push-up with
one arm, so he could grab her hand and move it to the fastening of his own attire. He let her go the moment she reached
the buttons, and then lowered himself, although this time he
wasn't putting his weight on her like before. He was in a
slant, on his knees, with one of them splitting her legs apart.
The blue dress was a froth of material all about his waist,
hiding the mass of him, the shape of him, the vision of him.
She pulled in breath after breath as she looked down. Then
she was shoving her own dress away, and over the side, where
it puddled somewhere on the floorboard, held to her only as
a ribbon of material about her waist.

The trouser fastening was on the side, and there were seven
buttons. They weren't moving easily, and she had to yank at
the last two to make them give up their command of the
holes.

"Oh God. Oh! Sweet . . . sweet, Lisle." He was murmuring
the words in her hair as she got his pants undone, and then he
was helping her by slithering himself out of them. That was
putting his weight and depth and the heat of him against her,
and keeping her from seeing what she was determined to see
at the same time. Lisle pushed at him when he had the pants
down to his knees, but he wasn't budging. So she used her
hands; roaming them about his back, all over the large, funnel
shape of him, until she reached what was probably the waist
of men's English underdrawers.

The sound she made was ground through her gritted teeth,
and this time it was one of anger. No Scotsman ever wore so
much. She knew that from her brothers. She was pounding
and hitting at him until the slight sound of soft laughter

stopped her. Lisle looked up into such a tender expression that everything on her felt frozen in space and time and intellect for one tiny, infinitesimal moment.

I love you. He mouthed it, and her eyes flew wide . . . wider. Then he had her mouth again. It was as if he was punishing her for being able to see what he'd just said as he shoved at her with his face, scratching her chin with the slight growth of whisker on his jaw, and sending a feeling of power to every pore.

Heat flowed into being; moist heat. And the fire, kindled at her core, was a driving force, fueled with anger and sensation and lust and passion. Lisle bucked her hips against his, against the thing of power, rigidity, and strength that he was denying her, and then she was moving her hands to the front of him. Drawers had openings. They had to. They just had to.

Then she had him in her hands—both hands—and was absorbing the shock and amazement. That wasn't a far cry from his reaction as everything on him went still and straight and taut.

"Oh . . . my God!"

The cry came from the depth of him, and then he was pushing her petticoat to the side, lifting himself to run his hands along her thighs; learning them, defining them, preparing them. Lisle wasn't still. She was lunging and kicking at him. He caught both legs effortlessly and then he was between them, and putting such a torment of pain and fire against her that her heart stalled in place and she forgot to breathe.

"Oh . . . dear God . . . you're a virgin." He lifted his head, his eyes wide, his hair ruffled about him like he'd just shaken himself like a dog might, and surprise evident everywhere.

"Aye," she replied.

Then she had to pull at the surprise and pain as he pushed again at her, frightening and hurting and making her lash out and kick, and this time it was to get away.

"Oh nae, you doona'." He used the muscles so evident all

along him to hold her in place, his hands pinioning her like bands of iron, and it was so he could shove himself even farther into her.

Lisle screamed. He was impaling her . . . hurting and paining, and doing a hundred other horrible things to her.

"Stop! Doona! Stop." Her words dribbled to a whisper, and her head moved side to side, and it didn't stop him a bit. It only seemed to inflame him.

He was making little grunt sounds as he continued shoving into her; low-in-the-throat kind of sounds; and then he slowed in a slide of movement, flexed himself to another of her moans, and stilled.

"Lisle?" His whisper didn't match the man of torture who was between her legs, but Lisle wasn't listening. She was still moving her head from side to side in denial.

"Lisle . . . love?" He whispered it again, only this time he added the false word he used. She swung upward at him, and managed to connect with his jaw, to the detriment of her own hand.

That had him leaning forward, those eyes so close to hers she could see each and every eyelash, and he was looking deeper into her than anyone had a right to.

"Doona' speak so to me!"

"Why not?" he asked softly, blowing the words across her nose and cheek as he pulled himself a little of the way out of her.

"Because you hurt me," she replied before she could stop the words she'd rather die than admit.

"I dinna' do it on purpose," he replied, using his voice as his newest drug.

"You do everything on purpose," she whispered to that.

He chuckled, and her lower body lunged at how that felt. "Well, maybe I did intend to hurt this time, but only because of your maidenhood, love. I promise. It does na' pain again. Ever. I promise."

He pushed himself again, sliding back to where her body had to absorb the pain, or do something to stop it.

"Then cease hurting me!" Lisle couldn't stay the tears, and he kissed at each one, and that sent the emotion straight to her heart, where it hurt almost as badly as where he'd joined them.

"Oh, love . . . so innocent. So precious. So pure." He finished the words to her ears and went onto his arms, like he was going to do push-ups, and he just stayed that way, looking down at her, and there wasn't any emotion showing anywhere on him.

"Put your legs about me. It will na' hurt as much that way."

"Nae," she replied, but tried anyway. The act of lifting anything was making everything worse.

"Then, hold to me. Stay with me, love."

"Where else . . . am I going to go?" she asked.

The grunt of amusement went directly through him and from there, into her. Lisle held onto the shock of how that felt, and then he was moving again.

Torrents of rain felt like they were lashing her, stealing her breath and making her struggle for each one. Then, it was fire doing the same thing. Flames licked at her ankles, her legs, her thighs, her core. . . .

Then it really was clouds, and they were thick and full of destructive force, and always there was Langston . . . moving, thrusting, pushing; willing himself into her. He was making certain she knew she'd never, ever be free. And there was lightning, sparking so swiftly into her she had trouble gathering her breath, and then she had to struggle for the next one, and the next, and hold to the man who was keeping the drumbeat of rhythm thumping in her ears, in her eyes, and in her very soul.

Langston cried aloud, almost like a man in torment, and then he was shuddering and shaking and quivering, and sounding very much like he was crying. Lisle held onto him, as he dropped onto her, then rolled to one side, so he could tumble off the cushion, the momentum taking her with him. While it was a soft landing atop him, in the depths of the coach where their feet should be, she didn't think he had the same luxury, since his head hit something, and then his heels hit on the other side.

"Oh. Dearest. Sweet. Heaven," he said finally, each word making her rise and fall with how he used a full breath for it.

"Is it this way every time?" Lisle asked, although the words were slurred, since she had her lips against his throat.

"What way?" he asked.

"Are you denying it?"

He must have known she was about to lift her head in order to see him while he spoke, because a hand immediately cupped her head, keeping her right where she was, atop him.

"I'm denying nothing. I merely ask what you mean."

"When you're in love . . . is it different?"

"Who said anything about love?" he asked.

Lisle gasped. He felt it. He couldn't help but feel it. "You did," she replied finally.

"I did?" He really was as surprised as it sounded, unless he'd found a way to control his own heartbeat. It wasn't in any rhythm. It was in a distinct pounding that had quickened, stopped for a beat, and then restarted.

"Aye." Lisle moved her free hand, rubbing it along his side, and wiping at what had to be sweat as she went. Then, she moved her hand back down, then back up, feeling every ridge and bump and muscle as she went.

"Are you trying to start something again?" he asked.

"Is it working?" she replied.

He sighed, and she rose and fell with it. "Better than you think."

"Oh good. I think you'll have to give this hand to me, Langston, my dear. I definitely know what wanton is, and I know how to use it."

He sucked in breath on that one and held it, keeping her

nearly level with the bottom of their satin seats, before he exhaled.

"I am defeated, Mistress Monteith. I shall have to forfeit. I hope you'll accept it with the proper gallantry."

"I know," she said. She slid her hand back down him.

"Knowledge is very dangerous."

"I know."

"I want to trust you. You have nae idea how much I want to."

"I know," she said, yet again, using a soothing voice, as well as another stroke along his side. He had very interesting ridges and bumps all along him, especially when she got near his hips and ran a hand along his upper thigh. That had muscles bunching beneath her fingertips that were definitely interesting.

"Lives are at stake here."

"I know that as well," she replied, and started the return journey up his side, around the line of muscle at his waist, over his ribs, along ridges of sinew . . . his upper arms . . .

"And we still have to get to our chambers."

Her hand stopped.

Chapter Twenty-One

Langston donned the Monteith chieftain attire, according it the reverence it deserved from over four centuries of pride, pain, glory, and bloodlust. He'd worn it before, but it had never felt so poignant. He looked up once, checking the connecting door, through where the woman who held his heart lay, and touched his fingers to his lips before releasing them toward her. She had turned into the woman every man lusts after and seeks—a woman of fire in his bed, with only the slightest hint of it everywhere else. He wasn't ever going to bargain for anything she wanted.

He was terrified that she would want her freedom.

He knew she still slept, because he'd been at her side watching her. Now, it was deep into the night. Time to let the Mac-Donalds know they'd found the clan they'd sought, and they could start acting like the men they were, rather than the animals they had become. He slipped the sett across one shoulder, strapped it beneath the silver-and-gold-embossed belt, and pulled until it slapped against the backs of his calves where it was supposed to. Then, he was donning the band covered in medals, the garter that belonged to one of his ancestors as a Knight Templar in the Crusades, the silver-embossed sporran, and the row of skeans that swung from a cord at his hip.

Last of all, he put the tam atop his head, slipped his broadsword into the scabbard at his side, and opened the door to be met by fifty men of his clan, all honored to be at the laird's side.

They moved soundlessly, as they'd been doing for almost a year now, down the steps and then into the door beneath the hall, and he didn't allow the pipes and drums to start until they were at the bottom of the dungeons, lighting torches as they went.

MacDonalds were getting to their feet, rustling the straw he'd given them to camp on, and they were pressing their faces to the bars of the prisons, staring. Then, one of them sent a dirk right into Langston's chest, where by luck of his ancestry, a medal sent it astray and into the flesh of his upper chest, instead of his heart.

Langston didn't even break stride, although he could feel the heat scoring his shoulder and instantly numbing his left arm. He didn't even look down. The drums and pipes halted and he waited until the echo of them died away before speaking.

"They tell me you are MacDonald clansmen!" he shouted. "You doona' look like MacDonald clansmen to me!"

The answer was garbled from more than one throat. Langston stepped forward, narrowed his eyes, and glared at each in turn. "I came for MacDonald clansmen! And I doona' like to repeat myself . . . are you the MacDonald I seek?"

This time there was a chorus of noise, and it grew until he stepped back, with a satisfied nod.

"That is very good. For you see before you what you seek. You see the clan you'll join, the one you'll live, and the colors you'll wear!"

"Monteith?" one of them said derisively.

"There is nae clan better," Langston replied loudly.

"The traitor?" someone yelled.

"Who better?" he yelled right back, his voice hollow-sounding in the stone and damp and decay of centuries. "Who better to make certain the ship got Prince Charles Stuart from this country? Who better to supply the gold that keeps him alive and ready for us in France? Who better to supply an army of clansmen with cannon and arms and horses, and everything else needed to get our country back? And who better to keep the cursed Sassenach from ever . . . *ever* . . . thinking different?"

He waited until the echo of his words died away.

"I say again—see before you the Clan Monteith!"

There was a sound rising, glancing off the stone and reaching the span of beams at the ceiling before falling back down. It was almost a cheer, from throats too parched and weak to make one. Langston waited for it to settle about him. His arm was turning into a throb of ache, and he suspected the damp feeling beneath the large sleeve of his shirt was his own blood, but he reached across his body to pull his broadsword and lift it with that arm anyway.

"The Monteith Clan now opens its arms for MacDonald! I need men. I need strong-willed men, with aims straight and true, and hearts pumping out red-hued Scot's blood. And I need them now! Now! Are you these men?" He was yelling it until the cords of his throat felt like they'd burst.

Their answer wasn't distinguishable as an aye or a nae, but was loud enough to make the rafters tremble above them. Langston slowly lowered his sword.

"Then take that MacDonald sett from your bodies. Cut a piece for remembrance, and know that when this is finished, they'll be more setts crafted, and more clans created. And get these auld plaides ready for the Sassenach bastards that I have stolen from beneath Captain Barton's stiff English nose, to replace your sorry arses!"

There was chatter and a bit of grumbling and laughter at that.

"And then don the Monteith green and gold. Etheridge?" Langston stepped aside, slid his sword back into its scabbard with a hand that trembled visibly if anyone chanced to look that way, and motioned his men forward with his right arm.

The iron gate was unbarred, plaides were divvied out, and there were flashes of bare skin amid clanging of belts, arm-bands, and weapons.

"You'll each be given a knight portion. You'll be fed—well fed. As much as you can hold and still keep up your regimen. You'll each be given the weapons to train with. If you have a skill, speak up! We need blacksmiths. We need archers. We need marksmen. We need cannoneers. We train. Hard. With an exact perfection they canna' match! Daily. And then we hide. We have a strict regimen. The man who does na' follow it dies. By the hand of the clansman at his side. Without jury, without trial. You ken all of this?"

There were murmurs of assent. Langston stepped back far-ther, keeping his left side in the shadows to the fullest extent possible. No clan army would follow a leader that wasn't strong, fit, had stamina, and was healthy. That was the busi-ness he was in. It had been since he was too young to think differently.

He turned away, and had men at his heels as he left the dun-geons. He still had to select fifty of his best Arabian stallions to send over to MacCullough Castle, and he had to find the other eighteen volunteers to go into service to Barton. That had to be a man's greatest nightmare, serving the enemy, wearing his colors, and acting like it was a normal state of af-fairs. He didn't envy them . . . except for the one thing he had left to do after all the other things were seen to. The thing that was making the knife wound feel like a scratch.

He had to say good-bye to Saladin.

Lisle rolled over, flung her arm over the lump that was Monteith, and squeezed until feathers puffed out. Her nose twitched. Her eyes opened and she sneezed. She lifted her head and then she narrowed her eyes. It wasn't Langston. It should have been. He'd carried her, wrapped in the remnants of her wire-enhanced petticoat, that beautiful ballgown, and covered over with a Monteith green and gold cloak, up the steps and set her in this bed with a reverence that was akin to awe.

She lay back and stretched, and there wasn't any tight bodice restricting that movement. Lisle gasped and lifted the covers and gasped again. She hadn't been dreaming. Monteith had slept beside her, just as she'd dreamt. The entire episode felt that way. Her body told her it was no dream, the destroyed ballgown that she was still semiwearing told her it was no dream, but the man she'd given herself to in the white, satin-lined coach had been a dream of a man.

She slid out of the sheets and snuck over to the connecting door. She wanted to see him, just to reassure her. He was no dream. He was the most handsome man birthed. He was very stirring and rousing and passionate and all those other illicit things she'd whispered of. He was also hers.

He wasn't snoring. That must happen only when he was severely exhausted. Lisle lifted onto her tiptoes to look. His bed was empty. The entire chamber reeked of emptiness, and she spun in place. He hadn't stayed? After what had happened, he'd been out marching, or practicing with that claymore, or deciding on yet another torment for his prisoners?

She was rushing to find a serviceable gown, or at least one that she could fasten by herself, and pulled a dark blue daygown from the dressing room that had more than fifteen gowns already hanging in it. Although it was costly, it would get her about the rafters without too much trouble.

She just had to get out of the room before Mary MacGreggor came looking for her, and from the amount of light entering the chamber through those diamond-paned windows and the small slits above, it was almost time for Mary MacGreggor and the bath that was designed to sap her energy, take her will, and make her groggy with nothing better to do than look about her and continue breathing.

She shoved her feet into shoes, ignoring socks. She was buttoning the front of her gown as she ran. She didn't bother checking her door. She knew it would be locked. She went through the connecting door, locking it behind her and tossing the key high up on one of his armoires before she realized how self-destructive that was. It was too late to wish it undone. The sun was licking across the floor in front of her, warming everywhere it touched, and if she didn't hurry, she was going to have to use his fireplace for beam access, rather than the staircase right outside his door.

Lisle slid through to his antechamber, caught a glimpse of herself in the mirror, and groaned. Then she was taking out what pins were left as she walked until she had a handful of them and nowhere to put them. There wasn't anyone in the hall, although she could hear voices below from Mabel Beamans's crew of housemaids, and the smell of breakfast meats was wafting through from the kitchens. Lisle didn't know the first place to look, and had to duck into a hallway as a grouping of seamstresses passed by. The maze of halls was still an impossibility to learn, and then luck had her spotting Langston in a passing window, racing his black stallion across the lawn, before they were both disappearing just outside of her range of view.

Lisle pressed her nose to glass that hadn't one disguising diamond cut into it, and fogged her own view. She still couldn't see him. She made up her mind. She was marching to the stables. She was going to tell anyone stupid enough to get in her way that she was the lady of the house, and she was doing inspections of some kind, and they had better not try to stop her.

No one stopped her. It wasn't that she was brave enough to test her plan. It was because she didn't give them a chance. If she heard anyone, she ducked into a room and waited until they passed. It took so long, she was hopelessly lost amid yet another series of halls before she found her egress. It was a set of large, French-inspired doors opening onto a vista of garden that would shame many a landlord. Lisle stepped down the rounded series of steps that zigzagged their way into the blooms and shrubs and trees and benches that had to make up the castle gardens.

At least she was outside. That was part of her agenda, although she didn't know in which direction the stables lay, or even if she would have to swim the loch before she reached it. Lisle giggled. The dew was wetting the bottom of her skirt, hampering her movements as it slapped against her ankles, and she told herself that Mary MacGreggor was probably into her smelling salts right about this time due to her mistress's absence.

The garden ended at more of the yellow-cast wall, and she raced along it until it ended in another abutment. The one contained the same three hundred or so long, low steps. It wasn't empty, however. There were men on horseback from a point halfway up the wall, and farther along it as well.

Lisle ducked back around the wall, going into a small ball while she waited for her heart to continue to support her life and not thud its way right out of her chest with the surprise. He'd crafted those long steps for horses to traverse. It was so simple, she felt stupid for not realizing it before. Such a stairway was also necessary for moving cannon up it, and whatever else he had a use for up on the walls.

Lisle caught her breath, stood, and walked in a crouched-over hunch of a walk, back the way she'd come. The gardens might have another exit. She'd look for that. If she didn't hurry, she'd probably miss Langston entirely, and then she really would feel like a complete fool for not having the smarts to climb up onto a window ledge in his room and simply wait for his reappearance.

The gardens had another exit, but to find it she had to follow two meandering pathways through groves of trees and gardenias and roses, and all sorts of ferns and bushes and shrubs that she didn't know existed. Her hands were trembling, her lungs were burning, and her belly wasn't too fond of her either as she pushed, with too much emphasis, on a wooden door. Since it was as oiled and well maintained as everything else at Monteith Castle, it swung open swiftly and rapidly. Lisle fell headlong into the stableyard.

Her abrupt entry into the muddy enclosure went unnoticed, but not due to anything other than the melee of horses all getting saddled and groomed, and pawing restlessly while an army of groomsmen worked on them. There was also the fact that she'd chosen a dark blue dress, she was now coated with mud, and there wasn't any activity happening at the side where she'd entered. There was also the bit of luck that there was a bench right next to her that she crawled beneath the moment she had her breath back.

From that vantage point, it was impossible to pick out Langston. It was impossible to do more than watch horse legs, trouser-clad legs, and at the far end what looked to be three black coaches. There was a loud whistle given. That must have meant to mount up, because they were forming columns and riding out, emptying the yard within moments, without one word spoken between any of them.

That was exactly what she would have expected of a well-trained army that was sending horses over to Captain Barton. Lisle watched and listened, and beyond the sounds of hooves and coach wheels turning, there wasn't any other sound. There was silence.

And then there was the sound of sobbing.

Lisle crawled from beneath the bench and went to the same hunched-over walk as she circled the stableyard, keeping to the wall and using what trees there were for covering. Her dress was beyond repair. She'd never be able to explain it. The seamstresses would probably be in fits of gossipy whispers over the extent of damage done to her ballgown anyway. First, her clothing was ripped off of her, and now she was plowing through stable mud with this one.

They probably should use less costly materials.

Monteith's stables were dank, and dark, and smelled of

musk and horseflesh and a thousand other interesting things that she didn't know enough about to name. The heart-rending sound of loss pulled at her, drawing her past row upon row of stalls, some vacant, some holding one horse, until there was only one left. Lisle approached it with a stealth she didn't know she possessed.

The sound of sobs had since ended, although there were still rustling noises coming from the stall that had to have held a very special horse. Lisle couldn't read the strange symbol that was etched into the nameplate on the door. She dropped to her knees to peek through the bottom bar, and then she was peering in and shoving her own hand into her mouth to stop the cry.

Langston was hunched into a ball of misery about a saddle that she instinctively knew belonged to the stallion Saladin, and he was covered in muck, and blood, and turf. He was rocking in a version of abject misery that made her own eyes fill until she couldn't see through the blur of moisture. This was the hidden Langston no one ever got to see. This was the man who'd been hated by his own father to the extent he'd been tossed out. This was the man who was trying to build a future for his country, and having to fight the very people he was working for. Here was the man who was vilified, hated, and detested by foe and friend alike, and here was the man who had just given away something he loved very much . . . because he had to.

Lisle crawled backward, disturbing the straw enough that he lifted his head and looked her way. She prayed for the cover of obscurity in the black ranks of the stable floor as she had never winged a prayer before, and it must have been heard, because Langston bowed his head and turned back to the saddle. His shoulders started heaving again with misery and loss and pain.

Lisle clapped a hand to her mouth, scuttled as far away from him as she could before she dared risk it, and then started running.

God was with her the entire flight. He gave her feet wings, and her body stealth, and her mind direction. She was on her knees thanking Him the moment she reached her unlocked chamber and stumbled over to the bed. Langston wasn't ever going to hear of this from her. No one was . . . ever.

She was still on her knees when Mary MacGreggor came back, clucking her tongue over Lisle's attire, and her ball-gown, and then she was ordering another bath and making everyone else leave. There wasn't a hint of salts poured into this water to send any fragrance into the air, or make the water silken-smooth to the touch.

It wouldn't have changed anything. It was still flavored with tears.

Chapter Twenty-Two

She was on the wrong beam.

Lisle looked over her head at the proof and groaned the frustration aloud. Since she was in the castle's chapel, and almost directly over the center, the sound seemed to search out every corner of the room far below before it came thundering back. She laid her head down on the beam she would be straddling if it were small enough, and waited for the sound to dim. She'd been so sure! After what seemed like hours of inching along this one, it was all for nothing. It looked to be much higher once she'd crossed over the wooden entry doors, too. Her question was answered for her, also. The wooden doors were thick enough that any perpetrator would need a battering ram to get through them.

It had taken some time to clear the doors, and her nerve had almost completely deserted her then. It seemed so much higher than the starting point she'd taken, which had been a large step up from the top shelf of what was probably the castle's library.

Mabel Beamans wasn't going to have to worry about dust on this great piece of wood. Lisle had taken care to get a light blue daygown this time, and a petticoat, both of which were looped through the ties at her waist, making a balloon affair.

That bunching of skirts, her woolen socks, and her pantaloons were doing a very good job of dusting the entire beam, especially since she was so afraid of moving that she'd slithered along inch by inch. It was wide enough they could probably walk two abreast along it, but she wasn't a marksman set on getting to his perch. She was a lady of a castle—one that should have better things to do than sneak across the beams into her husband's empty chamber, get lost twice trying to find the chapel, and then follow a beam backward to the starting point amid the bookshelves. And never once had she checked and looked to see her destination. If such a thing had happened, she was afraid she might look down. That was enough to make her hands wet with sweat again . . . all of which made the dust turn into grime on her palms and required wiping them on her skirt again. There was no way she was going to able to explain further clothing damage of this nature to Mary MacGreggor, and her partner the maid, Betsy.

It was a good thing Langston had hired her lady's maids that were closemouthed about such things, and didn't question shredded ballgowns, mud-streaked daydresses, and now a morning dress that would need a place in the nearest dustbin.

All of which made the frustration greater when another beam seemed to come out of nowhere and cross a good four feet over her head. Her eyes followed it again . . . right to the pipe organ.

It was a good thing she had been raised among brothers, for a more ladylike woman would have started sliding back the way she'd come. A girl who'd successfully finished the convent school wouldn't even think of getting to her feet and trying to climb even higher. Why, any one of a thousand other girls wouldn't be up on a beam so high above the floor for no reason other than there was something hidden in the chapel, and she wanted to know what it was.

Lisle took a deep breath, gathered her courage to get to her knees, and was forestalled by the sound of footsteps across the floor below her. She eased the breath out slowly, said a prayer of thankfulness that she'd been saved from her own plan, and moved her face a little closer to the edge . . . not enough for danger, but enough to see what was happening.

It was a clergyman. It was probably the largest one of them, but he looked very small from her vantage point. He was lifting the bolt by using a lever at one side, unlocking the doors, swinging one of them wide, and the entire chapel floor seemed to be filling with two lines of armed men . . . very armed men.

The other clergy fellows were standing at the massive wall organ, and as each man approached, he was taking bows, arrows, claymores and muskets, and skeans and daggers, swords, and things Lisle hadn't any experience with, and handing some over before going behind the pipe organ. Then, they'd disappear inside.

Lisle narrowed her eyes and slid a little closer to the edge, tipping her head straight so the view wouldn't be so distorted. After tens of men had gone behind the pipe organ and none had reappeared, she had to accept the obvious. It was a tunnel. It had to be.

She saw a flash of movement on the other side . . . near the statue of Mary and her child that Mary MacGreggor had told her of, what seemed like months ago. Lisle slid to the opposite side and watched as the men started coming back up, still in Highland dress, but without a sign of weaponry anywhere.

It was an arsenal! That's what he used the chapel for, and while it was sacrilegious, it was also cunning and wily and smart, and everything Langston Monteith obviously was. She'd conjured him, for the next moment she heard his name spoken, but it was coming from behind her, and that meant she had to swivel in place.

It wasn't as hazardous as she'd suspected, she wasn't going to have to risk her life getting to another beam, and she had everything she wanted.

"Prepare, lads."

Monteith's words carried up to her, and she inched her way

to the side of the beam again to see what he was doing. He was at the entry doors, he was nodding to each man who passed him by, and he wasn't looking anything like the fellow who'd been in Saladin's stables yestermorn. He looked like a full-blooded Scot, who was proud to be a Scot, and not ashamed to show it.

Lisle's smile widened. He was also her Scot . . . *hers*. The thrill that thought brought made every bit of her tingle. It also made every bit of her aware of him. She peeked over and looked at him and caught the sigh. He made an efficient guardian of the room. He was also well aware of what was happening throughout the chapel. She watched as he put his hands on his hips and looked about, almost as if he sensed something. Then he looked up, although she saw the movement coming and ducked her head out of sight while she waited for her heart to calm enough that she could hear what else was going on.

"Laird Monteith?" a voice said in a low, soft tone that carried to her perch and was such an odd thing that it caught her ear.

"Aye?"

"Green reporting in."

"Very good."

The men were leaving and Lisle let out the sigh. It was followed by the intake gasp of breath as men began filing in again, making the same strange sound of a very large, silent crowd. They weren't talking. There was just the sound of boots on stone, steel against leather, blade to scabbard. She slid close to the edge, not so much that Langston might see her if he looked up, but close enough that she could see what she suspected was happening. The chapel was filling with a double column of men again. The same kilts, the same amount of arms, the same purpose of movement.

At least they had that much freedom. She wasn't going anywhere . . . and she'd done such a thing to herself! She watched until they were filing out, counted to a hundred, another hundred.

It was stupid to count; she didn't have a starting point, and they all looked alike, except for the colors of their hair, and the occasional balding head tossed in. She yawned.

"Laird Monteith?" a voice said again in the same soft, low tone.

"Aye?"

"Yellow reporting in."

"Very good."

Lisle watched him nod. The men filed out. There was a moment of silence from the almost empty aisles. Then another stream of men filled the gap . . . then another: red, blue, black, orange, white, brown, and purple. After that, they started on jewel tones. Her eyes were wide on the ninth or tenth company of men, and she was growing more and more astonished as the morning progressed, and her belly grumbled with hunger, and there was nothing to do for it but stay where she was and try to keep her mind on how many companies of men he had. Hundreds? Thousands? Tens of thousands?

It was incredible. It was impossible. It was unbelievable. Captain Barton would have fallen off his new stallion if he knew. Ruby, emerald, sapphire. . . . When they listed pearl, Lisle had to catch the giggle. The men in that company must have done something to deserve such a moniker.

The sun rose higher, sending the colors of the stained glass window across the floor and to the pews, and still there were men milling about, in the same silence, giving the same salute to Langston, receiving the same response in reply. They were probably receiving breakfast, too, she told herself. They'd be sitting down to a feast of rolls and meats, some cooked, some chilled, some in gravy, some sliced, and Lisle had her belly growling again with her own salivating thoughts.

Mary MacGreggor had been right that first morning. They didn't have any food that went to waste. It probably took another fortune to feed them, and she wondered again just how much gold Monteith had, and if it really was earned in the fashion he'd told the captain, and then a shiver of dread crossed over her spine, pressing her into the wood with the force of it.

She knew what he was doing.

He was planning on waging war with England again! The same war they'd lost, Monteith was trying to change. He was trying to buy a win. It wasn't possible. Such a thing took The Stuart, and rumor had it Bonnie Prince Charlie was on the continent, living a life of luxury in Germany, or Austria, or France, or any number of places that didn't resemble Scotland.

She had to stop her husband, but her attempt at negotiating for his prisoners had gone so far astray, it hadn't been Langston that should have declared himself the loser. It was her, and that beautiful ballgown. Lisle felt the blush, lying flat on a beam stories above the chapel floor which kept filling with men and emptying of them, until there couldn't possibly be any room beneath the castle for more armament. And more just kept coming.

Monteith was insane. He was going to ruin everything he'd worked for. He was going to reap the same punishment, and all these men were going to be the same as those at Culloden . . . dead and rotting beneath the sod. All of them. The dread was like a blanket, holding her down, punishing her with the future, frightening her more than a walk across any number of beams, and still men kept coming in.

She was going to be up there forever. She was going to fall asleep and roll and then she was going to fall off, and they'd find her body on the chapel floor, with her petticoat and skirts in a bundle of material about her waist and covered in dust. Worse . . . she was going to be found years from now, her skeleton still clinging to the beams, dead of starvation. She told her own mind to hush, but there wasn't anything else to pass the time except the litany of troops filing in, disarming, filing back out. She was being ridiculous. She knew she was, but it didn't help. She could curse her imagination. That never helped, either. She could curse Langston. He should be hungry by now. He should be exhausted again. He'd stayed out almost all night again. He'd been standing and accepting their honor and recognition for hours. She'd been in the same position for hours. Her legs were cramped. Her belly was cramped. Her mind was cramped.

She peered over the edge again. The splash of color from the stained glass window had barely moved. Such a thing wasn't possible. Time was passing with a slowness she hadn't felt since she'd been sent to the Mother Superior's office and made to sit in the corner, fingering her rosary and saying her prayers, all of which had happened too often to recall the times individually.

The names changed after ruby. They started on the elements: storm, blizzom—for the winter holocaust, fury, and rain. Lisle's lips twitched. Rain? That wasn't very original.

It didn't occur to her that the process of disarmament was complete until a span had passed with no new names said and no words of "very good" by Monteith, either. Lisle tilted her head back upright so she could look down. There was only Langston left. There wasn't even a clergyman with him.

Of course there wasn't a clergy fellow available to assist anyone. They weren't going to be able to do a proper sermon, either. They were probably going to be busy for the next fortnight trying to get all that weaponry put back away, Lisle thought, and then everything went still as Langston looked up toward the organ, and grimaced a bit as he moved his left arm.

And then he whispered her name.

"Well! You are one for scrapes and such, aren't you, my lady?"

Lisle took back everything she'd thought about Mary Mac-Greggor being even remotely closemouthed. The woman hadn't stopped, except for breath, ever since Lisle had come running up the stairs and been caught even before she got to her door. There was no way to explain attire such as hers, nor how it got there, so she didn't try. She let Mary come up with the explanations, and left it to Betsy to either agree or disagree.

She almost choked with laughter when Mary came up with digging a tunnel with which to find her own gold, and why Laird Monteith's wasn't good enough for her. Betsy nodded to that, like it made sense. Lisle didn't say anything. Her mind was elsewhere. She had to shove as much food in her as she could fit, since it was almost noon by the time she gained her chamber; she had to get a bath, luxuriate in any fragrance and oil they brought, except one with opiate; and she had to decide which of her various nightgowns and chemises were going to be enough to get him to negotiate.

He'd gained so much! To toss it away was the height of idiocy. She had to save him from ruin. She had to save everyone who relied on him from ruin. She had to do whatever it took to get him to bargain for dropping his plans. She only hoped he'd stay true to his word once he gave it.

He was going to give it, all right. She was doing everything in her power to get him to. He wasn't going to get Lisle Monteith into his bed without negotiating first, and striking a bargain second, and she prayed for the fortitude to make certain he didn't.

And he'd almost caught her, too! That part was the most frightening. After whispering her name, he started looking along the pipe organ and to the wrong beam, all of which gave Lisle time to roll onto her side, making the smallest image possible, and try to keep her own breathing from giving her away. She'd had to resort to breathing out her mouth, shoving the breath through a ring of space with her lips to mute it, and then suck in another one. Anything else would have been too loud. Her heartbeat certainly was. Then, she heard him sigh, call himself a fool, and walk out. *He was the fool?* she wondered. At least he got to eat breakfast. She got to wait for the trembling to die down enough she could inch her way back to the library, and hope the entire time that the army of men hadn't eaten everything involved with breakfast before she got there.

Then, Angus MacHugh arrived.

The morning stalled when they announced that the Laird MacHugh was awaiting her below. Monteith could have spoken to him, but he'd disappeared—along with thousands of other fellows—and Lisle had to rush through the rest of her toiletry to see to Angus. Mary wouldn't let her out without her hair properly braided and everything perfectly in place, making it feel like another hour had passed. Lisle ground the frustration with her teeth. If she said anything, they'd double their efforts to delay her, and Angus was probably getting more and more angered at being kept waiting by what was, in essence, a Monteith.

Angus wasn't angered. He was fidgeting and going from foot to foot and he wasn't looking up at anything or anyone when she entered the salon. Any other visitor would have chanced to look up at where furniture still dangled haphazardly, although it didn't appear as cramped as before. Lisle frowned for a moment as she wondered what Langston was doing with the tables, chairs, bedsteads, and other items. He wouldn't be paying good gold to dismantle them as firewood, would he?

Surely he wasn't that wasteful . . . was he?

Angus had a dejected air about him that went straight to Lisle's heart, like a skean-thrust. She had to suck in the gasp so he wouldn't hear it, instinctively knowing what he'd think if he did. Angus MacHugh looked like a shadow of himself; a saddened, wizened, diminished shadow. Lisle swallowed. It didn't work. Her eyes still filled with tears.

"Angus?" she asked.

He looked up at her, and the red-rimmed eyes told their own story, as did the ashen color of his skin and the tremble of his lips.

"What's happened to you?" she asked.

"'Tis very good whiskey that gold buys, lassie. Very good."

"You're drinking?"

"It takes the sharpness from women's tongues away," he answered. "Makes other things . . . nice, too."

"Oh, Angus. I'm so sorry," Lisle said.

"Now, lassie—" he began.

The door swung open with such force it slammed against the wall support at its side, and Langston strode in, dressed in full Highland attire, covered in a sheen of sweat and grime, dripping blood down his left arm, and there was a very large claymore pointing straight at Angus. There wasn't a hint of tremble anywhere along him. There were two other green-and-gold-plaide-wearing Highlanders with him, equally attired, and equally frightening.

Langston took in the man standing in front of him, and his broadsword dipped until it touched the stone floor with a thud of noise. It was followed by the other two. He turned his head and glared at her for a moment before turning what was probably the same look at Angus.

"They told me a MacHugh was here!" Langston thundered.

"Aye," Angus whispered.

"This is na' the MacHugh I requested!" Langston replied.

"I am Angus MacHugh."

"You canna' be. Angus MacHugh is a man!"

Lisle couldn't defend him. She was in shock. Her entire body seemed filled with water colder than a loch-emptying burn, and there wasn't anything on her that could move . . . except her eyes. They were wide and watched as Angus actually straightened, and then his eyes narrowed, and he gave Langston back a look that was probably as good as the one he was getting.

"I am Angus MacHugh, you black bastard!"

Monteith handed the sword to one of his men and then crossed his arms.

"You the MacHugh that plays the pipes?" he asked, still in the aggressive tone he'd been using since he first strode into the room.

"Aye."

"You any good?"

"Angus MacHugh is one of the best, Monteith. Always was."

"Good. You make pipes, then?"

"None said anything about making pipes."

"The best pipers always make their own bagpipes. I ask again. You make pipes?"

"I've been known to craft a set or two," Angus replied, and there wasn't a hint of a warble to his voice or his frame.

"Good. Craft me a set or two. Fifty gold pieces per set."

"Fifty?" Angus asked, and his eyes were wide.

"You having trouble hearing, auld man?" Langston replied.

Angus's expression changed to a sneer. "You're mad. Any man can buy a set of bagpipes for shillings. Less. 'Tis a bane of this Sassenach law. Pipes are so much baggage, anymore. Nae pipes can be played, and owning pipes can get a man imprisoned. They certainly canna' feed a family. Pipes sell for a pittance, and you want them made for a fortune."

"Let me tell you a little secret, MacHugh. I am a black bastard, and I am mad. I'm also a devil when it comes to getting my way. I always get it. Always. I put my Monteith mark on pipes, they'll be the best money can buy, or I'll na' do it. I craft pipes, I expect the best. I expect the best pipers to make them. I expect to pay for the best. I ask again, and I pay fifty gold pieces per set."

"Very well," Angus replied. "You've got your set or two."

"Good. Now, see to cleaning the whiskey drunk smell from yourself. I doona' allow a man of mine to smell."

"You black—!"

"We already went through the names, MacHugh. I'm na' interested in what you call me. I'm only interested in your skills."

"You show nae respect for your elders," Angus replied. He sounded like he was in the same shock Lisle still was.

"You want respect from me, auld man? Earn it."

Angus sucked in the reaction. He went straighter still.

"Good. We see eye to eye, finally. I hire a man, I expect to get a man," Langston said, loudly.

"I'll na' work for you," Angus replied.

"Oh. You're going to do more than work for me. You're going to wash that smell from yourself; you're going to get a healthy meal, and a clean place of your own. You're going to doff that Sassenach attire and get good Monteith plaide on. You're going to craft me some pipes, and you're going to make certain they're good, because you're going to test each and every one of them with a good, solid, lung full of air. You're going to get some self-respect back. That's what you're going to do. Were you na' at Culloden?"

"Doona' let the name cross your black lips!"

"You were, weren't you?"

"Aye!" Angus was yelling, bulging the cords out of his neck.

"Good! I expect my men clean. I expect my men sober. I expect my men prompt. I request a man, I expect him to report immediately, na' the next day, wandering into my house, soused in whiskey!"

"Why—you young braggart!"

Angus was still yelling. They were both yelling. Lisle looked from one to the other. Angus no longer looked like he needed a champion, or anything other than his own claymore, so he could challenge the other.

"I expect my men to act like a man, and na' a sniveling lad. I'll ask it one more time—and I would na' waste words with me further, if I were you. Were you at Culloden?"

"Aye!" Angus replied.

"And were you injured?"

"I took a cleaving or two."

Langston absorbed that information. Then, he strode across the floor to stand directly in front of Angus.

"Allow me to shake your hand, MacHugh." He said it quietly, with a reverence better suited to the chapel. Then, he put his hand out and waited.

Angus eyed him a bit. Then he put his own hand out.

"Welcome back to the Highlands," Langston said. "Etheridge? See that he's put with the others. Get him a horse. Fit him."

Angus's look was priceless at that information. His mouth had dropped open. Then he was following one of them, who didn't resemble the man who was Langston's personal valet at all, out the door.

Langston turned to her and shook his head. "I was just in time," he said softly.

"You yelled at him."

"I had to. You were doing worse."

"I was na'!"

"You doona' understand. You canna' coddle an auld warrior, Lisle. You'll ruin him."

"I was na' coddling him . . . much," she replied.

He sighed, and lifted his left shoulder with a grimace. "Come. 'Tis time for my own bath. I believe you owe me one of those."

Lisle's eyes were huge. She was very afraid her mouth made the same motion. "'Tis midday," she replied finally.

He grinned, bringing those laugh lines into play about his eyes. A thunderbolt struck her in place, and Lisle felt the reaction clear to her toes.

"Aye. So 'tis." He was striding toward her and wrapping his right arm about her, and pulling her close to the healthy, sweaty, raw smell of him. "Saves a bit on torchlight this way," he whispered. "And you ken how I feel about such waste."

"Langston—"

"Save it for the chamber, sweet."

The endearment twisted her tongue into knots, and then he made it worse when he dropped a kiss to her temple.

Chapter Twenty-Three

Invisible hands had been at work on Monteith's chamber.

Lisle looked about and kept the intake of air to herself. There was a larger tub than she'd ever seen beside his armoire, catching the afternoon light; there was a feast of so many various dishes her eyes couldn't absorb them all, on three of his four tables; and there was a strange hip-high iron object between the chairs fronting his unlit fireplace. Lisle focused on the iron thing. It had one thin, iron leg atop a footing of four decorated ones. Toward the top was a sheltered area where she could see a small flame flickering through the amber-colored glass, and above that was a bowl shape, full of glowing coals.

"A brazier," Langston said at her side before she had a chance to ask.

"What's it for?"

"Cooking things."

"You've a stone-weight of foods lying about, Monteith. There is nae need for cooking that I can tell."

He smiled down at her. "I brought them from Persia. The desert. There is so much sand and heat and sun, it hurts the eye to contemplate it all. Everything is already roasting in the heat, making fire a useless thing to pursue, as well as nearly impossible to make. Nae wood about, unless you carry it with you."

"So, why make a fire?"

His smile widened. "To cook. 'Tis also useful for heating things."

"Things?" Those ale-colored eyes were doing strange things to her heart, making it skip a beat, pump mightily, skip another. Lisle swallowed to keep it to herself, but she couldn't look away.

"Things like incense, coffee . . . skeans."

Lisle's eyes widened, and her heart decided to pump itself into the area just below her throat, making it difficult to breathe and impossible to swallow. *Skeans?* she wondered. "What are you planning on using it for?" she asked, with a voice that was almost nonexistent.

He didn't answer, but he released her gaze to look down at himself. Lisle also watched as he pulled a long, wide blade from his belt and twirled it, catching the light.

"Skeans," he replied finally.

She gasped. He ignored it to walk over to the brazier and stir the coals a bit before settling his knife underneath them. Then, he reached to start pulling more knives from his belt, dumping them on the chair seat in front of him, and always using his right hand to do so. When he came across another wide, flat blade, he put it in the coals, too.

Lisle watched, mentally storing the information of where not to sit, in the event she got to do so, since he'd had close to twenty blades tucked into his belt. She didn't know how many for certain. She hadn't been counting until he already had them jumping about on the padded seat. She was trying to keep the same fear that was clogging her throat from transferring to the rest of her. It was a forlorn idea. Her back was already tight with dread, and her palms clammy with moisture.

He was heating blades . . . and such a thing was used to brand things like sheep. Sheep were branded. Wives weren't branded . . . were they? He wouldn't dare! She'd fight him! She didn't fight well, though. She was worse than clay in his hands. Despite her imagination and the cold water that felt like it was filling her veins, replacing the blood that should be there, Lisle colored. She didn't fight him well, at all.

She should have kept to herself. She knew, without asking, that he knew she'd been in the chapel this morning. She knew his plot. She was going to be punished. Or . . . she shouldn't have spoken to Angus. She should have stayed out of it. She should have stayed in ignorance. She should have stayed in her room, and never snuck about his castle.

Langston looked her way and frowned slightly. "Something bother you, sweet?" he asked.

You. She answered it in her mind. *And what you're going to do.* She shook her head. Her tongue wasn't working for anything other than adding to her misery by giving her a mouthful of spittle she couldn't force her throat to swallow.

His lips twitched, and then he was raising his hand to push the kilt band that was across his left shoulder away, revealing a lot of blood on his shirt. He was cursing, too, softly and viciously. The chest band of his sett dropped to his side, held in place by his belt, and then it wasn't held at all, as he unclasped the belt and let it fall to the floor with a thud of sound. He didn't help the plaide fall off. He didn't need to. Lisle watched as green and gold material unwound itself from his frame and joined the belt at his ankles.

Lisle already had both hands to her mouth. It was to stop the sound at seeing him, and then it was to stop the disappointment. He was wearing a shirt of broadcloth and the ends of it curved to midthigh. He had wonderful, full-muscled thighs, she noted, and they were especially visual as he stepped from the pile of clothing he'd just made. He glanced her way and stalled for a moment, in perfect statue form. It had to be obvious what was on her face, because his lips went into a smile he was trying not to make and he looked away, while two spots of color touched the tops of his cheeks.

Lisle made a strangled noise and turned her back on him. It helped control the burn of her blush and confuse it with anger. He had no right to be so beautiful! None. No man should be as gifted. The black hair was striking enough, especially with the way he kept his jaw clean-shaven of any beard. The ale color of his eyes was another striking feature, as was such handsomeness that women had probably swooned over it well before she almost did. There was no excuse for adding to his handsomeness by creating such a muscled physique. That was totally unfair! And it was unfair of him to show it so easily to any woman . . . even if she was his wife and watching him with such speechless admiration on her entire frame that he flushed over it!

She heard material ripping and her back clenched. She heard the swish of cloth as it moved, followed by the sound of his movement. Her shoulders and neck joined the fray with her back, stiffening before he could reach her. She knew he was coming. Then, she heard the sound of rocks moving, followed by a hissing noise that was immediately pursued by a sharp intake of breath, one that came with his groan attached. Lisle glanced over her shoulder. He was sitting in the chair he hadn't peppered with weapons, and he was branding himself!

She wasn't far away, but the walk took forever. Then, she was at his side and on her knees, her eyes filling with tears as he held the blade to his shoulder. He had unbuttoned his shirt to his waist and peeled it off his left shoulder, proving where the ripping noise had come from since he'd torn the material in the process, and also showing why there was so much blood, and it just kept trickling out as she watched.

"Oh, Lang . . . ston," she said, splitting his name into two syllables with a sobbing sound between them.

"Lisle," he said finally, in a gruff tone.

"Aye?" she asked, lifting her eyes to his.

"You canna' coddle a young warrior, either," he told her. He was moving the cooled blade away and dropping it, where it fell soundlessly to the pile he'd already made. He didn't move his gaze from hers as he did it.

Then he narrowed his eyes, blackening them and shutting her out. Such a thing had her moving her hands, clasping them together, and then plunging them against her breast where her own flesh moved to allow them the space. It didn't help. Everything was hurting, and it was emanating from the spot her hands were pushing into.

Langston grabbed up another blade and held it against his shoulder, tensing everything along his entire frame to absorb what had to be agony. He didn't make a sound this time. The tears slid from her eyes, coated her cheeks, and dropped from there to the ball of her conjoined hands.

He dropped the other skean, let go of the tenseness, and allowed himself to fall back against the chair. He didn't say a thing. He had his eyes closed, his lips pursed as he breathed shallowly, and there was more than one line creasing his forehead.

Lisle dropped her view to his wound. It was black and red and angry-looking, with a line of white flesh encircling it. There wasn't a sign of fresh bleeding.

"You're hurt," Lisle said.

"'Tis but a scratch," he answered the air, since he hadn't opened his eyes and would have been looking more toward the beams above them than anywhere else.

"What happened?" she asked.

"I got careless."

"You fight your own men? Must you be so stupid?"

A smile touched his lips, moving them out of the kissable look he held them in. "Nae, and nae," he replied.

"I doona' ken you," Lisle said to that.

"I'm na' fighting my own men . . . or at least, they weren't at the time, and nae, I am na' that stupid."

"You go about with an untended wound, acting like 'tis naught, and call yourself smart?" she asked.

It was definitely a smile. Lisle watched as his lips curved, then went back to a pout.

"I did have it tended when it happened . . . well, shortly after, anyway. And I had excellent care. I pay the best surgeons, you know."

"Then why is it you have to tend it yourself now?"

He opened his eyes to slits and moved his jaw down prior to rolling his head toward where she still knelt. "Because they seared the opening, na' the sides. Such a method requires time to heal. I dinna' give it time."

"So you had to seal both sides, which will make a wicked scar."

He nodded.

"Because both sides were bleeding too much to keep it secret, and it was getting too painful to do your business without someone knowing you get hurt, too. You bleed. You're not invincible."

"You ken this?"

She nodded. "I had brothers."

He grinned. "I keep forgetting. What else do you ken?"

"That such a wound would need searing to stop the bleeding only if it was deep."

He shrugged by lifting his right shoulder. "It was deep. Is that what you wish to hear?"

"It was nae scratch, was it?" Lisle replied, innocently.

He shook his head, rolling it along the back of his chair with the motion.

"Then, you lied to me," she said.

His lips held the smile for a moment, then let it out. "I always lie. I live a lie. Haven't you listened to a thing I've said to you?"

"I've listened. I just doona' believe my ears anymore, though."

"Truly?"

"Aye. I've found something better."

"And what would that be?" he asked.

She moved her hands away from where they were clasped between her breasts and put them on her knees. "Trust," she whispered.

"Trust," he replied. "Good word. Harsh. Full of meaning. That word contains too much, means too much, and can destroy too much. It is too deep. Much like this wound of mine."

Lisle moved her hands away from where they were holding to her knees and wiped at the residue of tears on her face. "You can trust me," she replied.

"I know," he answered.

Those two words sent such a vicious spate of joy running through her, Lisle felt she could easily float about the chamber and wouldn't need any beam. Then it stopped, crashing about her and making it feel like it hurt her ears with the sound of it—much like breaking glass.

"Then, why doona' you?" she asked in a little voice.

He sighed heavily. He didn't move his gaze from hers. "Because you are too full of joy and love and compassion and everything that is light in this world. I've never come across one who breathes, eats, sleeps, and exudes such emotion. You're vivid with all that is light and life and bliss. One can reach out and sense it . . ." He put out a hand toward her. "One can almost feel it, just by being near you. It drew me the moment I saw you. It still does."

His hand dropped. "It is also easy to read. Transparent. Every thought in that beautiful little head, I can see. That means others can, too."

"You are starting to be insulting," she replied.

His eyebrows rose. "Oh. And why is that?"

"I can keep a secret."

"You, my dear, exude honesty. There isn't a secret safe with you in the entire world."

"I have never given away a secret!" she complained.

"I dinna' mean that. I have already said I can trust you. I ken how honest you are. That is the trouble. This honesty thing. Such a thing is of little use in negotiations and politics and chess."

"Chess?" Lisle asked, without hiding the confusion.

"Life is a chess game. With a really large, convoluted, constantly changing game board. We're all players. Everyone you come across. Some are pawns. Easily erased. Rarely missed. Easily replaced. Some are kings. Some are knights."

"You are a very strange man, Langston Monteith," she commented, since he seemed to be waiting for a reply.

"True," he stated.

"And you have very strange views of things. Nae one is easily erased and na' missed."

"Spend half your life in Persia and we'll see if you think the same. Forget I offered that. I would na' wish you to see anything so dark. I doona' want anything to change you. I doona' dare change perfection."

There was that floating sensation again, and Lisle's eyes were huge with it, while her mouth was trying to hold in the smile.

"I am na' perfect," she challenged him.

"True. But you are perfect . . . for me."

The floating feeling burst, sending her back to the floor, kneeling at his feet, and talking senseless things. "You are a very strange man, Monteith."

"You already said that, and I agreed."

"And I can keep a secret. I can keep it well."

"I know your mouth can. 'Tis the rest of you I am in doubt of."

"What? Why?"

"A moment ago, you were afire with happiness at hearing I found you perfect. And the next you were upset at me, for changing my definition of the word *perfection* to encompass only me. Tell me I'm wrong."

Her mouth was open. She couldn't speak it.

"You see? Everything on you is so open, so honest, so trusting. So opposite of everything I am. I'm ensnared."

"Ensnared?" Lisle asked.

"Tightly."

"By me?"

He nodded, moving his head on the backrest of the chair. "'Tis worse than an opiate. I have never tried the stuff, myself. I doona' dare. I watched it erase too many pawns in this chess game you say doesn't exist."

"But . . . you would use such a thing on me?" she asked in a very small voice.

His lips twitched. His eyes were so amber-dark there wasn't a hint of black. "I only told Mary MacGreggor what it was and how it acted on the senses. She did the rest."

"What?"

"You've been bathing in incense and jasmine oil, and naught else. I only allowed you to think otherwise."

"Why?"

"Because the mind is a powerful weapon, and if one thinks certain things are . . . then they are. 'Tis difficult to convince them otherwise."

"You played with me?"

"There you go, getting all upset with me again. And here you just said I could trust you."

"Langston Monteith! You are a devil."

"And you're going to have to change your definition . . . either of me, or what a devil is."

"Now, why would I do such a thing?" Lisle was moving to her knees so she could stand and finish this nonsensical conversation from a safe distance from him.

"Because the devil canna' feel love," he said softly, stopping everything in the world with the power of those words.

"Wh-what did you just say?" she asked, halfway between a crouch and standing upright.

"I love you," he replied.

Her legs decided it was easier to fall to the floor than try to stand and hold her up. Lisle slid back to her knees. "You do?" she asked.

He licked his lips. "More than I can say. Definitely more than I can show."

"Nae," she breathed.

He chuckled. "You are hard to convince, my love."

"You canna' love me, Monteith."

"Why na?"

"Because— I doona' know."

"You ken something else, sweet?" he asked.

She shook her head. Her voice wasn't working.

"You love me, too."

"I doona'!"

"And you will need to work on your lying skills to say something so false and make me believe it."

Lisle was on her feet now. So was he, and it looked easy. Then he was stalking . . . and there wasn't much left of his attire from what she was looking at.

"I doona'!"

She was backing from him; stumbling. There was a table in the way. It fell with a crashing noise, sending breads rolling all along his floor. She glanced down for the best path through the rolls, and thanking her luck it hadn't contained gravies to coat the floor and make it slick.

She shouldn't have looked down.

Langston had her with his right arm, lifting her easily above the floor, and then he was laughing and hauling her under his arm, while her kicking and pummeling didn't make a hint of difference.

Then she was tossed into the tub, on her back, and lunging herself into an arch, since he'd hooked her legs on the edge. That was sending water all about the floor with the sound of a waterfall. Then, he was there, lifting her against him and holding her to where the shirt wasn't any good as a covering since it was plastered to him now. Then he was lowering his head and kissing her, and Lisle forgot everything.

Hands flew about his back, along the curve of his buttocks, around to the front, and Langston was groaning into the depths of the mouth she'd opened in order to taste him more fully.

She felt her skirts lifting, water making the material much heavier than before, and then he was lifting her above him, sliding her along his chest and belly, before bringing her down to embrace where he was ready for her. Lisle felt the size of him as she enwrapped him, and there was nothing resembling the remembered pain, only the ecstasy and light and everything he'd told her she was.

Lisle looped her ankles together behind him, wrapped her arms about his neck, and leaned back, glorying in everything the tall, godlike man was. He had his hands about the mass of material he'd shoved to her waist, using his left merely to guide, and his right to maintain the rhythm of a silent drumbeat, as he took her to heights no beam could reach, and then even higher than that.

Water sloshed about with his every move, sounding like it was splashing more than the floor, and Lisle watched traces of the same ecstatic feeling flit across his face with every twinge he made, every heave, every move . . . every inhaled breath that he hung onto.

Then, he was taking them from the tub, balancing them for a moment on the rim, before settling down onto his haunches, keeping her with him, sealing his lips to hers, his body to hers, and pounding every bit of what he considered love into her until there wasn't any excuse for not screaming. So she did, with abandon, until her throat hoarsened and his laughter was making everything more vivid and life-stirring and wonderful. He drew her toward him, holding her so closely to his chest that every breath was pushed into her. She did the same, although there wasn't much air she could suck in and hold before having to do it again. He was moving them again, this time laying her on her back, on what could be a rug, but could just as easily be stone, or wood, or any number of things. The position caused the wad of skirts and underthings that were still about her waist to lift her more fully for him, and against him, and everywhere to him, and added even more to the throes of abandonment she didn't have a voice left to scream with.

And so this time he screamed, yanking his mouth from hers, lifting his upper body in a complete arc, and doing the sound for her, only he made it lower and deeper, resembling a groan that gained in volume to her own ears. Lisle moved her hands to his throat, held to the thick cords there, as he sent the cry to the rafters and waited for it to come back down.

The drumbeat was still there; harder, thicker, and stronger. It was in his heartbeat against hers. It was in the trembling of his frame to hers. It was in the sound of lungs sucking in air and releasing it. It was in the sound of everything about them. He was probably right about this love thing, too, but she wasn't going to let him know of it that easily.

He rolled to his side, the movement separating them, and then he was on his back and staring without blinking up at the beams intersecting the ceiling.

"Langston?" she whispered.

"I'm afraid you're a *bruadair*—a dream," he replied.

She lifted onto an elbow to look over at him. "I am nae dream. You ken?" Her voice came out in a whisper of sound that hurt her throat. She frowned a bit at that.

"You must be. For a man to experience this, he would have to be in heaven. I'm na' in heaven, therefore you are na' real."

Lisle giggled. That didn't hurt her throat. Then, she reached over and traced along his ribcage until she got to the wound that was starting to seep a little.

"You've opened your wound," she whispered.

"What wound?" he asked, and put the little frown line in his forehead into existence with the question.

"The one you have here." She touched along his shoulder.

"Oh. That one."

"Does it pain?"

"There isn't a portion of my body that feels pain, love," he replied.

"Must you lie all the time?" Lisle went to a sitting position, and shoved all the wet, cold garments all about her legs as she did so, where they started warming.

"I doona' lie at the moment. I swear it."

"Then . . . explain."

"I have naught but happiness and joy and life and love flowing all over me at present, Lisle love. That is what is so unreal about you . . . about this. I canna' feel pain. Anywhere. I swear it. I vow it."

"Oh. That's better, then."

He snorted, and turned his head. Their eyes locked. Lisle's heart fell in a swoop of movement, to land in the lowest echelons of her belly where it started pounding everything that was real through every part of her.

"You swear you're real?" he asked in such a low tone she had to move forward to hear it.

She nodded.

"And this is real?"

"What . . . this?" she asked.

His eyebrows went up and down several times. Then, he was running his right hand over his chest, his belly, under the shirt ends that had miraculously stayed fastened, and growling before he brought it back out. "This. Life. You . . . me. This."

"Oh. That." She shrugged. "'Tis real enough, I suppose."

He reached out to flick her nose. "You are a horrendous liar, Mistress Monteith," he announced.

"I am not!"

"Tell me you doona' love me."

Lisle looked at him as evenly as possible, and made her face as expressionless as possible. "I doona' love you," she said, although her voice warbled.

"Then I shall try harder."

"This is trying?" she asked.

"Nae. This." He pointed to her, then back at himself, and did it several times. "This . . . between us . . . is love. Real. Love. And it's ours. I'll just have to try harder to get you to see it."

"How do you propose to do that?" she asked.

"By taking you on a honeymoon, of course."

Lisle's ears heard it, but nothing else did. She was gazing into those beautiful eyes, watching the little crinkles about them that came into being when he teased or grinned, or all-out laughed, and not much else occurred to her.

"A—a . . . honey . . . moon?" she queried.

"Aye. To Paris. You need a wardrobe."

Lisle stared. "I am gaining a wardrobe."

"You need seamstresses with more use of wire."

"I beg your pardon?"

"Your clothing rips too easily. It's in disgraceful condition. We need more sturdy fabrics, and we'll need to start using wire for thread."

Lisle reached out and smacked him on that beautiful, rippled abdomen, and nothing even bounced. Then, her fingers opened from the fist they were in and started running over the lumps and bumps and sinews of him that all appeared to be rippling just for her.

"Are you trying to start something again, Mistress?" he asked.

She looked up at him, and kept her face as emotionless as possible. "I am checking for further injury. I need to do this before I assist you with your bath. That is what I'm here for, you ken?"

"This is what you call assisting me?"

"Oh. Aye. I do it rather well, doona' I?"

"You're wicked."

"Thank you," she replied. "I do try to please."

"And you'll do the same again?"

In answer, she moved her hand from him and started unbuttoning her own dress. Then, she flicked her tongue out over her upper lip. He pulsed along the floor with the movement.

"But, of course, *monsieur*," she replied in French. "I shall need to be dressed more appropriately the next time. I dinna' know you required a personal assist in your water, but I am learning."

That got her a growl, and his complete attention.

Chapter Twenty-Four

Langston had invited Captain Barton to a dinner soiree. There were going to be Inverness women invited. There were probably going to be two certain MacHugh lasses invited. Lisle was the only one without an invitation. She was under orders to appear and be the proper hostess to English trash she'd rather spit on than watch served. And if all of that wasn't bad enough, Monteith wasn't listening to one word of argument about this honeymoon trip he was planning, either.

Lisle sat with the seamstresses, listening to the ebb and flow of words, twitters of amusement, and not a whole lot else, and wondered what she could use to sway Langston this time.

He was immune to further negotiation. He seemed to know what she was doing the moment she started, and it didn't take much effort to get that man interested enough that he joined in with her seduction, and then there was no telling the winner. He had too great a weapon to use. He called it passion. He'd told her she had the same, and once she learned how to wield it, they were in for a whole lot of trouble.

She was also going through sheer underthings faster than the castle seamstresses could sew them. Lisle looked across the sewing room that felt like a prison, and thought she'd much rather be a male, outside in the open air, instead of with a roomful of women whose mouths moved as fast as their needles did. Then again, no male got to design and wear chemises like the one Maggie had designed for tonight's use.

Despite the bevy of women all about her, Lisle blushed, and had to fan herself with the parchment listing of foods he wanted her to peruse and give her opinion over. She looked down at listings of dishes that were next to impossible to imagine in these austere times, and wondered why he'd given it to her to approve. There wasn't time to change the menu.

She sighed and fanned more. She didn't bother looking over the menu further. There wasn't time to change anything. He was rushing them toward the clan's demise, and he couldn't even see it. It was as if the entire castle was holding its breath, waiting. And it wasn't waiting for Captain Barton.

Lisle descended the staircase, after tiring of waiting for Langston to appear to escort her. The castle was alive with music and laughter and flowing wine and ales, and all kinds of appetizing smells. The only thing missing was its owner.

Lisle looked down at the translucent upper layer that belonged to one of her first ballgowns. This one had been made with a large bodice band of shimmering blue-green fabric that looked molded to her and gave her a moment of shyness when she'd first seen it. The seamstresses had then attached long strips of filmy sea-blue netting that overlaid such a pristine, white satin skirt, it looked like she was a mermaid rising from the depths of the deepest loch.

Lisle's body was changing. It had to be. Her bosom had never been this large, and she was tired of constantly having to be measured to capture her increasing proportions. She smiled slyly. Perhaps Laird Monteith should have waited until she completely finished growing before he ordered and paid for entire wardrobes, if someone decided when that would be. Lisle pulled on the low-cut neckline, managing to do nothing more than put a thumb and fingerprint on the fabric, and then she sighed.

"There you are, my dear. Right in time for—"

Langston's voice stopped as he looked fully at her. What was worse was Captain Barton's expression right next to him.

"I'm speechless, Monteith. A tad jealous, too, I might add."

The captain broke the silence. Lisle felt her skin crawl from where the man was looking. She raised her eyes to Langston's. They were black, expressionless . . . hard. She gulped.

"You . . . look lovely, Lisle," Langston said, and pulled her to his right side, away from the captain.

"You might want to keep her under wraps next month, Monteith. Cumberland has an eye for the wenches, and one so well served up as this one will definitely whet his appetite, and make your life misery. Unless, of course, that's your object."

"My wife forgot her shawl. Lisle? Your shawl?"

Captain Barton chuckled from the far side of him. "In that event, I'd keep her locked well away from him. He's got a reputation for that, you know."

"He steals men's wives?"

"He doesn't need to steal. He can make any woman a mistress. If she's available. And even if she's not. I don't think he quibbles over marital status. Wait until you meet the man. You'll see."

"Lisle?" Langston bowed his head to put his forehead near hers. "Does that dress come with a shawl?"

"I'll find one," she whispered back.

"Good. I'll wait. Captain? Go ahead. I'll join you in a moment. I've got to await my wife."

"That woman has certainly changed, Monteith, and all for the better that I can see. Makes me almost want my own Highland lass. Is that what carrying your heir is doing to her?"

Lisle was on the fourth step, then the fifth; then she was moving up them automatically and without any more thought to anything other than the obvious. She was carrying Langston's heir! Chills ran her arms, wings of nervousness fluttered about in her belly, and she swung the wardrobe door open with a movement that made all the shawls dance about in the interior. Then, she dropped her hands to the flatness that was her belly, despite the inner conviction that it was true.

She was carrying a baby—Langston's baby! Lisle tied a ring stole about her shoulders and turned the knot to the back so the gossamer fabric created a curtain effect, hiding what she should have already had the smarts to keep hidden. She wondered if Langston suspected. She wondered why the captain had, and then she remembered. Langston had given him that excuse for wedding her in the first place. She slammed the armoire door shut.

The captain was still there, he was still talking, and she was almost down the staircase before she knew what they were talking of. Langston was still talking of what this William wanted, and why it was important, and food likes and dislikes, and then her stomach felt like it caved on her.

He wouldn't—! He couldn't —! Monteith Castle was going to host the Duke of Cumberland, the man called Butcher Willie? The man who had ordered and executed the razing of the Highlands following his victory at Culloden? Everything in her recoiled. She was surprised to see her hand still skimming down the banister and her feet still moving underneath her without a sign of the devastation that was happening inside.

"He'll bring troops?"

"Of course, although I've told him it's not necessary. We've got the barbarians cowed—and their women beaten. There's not a Highlander about with any intellect, strength, or power to give William a difficult time. And if they do, we'll just have us another Culloden, won't we?" The captain laughed at the end of his words. Lisle clenched her hand on the wooden railing.

"They'll bring their own horses?"

"Why? You want to put them on your own stud?"

"Of course. A testimony from Cumberland will further my ambitions a hundredfold in London."

"I've heard he's much too corpulent to put such a thing into action."

"He still likes horseflesh, though? Riding?"

"When his gout allows it. You'll see. Ah. Here's the lovely Mistress Monteith. My dear, allow me to escort you in."

Lisle looked toward Langston for help, and all he did was nod. Everything was cringing, screaming, raging. She reached a hand that trembled and placed it on the captain's arm. Then she was matching her steps to his and trying everything she knew to keep from crying aloud with the hatred of it.

"You have the oddest luck, Monteith," the captain said when they were at the largest dining room. "You choose a woman I'd have run from, turn her into the loveliest creature on the earth, and manage to subdue her into submission. She keeps quiet. I am very envious, I've decided."

Lisle's teeth were grinding in step with her feet, and then they were in what used to be a room full of furniture, with more hanging from the beams. She looked up. Now all that was up there were full chandeliers of lit oil lamps. Lisle looked about the room with awe at how lovely it all was, and an instant curiosity in where he'd put the furniture.

Then, it occurred to her. There hadn't been one stick of anything strange hanging from any beam, anywhere. The furniture was gone . . . all of it.

"You're going to have to work on your conversation skills, my dear Lady Monteith. A bit of light conversation wouldn't go amiss, and would have any man tied to your side. I vow it."

A bit of light conversation? she repeated to herself. A shiver went right up her spine and climbed the back of her head. Lisle's face probably showed it. She was going to gag.

"Then again, a man can't help but look brilliant when around a woman with such a skill for quiet."

"I—" Lisle tried to say something but it got stuck in her throat.

"No words means no arguments. You understand?" He was leaning toward her, and then he was winking at her.

Lisle's eyes went huge. He mistook that look, too, as he squeezed the arm she was holding against his side.

"If you'll pardon me, Captain?" Lisle smiled slightly up at him, pulled her hand out of his grasp, and turned, right into Langston.

"Langston?"

His arm enveloped her, taking away all the panic and dulling the shaking she wasn't very good at disguising. Langston was absolutely right about her. She was a terrible liar. Everything on her body had been in a state of amazement and surprise at carrying a baby, and then it turned to disgust at what she'd had to touch; what he'd made her touch. Her eyes narrowed.

"You made me do that!" she hissed.

Langston frowned.

"You wanted me to learn, and so you made me touch him!"

"Not exactly," he replied softly.

"Well, you succeeded. I learned. Doona' let that man touch me again. He won't survive the skean I put into him."

"Lisle."

"Doona' 'Lisle' me!"

"At least keep your voice down then."

"My voice is down. Otherwise I'd be tearing out handfuls of that black hair from your scalp and screaming you into a deaf state."

His lips twisted. "Visual," he said.

"Why would you do this to yourself? Isn't it enough to host that snake? Must we add the Butcher?"

"Cumberland is a learned man. He'll be a wonderful conversationalist. I doona' even think he likes to argue. It would take too much effort, and that he doesn't give." He was smiling and talking and moving her over to a seat at the very end of the very long table, and then he was helping seat her.

"Entertain your guests, Lisle."

"I detest this about you, Langston."

He sighed. "Take some time to introduce my new valet, Percy, to a certain Mistress Angela. I believe they'll make a fine coupling."

"How would you know?"

"I believe I spoke too soon, Monteith. She has a vicious tongue, and turns it on you. That's interesting and enlightening." It was the captain again. He was seating himself to Lisle's right.

She tried glaring at Langston. It didn't do much. He simply lifted one brow, his right shoulder in a shrug that wouldn't hurt him, and turned his back on her. She told herself she was never speaking to him again.

Langston had three ships awaiting them in the harbor, and three more just barely visible on this horizon, although you needed a spyglass to make certain. At least that was what she was told. She didn't ask anyone about anything. She wasn't speaking to anyone. She told herself it was for the practice, since he was denying her his presence.

She was getting all her information from her maid, Betsy, who had now been joined by two more young girls named Bess and Cassie. Mary MacGreggor wasn't going anywhere where her feet weren't on solid ground. Betsy was made of more adventuresome material. Then again, she seemed to be on very good terms with one of the lads flitting about through the sails and across the decks, and handling baggage, and then they were escorting her and her little entourage to what was probably the largest cabin aboard any ship, ever.

Lisle stood in the doorway with her mouth open slightly, and looked at a scene someone had dreamt up from an inferno of some kind. There was dark wood everywhere, and it was sliced in a diagonal pattern with ruby-red strips of what looked to be velvet. And there were mirrors . . . everywhere, making everything look like a kaleidoscope of colors—red and black—wherever she looked. It gave her an instant headache.

"They tell me His Lordship designed this cabin."

"Nae doubt," Lisle replied.

"Isn't it grand?"

That was Betsy again. She was walking into the room, looking about and up and all along, at every black lacquered piece of furniture, and the slick black wood that encased their bed.

"It looks like hell," Lisle replied.

That got her a gasp, and reinforced her vow not to speak. All that came out were spates of angered words that should be directed toward one man, and since he was denying her that, got to be lashed out at whoever was available.

It was better to remain silent . . . and alone. All too soon, the cabin emptied. Lisle sat in one of the red velvet–covered chairs and watched as her maids unpacked her clothing, hung it in all four of the wardrobe closets he had lined against one wall for that purpose, and then served her a light supper of a hard roll, sliced ham, and a mustard seed spread that made her nose itch.

The cabin emptied again, and when the ship left the dock she was very grateful to be alone. No one needed to know that she was a dreadful sailor and that everything she'd eaten for the last month wasn't going to stay there.

Then Langston was there, hauling her into his arms from her position at the chamber pot, and rocking her and soothing her brow. He was speaking words of such devotion and love that she forgot she wasn't ever speaking to him again, and she just let him hold her until the next bout of mal de mer hit.

"This all your fault!" she wailed when her stomach settled enough she could use her voice.

Langston got onto the mattress with her, although he did it slowly. The movement still made her retch. She opened her eyes to slits and glared at him.

"Dinna' you hear me?" she asked.

"You've got the sickness. That isn't my fault."

"You brought me here, dinna' you?"

He couldn't deny that, and after a few moments, he didn't try.

"You also made certain I'd be put in a cabin resembling hell. You ken what that does to one?"

"Hell?" He lifted his head to look around. "I fancied it more like a rich, elegant, calabash tent. They're everywhere. One could always find something to look at while smoking oneself into a state of lethargy."

"Aye. Yourself."

He grinned. "Some say it's not such a bad thing to look at."

Lisle looked at him until the grin faded. "You design this cabin?"

"Nae," he replied.

"But you left it this way? With all your gold?"

"I rather like it."

"Ugh." Lisle was rolling back off the bed and running back over to the privy closet, her hand plastered to her mouth.

He was sitting on the bed, looking at his hands, when she groped her way back, using the wood along the sides for handholds. If every shard of mirror was telling the truth, she was pale to the point that her hair looked flame-colored and theatrical. She grimaced at herself. He must have thought it was at him.

"You finished raging at me?"

"I wasn't raging," she replied nastily.

He snorted. "You keep so little hidden. It's a real joy to spar with you when you try to do so."

"I wasn't raging. You want to see me raging? Wait until I have firm ground beneath my feet, and a kitchen full of pots to launch at you."

He was laughing at that. Lisle lay carefully on the bed, waiting for the pitch and roll of the thing to make her belly wish it had never eaten anything—again.

"It won't last, love."

"Doona' call me love!" she replied.

"Very well . . . sweet."

"Doona' call me sweet, either!"

"You are difficult to please tonight."

"You left me with that Captain Barton arse the other night, and you want pleasure tonight? Find yourself a tavern wench!"

"There's a shortage of taverns aboard my flagship. Consequently, that would also mean there is a shortage of tavern wenches. Aside from all of that, I happen to find myself enamored of just one woman in this world, and there is nae woman that could possibly compete."

"Would you please cease talking?"

He laughed for an answer, and then kept talking. "Cool water is what you need. I'll be back. Doona' move."

"I couldn't move if I wanted to," she grumbled.

"That would also mean that you're unable to climb about, seeing things that should remain unseen, and learning things that are best left undiscovered?"

He was out the door before she could answer, and beyond a weak toss of her head, there wasn't much she felt like answering, anyway. But he was going to be back, and she was going to give him an earful. Just as soon as she finished retching and crying and sobbing. He returned, wiping cool cloths about her cheeks and across her forehead, and crooning nonsensical things to her, until she was ready to cry again over his stupidity.

"This is all your fault!" she wailed when he wouldn't cease.

"You already said that. I already replied."

"You doona' know the whole of it!"

"Apprise me." He had her head pillowed on those two lumps of his chest, which, when he didn't make them taut, had the consistency of a warm mattress, except for his heartbeat. It also made his voice sound like it was coming from very far away.

"You should have let me stay. I wouldn't have been trouble."

"And go without you? This is a honeymoon. I'd look a fool."

"You already look like that."

"My thanks. At least my acting isn't in question."

"You wish to look like a fool?"

"Fools can't do much. Therefore, they're not looked at closely."

"I hate travel by ship!" Lisle replied.

"It's just down the coast. We'll be there a-fore you know it."

"And I failed at music! I can't even read notes."

Langston stopped breathing for a moment, and then he restarted it. Lisle wondered if he noticed. "Music?" he asked.

"You have them play music. With horns."

"Horns?"

"Aye. One long note. Sometimes two or three of them. Spaced far apart. Always the same tone—always. I doona' know which note you have them use. It's like this." Lisle moved her head a bit, sucked in a breath, and mimicked the note.

"Really?" The one word was accompanied by a stroke of his finger along her cheek and to her jaw.

She nodded. The support of his chest moved as his arm moved. Lisle let her head roll with the motion. He was pulling her closer to him, and that was making the heartbeat thicken in her ear. That was interesting.

"What else is my fault?" he asked.

"The three notes. They mean something. Something like hide or run, or the rangers arc coming. Something like that. One note means all is clear. I think. I'm na' certain since I've heard it but once and we weren't home at the time. He must come in your direction a lot."

"Home. You just called my castle home." He wasn't in control of his breathing, but that was all right. The arms tightened for a moment too, tucking her nose between the muscles of his chest, and then he released her, although one arm stayed at her back.

"I have nae other place to stay," she replied finally.

"Having nae other place to stay, and calling a place home, are two incredibly different things, Lisle."

"I doona' ken what two notes mean," she replied.

"What?" He wasn't feigning the confusion.

"I know what one means. I ken what three means. I doona' know what two means."

"Why na'?"

"I've never heard it. I imagine it means to keep an eye out."

"Hmn." The moan of sound rumbled through his chest. It sounded like acquiescence, so she just continued her complaints.

"Then, there are the beams. You spent so much time putting them in all your chambers. It was a total waste of gold, clutters up good space, and they're very difficult to keep clean . . . when you're not hanging furniture from them."

"All of which has kept several carpenters, masons, and woodcutters employed that I recall. It still does."

"Right." She nuzzled her nose against the mound that had the heartbeats coming from it.

"You think I have another reason?"

"I know you do," she answered.

"Really? Do tell."

"You have steps cut into your walls, or hidden into fireplaces, or you have them fashioned right out of your bookshelves without any subtlety at all. They've been designed into the very walls. They all lead to a beam, and from there you can reach any number of your perfect little windows without much effort. You could even bring a weapon while you did so."

"A weapon? You have strange ideas, my dear. You don't think I did it to correct the symmetry of each room?"

"Oh nae, not with you. They have another reason."

"What would that be, if I may be so bold?"

"They're for defense. The same as your cannons."

"Cannons?" He was still stroking a hand along her back, and his breathing hadn't changed, but he was going to have to work on the rest of his body, for his heart had definitely gotten stronger and faster. She smiled slightly. He wasn't a perfect liar after all.

"Aye. Cannons, and then there's the complete armory that's in your chapel. You can defend just about anything against just about any foe. Only you're willing to risk it all for naught."

"I am? This doesn't sound like me."

"You want to fight the battle of Drumossie Moor again, and you want it to come out differently this time."

"What Scot doesn't?"

"You think you can change history, and I'm afraid that you're planning on that very thing."

"How am I doing that?"

"You're trying to buy it with this gold of ours. How much of it do we have, anyway?"

"More than we can count in this lifetime."

"Why?"

"Commodities and exchange."

"What?" Lisle wrinkled her nose.

"Commodities are things people want and I offer. Exchange is what they get for spending their gold for my commodity. Simple. Complex."

"Are you—we . . . also slavers?"

"You believed that?"

"You're a good actor, Langston."

"Thank God. I was beginning to think myself pathetic at it."

"Why so?"

"All these tales you have of my—our home."

"So . . . are we?"

Langston sighed. She rose and fell with it. "Solomon tried it once. It wasn't worth the gold. There are easier ways. He sold the ship. 'Tis a shame, actually."

"Your partner is nae longer a slaver, and that's a shame?"

"He always treated the cargo humanely. That isn't always the case. It rarely is."

"Then put a stop to it."

"Me? How?"

"Use your gold. Buy a stop to it."

"I have nae power to do such. You can't change the world."

"Aha!" The word was accompanied by lifting her head sharply. She wanted to see his face as he heard it. Unfortunately, her movement made the room swim again, her belly rumble warningly, and she put her head back down almost as swiftly as she'd lifted it.

His chuckle sounded even stranger that his voice had. Lisle listened to it.

"A man can only change a portion of it, Lisle love."

"You can also . . . die."

"I know. That's why I had a dower house built."

"A dower house?"

"For a dowager. That's what you'd be. In the event of my death, that is. You wondered where all the furniture went, dinna' you? At least, that's what I ken you were thinking when we first reached the dining room the other night. Tell me I'm wrong."

"You're wrong."

He chuckled again. "Tell me I'm wrong, and make it believable."

"That wasn't what you said. You think you ken everything about me, Langston Monteith?"

"You're very easy to read, love. It isn't your fault. 'Tis those clear, sky-blue eyes, and the way you grasp and feel this life of ours. You almost have me feeling it, too. That's what makes you so special to me."

"You doona' know anything about me."

He sighed long and deeply. "Very well. You wish to argue? Carry on. I do ken one thing, though."

"What?" she asked.

"It was a very good idea to take this honeymoon trip. Very."

"In the midst of all your planning and intriguing and work, you leave? There must be a reason, and I knew right away what it was."

"Really?" Langston asked.

"You wanted me out of the castle. You're moving things. Changing things. I'm too observant. I might find out, and then what? The captain might be able to guess my knowledge from my face? I never even spoke to the man."

That got her another large sigh. "I know. All eve he looked at me closer than he's ever looked at me before because of it."

"What? Why? I did naught!"

"You do so much. You just doonna' see it. The scarf was a dreadful idea, too. I lost my mind. I was jealous. I can't afford such emotion. Not now. That is why you're with me, love. That . . . and I'd be incredibly lonely otherwise. This is a honeymoon, you ken?"

Chapter Twenty-Five

Lisle's version of hell lasted four days, although she lost track of time after the second day, and definitely after the second night. The only constant was Langston. He was always there, wiping at her face, assisting her to and from the privy closet, helping her take the sweat-soaked nightgowns off, and putting clean ones on, although he did that with a black look to his eyes and a set line to his jaw. His were the hands sponging off her body and forcing broth down her throat, when he knew it wouldn't stay.

On the fifth day, she opened her eyes to a room filled with waning sunlight, a snoring Monteith, who was sleeping on his belly and taking up way too much of the bed, and not a ripple of movement happening anywhere to tilt her belly and make it decide to destroy her again.

Lisle slid to the side of the bed, walked over to a window, and pressed her face against the glass, fully expecting to see the city of Paris, or a port of some kind, and totally mystified that there was nothing but water and two ships to look at. She crossed the cabin to the other side and did the exact same thing, although she had to push the draperies aside in order to see. Water. There was nothing but smooth-looking water, and the other three ships.

There wasn't any sign of land anywhere. She went back to the bed, got back up on the mattress, and started shoving at the sleeping male that was behind all her agony.

"Langston?"

His snore interrupted midbreath, and then she got an eye opened to regard her. "Aye?" he asked.

"We're na' moving."

His lips tipped. "You woke me to tell me that?"

"And 'tis eve."

That got her a groan of a reply. There didn't seem to be any words to it.

"And nae man should be sleeping away the day."

"A man exhausted by taking care of his wife would be. Why, such a man has to get his sleep when he can."

"Good," she replied.

"Good?" he asked, lifting his head to look at her.

"Aye. 'Tis your own fault, remember?"

That had him turning on his side toward her, showing that he wasn't wearing much, and the covers weren't keeping that tale to themselves as they followed him to the extent they could. Lisle was holding down a portion of them, and that was making the material twist about him. She forced herself not to look.

"Seems to me we were at a decided dispute over that particular phrasing when last we were discussing it, but I could be wrong."

"You still wish to argue with me?" she asked.

"Argue? Nae. Negotiate? Definitely."

"What are you negotiating with?"

"The ship."

Lisle stared. "You'd give me your ship?"

"I doona' need to gift you with it, Lisle. 'Tis already yours. I vowed as much in my wedding words. At least, I recall saying as much. Since I was na' paying attention to much at the time, I could have vowed to anything. Enlighten me."

"You twist words."

That got her a smile. "True. That's one of the things I do. I happen to be very good at it."

"What are the others?"

"Other what?"

"Things that you do?"

"Oh."

He sat, the covers slid to his belly, and Lisle had to force herself not to look. She could tell it wasn't working as her face heated up, and telling herself she was being ridiculous didn't help.

"I twist all kinds of other things as well."

"You wish me to note the way you've twisted the covers now?" she asked. Her face was flaming.

"Are you?"

At that question he rolled completely onto his back, making the traitorous coverlet cling to every hidden portion of that frame, and then he was raising a thigh to keep her guessing at the rest.

"I'm actually starved," she replied.

"Is it near eight?" he asked.

"How am I to tell?"

"They ring bells. On the hour. What was the last one you heard?"

She wrinkled her nose. "Twelve," she replied.

He blew the sigh, lifting hair that only thought to curtain any part of his forehead. "I believe it's nearer eight. That's good."

"Why?"

"Because I ordered certain things to happen at eight."

"What certain things?"

"What are you willing to give to find out?" he asked and folded his arms.

Lisle regarded him. Then, she smiled. "Na' much," she admitted finally.

"Why na'?"

"Because whatever you have ordered will happen at eight,

whether I ken what it is or na'. My guess is, it's fairly near eight. I will na' have much time with which to puzzle it out. Why would I give anything for that?"

"What would it take to get that nightgown from you?"

Lisle's eyes went wide. "You're na' serious."

"Of course I'm serious. Does it look like I'm na' serious?"

Lisle put a hand to the little ribbon tie at her throat. "But . . . why?"

"Because I'm on my honeymoon, and doing my damnedest to pretend it's been everything I dreamed it would be."

"You did that?"

"Are you na' grateful?"

"Where are we, Langston?"

"In my bed, that's in my cabin, aboard the *Adventurer*, although to be truthful, you're on the bed, na' in it."

"I mean, where are we?"

"Oh. On the ocean. The North Sea."

"I mean, where are we?"

"You want exact locations? Na' possible, love. I did a bit of navigating while I was out and about as a lad. There's nae such thing as exact out here."

"Langston."

"What? You wish to hear of my navigating? Very well. I did a bit with a sextant, learned to follow the stars, look for the winds, follow charts, that sort of thing."

"That's na' what I meant."

"Well, I had to do something when I was sailing. 'Tis a long voyage to Persia. Bores an enterprising lad who has to learn everything he can in the smallest amount of time possible."

"Why?"

"Why was I a lad? Why did I have to learn everything quickly? Why was I bored? Which one?"

"I have to admit it, Langston. You are very good at this word twisting you do."

That got her a wide grin. Then he sobered. "You're a quick student. I like that. What did you wish to know, again?"

"Why are we na' moving?"

"Are you willing to part with that nightgown for the information?"

"I will part with the ribbon tie," she replied.

He looked away, as if considering that. Lisle watched him do it. Then he looked back at her and held out his hand.

"You're jesting," she said.

His eyebrows rose, but the hand stayed where it was, although he waved with his fingers.

Lisle pulled the bow apart and tugged on one end until the entire blue ribbon came out. Since it wasn't holding her nightgown close to her throat any more, the neckline gapped to her shoulders as it opened.

The look on his face was unreadable. Lisle wound the ribbon about her fingers into a little swirl of it, and placed it on his palm, which closed immediately. Then he was pulling his crazed mane of hair into a queue and tying it with her ribbon. Everything was moving and rippling on him while he did so. Lisle ordered her eyes not to watch. They weren't obeying. When he was finished, he folded his arms again, and answered her. "We're na' moving because I ordered it so."

"Now wait a moment. That's na' an answer."

"'Tis exactly what you asked and paid to know."

"That's unfair."

"Negotiations are na' fair, Lisle. They never were. They're meant to find a compromise. Do you ken what that is?"

She shook her head.

"'Tis a deal that both sides can agree to abide by. Nae one wins, nae one loses. Both sides have less than they wanted, but more than they started with."

"Teach me how." She sat, cross-legged, pulled her nightgown over her toes, and watched the corresponding shift as it dropped off her shoulders and met the resistance of her increasing bosom. She watched him look there.

"Oh. You have the skills already, love."

"I do?"

He licked his lips to wet them, slid his glance to the shadow she was making between her breasts, and then back to her face. "Aye," he answered finally.

"Good."

"A negotiation can only take place if both sides want something the other side has. Take us, for instance."

"What about us?"

"You want information. I want you. More specifically, I want you naked. Warm. Willing. In my bed. Passionate. Christ. I have to stop while I'm ahead."

He had both legs bowed at the knees now and was running his hands over the covered tops of his thighs. Lisle watched him.

"Why?"

"Why must I stop? Why do I want you? Naked? Willing? Why should we negotiate? What?"

"Why are we na' moving?"

His lips twisted, but he didn't smile. He regarded her solemnly until his eyes lightened again. "You're a very stubborn woman, Lisle Monteith."

"So I've been told. Why, please? I paid, and I want to know."

"You paid for information. You got it."

"I could have figured that out for myself!"

"What more do you wish to know, then?"

"Why did you order the ships to stop moving?"

"Oh. What are you willing to pay for that information?"

Lisle moved her elbows, making her breasts brush against each other and create an indentation in the front of her nightgown. She watched him look there. She slid her toes from beneath the fabric to impart more softness to it, more cling. She watched the reaction as he trembled, although he had it under control almost immediately. He didn't have the same control over his breathing, for his lips opened slightly to allow the increase in it.

"Well?" she asked.

"Well . . . what?"

"Why did you order the ships to stop moving?"

"Oh. My wife is a terrible sailor."

"You stopped six ships for that?"

Langston lifted a finger and wagged it back and forth. Lisle narrowed her eyes.

"You want to know what more I'm willing to part with for that information?"

He nodded.

"That depends. What am I wearing?"

He thought about that. "That nightgown. A chemise thing. Drawers. Stocking . . . long stockings. Midthigh."

"You put all that on me?"

"I had to."

"Why?"

"Because someone had to."

"What? Why?"

"Your maids were na' up to that sort of movement at present."

"They suffer the mal de mer, too?"

He nodded.

"There's more, is there na'?"

"You are a very quick learner, wife."

"What is it, now?"

"I also put that much clothing on my wife because I dinna' trust myself without it."

"That's disgusting."

"Is it?"

"You're na' a very nice man, Langston Monteith."

"When did you ever think otherwise?"

"While I've been sick? You tended me, and . . . you— you—?"

"The word is lusted, love," he said softly.

"You lusted for me?"

He nodded.

"Nae," she replied.

"I have the utmost regard for you and that amazing body of yours, Lisle Monteith. I love you. I lust for you. Jealousy hit me right between the eyes when I saw you in that ballgown the other night, with Barton. I admit it. Freely. You ken? I lust for you. I probably will always lust for you. 'Tis a bane I dinna' ask for, let me assure you, but I doona' fight it. I canna'. 'Tis against human creation. Pay up." He put his hand out.

"Why? I dinna' ask anything."

"You've been asking and receiving and na' making a hint of a payment on the whole. That is most against protocol. Most."

"'Tis your own fault, again. You've been the one answering and giving and na' making any of it a condition," she answered with a lift to her chin.

He was grinning then. "Very good," he said.

"Why would you stop six ships in the midst of the North Sea, when you should be in France, or wherever we're going, and there's nae time to do all of that and return to Monteith Castle a-fore Butcher Willie arrives, since you doona' think I ken that much about this trip?"

He whistled softly, and Lisle felt the flare of pleasure all the way from her toes, over her shoulders, and centered right where she didn't need it, at her nipples, making them taut against the fabric and itch where it touched. She watched Langston look there, and then he gulped.

"Your query has too many parts," he answered finally.

"Truly? What are they?"

"That, in itself, is another query. Pay up."

"What is it you wish?"

"You have a chemise beneath that."

"You just said I did."

"Hand over the nightgown then."

"Will I get an answer to all my questions?"

"Why did I order the ships to stop? Where are we really going, and is it to France? Why dinna' I think you would know about this trip coinciding with Cumberland's visit? Does it coincide with Cumberland's visit? Aye. All of that."

"You're too easy, my love," Lisle answered.

His eyes flew wide, opening them to their warm ale color,

and he was definitely flushing all over that massive chest, and then up into his cheeks. Lisle watched it, and felt like giggling. Then she just did it.

He cleared his throat. "How so?" he finally asked.

"You gave me an answer and I dinna' even have to pay."

"What answer was that?"

"The one about the parts of my query. You just listed them. I wonder what else I can get you to confess to, if I just let a little bit of this slide right here." Lisle tipped an arm, and assisted the nightgown to move a bit down to her elbow. She was wearing a chemise all right, but it hadn't a strap to hold up the thing, and it wasn't doing its job very well.

She looked down at herself and then over at Langston. He hadn't moved.

"You chose this?" she asked.

He tipped his head, and then smiled. "It was the first thing I grabbed."

"Right."

"You saying I lie?"

"I'm saying you rarely tell the truth, and this one's even more full of holes than your usual."

He was grinning again. Lisle wet her lips with her tongue. "If I give you this bit of cotton and lace . . . am I going to get the truth?"

"There's usually more than one bit of truth to everything."

"What?"

"I'm saying there are several layers to every bit of truth, and if you part with that nightgown, I'll give you one of the layers. One of the lower ones."

"Truth is truth. Anyone who says different is a liar."

"As I've already claimed that title, you've na' much else to your argument, *madame*. Hand over the nightgown."

He had his hand out again. Lisle unfolded her legs and put her toes against his side, and squirmed beneath the material he was requesting.

"Explain this truth thing, Monteith."

"Will I get the nightgown if I do?"

"That depends on what you say."

He licked his lips. "Start undressing. I'll start talking. Stop if you feel it merits it. I'll do the same."

Lisle brought her legs back underneath her and rose to her knees.

"There are many reasons people do things. Many reasons they call the truth. Take this thing between us. I wed with you because it was like a blizzom hit me right square between the eyes. It was also because the MacHughs would na' take my gold, and they needed it to keep them from starving. They had something I wanted. 'Tis something I would give anything for. You. They think it was for the gold. So do you. All of it is truth. All of it. Which one is the real truth?"

Lisle lifted the nightgown over her head and handed it to him. He had his eyes on the cleavage her bone-enhanced chemise was holding in place. She couldn't believe he'd taken the time to strap her into it when she was ill.

"You put me in this chemise on purpose, Langston."

"There's another truth thing. It truly was the first thing I grabbed, and it was something I would have looked for if I knew you had it. It was my pleasure to strap you into the thing. It still is. Damn you, woman."

"You are a very strange man, Langston Monteith."

"And you are a viciously desirable woman. What do you want for the drawers?"

He shook after asking it and Lisle watched him do it. Her own body was doing antics that weren't far behind, and every breath was pushing her further to the edge of her chemise cups. She watched him look there and close his eyes while another shudder ran him, and then open his eyes back on her.

Lisle had never felt such a feeling. She went back on her haunches, stretched out with her legs, and toyed along the buried side of him with her toes. "Doona' you think we should wait for eight?"

"What the hell for?" he asked.

"You probably ordered sup, and other things."

He looked away, sucked in several breaths, and let them out, and that was fascinating to watch. The man was more than handsome, and he knew it. He looked back to her.

"Eight o'clock better hurry along then, or it will be damned, like the rest of this."

"What does that mean?"

"Give me the drawers to find out."

"I'd rather puzzle it out myself."

"I ordered a bath. I ordered food. Roast, duckling, salmon. Vegetables . . . I forget which. Damn you, Lisle Monteith!"

He was shouting it across at her. She reached for the pantaloon tie. He was heaving great breaths as she lay back, using her arms to wriggle out of the drawers, and careful not to disturb the thigh-high stockings he'd put on her. And then she was pulling her legs back beneath her, keeping the chemise about her upper thighs, so there was only a gap of a finger-length or so between the two materials, and handing him the drawers.

He plucked them from her and tossed them to the side, where they landed somewhere on the floor beyond the bed. Then he was moving, coming at her, and the covers were showing their traitorous side as they gave up any hint of clinging to him and hiding him. There wasn't anything she could do about it, except lie back down and take the brunt of his weight with her hands on his chest, her elbows bent and her belly feeling every bit of every breath, while all that was male about him was searching, pushing, straining against where she was denying.

Lisle's arms flexed with the weight, and held him precariously as he bent his head and brushed a kiss down her nose, and from there onto her lips.

"We have . . . to speak about . . . your negotiating skills, my lord." Lisle turned her head to pant the words to the mountain of covers he'd shoved to the side of them.

His answer was garbled, since he had her chin in his mouth

and was sucking on it, and that had her bucking and heaving and doing everything but opening for him, while he slid along her . . . to her knees. Back. To her knees . . . . back.

"Open for me, love," he whispered when he got his lips to her neck and was doing things on her skin that were sending rushes of sensation to every part that she was denying him.

"What . . . will I get . . . if I do?" she asked.

A growl answered her and then he was peeling the cups of her chemise down to reach her, punish her, suckle her, and Lisle was spiraling into a world that didn't resemble anything like the red and black calabash room they were in, for it had too much light.

Her arms were shaking with holding him aloft, and then he wasn't helping her with it at all, as one hand moved to lift her for his delectation, bringing her to a point of ecstasy, and then passing it. Lisle cried it aloud, and then he chuckled, cooling flesh that he'd just moistened and heated, and making her buck at him in earnest, to unlatch him.

All that gained her was more of his mouth, and more of his weight, as he gave up helping her hold him aloft and reached down to hold all of her in position for him. Lisle watched him, and then he looked up, met her eyes, and the flash of something that hit her looked like it hit him at exactly the same time as he shuddered, eyes half-lidded and locked with hers.

"I ordered the ships to anchor for this," he said, although his voice trembled, and then he looked down at her and licked her.

Lisle screamed again.

"And for this."

He licked the other peak, and her cry was turning into a keening note of passion, pain, and joy. Then, he was lifting his upper body away from her, taking the heat and sensation and all that was glorious away from her; denying her. She was after him, straddling him as he lay back, opening for him, encasing him, and then she was swimming, filling her lungs with air in order to make it to the next space when breath would be allowed her. Oceans were cresting on a waveless sea, and she heard them, gloried in them.

Langston had her waist and was manipulating her up . . . down. Up . . . down. Over and over, until she was crying again with it, ignoring the tears that streamed everywhere, blotting where the chemise bodice was still pushed down, sliding over her flesh, and dropping onto him, where she was wetting both of them.

Breathing deepened, filling the cabin with the drumbeat of sound, the cadence of life, the thunder of passion and desire and hunger, and pure, unadulterated lust. Then Langston was crying with her, his voice blending with hers, in a groan of time-defying length and depth. Lisle clung to him, held onto him, as he arched against her, shuddered, and emptied himself into her.

There was the flow of the ocean in her ears, although it sounded more like a friendly Scot's burn than the torrent of sea that made her belly recoil in an agony of ache. Lisle slid down onto him, slowly, suspending herself in time as she did so, making it an ooze of movement rather than the freefall of disjointed flesh she felt like she was.

Langston's chest was heaving, he was covered in a fine sheen of sweat, and there were definite tracings of tears leading from both eyes down into the black hair behind his ears. He was watching the ceiling above them, and he wasn't seeing any of it. She could tell. Lisle forced her neck to support her head to turn it from where it lay, so she could regard him.

"Langston?" she whispered, reaching with a hand to follow a tear path from his eye.

Her action made him twitch, and brought him back from wherever he'd been. It wasn't an easy journey, if the confused look in his eyes was any indication. He licked his lips. Lisle shifted, lifting herself a bit higher so she could look fully at him.

"Aye?" he asked, finally.

"What are you willing to give me for the stockings?"

Her answer was a whoosh of air that was probably meant to be a chuckle, but fell woefully short. She giggled for him, lay back down atop his chest, snuggled into him, and slept. Neither of them heard the knock he'd scheduled for eight.

Chapter Twenty-Six

Langston Leed Monteith wasn't just a liar. He was a cheat, and evil, and a devil, and everything they'd ever called him, and Lisle didn't need the eighteen ships that had joined them the very same evening he was loving her and telling her he'd stopped his ships just for her, to convince her of it. She toyed with asking him if he was planning on invading France now, since he appeared to have an armada of more than twenty ships. It was impressive, and it created quite a stir all the way up the French coast until they anchored just off the port of Calais.

She assumed word would get back to England about the armada of caravels, all flying a dark green flag with a golden lion passant at the center, and anyone who didn't have a clue who Clan Monteith was would certainly know now. She was treated to the sight of hundreds of troops atop hundreds of horses, all in green and gold, and all in kilts, and all waiting, to escort them to Paris.

Lisle was given herself for company in the carriage, and that was all right with her. If Monteith had shown her his face, she'd have been scratching it. If he gave her sight of an ear, she'd have been screeching in it, and if he so much as gave her a glimpse of his back, she'd have been stabbing something into him and finishing the job started with his left shoulder. That's how much he, and his lying tongue, meant to her!

The tears started before they'd gone a league, and then she was very grateful she had the carriage all to herself. Betsy, Cassie, and Bess had their own carriage, and there were eleven more of them trailing behind, with the baggage and all the arms and food that men needed to make such a spectacle. She was grateful they didn't stop until they reached Paris. Even if she had to bed down in her quiet carriage, and cry herself to sleep. That was better than looking across at Monteith and knowing she'd given her heart to a man who could lie to her in the throes of his own ecstasy, and not even worry over it.

She hadn't told him of the baby, either. He was just going to have to ferret that one out for himself. She wasn't going to give him anything more to bind her to him than he already had. King Louis was expecting them. He'd given them a portion of the Louvre Palace in which to stay, but that was probably more due to having all these troops in his capital. Apparently he already knew that it was better to know where the devil was, than to have to guess at it.

That much of what he'd told her, Langston hadn't lied about. It took them four days to reach Paris, in which time Langston hadn't done a thing toward purchasing her a larger wardrobe that she could see. The most he'd done was send off a contingency of men with orders to purchase goods that he was going to transport home, and even that she questioned. They were probably doing something else. Sneaking about, creating customers for his commodities, with calabash pipes full of opiate, or whatever they smoked in them. She didn't trust anything Monteith said. She never would again, either.

She was given a parchment with her own marching orders, and they weren't open for discussion. The Monteith had apparently finished with one of his false truths, which was the excuse that he was here to honeymoon with her, although he'd been shopping all right. He'd been to a jeweler. He'd had a dress made and sent to her. He had Betsy, Cassie, and Bess there to assist, although they mostly stood about with their mouths open at the lavish rooms the Louvre Palace boasted. Monteith wanted her to report at seven, sharp, dressed head to toe in dark Monteith green, and wearing as much gold as a woman could possibly wear and not be bowed down with the weight of it.

It was positively Medieval looking, and Lisle looked at her reflection with distaste. It was effective, though. She moved sideways and then back, and felt the large, voluminous velvet of her skirt sway with it. There was golden embroidery, sewn with real gold in the threads, all through her green skirt, making vines that trailed from the bodice to the bottom, and then turned into leaves of almost solid gold all about the hem and the train that swept the floor behind her.

There was a golden girdle about her hips, and it was so heavy it had taken both Cassie and Bess to hold it in place while Betsy hooked it into the dress at the back, where at least the material had to assist with holding it up. The sleeves had been sewn with golden leaves at the tops, and it was probably more for strength than visual impact, although it had that. About the only thing that wasn't gold was the crisp white puff of lace above a bodice that peeked out from the neckline, which was intentionally cut low, barely covering what it needed to cover. That way the emeralds he'd sent hadn't a chance of being overlooked, either.

They had even threaded gold-ribbed ribbons all through her hair, which was loose and rippled to her waist, disguising the layers of strapping that went from her shoulders to her belt and back up, to also assist with the weight of her belt. It was ridiculous. It was incredibly heavy. It was extremely impressive.

As was Langston Monteith, when he arrived for her, in his Highland Chieftain ensemble, with the retinue of Monteith men at his heels; all moving with such a perfection of stride that it sounded like one set of footsteps rather than twenty-some-odd.

Lisle eyed him as he came toward her. Then he went to his knee, lifted her hand to his lips, and moved his eyes to hers.

It was for show, it had to be, and Betsy, Cassie, and Bess gave him what he expected with their sighs behind her. Lisle ignored them and looked down at him with as cold an expression as she could manage. He rose to stand beside her, tucked her hand in his, and acted like she really was a loved wife that spent every night with him rather than one that had been sentenced and kept in solitary confinement for almost a week now.

"You look exactly as I imagined you would, Lisle." He whispered it as they started their procession, passing hall after hall filled with the nobility of King Louis's court, and looking at bowed head after bowed head as they went.

"We're being treated as royalty," Lisle whispered back.

"Of course. We are. Or close to it."

"Langston?"

"Quiet, love. We're going to be introduced."

"I've met King Louis. I was na' impressed. He wears more powder than half the ladies in court must own. All at once. On his face. 'Tis unmanly, and ugly. Makes me wonder what pocks he hides."

"Na' him. Our prince. Charles. Charles Stuart. My patron. My liege. My only true liege."

"Our—?" Her voice was failing her, as were her knees, and Langston must have known or guessed, because he had an arm snaked about her, and it was holding her up by her golden belt, and forcing her to remain standing at his side, whether her legs helped with it or not.

"Hold steady, Lisle love. You'll see very soon what this has all been about. What it's always been about. I need you now. I need to put you on your own stallion, and I need to show all the people of France what kind of backing Prince Charlie has now . . . has always had."

"Prince . . . Charles?" she whispered, her eyes still wide.

"Aye."

"You know where he is?"

"Of course. 'Tis my gold that supports him."

Her legs did lose her with that one, and she stumbled, but Langston had that hand looped into the back of her belt and had her against him, so it barely showed.

The steps outside were teeming with horses, Highland men all wearing the Monteith colors, and people, everywhere she looked there were people, some clapping, some talking, all looking. It didn't appear that a stray dog could get through, and he expected to get an entire column of men through them?

"Langston?" Lisle's hand shook on his arm, and that wasn't a far cry from how her voice was acting.

"You'll be fine, Lisle. You'll ride at my side. See? Torment and Blizzom. I felt it appropriate."

"You brought over your own horses?"

"Of course. There are very few Arabian stallions in France. King Louis has na' given an order for mine, as of yet. This should convince him otherwise, I think."

"You doona' let an opportunity pass you, do you?"

He grinned. "Very good. Come. I'll mount you."

Lisle caught her breath and scanned him from beneath her lashes. Then, she smiled. Softly. Sweetly. "I believe I shall allow you to do so," she replied.

"Lisle, I have a prince to sway, negotiations to make, and I need to be sharp, focused. I canna' have you turning my lust on me. Not now."

"I am na'," she replied.

"Why do you ken I stayed away from you?"

"You knew I was planning on flaying you alive?" she replied.

He grinned wider. "I have to be focused. Sharp. I had to set this up. I had to put my gold in the right palms. I had to do a thousand things that the sight, smell, and touch of you and your body just seem to interfere with. Will you cease that?"

"What?" she asked innocently, although she had been running her hand along his arm, in a suggestive manner.

"I'll pay that back later. When I have the prince safely aboard."

"Oh dear God. You're planning on ransoming Cumberland. You're going to use him to make them accept Prince Charles and Scotland."

"Smart. I'll say it again. You're quick."

"'Tis too dangerous. Nae. Doona' do this, Langston. Nae. You canna' do it. I beg it of you."

His smile died. His eyes went black. "Doona' ask for what you canna' get. Such a thing is na' open for negotiation."

"Please?"

"I've still a prince to sway with my plans, Lisle. I canna' afford dissent in my own bed."

"Please, Langston?"

They had reached the stallions. There was a mounting block beside Blizzom. Langston ignored it and put his hands about the golden girdle that was around her waist, and had to try twice before he could lift her.

"You weigh five stone more, wife."

"'Tis your gold creating such," she replied. "I can scarce walk."

"Forgive me."

The words were meant to convey more. Lisle watched him mount Torment, who tossed his head a couple of times before coming under control.

"Come. Stay close to me. I will na' let you from my sight this eve. I daren't."

"Truth?" she asked, without inflection.

"Of course. I'll na' let my lady get far. How can I? She's a fortune in gold on her."

"And it's easier to make certain of what she does and does na' do. As well as what she might say. I ken there's another reason to this truth."

He looked over at her, as he got close. "Truth has many layers, remember?"

"Oh, aye. I recollect that lesson very well. As well as I recollect the reason you gave me for stopping in the midst of the North Sea in order to calm my belly. It had naught to do with having to await the rest of your armada. None at all."

"I also wanted the other. 'Twas nae lie."

"'Twas nae truth, either."

"Very well. 'Twas half a truth. Fair?"

"Naught is fair, Monteith, recollect that as well? This is a negotiation. Very well. Carry on. Take me to this prince that cost us so heavily last year, and is preparing to do the same to the Highlands once again. He dinna' even have the heart to stay and fight and die like a man. He ran!"

"He had to run, Lisle. If he'd been taken, there'd be nae chance ever again. Never."

"There is nae chance now, Monteith. Remember I said it."

"I ken." He looked away from her and back at the columns of men that were of an uncountable number, the rows of bagpipers, the drums, the large banners held aloft every fifty or so men, that had a dark green background with the golden lion passant at the center of each. It was very impressive. It was all for one man, one reason, one unattainable vision that had already been proved impossible.

She wrapped her hands around the pommel of Blizzom's saddle, although the green-and-gold-bedecked riding platform that she was on didn't look remotely like the saddle she'd been on before. It was too richly appointed, and too large, and tassels of real gold trailed to the streets where the populace was probably hoping it would fray and lose some of it. She started praying, like she hadn't in months, fervently, and with her entire heart and soul.

Someone gave a signal. It was the long, drawn-out note, and the moment it ended the drums started, thumping in rhythm to her own pulse, or creating a beat that dragged her pulse into cadence with it, and then the skirl of pipes started up. The column didn't have to wend its way through anything because people immediately moved out of the way for them.

Their destination didn't merit the time it took to mount up and start a drumroll, since they were merely traveling down one *rue* and stopping at a large, imposing gate that was probably located on castle grounds still.

The word MONTBAZON was emblazoned into the ironwork gate.

They were at the front steps before a retinue of servants came out, one of whom appeared to have the authority to meet a contingency looking like an invading army, moving in perfect unison. Langston held up his arm, and two-by-two they all came to a halt.

"We've come to see my prince!" he shouted down at the group of servants, and the brave one stepped out and told them that the prince no longer kept Madame de Montbazon company. There was more to it, but Langston's lips simply thinned, and he dismounted. He took Etheridge in with him, and three more Lisle didn't recognize, and there was a thunderous look about his features when he returned.

They turned around with a precision that defied explanation, and Lisle watched as two-by-two they passed the column that was sitting, awaiting their own turn. There wasn't a sound made; no drum . . . no pipe, only horse hooves, only leather creaking and bridles jangling in the late afternoon sunlight.

Lisle leaned a bit to ask, "What has happened, Langston?"

"Our prince is a bonny fellow."

"So I've heard."

"I would go to the Chateau de Valmilarot, where he lives, but he is na' at his abode."

"How do you know?"

"I employ spies, Lisle. I do so when I have a need to know things."

"So . . . he was supposed to be here?"

He nodded.

"Why?"

"He keeps the Lady de Montbazon company while her husband is in military service."

"So . . . where is he?"

"Apparently, he was keeping Louise too much company, and now that she is expecting his child, he has left her to face the ruination alone. She is in seclusion. She is very unhappy. I doona' blame her."

Lisle gasped.

"You wish to hear the rest?"

She nodded.

"He has taken up with the Princess of Talmont. Apparently, this is news to all, especially the Lady de Montbazon."

"Is he with the princess now?"

"If I had paid to have him followed I wouldn't be in this situation, where I have legions following me, making a spectacle about me, and incapable of providing clear direction to any."

Lisle's lips were twisting, but she kept the glee inside. God was answering her prayers . . . already. "Is this the man you would give your life's blood for?" she asked.

His eyes were black, so he wasn't going to be open with her. He was probably keeping it from himself, as well.

"I would go to the grave for my prince. I would do whatever it takes to get my respect, life, and liberty back. That is what I will do. Even if I have to sober him up, button up his trousers, and prop him onto a throne in order to make it happen!"

"I hope your men feel the same," she replied.

"They doona' know what you know. I would prefer it kept that way."

Lisle nodded. She didn't wish to foul her mouth with tales, even if they were truth. Besides, she didn't have anyone to impart the story to, even if she wanted to. Betsy, Cassie, and Bess were all starry-eyed at the prospect of staying in a real royal palace. If she dared mention anything scandalous about Bonnie Prince Charlie, she'd probably find herself stuck with a sewing pin, instead of using them to hold the fabric together.

* * *

The Princess of Talmont was in, the prince of the House of Stuart was said to be with her, and Monteith would be granted an audience if he waited for the household to prepare for such an honor.

Langston sat atop Torment, clenched his jaw until a nerve poked out the side, and held the black anger inside where no one could see it. He should have checked with his spies instead of trusting to details that were days old. He should have prepared for contingencies. He'd taught himself better; no loose openings, no unknown quantities, no women. He glanced sidelong at Lisle again, and felt the same stutter in his ribcage that had him going to a knee the moment he'd seen her.

He knew she was the loveliest woman alive. There was something about the light behind her blue eyes, and the joy behind her smile, and even the anger behind the words she used to flay him with. She had fire. That's what it was, and everything he'd purchased and designed was putting that on display. She was the fire that burned deep in his heart, making him stumble when he couldn't afford to.

He was a diplomat with a prince to sway, and a country to gain. He was an actor with a part to play. He was a liar, and an expert one. He couldn't afford to just be Lisle Monteith's husband.

He groaned.

"Her Highness will see you now."

A bewigged butler announced it, and Langston held up his hand for the three men he'd chosen to come with him, and dismounted. He thought for a scant moment about bringing Lisle. He didn't dare. He turned his back on her and walked up the steps.

The princess was nearing her fortieth winter, if Langston's eye was correct, and she was alone. Langston eyed the remains of a feast, several wine decanters, and more than one tankard brimming with ale.

Such a thing could be used to his advantage. Many a man had found himself locked into things he wouldn't have agreed to if he'd been sober. He approached the high-backed chair the princess was perched in and went to his knee, clanging the broadsword at his hip with the movement. Beside him, the three men did the exact same movement with the exact same sound, although it was behind his.

"Langston Leed Monteith, laird of Clan Monteith; protector of Clans MacDugall, MacDonald, and MacIntyre, to see my one true lord and liege."

"You . . . come too late, my lord," came the answer. The princess was frightened. Either that, or she'd imbibed too freely.

Langston went back to his feet, the others following suit with the exact motion. "What do you mean . . . too late?"

She smiled. It wasn't comely. Langston blinked. The woman was forty, and she wasn't attractive. There was no accounting for a man's taste, however. He'd long ago learned not to puzzle it.

"Your prince . . . has fled."

"Fled!" The word exploded from his lips. The princess jumped. "He knew the dates! He knew the plans! I left nothing to chance. Nothing."

"You left human nature to chance, my lord."

She looked wise beyond her years all of a sudden. Langston's eyes narrowed. "Go on," he said.

She shrugged, lifting a tired bosom with the motion. Everything she did looked tired, he decided.

"Well?" Langston put a hand to his hip. The other still rested on his sword hilt.

"Prince Charlie left this morn. Before the gossip broke."

"What gossip?"

"Surely you've just come from Montbazon?" she supplied. He nodded, the motion curt.

"And Madame de Montbazon kept her silence from you? That is a surprise. She has been spouting her misfortune on every ear that will listen since yestermorn, when your prince joined with me."

"I haven't time for this! I must find my prince!"

"He sailed already. It's too late."

"Sailed?" Langston's heart was falling, inch by tormenting inch. It was paining clear to his fingertips with how it felt, too. He swallowed. "To where?"

She shrugged again.

"You know. You're paying."

She smiled again. "True."

"Tell me the direction. I may yet stop this!"

"I'm not so certain I should."

"What?" It was the second time he'd shouted at her. She didn't look like it was a normal occurrence. Etheridge put a broadsword against Langston's thigh in warning.

"If I tell you where he is, you'll go after him?"

Langston nodded. He didn't trust his tongue. Rage was difficult to control when combined with the impotence of his position. He twisted the hilt of his sword until it felt like the gold was being moved and molded by his fingers.

"And if you reach him, what happens?"

"He gains his country back. What else?"

"And I lose him."

Langston narrowed his eyes and pinned her in place. "Tell me the direction and the tide."

"Or . . . ?" she asked.

He pulled his sword. Three other blades joined his. She waved her hand, and guards stepped forward, filling the sides of the room. Langston counted eleven without his eyes leaving her face. She was smiling again. She was still unpleasant to look upon, he decided.

"He doesn't wish to go with you."

"How do you know?"

She shifted her head slightly, and a missive was held out to him from his left side. Langston swallowed before reaching for it. He wondered if this was how Lisle had felt. How he'd made her feel. He didn't like the comparison.

"You would wish to support a sovereign, without a country, at your side?"

"It's that, or no sovereign at all. Read. Don't listen to just me. Read."

There were four words on the paper, and the distinctive seal of the House of Stuart at the bottom of it. *God go with you.*

"He will na' come with us?" Etheridge asked at his side.

Langston handed the parchment to him. There was a grunt as he also read it. The swords were lowered.

"What shall we do now, my laird?" his second-in-command asked.

"We do what we need to do. Without him."

He swung on his heel and marched out of the room without a backward glance. The three clansmen were with him every step.

Chapter Twenty-Seven

Langston Monteith was known as the Black Monteith, and it was due to his temperament. It had to be. Lisle had been ill every morning they were sailing, although the ship was making very good headway with a healthy wind behind it, making any wave unnoticeable. By afternoon, she was always feeling better, drinking broth, and trying to sway him.

There was only one thing left in her arsenal, and she was afraid to use it. He wasn't speaking with her anyway. He was studying things at his table, spreading maps and charts and drawing lines, and coloring in glens and shading forests, delineating even the gulches and moors, and if she chanced to try and look, he was bundling it all into a large roll and walking out.

He hadn't said a word to her after leaving the residence where their prince was staying. He hadn't said whether his plan to sway the prince had been successful or not. He had such a dark look about him, she thought it must not have been. Then again, if his plan had worked, and the prince was aboard any other ship, then Langston was planning and preparing and gearing up for a large confrontation that might result in death, in which event he might look just as grim.

Any man would.

He wasn't sleeping, either. Or he wasn't sleeping with her.

Lisle reached out every night for the place he'd been, and never once did she connect with him; until the last night. He must have finalized what he had to do, for when she woke the final day, he was there, watching her, and he was smiling.

"'Tis been rough, Lisle love," he said in a gruff voice that probably went for an apology.

"Better than my first crossing," she replied.

"Truth. You are a horrid sailor. You'd have been tossed overboard had this been Solomon at the helm."

"Nae!" she responded.

He smiled. "I'd say I jest, but it would be a lie. Then again, since I lie very well, how would you know?"

"'Tis a strange honeymoon you accorded me, Langston," she remarked when all he did was sit there and trace little circles about the coverlet's quilting threads.

He looked across at her and smiled. "Aye. That it was."

Lisle gathered her nerve and asked it. "Does the prince sail with us?"

"Does it matter?" he asked.

"Of course! There is a huge bounty on his head. He'll na' be safe anywhere in the country."

"I've enough men to guarantee his safety."

"The Sassenach have more, Langston. They always have more. That's why they always win."

"Not always. Recollect I told you of . . . Saladin, the Arabian general?" His voice broke before the name, and a shadow went across his face.

"Was there huge loss of life?" she asked.

He looked at her, and made her wonder if he was going to tell her the truth. "Aye," he replied finally.

"Then . . . was it worth it?"

"To gain what we must, it will be worth it. Trust me."

"I canna' trust you, Langston."

He sucked in air at the surprise. "Why na'?" he asked.

"Because to be trusted, a man must be trustworthy. His

word must be his bond. He canna' tell lies, and expect to be believed when he is na' telling a lie."

"I doona' think I like this conversation very much, Lisle love."

"You're going to like it a lot less in a moment, Langston Leed."

He smiled at her use of his names, since she'd given them the same inflection he had. "Go on," he said finally.

"I doona' wish you to risk it. There is too much to lose."

"There is too much not to try."

"You've given them back their self-respect. You've given clansmen back their joy, their worth, made them walk like men again, rather than slink about like shadows. You've given the glens new life, and you're willing to toss it all away? For what?"

"Freedom," he replied.

"There is nae such thing."

"There is. It's in everything about us. Do you na' see? It's in every drop of rain that hits the ground. It's in every wisp of fog, every gurgle of every burn, and it's in every whisper of the grasses out on the moors. It's everywhere. It's just not in here." He thumped his chest with a sideways fist. "And that hurts too much to let it go."

"What if you're . . . taken?"

"I had the dower house constructed for a reason, Lisle. 'Tis very fine, the best stone, the finest furniture from the finest craftsmen. I had it hidden away, cleared forest to make it as sheltered as possible. 'Tis na' even possible to see it, unless one knows where it is."

"I canna' live in a dower house, Langston," she whispered.

"Why na'?"

"Because I am na' a widow."

"You'll na' need to take up residency anytime soon. I'm simply preparing for everything that could happen."

"Langston." Lisle reached out and touched his hand with her forefinger. Then, she opened her hand and spread it atop his, much like she had in the carriage following their wedding.

"Aye?"

Something had shifted, turning the black back into the amber brown she loved. Lisle knew what it was. He couldn't pretend when his emotions were involved, and that was the only hold she had.

"You dinna' plan for our son," she whispered.

His eyes went huge as he stared at her. Then he was grinning, and then he was whooping great, loud gusts of sound, until the cabin rang with it.

"You're na' unhappy?" Lisle teased.

The Langston she loved pulled her into his arms, put her against the solid pounding of his heart, and held her there, soothing her with the drumlike rhythm of it. The entire time he had her clasped to him, he was cupping the place that held their son, with hands that contained reverence to each finger.

"I love you, Lisle Monteith. You are the life in every breath I take, and the joy in everything I see, and I'm a-feared you're in every thought I am having, and will ever have."

She reached up to ruffle the edge of where the black hair was just deciding to drop onto his forehead, and then she moved her gaze down to his.

"Then, doona' do this thing," she said softly.

He went rigid. Cold. Dark. The arms about her dropped away and then he was moving from her, standing, and there wasn't anything on him that was loving.

"There is nae bargaining tool you can use to stay my destiny, Lisle. None. You canna' even use my son."

He turned his back on her and strode out.

The Duke of Cumberland was exactly on time. Lisle stood in her chamber, the white and maroon one with the light wooden beams crossing it, and listened to the horns the Sassenach were blasting as they entered the enclosure of the castle yard. She could almost hear the portcullis falling at every gate they went through, and she was surprised they didn't hear it and take note of it, or at least feel a brush of suspicion about the entire thing.

But no. This William was an arrogant, pompous, overly proud son, the favored son of their King George, and he had subdued the Highlands as no man before him could have hoped to. He was making a triumphant return journey, since, being a second son, military success was the most he could hope for from his father.

Lisle was under house arrest, although there was no order given, and no room denied her. It was an understanding, and she'd been made aware of it ever since she'd decided to try and use her own son for negotiating. There was a Highlander in Sassenach dress at every door she decided to try, and in every window she peered out of, and they also seemed to know what she was being punished for and had tried to do.

Lisle felt the tears filling her eyes and forced them back down. She wasn't going to cry! She was going to go down to the amazing feast Monteith Castle had prepared and she was going to charm the socks off that Sassenach bastard, if she had to learn how to be an actress in order to do it. And she was going to wear the dress Langston had ordered her to, although she felt like a kept woman in it. He knew what he was doing. He was keeping Cumberland's eyes on her, or on anything other than the obvious, until the trap was sprung.

Then, there came the sound of a long, drawn-out note, overriding the Sassenach flare of noise and making everything stop and listen. It was followed by two short blasts of a horn. Two. Lisle waited for the third, but it never came. Two? What did two mean?

"Show him the prisoners, Monteith."

Captain Barton's eyes were gleaming, and the mug of chilled ale he'd swigged only seemed to intensify them. Langston swung his glance away from where all the troops they'd brought with them were also partaking, and smiled with a sardonic, evil expression.

"I'd best prepare them first."

"For what?"

"Viewing."

Barton laughed heartily. William didn't look like he had much intelligence for the jest, but he was drinking fully of the ale, too. That was a good omen, a very good one.

Servant women flitted about, taking tankards, filling others, and always slipping a sleeve down onto an arm with the movement, showing every red-blooded male there that a Highland wench was just as well endowed as any they'd find in any of the finest taverns in London. Langston smiled.

"My dungeon, it is. Gentlemen?"

They rose from the thick, overstuffed chairs they'd been in, and followed him. They were joined immediately by at least thirty men to accompany them, coming from the ranks of William's personal guard. It was obvious they were a well-trained unit, too. They hadn't partaken of a drop of anything offered, nor had they shifted glances to anything the women displayed.

He knew that Etheridge and the Green Company were also aware of it. As the most elite corps, it was going to be their chore to subdue any that hadn't had a tankard of the ale.

"These are the MacDonald clan you spoke of?" William asked as they went down first one hall, and then another.

"Oh, yes. And wait until you see them. Twenty-seven of them! All trussed up and ready to haul to London. Just like I promised." It was Captain Barton answering, and the drug only seemed to heighten his arrogance and make him louder.

"You gave them to a Highland laird for safekeeping? Isn't that highly unusual?" It was obvious William was searching for the correct word.

It was probably damned unusual, Langston thought.

"This is no normal Highland laird, Wills, old boy!" Captain Barton clapped the duke on the back, and received a stern look for his effort. It didn't affect him much. "This is Monteith. Hated by both sides, loyal to none. Isn't that right, Monteith?"

"It would seem you have me directly in your sights, Captain. My congratulations," Langston replied, drawing out the words with a bored tone. They were at the door to the dungeons. Langston turned to prepare them. "Don't go too close to the bars."

"The bars?" William asked.

"Why ever not?" Captain Barton wanted to know.

"Because desperate men do desperate things. The Mac-Donalds are that."

The men, wearing MacDonald plaide and posing as Mac-Donalds, were desperate, all right, but it wasn't for any escape. They were also writhing and screaming and one of them appeared to be trying to climb the walls, while another was looking at his toes as if they held all the secrets of his world. There was one beneath a bed of straw, splashing in the film of water coating the floor, and the smell of filth assailed their nostrils to the point that William started gagging. Langston smiled. He'd ordered it prepared, and the men they were watching had but been placed there an hour earlier. They were also well into the bane of every opiate addict—withdrawal.

"My God, Monteith! What have you done to them?"

It was Captain Barton, and he wasn't going anywhere near the bars. He was staring at the men inside and then at Monteith as if he were a demon only Satan could have dreamt up.

"I tortured them. Exactly as you specified. Think nothing of it. They'll be on their feet and ready for travel in a matter of days. Those that survive, that is."

He yawned, and watched as William looked like he was ready to retch into the perfumed handkerchief he had held to his nose.

"Have you seen enough, Captain?"

Barton nodded. Langston smiled and waved the way back up the stairs. He could hear the stones of the secret passage moving before the door was shut, and made a mental note of reprimand. They were not to move the prisoners until it was time, and it wasn't time . . . yet.

Supper was served exactly on schedule, and with a gaiety that seemed to permeate the air until even the wine sparkled like it was champagne. Lisle made her entrance, and Langston's heart felt every bit of the hurt and pain that was reflecting from those sky-blue eyes at him. She looked across the room at him and nodded. Then, she was walking over to take her assigned place, and holding her hand out to the butcher of the Highlands and introducing herself with the slightest warble to her voice, enchanting that fellow until his eyes looked like they'd forgotten how to blink.

Langston was halfway to a stand before he caught himself. She was wearing a sky-blue taffeta dress that he'd selected, but once again he'd forgotten that she had a very lovely bosom, and only an idiot put such a thing on display when there was a man known for his sexual appetites as her dining partner. Langston groaned, and stabbed his fork into his gelled cranberry mold, separating it with the thrust and watching the filling ooze out with a strange feeling of satisfaction that was only tempered when he looked up and watched William Cumberland fawning over his wife.

As if she'd felt his gaze, she looked up, speared him into place with the pain luminating out at him, and making him wrench the silver spoon in his hand until it warped. She looked away, placed her hand on the duke's arm, and laughed lightly at something he'd said. All of which had Langston rising from his seat again, and feeling nothing over the blood-pounding heartbeat in his ears but pure and absolute hate.

Then Lisle was turning to the captain at her other side, and leaning slightly as she conversed with him. The movement had the front of her gown gaping farther open, and she made certain the gentlemen were looking there, as she brushed a stray lock of her hair from where it was at least trying to shield some of her. Langston groaned.

He'd planned everything to the smallest detail, except for one thing: his own reaction to his wife.

Langston controlled the tremble of his own hand as he reached for, and downed, the water in his goblet. He needed her tonight; her beauty, her power, her charm. He was trusting her more than he should, but he was prepared for a betrayal by making certain every one of the chairs had a servant directly behind it, and that servant wasn't just a footman. They were Yellow Company, well trained, and well armed. The duke had even done him the great honor of dismissing his own guard, since he felt so certain of Monteith, and so safe in his hands.

Lisle was laughing, and Langston was not. He watched her pose and flirt with the men at either side of her, and knew he was turning red with an emotion he should have killed off years before. The sweat was making the shirt stick to his backbone, and run from there to the edge of his English trousers, and he couldn't wait to shed them and put on his rightful raiment, and take his rightful place.

She damn well better get her hand off the duke's sleeve!

Langston had his napkin tossed to the table and his chair already sliding out before he caught the motion, and stared down at the plate of squab pie they'd served him, looking at it like it was something that hadn't been invented yet. He took great gulps of air, pulled his collar from his neck, and wondered what was wrong with him that he couldn't control his emotion any better than this.

She truly was ruining him. He was going to be useless as an actor and a liar if this kept up. He sat back down, put half the pie in his mouth in one bite, and started chewing, viciously, with intent, and with a look down the table that if she'd chanced to glance up she'd have gasped in shock at.

They served another course. She was laughing and hiding her mouth and saying things that made them laugh, and everything he put in his mouth was as tasteless as the next, and then everything went completely still as he saw her lift a wine glass and take a sip of it.

Langston was on his feet, and halfway down the table before she set the glass down. Then she was looking up at him with those beautiful, brittle-looking, sky-blue eyes, although anyone else would have a hard time looking anywhere but at how much bosom she was putting on display, and pleading with him not to hold the matter against her anymore.

"Gentlemen. I'm afraid my wife has taken ill," Langston said, nodding his head for one of the servants to assist her with her chair.

She was in his arms, and she was pliant and looking at him with a dazed expression, while he was kicking himself for every kind of a fool for allowing her to come into close contact with anything that might harm her, or their baby. Langston's eyes filled and he had to blink them rapidly before the two Englishmen noticed that the laird was close to sobbing, and then they'd want to know why. It was at what he'd done. Very little was going according to plan.

Lisle looked up at him with eyes that were swimming with her own tears. Then she was pouting and smiling and making little kissing noises. All of it was driving him insane with all he had to keep in his mind; the things he had left to do. There was nothing for it but to get her into competent hands.

"Excuse me, gentlemen. I have to see my wife to her room. I'll be down shortly." Langston ran up the steps. He was calling for Mary MacGreggor and giving her heartless instructions to keep Lisle up and sober and walking. Then he was running back down the steps before any of the men got the idea to leave.

He reassured himself with his instructions. There hadn't been much opiate in any glass of wine, or in any of the ale. There hadn't been enough to harm anyone. He just wanted their senses dulled, not obliterated. He needed every one of them well and alive, and healthy; exactly as he'd told Captain Barton a prisoner needed to be.

"Well! It's been a lovely evening, Monteith. Congratulate

your wife when you see her again. Tell her Big Wills has a surprise for her. I'll be happy to let her see it."

Langston had his hand in a fist, and was ready to swing it before sanity returned, and with it time and reason and everything he'd prepared and worked for. He uncoiled his fist by act of will, and worked his fingers loose.

"My pleasure, my lord duke. If you'll be so good as to come outside. We've got everything prepared."

"You're a wonderful host, Monteith. I'll recommend you to all my friends back in the civilized world. I vow it—"

The words died, as well as his breath, as they stepped out onto the front steps, and then went out farther onto the grass, as the number of English soldiers coming from behind them pushed them out. The door shut, loudly, and there was a sound of a bolt being drawn. Langston stood on the steps, folded his arms, and waited while both the captain and the duke, and those men who were sober enough to be with them, took in the sea of Highlanders facing them, and filling the castle grounds in perfect rows and with perfect precision. Each division had a banner held high that had a golden lion passant at the center of green, while the only difference was the color or design of the ribbon clasped in its claws.

On perfect signal, and in perfect unison, the pipers, standing two hundred deep, started the skirl of their pipes, while the drums all about the edge of the courtyard started in, thumping a beat that felt like it went across the turf and climbed into every man's back.

"I don't understand, Monteith. These are Highlanders . . . and they play the pipes, and they're armed, and they're in kilts! Captain?"

The duke's voice was gaining in volume, and then there was a general sound of noise and confusion coming from the sides of his courtyard as English soldiers appeared, all carrying muskets and all looking like they'd just as soon bed down and sleep it off.

Langston nodded, and a thunder of noise started filling the

enclosure until it echoed off the walls and reverberated into the sky. One by one every crenellation in every bit of every wall filled with the round barrel of cannon and they were all pointed directly down at the courtyard before them.

"Monteith!"

Langston nodded again, and there was a sound of windows being opened. He didn't have to look up to see how every window in every portion of his home was filling with a musket or a crossbow, and they were also pointing at each and every Englishman in the enclosure.

"You have an explanation of this?"

Cumberland was trying to ask it over the drums and the pipes and Langston lifted his arm for a silence that, when it fell, seemed to make the very sounds of their sweat breaking out on their bodies audible.

"Of course I have an explanation," he said slowly and distinctly. "I am a Highlander, born and bred. Forever."

"You are a bloody, conniving, barbaric bastard!"

That was Captain Barton, and he was spitting between the words, with anger that was turning him red.

"True," Langston replied loudly. "Now, what are you going to do about it? The answer has to be, not much. In point of fact, I'd ask you to lay down your weapon, but you're na' even wearing one, so it would be a moot request."

"What do you want?" The duke asked it, perfectly sober-sounding and lethal. He was cunning. He'd just kept it well hidden.

"To negotiate, of course."

"Speak up."

"Not with you. You're but a pawn. I want to speak with your father."

"The king doesn't speak with rabble."

"Oh . . . I think he will. You see, I have something of his. I think he'll want it back. Especially if I sweeten the pot and keep it quiet."

"You're holding me for ransom?"

"Na' exactly. I'm holding you for peace. I'm even paying the ransom to get rid of you."

"What?"

"I've got something King George will want back. He's got something that I want back."

"What is that?"

Langston sighed heavily. "I have prepared my dower house for you and Captain Barton, and even the Highland Rangers to use. You're to be my guests, enjoying my hospitality. There will be meals served, ales, wines; you'll want for nothing, and there will be nothing spared for your comfort."

"How long are we going to be your . . . guests?"

"That will depend on how amenable your father is. I imagine he's hearing about this just about now, and I daresay he'll want this little episode closed rather quickly, because otherwise he has to face the embarrassment of how easily it was to kidnap his favored son in a country he thought subdued."

"He knows already?"

"I sent my emissary a sennight past. I doona' wish to be your host for an overlong period. I'd prefer it to be brief."

"What do you want?"

"I already told you. I doona' negotiate with pawns. Only kings."

"I'll not stand by and allow you to—!"

Langston swiveled to glare at the captain. "Barton, please. I already had to weigh heavily on if it was worth keeping your sorry neck unsliced for the duration of the negotiations. I doona' think you are worth much. But then, I had a thought. There might actually be someone out there that thinks you have some worth. Every man has to have a mother, at least. Do you think she'll pay much for your return?"

"You miserable, low bastard!"

There was a sword to the captain's throat before he finished, and it was Angus MacHugh holding it. Langston watched as the old warrior looked the man up and down and then turned toward him.

"You want me to slice him for you, my laird?" he asked.

"Nae. Na' yet."

"Langston." Captain Barton had a bit of trouble talking with a blade against his throat. It sounded in the way the word choked out.

"Aye?" Langston replied.

"What . . . do you want?"

"From you?"

Barton nodded, although it scraped his skin against the blade, starting a small trickle of blood he probably couldn't even feel.

"Saladin."

Langston turned and went back into the house, and waited until the sound of the large, heavy doors were shutting before he was running up the stairs like life and joy depended on it.

Epilogue

Randolph Dugall Monteith arrived on the exact day his father conceded there would be no win, only a compromise. It was a good compromise, though, and there was cannon fired over it, making the sound of thunder rumble through the glens and across the lochs and causing more than one of the clansmen that had joined Monteith to raise their voices in prayer.

That was what a round of cannon fire meant, in case any wondered over it, although from that day forward, it was also used to announce a birth in the clan.

It had taken two rounds of negotiations before the treaty was written, gold changed hands, and Monteith Castle could bid adieu to its guests. In that time, King George had, at first, tried to put a limit on the size of army Langston Monteith wanted to maintain, while it was already increasing daily; he wanted twice the gold that was offered and wanted it delivered in half the time; and he wanted to put limits on the size and amount of armament they'd be allowed. Then there was the bagpipe issue, and the debate on if it truly was an instrument of war or not.

It was a compromise, and the fact that he'd agreed never to

bear arms against England was the hardest to swallow. Langston looked down at the grapefruit and toasted bread that he'd ordered for his breakfast and swallowed his disappointment. It could be worse. It could be a lot worse.

He knew it, as the final draft was delivered to him nearly seven months to the day after he'd first sent word that he had something to negotiate. Langston took his time opening it. He knew what it would contain, and so he set it aside to read to Lisle when she woke and let him in to see her. She was getting so large and unwieldy that she rarely came down the steps anymore to have her meals with him at all.

She didn't want him to visit her until she'd had her breakfast and her bath, and was covering over every part of the shape she'd grown into. He couldn't convince her she was the most lovely woman in the world still, and had gotten so bad at trying, she called him the worst liar born.

The sound of heavy quick steps filled the rooms, echoing from the front hall. "My lord! Come quick! It's Her Ladyship!"

Langston was on his feet and passing the maid up the stairs and then he was in the room, and there wasn't anything amiss, other than Lisle was taking her time getting out of her bed, and then she was moaning and calling to him.

"The bairn," she whispered. "It thinks 'tis time to arrive."

That began the longest day of his life, where there wasn't a square of his castle that was safe from his pacing and roaming, sweating and fretting. Sometimes he had company, like Angus, who was keeping perfect marching time with the laird; and at others, he was accompanied by every clansman that had perished on every battlefield in every battle. Then it was over, and Langston got to see the result of an entire day of labor by the woman he loved, and there wasn't much of substance to say about the little red-faced bundle they handed him, except it had a healthy head of thick black hair.

"'Tis a lad, my love," Lisle said, and there was the softest, most loving look on her face that Langston's head felt like it might come loose with the explosion of peace, love, and joy.

And there came a time when Highlanders again owned and walked across their own land, and Clan Monteith coveted a new, most valuable asset—its children.